COLLECTED NOVELLAS

VOLUME TWO

Josh Lanyon

mlrpress

This book is a work of fiction. Names, characters, places, and incidents either are products of the author's imagination or are used fictitiously. Any resemblance to actual events or locales or persons, living or dead, is entirely coincidental.

Copyright 2009 by Josh Lanyon

All rights reserved, including the right of reproduction in whole or in part in any form.

Published by
MLR Press, LLC
3052 Gaines Waterport Rd.
Albion, NY 14411

Visit ManLoveRomance Press, LLC on the Internet:
www.mlrpress.com

Cover Art by Anne Cain
Editing by Judith David
Printed in the United States of America.

ISBN# 978-1-60820-052-8

Re-issued 2009

In a Dark Wood... *1*

I Spy Something Bloody... *43*

A Limited Engagement... *141*

Dark Horse *161*

Ghost of a Chance *281*

IN A DARK WOOD

In a dark, dark wood there was a dark, dark house... Years ago I read on the Internet about this creepy old house in the eastern woods — there were even photos — and then when the idea came to write this story and I tried to find the page again, I couldn't. Which seemed appropriately eerie. Anyway, Tim's problems came as a revelation to me. I kept trying to write away from them, but they just wouldn't go away.

"We're lost."

Luke came up behind me. I pointed, hand shaking, at the cross carved into the white bark of the tree. "We're going in goddamned circles!"

He was silent. Beneath the drone of insects I could hear the even tenor of his breathing although we'd hiked a good nine miles already that autumn afternoon — and no end to it in sight. My head ached and I had a stitch in my side like someone was jabbing me with a hot poker.

I lowered my pack to the ground, lowered myself to a fallen tree — this time not bothering to check for ant nests or coiled rattlers — lowered my face in my hands and lost it. I mean, *lost it*. Tears…oh, yeah. Shoulders shaking, shuddering sobs. I didn't even care anymore what he thought.

"Tim…" He dropped his pack too, sat down next to me on the log. He sounded sort of at a loss. After a minute he patted my shoulder. Awkwardly.

I turned away from him and tried to wipe my face on my shirt sleeve.

Feeling him fumbling around with his pack, I watched him through wet lashes. He pulled out his canteen, unscrewed the top and offered it to me.

I took the canteen, swallowed the warm stale water, handed it back. Wiped my face again. Perfect. My nose was running. Not that it mattered. It wasn't like I had a shred of dignity left.

First dates. You've got to love 'em.

But I mean, what kind of fucking sadist chooses camping for a first date?

Fast forward to the end of this one: we'd shake hands at my brownstone door — assuming we got out of this field trip into Hell alive — and he'd promise to call, and with equal insincerity I'd say I looked forward to it.

I'd never see him again — and that was the only bright side to this whole — literally — walking nightmare.

Luke pulled a cloth out of his pack and wet it with the canteen. "Here, look at me."

I looked at him. He wiped my face with the wet cloth, shocking me into immobility. His own face was serious, his hazel eyes studied me. I closed my eyes and he gently swiped my eyelids, washing away the sweat and tears.

"Better?"

I lifted my lashes, got my lips steady enough to form words. "Oh, sure. Great."

"I thought you were a travel writer?"

"I'm not an explorer! I write about comfortable hotels with clean sheets and hot water. My idea of roughing it is a two-star restaurant!"

The corner of his mouth tugged as though, against his will, he found this just a little bit comical. What the hell could be funny about any of this?

"Listen, we're not lost."

I opened my mouth and he said, "I don't mean I know where we are. But I can get us out of here, if that's what you want. I've got a compass and we can start walking east and be back to civilization within a few hours."

I swallowed hard. First off, there was no place in New Jersey that even remotely qualified as "civilization," but that was beside the point.

Luke said, "And, for the record, we're not going in circles. Look again at that carving on the tree. It's not a fresh cut. Look at the edges. They curl, but they're worn. It's not your mark. At least, it's not the mark you made today."

I blinked at him stupidly.

He said, "I think it's your mark from twelve years ago."

§ § § §

Flash back four days ago to a dinner party at my best friend Rob's place in Manhattan. Rob'd gone all out: Chinese lanterns hang over the table, shadows bobbing against the wall, all of us fumbling around with chopsticks, and the Peking duck from Chef Ho's exquisite. I'd had three cocktails too many and Rob was egging me on.

"Tim, tell the story about the skull house, come on!"

I laughed, shaking my head.

"Come on," Rob urged. "Luke wants to hear it. Luke! Tell Tim you want to hear about the skull house in New Jersey."

Across the table and two faces down there was this very attractive guy, a few years older than me, with dark hair and crinkly hazel eyes. He gave me a wry grin.

This was Luke, the cop who Rob kept trying to fix me up with. "A cop?" I always said doubtfully. "I don't know."

"He's a detective, not a beat cop," Rob always replied. "He doesn't give speeding tickets."

Speeding tickets being kind of a sore subject with me. "I'm not really into cops," I always said.

"You're not into anybody," was Rob's standard answer. "And nobody is into you, which is your problem. One of your problems."

And that's where the conversation ended, except that night Luke was actually present and could speak up for himself.

"Sure, Tim," he said. "I'd like to hear."

He had a nice voice, not at all the voice cops use when they're slapping a parking ticket on your windshield or asking you to pull out your vehicle registration. He had very white teeth and a very nice smile. Did he know Rob wanted to set us up? Er — fix us up, I mean. He probably did, and he'd probably been resisting just as hard as me. He'd certainly kept a polite distance all evening.

I gave Rob a look that promised all kinds of retribution that I wouldn't remember once I sobered up. He just laughed and poured me another scorpion.

"Come on, Tim," someone else urged.

Someone else I didn't know. Rob knew everybody and everybody knew Rob. Most of them didn't know Rob as long as I'd known him, which was since we were the two most unpopular guys in Trinity School.

I gave in to peer pressure — not for the first time — with a sigh.

"I was thirteen and I was staying with a friend in the Pine Barrens for a couple of weeks during the summer. There wasn't a lot to do. Mostly we went swimming in this little lake and we spent a lot of time prowling through woods."

I glanced over at Luke. He set his glass back down, but his lashes lifted and he caught my eye. I couldn't look away. He didn't look away either. It's like tractor beams locking on. People were going to notice. My face felt hot, but that was probably the spicy sea dragon bass.

Managing to tear my gaze away, I said, "Anyway, one day we wandered farther into the woods then we were supposed to go. We get really turned around. Totally lost. Oh wait, I'm forgetting. There was supposed to be this house, see, where — I don't remember what the exact story was now — the Boogey Man or somebody like that was supposed to live in the heart of the woods. And when hikers or nosey kids like us disappeared, The Forester was supposed to have grabbed them."

"The Forester?" Luke asked. Everyone else chuckled, reaching for glasses or forks. Only Luke was paying close attention.

I focused inward. "Uh, yeah. I think that's right." Weird. I'd forgotten that he was called the Forester.

"So, anyway, we wander around, lost. We're afraid we're going in circles, and it's getting dark. I start marking the trees, making a little cross with my penknife in the bark, which is all white and shimmery that time of evening."

My heart started to thud against my ribs as it came back to me: the deepening shadows, the ghostly trees, the creeping chill of the woods closing in on us. "And then all at once there's a house right in front of us. Two stories, really old, falling down. There's a tree growing out through a big hole in the roof."

I gestured with my hands trying to make them see this creepy old house being claimed by the woods. "It has an ornate portico thing and little gable windows. Some of the other windows are broken, some of them are still there. The front door is hanging off its hinges…"

I stopped. For a moment it was like I was back in the woods. The smell of moldering house and weird animal scents and…the woods. The hush of evening — even the crickets were silent.

Too silent.

Rob laughed. He'd heard the story before — always when I was drunk. I don't tell this story sober. I couldn't help stealing another look at Luke. He wasn't smiling anymore; his brows were drawn together like he was studying me from a distance and not sure about what he was seeing.

"I took a step forward and something crunched under my foot. When I looked down it was part of a skull."

Laughter, some expelled breaths, Luke still stared, still frowning. "Skull or a bone?"

"Skull."

"Human?" someone else asked.

"I don't know," I admitted. "At the time we thought so, but we kind of wanted to think so, you know? I don't think it was."

I did think it was human, actually, but I sure as hell didn't want to admit it.

"So what happened?" a woman asked. The light from the blue lanterns bounced off her glasses and made her look blind. A blind lady insect.

"Nothing. We freaked out and ran home." I laughed. It wasn't a convincing laugh, but everyone else laughed too.

Everyone but Luke. "Did you tell anyone?"

I shook my head. "We weren't supposed to be there. We were afraid…"

We were afraid all right, and getting into trouble was only a little part of it.

"Did you ever go back?" the woman asked again.

Even her voice has a kind of insect whine to it. It hurt my head. I reached for my glass. "No."

"Do you think you could find the house again?" Rob asked slyly, looking from Luke to me. "If you had to?"

"No."

Luke asked, with a funny smile, "Would you want to try?"

§ § § §

I should have known the weekend would be a disaster when Luke told me later that evening that he would pick me up Saturday at six a.m.

"Morning?" I said uncertainly, hoping against hope that he'd got the a.m. and p.m. thing mixed up.

"Well, yeah. We'll need to get an early start. There's a lot of ground to cover, especially if we don't know where we're going."

He was smiling. He had a great smile: his hazel eyes tilted at the corners and his mouth — he had a very sexy mouth — did this little quirky thing. I felt a powerful tug of attraction — something I hadn't felt in a long time.

Still, I knew myself pretty well by then, and I wasn't at my best and brightest before noon on the weekends. Or any day. "Uh...I'm not much of a morning person."

"Mornings can be the best part of the day," Luke said softly, and it was clear he wasn't talking cornflakes. His gaze held mine; I literally couldn't look away. My heart did a little flip.

"Do you have a sleeping bag?" he added.

"A...sleeping...bag?"

"We'll be spending the night, right? Camping?"

"Uh...probably. Yeah." Oh. My. God. Did he mean—? Were we going to—?

"Don't sweat it," he said. "I've got you covered." His eyes actually twinkled. A cop with twinkly eyes? How much had I had to drink? I checked my glass.

So, yeah, the upshot: I went to dinner at Rob's on Thursday night and somehow walked out with a date — my first in over a year — for the weekend.

"Isn't Luke *hot?*" Rob demanded, when he called on Friday afternoon.

"He's pretty cute," I admitted, massaging my throbbing temples. I tried to focus on the monitor screen.

"Cute?" Rob exclaimed. "That's like saying Tom Cruise has nice teeth. He's gorgeous! That grin. Those eyes. That *ass.*"

"Enough with Tom Cruise."

"I'm talking about Luke!"

I rubbed my eyes. Tried to read back what I'd written. Garbage. I mean, really, who gave a flying fuck about Scenic Hudson?

"I didn't even catch his last name," I said.

"O'Brien."

"Swell. He probably comes from a long line of Irish cops."

"Sure, and don't you know the way of it, boyo," Rob returned in a tooth-peeling brogue.

"I don't think he's my type."

"What are you talking about? He's attractive, smart, funny — and he has a steady job."

"He carries a gun."

"He rarely shoots people on the first date."

"I may beg him to; he's taking me camping." Against my will, I was smiling.

"Camping?" Rob recovered quickly. "Camping is a *great* idea. You'll love camping. Fresh air, sunshine, exercise…"

"I hate fresh air, sunshine and exercise. I haven't been camping since I was thirteen."

Rob ignored this. He knows me pretty well. "Where are you going camping?"

"New Jersey."

"Jersey?"

"Yeah, we're staying with the Jersey Devil."

Rob snickered.

I added, a little uncomfortable because part of the evening — including the part where I'd agreed to go camping — was fuzzy, "I think he just wanted an excuse to get me to take him to the skull house."

"You're taking him to the skull house?"

My head was really pounding now. I was going to have to take more painkillers. A lot more painkillers. My poor liver. "I don't think I could find it if my life depended on it. But Luke seems to think it would be fun to try."

Luke. His name felt alien on my tongue. Like it was the first word I'd learned in a foreign language.

"Wow." Rob's single word seemed a little inadequate. I'd have phrased it more like…WTF? "Well, for the record," he said, "he wanted to meet you before he ever heard about the skull house. He loves that column you write for the New York Blade."

Against my will, I was flattered.

"And," Rob added, "He said you were really cute."

"Cute? That's like saying Marcelo Gomes has nice legs! I'm gorgeous!"

§ § § §

At five fifty-nine a.m. on Saturday morning, my doorbell rang. I stared blearily into the peephole. A tiny Luke stood at the end of what appeared to be an inverted telescope. As I studied him, he raked a self-conscious hand through his hair.

I stepped back, unlocked the slide and the three deadbolts, and opened the door.

"You're early," I said.

He laughed. He had a very nice laugh. I laughed too, although I was still convinced the weekend was a mistake. It sort of worried me that I was looking forward to it so much. Looking forward to seeing Luke again.

He really was good-looking: just over medium height, wide shoulders, narrow hips, long legs. He wore faded Levi's and a white tee-shirt that read, *OK, so I like donuts!!* The tee emphasized the rock-hard muscles in his arms.

"Ready to roll?"

"I guess."

His mouth twitched at the lack of enthusiasm in my voice. He nodded to my backpack. "That it?"

"Yeah." I gave him a doubtful look. "You said you'd bring the gear…"

He picked up my bag. "Yep. We're good."

Were we?

I followed him out, locked the door with shaking hands and tottered down the street to where he'd parked. He unlocked the passenger side and I crawled inside, slumping with relief in the front seat.

He stowed my gear in the back of the SUV, came around to his side. "Buckle up." He smiled, but he was obviously serious.

I fumbled with the seat belt.

He started the engine and Springsteen's *We Shall Overcome: The Seeger Sessions* picked up where it had left off on the CD player. I was a little surprised. I'm not sure what I was expecting. The Stones? *The Seeger Sessions* was a good sign; hours of "I Can't Get No Satisfaction" would have been daunting.

Somehow the close confines of the car heightened my awareness of him. He smelled like he had just stepped out of the shower. There was another smell too, straight from my idyllic childhood — Hoppes gun cleaner. And here I'd hoped I was kidding about his carrying.

I asked, "Can we stop and get coffee or something?"

He glanced at me. "Rough night?"

"Late night."

He nodded like that's what he'd thought. He found a Starbucks and we got coffee and pastries to go — which Luke insisted on paying for. I felt a little better after the coffee and sugar.

We started talking. It had been a long time since I had to make dating conversation. Maybe the effort showed.

Luke asked, "How's the hangover?"

I glanced at him. "Wow," I drawled, "you really are a detective."

He lifted a shoulder. "Hey."

Hey yourself, I thought irritably, but I let it go. He probably didn't miss a hell of a lot.

"How long have you been a detective?"

"Nine years. In New York, detectives are the equivalent rank of police officers." He added very casually, "I'm a Detective Second Grade now."

I gave him another look. He wasn't a lot older than me in years, but in experience…light-years. "What's that like: being a queer cop?"

"I don't think of myself as a *queer* cop. I think of myself as a cop."

"Sorry. You know what I mean, though. Is it tough? Or are you not out at work?"

"I'm out." He drove with one hand on the wheel, very relaxed, and one hand resting on the seat behind me. My skin felt alive to the possibility of the brush of his fingertips. If he flexed his fingers he could stroke my neck or touch my shoulder.

"But you're right. Law enforcement is a macho gig. I don't go out of my way to stress that I like to sleep with other guys."

"Have you ever shot anyone?"

He laughed. "Why does everyone ask that? You know how rare it is for a cop to actually shoot someone?"

"Have you ever *wanted* to shoot someone?"

"All the time!" We both laughed.

When we reached the Garden State Parkway I began to reluctantly dig through my mostly forgotten memories of that long ago summer. My friend, Ricky, had lived outside of Batsto, that much I remembered, but how far outside, I couldn't seem to recall. Nothing looked the same.

We stopped for a late breakfast — or early lunch — at a little pub called Lighthouse Tavern and had a couple of thick, juicy "Alpine" burgers and a couple of beers. By then we were getting along pretty well, having discovered that we had a few vital things in common, namely love of Cuban-Chinese food, Irish music, and really, really bad kung fu movies.

I mentioned digging the Springsteen track on Jesse Malin's new album, and he suggested — very off-hand — getting tickets for Malin's Bowery Ballroom concert if I was interested.

I said, equally off-hand, yeah, I was probably interested.

I ordered another beer. Luke again declined on the basis of driving. He seemed thoughtful as I finished my drink. "So what's the deal with you and cops?" he asked.

"Huh?"

"Rob said you had this thing about cops. You get nailed for a DUI or something?"

What the hell was *that* supposed to mean? I set my mug down and stared at him, instantly offended. But he just seemed curious. "Hey, for the record, just a couple of drinks can put you over the legal limit if you haven't eaten."

"Sure," he said peaceably. "So that's it then?"

"Not really." I gave him a sheepish grin. "I mean, I guess everyone is a little intimidated."

"Some people are turned on."

Our eyes met. I said casually, "That too."

He grinned.

§ § § §

Just outside of a little hamlet we stopped at the one-hundred-fifty-year-old general store and picked up German sausages, smoke-cured bacon and insect repellent. On our way out of the market I noticed a glass-fronted bulletin board. Tacked on top of the faded flyers and browned cards was a recent poster of a smiling girl: Elizabeth Ann Chattam. Twenty-one years old, freckles, brown hair clipped in big daisy barrettes, blue eyes, last seen hiking in Wharton State Forest.

"Something wrong?" Luke asked.

I shook my head.

Historic villages and blueberry farms gave way to cranberry bogs and cemeteries and ghost towns as we wound through the deep oak-pine forest of the Pinelands National Reserve.

We left the SUV at Parkdale, an old ghost town with only a rusty railroad bridge and a couple of stone foundations to show civilization had ever made it that far. We loaded our gear onto our backs. Luke checked his cell phone. His mouth did that little wry quirk.

"No reception?"

"I didn't really think there would be." He put his phone away. Pulled out a compass and then checked the sun. "We've got plenty of time before it gets dark. Any idea of which direction we should head out?"

I had exhausted my small store of memory getting us this far. I shrugged on my pack, shook my head. "Even if I —" I realized what I was saying, and shut up.

"Even if you...wanted to?"

"Hey, this was your idea. I'm just along for the ride." I caught his expression, played my comment back in my head, and felt myself reddening.

He grinned that devilish grin.

We hiked the sugar sand road for a couple of miles, then moved off onto one of the narrower trails.

I knew Luke was hoping that something would trigger my memories, but Ricky and I had been lost for hours when we stumbled on the house. It could have been just a mile or so in, or it could have been a day's walk — we had *spent* a day walking, but that was as likely due to having lost our sense of direction as necessity.

"Let me know if anything looks familiar," he requested when we paused to drink from our canteens.

I gave him an ironic look, and he grinned back. *When Irish eyes are smiling*, I thought ruefully. I still couldn't believe I'd let him talk me into this.

We kept up a brisk pace until it started to get dark. Then Luke set about finding a good spot to camp. I left it up to him. I was out of shape and feeling it. My feet ached, my calf muscles ached, my back ached. I was just glad I'd done enough walking tours in my time to know how to avoid blisters and heat rash.

I looked forward to sitting down and having a drink. I wished we could have just...gone away for the weekend; I knew a wonderful little historic bed and breakfast in Crown Point. But I didn't kid myself after miles of splashing through creeks and climbing over logs; the main attraction for Luke was not me; it really was the skull house.

That was okay. We could still have some fun. I just hoped the ground wasn't too hard and the night wasn't too cold. Or wet.

Luke found a nice little clearing that already had a campfire ring. I was glad to see the campfire ring, glad to have proof we hadn't traveled too far off the map. It was weird how a few miles could take you so far from civilization. It was like another world out here. He made up a campfire and we spread our bags out. He unwrapped the brats we'd bought at the little market.

I made my own preparations. "Cocktails, anyone?" I pulled the carefully-wrapped bottle of Bushmills out of my pack.

Luke raised his eyebrows. "So that's what was sloshing around. I thought you'd brought an awful lot of mouthwash for the weekend."

§ § § §

We dined *al fresco* on barbecued brats wrapped in toasted French rolls, washed down by beer and a whisky chaser. I'm not big on picnics or barbecues, but even I had no complaints that night, not once I'd had a chance to catch my breath.

"What's for dessert?" I asked, kidding.

Luke wiggled his eyebrows suggestively. I laughed and raised the bottle, offering it to him.

He took it, drank, handed it back. He was still smiling at me. Nodding to our sleeping bags lying a friendly distance from each other, he said, "It's going to be cold tonight. Should I zip our bags together?"

It took me a second to get it. I felt my face warm, but I tried to sound indifferent. "Oh. I guess so. Yeah."

He zipped the bags, turning them into one giant bag, and before long we were stretched out on our sides, not touching, but within arm's reach. "Where do you come up with the ideas for the stuff you write?"

"Things I see. Things I hear." I shrugged. "Stuff strikes me funny, and I write about it."

"I laugh my ass off reading that column you do for the Blade. It's such a kick the way your mind works."

I was insanely flattered, although I tried to hide it. I watched him under my lashes to see if he was serious.

"And you've written books?"

"Two." I lifted a negligent shoulder. "Travel books, that's all."

"That's all? That's amazing." His smile was genuinely admiring. "Travel books about where?"

"Italy. France." I stopped myself from shrugging again. It wasn't like I was being unduly modest, I just did't think it was a big deal. I hadn't written the Great American Novel or anything. Not yet. Probably not ever, if I wanted to be realistic — which I rarely did.

It didn't matter. The alcohol was singing in my bloodstream, and I was the life of the party. And it was a lovely party: firelight and starlight and the wine-crisp night air, the smell of pines and woodsmoke and lube and latex.

We were lying next to each other on our doublewide sleeping bag, feet brushing, knees brushing, arms brushing. Gradually we shed our clothes as we passed the bottle back and forth. More back than forth, but then I was more nervous than Luke. He was smiling and relaxed, reaching over to brush the hair out of my eyes as I talked.

I totally forgot what I was saying. Luke prompted me by asking about the trip to France, and I answered that it would have been better with someone with me — and maybe he should come next time.

"Oh, yeah? Where are you going next time?"

"Ireland." I said at random, guessing that with a name like O'Brien, he might like to go to Ireland.

He was amused. His eyes sparkled. "When are you going?" He licked his thumb and reached out to circle my left nipple. I caught my breath, tried to catch his hand and press it to my chest. "I might like to come."

"You can come," I promised, leaning over him.

I ran my hands over the broad expanse of his chest, the wide shoulders...communing. I could feel the warm flush beneath my fingertips, the damp of perspiration. I loved the language of his bare skin, the delicate punctuation of freckles and a tiny velvety mole on his rib cage.

I liked the contrast of bristly face and hard jaw with the softness of lips and flickery eyelashes. I scooted closer still, savoring the solid rub of our erections.

"Are you an innie or an outie?" he inquired huskily, his hand resting on the small of my back, pressing me closer.

I glanced down at my flat belly, and then chuckled, meeting his eyes. I'd never heard it called that. "I want you to fuck me," I told him. "I *need* you to fuck me."

"Happy to oblige."

He was in great shape, and I liked that too, Rock hard pecs, the balls of muscles in his arms; what would it be like to be in that kind of shape? There was a lot of strength, a lot of power there. Big hard hands rested on my hips as he helped me ease onto that straight rigid cock.

I cried out and I could see he liked it. He liked it vocal. Oh, he was truly Irish with his love of the blarney.

"Oh, fuck, you feel so good. You're so big," I told him, throatily.

"You *beauty*," he whispered.

That's not something you hear everyday. I chuckled again. Settled more fully on him, adjusting to his size and length. It had been a good long while since I'd had a real live partner and not a silicone rubber substitute.

He raised his head and kissed my breastbone, and I bent forward latching onto his mouth.

All this and kisses too? I kissed him until I thought I'd pass out from lack of oxygen, and his mouth parted reluctantly from mine. I liked his reluctance. The wet smack of his lips letting me go. I liked the taste of alcohol in his mouth.

"God, that's sweet," he muttered.

I rocked back and forth…gently…rising up and scrape-sliding down. The smooth swooping glide of a merry-go-round, that's what it reminded me of, and the merry-go-round pole driving up my hot little hole. We were just playing, but I started to feel that urgent aching need.

I planted my hand in the cushion of solid pecs and I worked my hips more frantically. Luke matched my rhythm easily, bucking up against my ass, thrusting deeply. His grunts excited me even more. I arched my back, went wild, begged him to fuck me hard, harder, *harder*.

I needed so much. There was such a big gaping emptiness in me. I needed him to fill it with heat and hungry demands; I wanted his need to overwhelm my own. I almost sobbed as he reached up and took my solid erection into his fist. He pumped me. Sweat broke out across my back. I was on fire.

I looked up and the sky was spinning, the stars rolling across the night, trying to drop into the little pockets. A dizzy swirl of stars and tree tops and the sliding moon, faster and faster and faster....

Luke shouted and I felt that funny squish inside the condom, the rush of hot release. My hole pulsed in response to his orgasm, like a pink mouth trying to find the words. There were no words for this. I reached for the low-hanging stars and yelled right out loud as my own release shivered through me.

Like the cork popping on champagne, spumes of white shot out. Emptied, I slumped forward on Luke's sweaty chest. Closed my eyes. His arms fastened around me. The sparse hair tickled my nose pleasantly. His heart was thumping from a million miles out...echoing across the universe...

"Christ Almighty," he moaned. "Please tell me you're just the same sober."

The merry-go-round slowed...slowed...glided gradually to a stop. It was nice to lie there like that, skin on skin, listening to the faraway chirp of crickets and frogs.

His words finally registered. I laughed and lifted my head. "It's moot. I'm never sober."

His mouth was a kiss away. He said wryly, "You think you're joking."

That startled me. "I *am* joking." I shook my hair out of my eyes. "Listen, I like to drink, but I do *not* have a problem with alcohol."

"Okay, okay," he said, in the tone of someone who doesn't want to get into an argument.

It was like he dumped a bucket of ice water over me. I felt bewildered. Hurt. I pulled out of his arms and sat up. "Maybe you should work on your after-play technique."

"Sorry." He tugged me back down. "That really *was* amazing."

I didn't have an answer for him. He'd spoiled it for me. I lay there, head on his chest, more hurt than angry — but a bit of both. He stroked my hair. His touch was light, almost tender. I couldn't think of the last time someone was tender with me.

"Tim," he said quietly. That was all. I raised my head and he kissed me, his mouth warm and surprisingly sweet.

And we did it all again, only slowly, lingeringly.

§ § § §

The house loomed before me. Ten stories tall. The windows flashed red in the setting sun. The hinges of the broken front door shrieked as the door swung open…

I jerked awake. It was freezing. My head throbbed. My mouth tasted horrible. I needed a piss.

"Bad dream?" Luke asked softly.

Confused, I realized that we were somehow in the same sleeping bag, and I was lying plastered on top of him, my sweaty head resting in the curve of his shoulder. He was dressed again; we both were, although I didn't remember pulling my clothes back on, didn't remember zipping ourselves into the bag.

"I…No. I…don't remember." I answered in a whisper, responding to his own hushed tone, even as I wondered why we were whispering.

Somewhere to the left, a twig snapped. I shivered.

He pulled the sleeping bag — wet with dew — over my shoulders, and slipped one arm around me again. It felt very good to be held. Even like this, in jeans and flannel shirts, I could feel and was comforted by the heat of his body. His hand slipped under my shirt, absently smoothing up and down my spine.

Despite the soothing touch, I heard the steady, swift thump of his heart beneath my ear.

His other arm, I slowly realized, rested on top of the sleeping bag — and he was holding a gun.

"Is something wrong?"

"Not sure. I think someone might be out there."

I sucked in a sharp breath, starting to pull away. He held me still. His put his mouth against my forehead. "Shhh. Don't let on."

I made myself lie still. Stared at what I could see of his profile in the dark. "What do we do?"

"Wait."

Wait?

For someone to pick us off as we lay by the cooling embers of our campfire? And I thought I had to pee *before?* My own heart was ricocheting around my ribcage. I felt for the zip of the sleeping bag, gently pulled it down. Luke nodded infinitesimal approval, continued to stroke my back in that automatic way, his eyes watching the line of trees surrounding the clearing.

We lay there not moving for what felt like an hour. Then I heard an owl call: not the drowsy nocturnal hoot, but the screech they make when they hunt.

A dank, damp breeze scented with the tangled undergrowth washed over my perspiring face. And all at once the night was alive with sound. From silence to deafening racket; I could practically hear ants marching up and down the grass blades, the dew drops crashing from the leaves overhead. Even the stars overhead seemed to crackle brightly in the black and bottomless sky. Too bright for my eyes…

§ § § §

I woke up sick and shaky, head pounding, my ass feeling thoroughly kicked.

"Morning, sunshine," Luke remarked in answer to my groan. He squatted next to the smoky campfire and held up a sauce pan. "Coffee?"

I muttered assent, crawled carefully out of the bag. Everything was wet, as though it had rained during the night. The smell of frying bacon made me want to puke. I staggered into the bushes and relieved myself.

As I wove my weary way back into camp the empty Bushmills bottle caught my eye. It lay near the ring of campfire stones, a tablespoon of amber glistening in its belly. Why the hell had we finished the entire bottle? Now there was nothing left for today.

My gut tightened remembering Luke's comments. Well, fuck him.

Oh yeah. I already did.

I took the lightweight aluminum cup he offered, picked up the bottle and tilted the dregs into my coffee. He watched in silence. "Hair of the dog." Against my will, I heard myself making an excuse. "Sometimes it helps a bad hangover if you have a little drink."

He eyed me for a long moment, then rose and went to the sleeping bags, unzipping them. He re-zipped his own bag and proceeded to roll it into a tight neat bundle.

I drank my coffee and tried to stop shaking.

He tied his bag with a couple of quick yanks, and said flatly, "My old man was a drunk."

It was like getting punched in the chest. I couldn't get my breath. *He can't really think….*

"He was what you'd call a functioning alcoholic," he added.

Maybe he's not talking about me. Maybe he's just…lousy at making morning after conversation. I said, "I…thought he was a cop?"

"He was. For thirty years. He drank and he did his job and he came home and drank some more. He was a decent cop and he tried to be a decent husband and a decent father, but he basically lived his entire adult life in a bottle. There's not a lot of room for other people in a bottle."

"I'm not…I don't have a drinking problem."

Luke didn't say anything.

"Look, I admit that I've gotten in the habit of drinking too much sometimes, but I'm not…I'm not an alcoholic." I offer him a twitchy smile. "Really. I'm not."

"I'm not judging you, Tim. It's an illness. It's like heart disease or HIV."

"The hell you're not judging," I said. "Not that I give a damn what you think. I just hope you're a better detective than you are…whatever this was supposed to be."

I threw out the rest of my coffee and went to tie my own sleeping bag up.

§ § § §

Which leads us to current events.

I stared at the ragged cross in the pale bark, my chest rising and falling.

"You couldn't be happy with dinner and a movie, could you?" I ask bitterly. "This is really all you dragged me out here for, to find this goddamned house. Why did you pretend it was anything else?"

"Look, I didn't kidnap you. You agreed to come. I assumed you wanted to."

"I wanted to see you again." It sounded pathetic, but I was so far beyond pride at this point, what did it matter?

His eyes flickered. "I wanted to see you too."

"Oh, please." Now it was my turn to be disgusted. "You were never interested in me. You're just looking to solve some big imaginary cold case. You're just…bucking for *Detective First Grade.*" I mimicked the quiet pride in his voice when he'd told me his rank.

He flushed. "That's bullshit. I wanted to ask you out before I ever heard about this skull house of yours. Rob said you weren't interested."

"I wasn't. I'm not." Now I was just being childish, but I didn't care. I hated him for dragging me out here, for seeing me break down sobbing, for making me face things I didn't want to face.

His mouth tightened. He said, "All right. That story about The Forester? That happens to be an urban legend that every cop in the northeast is familiar with."

"I didn't make it up!"

"I know." He was cool again. "The night of the party…I watched your eyes when you were talking. You weren't making it up."

What the hell had he seen? I had no idea. I stared sullenly at the carvings in the tree trunk.

"Whatever you saw all those years ago…it still scares you. And I thought if I offered you a chance to face whatever that was, you'd…take it."

"In other words, this is just a job opportunity for you."

"I already told you…" He stopped. Shrugged. "I thought maybe we'd have a few laughs while we were at it."

"A few laughs? It's *Lost Weekend*. In every *fucking* sense of the word."

"Hey —" But he didn't finish it, which was probably just as well. Instead he said, "It's your call. You want to turn back or you want to see what's ahead?"

I wanted to start back, no question about it. I looked at him. He met my eyes. I knew what he was thinking. I knew what he wanted. We'd come this far. I stared again at that little cross in the tree.

"After you, Jungle Jim," I said bitterly.

We continued walking.

And walking.

And walking.

The markings on the tree were mine, but now Luke led the way like he knew where we were going. It was all I could do to put one stumbling foot in front of the other. Maybe there was a path, but to me it seemed like an obstacle course of poison oak and sharp stones and snake holes and bug-infested logs and things that slithered and skittered reluctantly out of our way.

Miles of it in the humid, autumn heat. My head pounded nauseatingly with each step; I felt my heart hammering in my side. I took one step and then another, and I stopped, slid off my backpack. My head swam. I was coated in cold sweat, dizzy…

I dropped down on my knees, fell forward onto my hands. I was trying to decide if I would feel better or worse if I let myself throw up. I probably couldn't afford to get any more dehydrated than I already was.

Luke squatted down beside me. "You okay?"

I raised my head with an effort. "Of all the stupid questions..." I didn't have the energy to finish it. "I'm sick," I whispered.

"I know."

He opened his pack and pulled out a silver flask. "Medicinal purposes," he commented, measuring out a stingy little dose. "I think this qualifies."

I eased the rest of the way down and rested my head on my knees. I wanted to tell him to shove his little silver cup up his tight ass. There was no way that I could.

"Here." I looked up and he handed the cup to me, steadying my hand with his own.

I was a caricature, a movie drunk. I could hardly manage to get the cup to my mouth.

"Jesus," he said softly.

I drank. Put my hand still holding the flask cap over my eyes. Like the magic potion in a fairytale, I felt it begin to work, burning through my system, snapping on the lights, warming, calming, illuminating.... Maybe it would make me invisible to Luke; I didn't want him to keep looking at me like that. I wiped my face on my sleeve. "I'm okay."

Oh, yeah. Superb. Sick and shaking — but for God's sake: I was exhausted and sleep-deprived and out of shape; it wasn't all withdrawal. I didn't bother telling that to Luke, though. I'd already told him three times that weekend — possibly more — that I didn't have a drinking problem, so there was no point telling him again.

Even I knew by then that I was lying.

Follow the signs to journey's end: I couldn't get through the day without a drink. I was an alcoholic. A drunk.

"You can have another shot," Luke said. "But you may need it more later."

"I can wait." I didn't even know if that was true or not.

I didn't look into his eyes because I couldn't bear to see the reflection of what I already heard in his voice: attraction and liking replaced by pity — and distaste.

I heard myself say, "I've tried to stop. I can't." I listened in shock to the echo of those words.

Silence.

He said finally, "Have you ever thought about getting help?"

"You mean like…AA?"

"There are other organizations, but yeah, like AA"

"I…can't."

"You can't what?"

I swallowed hard. "I can't go and talk to a bunch of people about…my problems."

I couldn't believe I was talking to *him*. Just imagining standing up in a room full of strangers made me feel light-headed: *Hi, I'm Timothy…*

I looked at him shame-faced and said, "Besides, I don't…think it would work for me. I don't think I can stop on my own. I have…tried." I dropped my head on my folded arms.

Why was I *telling* him?

And yet, as humiliating and painful as this was, there was a terrible relief in just…saying it. Admitting it once and for all.

Luke rested his broad warm hand on my back. "What about getting medical treatment?"

"You mean…a hospital?"

"Rehab, yeah."

Voice hushed, I admitted the real truth. "I'm afraid."

"Of rehab?"

I moved my shoulders. "Of giving up control of my life."

He said gently, "Tim, you already gave up control."

§ § § §

The house leaned crookedly behind a wall of forbidding trees. I didn't remember the gingerbread trim. Those frivolous curlicues sweeping up and down the edge of the roof above the wall of trees seemed incongruous with the house of my memory. The vines and tree branches seemed to be all that was holding it rooted into place; I heard the old boards groaning like the building was ready to topple over any moment.

One or two of the upper story windows still had glass panes. The others gaped blackly or had been boarded up. The double wide front entrance was also boarded up. I couldn't remember if there had been a door before; I didn't remember the baby blue posts holding up the sagging portico. There was no giant tree growing out through the peeling roof; my imagination must have supplied that.

But there was no question it was the same house.

"There must have been a raised porch that ran the length of the house," Luke said, studying the high windows.

If there had been stairs they had disappeared with the long-ago porch, and the windows were too high to climb through unless one of us boosted the other.

The building creaked ominously in the breeze, like the laughter of some demented old crone. The sound snapped me out of my trance. "We have to get out of here."

I tried to brush past Luke. He said something, and reached for me, and I struck at his hand, ducking back when he lunged for me again. He swore. His foot caught on a tree root and he went down on one knee. I slipped out my pack and ran like a deer.

Only it wasn't running so much as trying to plough through the brush and bushes and trees. I didn't get more than a few yards when Luke caught me up. He grabbed my shoulder, and I turned around and swung at him.

He blocked me without particular trouble, not letting go of the steely grip he had on my shoulder.

I tried to slide out from under this hand, and when that didn't work I tried to slug him. He grasped my fist, yanked me forward, throwing me off balance, and I crashed against him. He still had hold of my arm and he twisted it behind me, turning me away from him.

The pain was instant and startling. I cried out.

"Don't struggle," he said, breathing fast. "I don't want to hurt you."

"You're breaking my fucking arm!"

"Then hold still, damn it." His other arm locked across my shoulders in a restraining hold that stopped just short of actually choking me. "Tim — stop."

I stopped. My arm felt wrenched out my shoulder socket. I clenched my jaw against the pain, and nodded. After a moment he let go of the arm twisted behind my back; it dropped limply to my side. I tried to move my other arm to rub my shoulder, but he kept me pinned against him.

"You *asshole.*" I hated him like I'd never hated anyone in my life.

Luke ignored my trembling rage. "What happened here, Tim?" His breath was warm against my ear. "Something happened twelve years ago. What was it?"

I shook my head. "*Nothing.*" I made another half-hearted attempt to wrest free. "Look, this was a bad idea. We need to get out of here."

His arms tightened. "Talk to me. What happened the first time you found this place?"

"I don't know. Please. Let me go."

I started shivering from head to foot — and the weirdest part was, I wasn't even sure why. I thought my heart was going to tear out of my chest. Maybe Luke felt it banging against his arm, because his grip changed, turning to support, comfort if I wanted it. I resisted it. I couldn't trust him anymore. This was all his fault.

"Where would you go, Tim? Think for a minute. You can't go barging through the bushes. If you go tearing out of here you'll just get lost or injured."

"I'll take my chances."

"I can't let you take that chance."

"Jesus, who died and made you John Wayne?"

He didn't bother to answer.

I thought how strange it was that at this time the night before we'd been settling down to sex and maybe the start of something. In twenty-four hours everything had changed.

I sagged against him. "Luke...I don't remember."

"The hell you don't."

I shook my head hopelessly. He just waited — like we had all the time in the world.

I said, finally, so quietly that he had to duck his head to hear, "There were pieces of bone all over the ground...like peanut shells or sea shells. Like gravel. Broken animal skulls and...human. I know they were..."

Luke's arms tightened. "You're okay. Go on."

"I picked up a little piece of a jaw. I could see where the...teeth were supposed to go." I swallowed dryly. "Ricky wanted to see if we could climb inside through one of the broken windows. We snuck up to the side of the house." I took a deep breath, trying to get control. "We got to one of the windows, looked up, and — and suddenly there was a man standing there."

"Inside the house?"

I nodded. "He just...stared at us. Straight at us. And we stared back. Frozen. Like a pair of rabbits. And then he raised his hand like he was waving hello." My voice broke. "It looked black. He pressed it against the window...and it left a bloody handprint."

My voice gave out as though I had run out of oxygen, which is how I felt. I stared up at Luke, stricken.

"What did you do?" he asked after a moment. His voice sounded thick.

"He turned away from the window...and we ran."

The dark woods of my memory opened up and swallowed me. That terrified scramble through briars, crawling and wriggling under when we couldn't push through, running blind as the night settled on the roof of treetops — and always the knowledge that *he* was behind us....

Luke said so calmly it was like a slap, "What happened when you got home?"

My mouth worked but I couldn't remember the words.

"You made it home safely," Luke said. "What happened then?"

"Nothing."

He let me go. "You didn't tell anyone?"

I shook my head, massaging my twisted shoulder. I could see the lack of comprehension on his face. "We were afraid. He saw us. We thought he would come after us."

"Then why the hell wouldn't you tell your parents?"

"Ricky — we weren't supposed to go into the woods. His dad said he would get the belt if he went back in there. We couldn't decide. We thought no one would believe us. And it's not like we could lead them back. We got lost so many times that day. I don't know how the hell we did finally get out."

Luck. And the fact that we were small enough to wriggle through places our pursuer couldn't. Mostly luck.

"But —"

"And my parents came the next day. I went home and it…all seemed like a dream. I told myself we imagined it."

Luke didn't say anything; I read condemnation in his silence.

"We left him free to keep killing, didn't we?" I said dully. "Everyone who disappeared after that…it's our fault."

"Let's get one thing straight," Luke said. "Nothing this sick fucker did is your fault. You were thirteen-years-old. And teenage boys don't have the greatest judgment in the world."

"I just…forgot about it," I whispered. "I let myself forget."

He said dryly, "Yeah, well, maybe you tried. I don't know how successful you were."

"That girl on the poster in the store…"

"Let it go, Tim. You have no idea what happened to her." He reached inside his shirt. He was wearing a shoulder holster. I already knew that. I'd felt it when I was leaning against him. He pulled out his gun, checked the chamber.

"Do you know how to handle a gun?"

I nodded wearily. My assent seemed to catch him by surprise.

"You do?"

"Yeah. My dad is ex-army. I know how to shoot. I grew up shooting." I understood his hesitation. In his shoes I wouldn't give me a gun either.

He knelt, opened his pack, pulled out a tightly-wrapped triangle, which, when unwrapped, turned out to be .38 revolver. He offered it to me.

I stepped back. "Don't. I'm not going back there. I'm not going with you."

His dark brows drew together. He continued to hold the gun out to me. "I can't. I can't. You *can't* ask this of me," I said.

"I *am* asking you."

"Luke...you of anybody knows that...there's a limit of what you can expect from me."

"I'm not asking anything more than you're capable of."

I gaped. "Are you...you can't be serious. Were you *here* five minutes ago?"

His hazel eyes met my own. "Tim, it's one thing to run away when you're thirteen. No one can blame you for that. But you're a man now. You have to stop running."

I blinked a couple of times, trying to focus on this idea. "But there's no need for us to go back. The Forester's dead by now." I rushed along, trying to convince him, convince myself. "The guy's dead. He has to be. He's not even there anymore. He can't be. We could just...call the cops."

"I *am* a cop. I have to check this out before I call anyone else in. Anyway, you don't believe that or you wouldn't be this frightened."

"Yes, I would! I am." I gulped. "If you want to go back...that's up to you. I'll...wait for you. I'll try to. But I can't..."

He just kept staring at me. *This is the face he wears when people try to talk him out of arresting them.*

"You have to. I can't leave you."

"Yes, you can, because I'm not going with you."

"Tim, for your own sake — you've got to face this before it destroys you."

"Jesus Christ. Stop it! You don't know me. You don't know what you're talking about."

"I know you this well. I need your help."

I couldn't look away from those hazel eyes. Finally, hand shaking, I took the gun, checked to make sure it was loaded, shoved it into my back waistband under my flannel shirt. I said unsteadily, "What the hell is this supposed to be? Intervention by serial killer?"

To my astonished rage, his mouth twitched like he actually found that funny.

I practically stuttered, "You laugh at me now, O'Brien, and I swear to Christ I'll deck you."

"You just keep channeling that anger and we'll be fine." His eyes assessed me.

"Do you need a drink?"

"Is that a trick question?"

"If it'll help you hold together…"

I couldn't hold his gaze. I looked away and nodded, and he got out the flask he'd brought for medicinal purposes and handed it to me.

I didn't bother with the little cup this time; I just tilted the flask.

* * * * *

From the cover of a thicket of berry bushes we studied the row of boarded windows. "Let's try the other side," Luke said, his voice low.

"If he was watching us last night, he could still be watching us. He could be following us and waiting for dark."

Luke glanced up at the fading sunlight. He nodded. "Stay frosty."

Stay frosty? Was he for real?

"Frosty the Snowman, that's me," I muttered. I moved around him, kneeling to pick up something white in the weeds. I handed it to Luke.

He studied the bone. "Animal. Not human."

I nodded, but I wasn't reassured.

Luke started toward the front of the house, skirting the bushes. I followed closely, watching the boarded face of the house. It didn't look like anyone had been there for years, and yet…it didn't quite feel dead, either.

If anyone lived in that wreck, he wasn't coming and going through the front entrance, which had been secured with thick planks. We picked our way around broken boards and tree roots, ducking under the sagging portico. I saw a snake slither into the underbrush a few feet ahead.

The first-story windows were boarded on the other side of the house as well, but the trees grew closer to the foundation, and I saw that it would be possible to climb up and get in through one of the open second-story windows. I kept this thought to myself. I was still hoping Luke might give up and decide we were wasting our time.

"Let's try the back," Luke said.

"Let's not and say we did."

He threw me a brief grin.

We scooted around the corner of the house and paused in the deep shade. Something crunched behind us. I froze, staring at the moving wall of bushes a few feet away. Was it only the breeze stirring the leaves?

"Do you have your cell phone?" I whispered to Luke.

He didn't bother to turn. "It's back with my pack. There's no signal out here."

Maybe not, but I'd have been willing to try. My phone, unfortunately, was in Luke's car.

"The back door's not boarded up," Luke said. He started forward across the carpet of autumn leaves.

I hesitated, still watching the bushes. The dusty purple berries hung in heavy clusters. I looked skyward. The sun looked distorted through the ragged tree-tops, splintered light glanced off the dark foliage and flaking paint of the house. White flakes in the weeds, too. I stooped. Picked up a sliver of white. Not paint. A bone chip. Bone chips dusting the grass. I swallowed hard, straightened.

We didn't have a lot of daylight left, and I didn't want to try and find our way out of the woods by flashlight. And I sure as hell didn't want to spend another night here.

"Tim."

I glanced back. Luke was at the rear door of the house. He gestured with his chin.

I threw one last uneasy look at the bushes and moved out from the shadow of the house. Bloodred autumn leaves blanketed the ground, crackling underfoot.

Just like that, the ground gave beneath me with the shriek of rotten wood and corroded hinges. I crashed down through a pair of crumbling cellar doors and slammed into the hard-packed dirt floor.

Stunned, I lay on my side for a few seconds trying to process what had happened while dry leaves floated gently down around me.

In a dark, dark wood... The words from the old children's song ran through my mind in dazed refrain. *There was a dark, dark house...*

My ankle hurt. My knee hurt. My hip hurt. My wrist felt broken. Somehow I'd managed to protect my head, but that had been hurting before I ever fell through the broken doors — and this wasn't helping.

Thank God I hadn't fallen on my back and shot myself.

And in that dark, dark house...

Light from the hole in the doors above me illuminated burnt and jagged timber — thank God I hadn't landed on any of that — wooden shelves with dusty jars and dusty cans, some broken furniture. A kerosene lantern swung precariously over my head, creaking on its rusty hook.

"Tim, can you hear me?"

I realized Luke was calling to me, that he had been calling for some time now.

"Tim? Can you answer me?"

"I'm okay." That was a slight overstatement.

"Tim!"

"I'm okay," I called more loudly. Gingerly, I made an effort to push up. My muscles screeched protest. Maybe my wrist was sprained, not broken. I cradled it against my chest, tried flexing the fingers.

"Jesus Christ," Luke's voice echoed with relief. "I thought...look, don't move. I'm coming down."

Don't move. Right...

I stared up. It was about a twelve-foot drop. Several steps led up to the broken doors, but they were blocked off by the broken timbers. The room itself was twenty feet long. Another set of stairs, probably leading up to the kitchen, vanished into the shadows.

Luke's head withdrew from the broken opening in the cellar doors. A moment later a shadow flashed across, and then was gone.

What...? Was that a bird?

I heard a thud. Swift, hard. And then another.

Hair prickled on the back of my neck. I yelled, "Luke?"

Nothing. No answer.

I listened tautly. Listened...and heard something like...a sodden dragging sound.

I opened my mouth to shout for Luke again, but something held me silent. I swallowed hard, and crawled out from under the opening in the cellar doors.

Grabbing onto one of the broken timbers, I painfully pulled myself upright. Okay, I was still in one working piece. Now I needed to focus on getting out of here. I could try climbing through the debris blocking the cellar doors and breaking out that way, but that might be what someone was expecting.

I picked my way across the junk-strewn floor and hesitated at the foot of the stairs. *And in that dark, dark house...*

Maybe I was...confused. Maybe everything was fine topside, and I needed to wait for Luke just like he told me to. The inner door was probably locked anyway.

Luke was pretty damned tough and pretty damned experienced. Nothing was going to happen to Luke that he couldn't handle. Me, on the other hand...

My gaze fell on the shelf of dusty mason jars next to me. I stared. Picked up one of the jars. Wiped the grimy front on my shirt, studying the murky contents. Not peaches. Not tomatoes.

I shook the jar gently and something small and round and unmistakable floated next to the glass, staring back at me.

I dropped the jar. It smashed on the floor, liquid mush spilling out.

"Oh, sweet Jesus…"

I reached out to steady myself on the shelf, and pain from my sprained wrist twisted through my nerves and muscles, snapping me back to awareness. I fumbled under my shirttail for the comforting weight of Luke's .38.

I went up the short flight of stairs and tried the door. It creaked open onto a short dim hallway. Faded wallpaper and moldering carpet gave way to an old-fashioned kitchen.

A sweetish sickly pall seemed to hang in the dead air. It was hard to see. The only light came from the small window in the door that led out to the clearing behind the house. I could just make out dingy wallpaper, a grimy wall thermometer in the shape of a fish, and some filthy decorative plates on the wall — all in shocking contrast to piles of empty jars, broken dishes and bones.

A meat cleaver lay on the counter. A butcher's knife lay on the floor. There were bones of all different sizes and shapes: like a macabre soup kitchen. Giant kettles sat on the cold stove and in the sinks and on tables.

There was a table in the center of the room. Feeling like I was sleepwalking, I moved over to it. The wooden top looked ink-stained. There were sheets and sheets of butcher paper covered with the crayon scrawls of a berserk child. Pictures of somber and serrated woods, tormented figures, and fire — fire or fountains of blood?

I crept over to the back door and peered out the grimy window. It would be dark soon. The clearing behind the house looked empty. No sign of Luke. No sign of anyone. But a shovel lay in plain sight on the bed of red and gold leaves. A shovel where there had been no shovel before.

I tried to hear over the thunder of my own heartbeat.

Evening sounds. Crickets. Birds. Frogs.

What the hell was I supposed to do? I had no idea. Even if it were possible for me to escape into the woods, I couldn't leave Luke. Not until I knew...for sure.

I looked across the kitchen, across the boiled bare carcasses and glass lanterns and knives, to another doorway leading into another dark room.

Would he have had time to drag Luke inside the house? Or was he butchering him out in the woods right now?

Or was he hunting for me?

I glanced back at the cellar door. It gaped blackly.

I picked up one of the candles from the table, scrabbled around till I found matches, and stepped inside the adjoining room. Leaves and branches were strewn over the wooden floor, but otherwise the room looked startlingly normal: old-fashioned moth-eaten furniture, tattered draperies, china. There was a fireplace with the burnt remains of clothing and a shoe. Over the fireplace hung a large, framed photo of a WWI soldier.

At the far end of the room stood another doorway and a staircase beyond. The upstairs windows were not boarded. I'd have a better chance of spotting Luke and his assailant from the second floor.

Glancing down at a little pie-shaped table my attention was caught by the small pile of odds and ends: coins, hair barrettes — *large daisy barrettes*. I stared at them for a long moment. No worse than any of the rest of it, right? If I was responsible for this, I was responsible for all of it. All of it. All of these things had belonged to someone: buttons, keys, a silver pen...and one boy's bone-handled penknife.

I reached out automatically. I recognized that knife. I'd lost it twelve years ago in these woods.

Picking it up, I was surprised to see that my hand was steady. Nothing like the anesthesia of total shock. I slipped it into my pocket, started warily up the stairs, gun at ready like I'd seen in a million TV shows. For all I knew there was a whole house full of these murdering freaks.

Halfway up the staircase I heard the kitchen door bang. I heard voices. An unfamiliar mumble and a groan that sounded like Luke.

He was alive.

My heart sped up with a hope I hadn't dared entertain until then. I snuck back down the squeaking staircase and darted over to the kitchen doorway. I had a quick glimpse of long gray hair, a massive back, giant hands the color of mahogany. He was dragging Luke by his hair and collar across the floor. I could tell Luke was only partially conscious; he struggled feebly, kicking out like he was trying to get to his feet. His hands struck ineffectively at the powerful arms hauling him towards the cellar.

The Forester slid him like a sack of potatoes across the floor.

Luke groped blindly, and his hand found the butcher's knife on the floor, closed on it.

The Forester, still muttering that incoherent litany, kicked the knife out of his hand, and then reached for the meat cleaver on the counter.

I stepped into the kitchen, thumb-cocked Luke's revolver. "Stop," I said breathlessly.

He tossed Luke back down, and turned, cleaver in hand. His face was seamed with scars and grime, tanned like old leather. There were leaves and twigs in his hair. His eyes were muddy and lifeless. I saw that there was not going to be any reasoning with him, but I said, "Don't do it."

He stepped toward me, and I instinctively stepped back, which I knew was a mistake. There was no way I was walking out of here while he was still standing. He lumbered toward me, and Luke grabbed for his ankle. The Forester slashed down at him with the cleaver — like you would swat at a mosquito.

I fired.

Saw the muzzle flash in the dim light, felt the gun kick in my hand. The bullet hit him in the shoulder. I'd been aiming for dead center, so that wasn't so good. But I'd been distracted by my abject relief that he hadn't cut Luke's head in two, the cleaver crunching into the table leg, and missing Luke by inches.

The bullet didn't seem to faze The Forester. He yanked the cleaver free and flew at me. I clamped down on the trigger and emptied the remaining five bullets into his chest. He piled right into me, heavy and hot and stinking like a bear, and I banged into the door frame and then crash-landed on the floor — with him on top.

The coppery smell of blood was in my nostrils; it was too dark to see him clearly anymore, just a black bulk crushing me. Wet warmth soaking into my jeans and shirt. I felt his teeth snapping against my throat, as I wriggled and kicked frantically to try and get free. Every second I expected to feel the meat cleaver chop into my bones. I swore and prayed and fought for my life.

I managed to get out from under him; he didn't come after me. I backed up along the floor. He just lay there twitching and shuddering, his breath rattling in his throat.

Blood drenched my clothes, but I was pretty sure none of it was mine.

"Tim?" Luke reeled into the doorway.

"Hi," I said faintly.

He staggered forward, nearly fell over the Forester's body, and then dropped down beside me, feeling me over blindly. "Are you okay? Did he get you?"

"No. I mean, yes, I'm okay. He didn't get me." I put my arms around him. I needed contact with someone alive and warm and reasonably sane. I needed to reassure myself that Luke really was alive.

He hugged me back. Hard. "You're *covered* in blood. Are you sure... ?"

"I'm sure."

And then neither of us said anything. After a time the thing on the floor stopped moving. Stopped breathing. I wondered if I should be feeling guilty about that too.

Head buried in Luke's shoulder I thought that somehow we were going to have to get back to Luke's car, drive to where we could call for help, lead the police back here, spend the rest of the night giving our statements. I would probably be arrested, self-defense or not. Not held for long, hopefully, and I was pretty sure Luke would help me every way he could, and if I was lucky it wouldn't even come to trial...

"You're sure you're okay?" he said, and his hands felt kind and familiar, once again running over my arms and back, checking for injuries because what other explanation could there be for the way I was clinging to him.

I didn't misread him. He felt guilty as hell that he'd nearly got me killed, and grateful that I'd saved his life, and worried about what this was going to do to me seeing that I wasn't exactly the Rock of Gibraltar. I wondered if killing monsters was a strong enough foundation for building a friendship. We could be friends, right? Because friends were good, too.

"Timmy?" The gentleness in his voice got me. I had to blink back the sting in my eyes.

"Yeah. I'm fine," I said, muffled. "I just… picked a really bad day to stop drinking."

§ § § §

I was dreaming that Luke was kissing me. His lips, a little chapped, pressed warmly, sweetly against my own. My mouth quivered. I wanted to kiss him back, but already he was withdrawing.

"Tim?"

I opened my eyes. Luke leaned over me.

"Hey," I mumbled, sitting up. Apparently I had been sleeping against his shoulder, which was more than a little embarrassing. It was late afternoon, and we were sitting in Luke's car on the street outside my brownstone. The sun shone brightly. The street was full of traffic, the sidewalk crowded with pedestrians. For a moment, I wondered if I'd dreamed the entire thing.

I glanced at Luke, who looked as battered as I felt. He had a funny look on his face. "How are you feeling?"

"Oh, you know. High on life." My neck felt broken and every muscle in my body felt bruised. I had a sprained wrist and a wrenched knee. I felt groggy, disoriented — and as always — thirsty. But…actually… it did feel very good to be alive. "Sorry for flaking out on you."

Luke said seriously, "Hey, you were there when I needed you."

I gave him a tired smile.

I realized he was waiting for me to say good-bye and get out of his car. I said, "Thanks for convincing the troopers not to arrest me"

"Nobody wanted to arrest you. It's a clear case of self-defense. I don't think it's even going to come to trial. Although there will probably be a hell of a lot of press."

"Yeah. Well." I reached in the backseat for my blood-stiff clothes. I wasn't sure why I'd brought them home; I was never going to wear them again. I stared at the gore-streaked bundle and hazily remembered stopping at a campsite with Luke, and showering, and changing into our spare clothes. After that...a comfortable gray blank. I didn't even remember climbing back into the car.

"Um..."

I glanced back at him.

"I can't promise that every time we go out we'll have this much fun, but...I'd really like to see you again."

I blinked.

"I mean," he said awkwardly, "If you're not too fed up about...everything."

"Are you serious?"

"Hell, yeah." He gave me that heart-stopping grin, but there was just a trace of uncertainty in his eyes. "Maybe next time we could just...I don't know...go to dinner."

I stared at him. He *was* serious.

I still had a chance with him. He knew...and he still wanted to see me. He had seen me at my absolute worst and he was still interested. Still attracted. He knew what to expect, and he was still willing to give it a try.

I so did not want to blow this second chance.

But I didn't want to be the guy responsible for taking the twinkle out of those eyes. I didn't want to see the affection and attraction die out — to be replaced with weariness and disgust when I slipped up and fell off the wagon — and there were going to be a lot of slips and falls ahead of me. As much as I wanted to believe I'd never let him down, I knew I was going to let us both down before I got better. If I got better. If I was strong enough.

It wasn't easy, but I said, "I'd like that too. But I... probably shouldn't answer till I'm...sober."

His gaze held mine and there was no disappointment, no impatience. In fact, his smile grew a little warmer, a little more confident. "Okay. I can respect that."

I realized I wanted his respect — among other things — almost as desperately as I wanted my own. All at once it was hard to control my face. I turned towards the door, and he put a hand on my arm.

"Listen, Tim. Sometimes it helps if a friend goes with you the first couple of times."

Oh. He meant to AA or wherever. I already knew I was going to need more help than that. "I don't need someone to go with me, but it would help to know I had a friend...waiting."

"You have a friend waiting." He leaned forward and kissed me, his mouth warm and insistent. His eyes met mine. "And just so you know, that's hello."

I Spy
Something Bloody

I find that readers either adore this story or they hate it. I wanted to try something with an older protagonist — a May/December relationship. In fact, almost an odd couple dynamic. Betrayal and forgiveness are frequent themes in my work — it's always interesting to see what the limits are for readers.

CHAPTER ONE

The telephone rang and rang. I stared through the window glass of the phone box at rugged green moorland and the distant snaggletoothed remains of a prehistoric circle. The rolling open hills of Devon looked blue and barren against the rain-washed sky. I'd read somewhere they'd filmed *The Hound of the Baskervilles* around here. It looked like a good day for a hellhound to be out and about, prowling the eerie ruins and chasing virgin squeak toys to their deaths.

To the north were the military firing zones, silent this afternoon.

The phone continued to ring — a faraway jangle on the other end of the line.

I closed my eyes for a moment. It felt years since I'd really slept. The glass was cool against my forehead. Why had I come back? What had I hoped to accomplish? It wasn't as though Barry Shelton and I had been best mates. He'd been a colleague. Quiet, tough, capable. I'd known a lot of Barry Sheltons through the years. Their faces all ran together. Just another anonymous young man — like me.

He died for nothing. A pointless, stupid, violent death. For nothing!

I could still hear Shelton's mother screaming at me, blaming me. Why not? It was as much my fault as anyone's. It didn't matter. I wasn't exactly the sensitive type. Neither had been Shelton. The only puzzle was why I'd imagined the news would come better from me. Wasn't even my style, really, dropping in on the widows and orphans and Aged Ps. That kind of thing was much better handled by the Old Man.

My leg was aching. And my ribs. Rain ticked against the glass. I opened my eyes. The wet-dark road was wide and empty. I could see miles in either direction. All clear. The wind whistled forlornly through the places where the door didn't join snugly; a mournful tune like a melody played on the *tula*.

Unexpectedly, the receiver was picked up. A deep voice — with just that hint of Virginia accent — said against my ear, "Stephen Thorpe."

I hadn't expected to be so moved by just the sound of his voice. Funny really, although laughter was the furthest thing from me. My throat closed and I had to work to get anything out.

"It's Mark," I managed huskily, after too long a pause.

Silence.

He was there, though. I could hear the live and open stillness on the other end of the line. "Stephen?" I said.

"What did you want, Mark?" he asked quietly. Too quietly.

"I'm in trouble." It was a mistake. I knew that the instant I said it. I should be apologizing, wooing him, not begging for help, not compounding my many errors. My hand clenched the receiver so hard my fingers felt numb. "Stephen?"

"I'm listening."

"Can I come home?"

He said without anger, "This isn't your home."

My heart pounded so hard I could hardly hear over the hollow thud. My mouth felt gummy-dry, the way it used to before an op. A long time ago. I licked my lips. No point arguing now. No time. I said, "I...don't have anywhere else to go."

Not his problem. I could hear him thinking it. And quite rightly.

He said with slow finality, "I don't think that coming here would be a good idea, Mark."

I didn't blame him. And I wasn't surprised. Not really. But surprised or not, it still hurt like hell. More than I expected. I'd been prepared to play desperate; it was a little shock to realize I didn't have to play. My voice shook as I said, "Please, Stephen. I wouldn't ask if it — please."

Nothing but the crackling emptiness of the open line. I feared he would hang up, that this tenuous connection would be lost — and then I would be lost. Stranded here at the ends of the Earth where bleak sky fused into wind-scoured wilderness.

Where the only person I knew was Barry Shelton's mother.

I opened my mouth — Stephen had once said I could talk him into anything — but I was out of arguments. Too tired to make them even if I'd known the magic words. All that came out was a long, shuddering sigh.

I don't know if Stephen heard it all the way across the Atlantic, but after another heartbeat he said abruptly, "All right then. Come."

I replaced the receiver very carefully and pushed open the door. The wind was cold against my face, laced with rain. Rain and a hint of the distant sea; I could taste the salty wet on my lips.

§ § § §

The flight from Heathrow to Dulles took eight hours. Eight hours through the stars and the clouds. Between my ribs and my leg, sleep was impossible — even if I'd felt safe enough to take a couple of painkillers and shut off. I tried reading a few pages of Dickens' *Little Dorrit,* then settled for numbing myself with alcohol and staring out the window. I don't remember thinking much of anything; I barely remember the flight. I just remember hurting and welcoming the hurt because it would keep me sharp. Which was proof of how drunk I was.

I waited longer for my connecting plane to Virginia than the flight itself took. By then I was sobering up, and my various aches and pains were fast reaching the point where I wanted to murder the bloke coughing incessantly behind me — and the baby screaming in front. I wasn't crazy about any of the other passengers either. Or the flight crew. Or the ground crew. Or anyone else on the ground. Or in the air. Or on the planet. Or in the solar system.

I tried to think happy thoughts, but happy thoughts weren't a big part of my job description. So I thought unhappy thoughts about Stephen not wanting me to come back. "This isn't your home," he'd said, and so much for Southern hospitality.

I waited my whole life for you. I can wait a few months more…

Time flies when you're having fun, I suppose.

Was it that easy for him to turn it off? Because I'd tried and I couldn't do it. If anything, my need for Stephen grew stronger with each passing day. It would be convenient to be able to turn off the memories: the way his green eyes crinkled at the corner when he smiled that slow, sexy grin; the way his damp hair smelled right out of the shower — a blend of orange and bamboo and vetiver that always inexplicably reminded me of the old open air market in Bengal; the way that soft Southern drawl got a little more pronounced when he was sleepy — or when we made love. Yeah, made love. It hadn't just been fucking. Stephen had loved me. I was sure of it.

He'd said so. And I didn't think he'd lie about it. Like it said in *Little Dorrit*, "Once a gentleman, and always a gentleman."

I was the liar. But I'd said the words too. And meant them.

§ § § §

We landed at Shenandoah Valley Airport just after eleven o'clock in the morning, and I stumbled off the plane, exhausted and edgy, tensing as hurrying passengers brushed past, crowding me. Too many people — and everyone's voice sounded harsh, too loud, nearly sending me out of my skin.

After what felt like several nerve-wrenching miles of this, Stephen appeared out of nowhere, striding towards me in that loose, easy way. I had never seen anything more beautiful. Tall and lean, broad shoulders and long legs, hair prematurely silver — striking with his youthful face. He was fifty now. I had missed his birthday. Missed it by a month. By a mile. Just one of many things I'd missed.

At the sight of me, he checked midstride, then came forward.

"What the hell happened to you?"

I offered a smile — to which he did not respond. "Long story."

There were tiny lines around his eyes that I didn't remember before — a sternness to his mouth that was new.

"Another one?" The tone was dry, but his expression gave me a little hope.

I hadn't realized how much I missed him till he was standing arm's length from me, and then it was like physical pain: He was so familiar, so…dear — like a glimpse of land after months at sea. The boyishly ruffled pale hair, the spring green of his eyes…

I thought for an instant he might even take me into his arms, but no. Instead he took my bag, took my elbow, took charge. His fingers were warm — if a little steely — wrapping around my arm. And although it was not exactly what I wanted, it was a relief. A welcome relief to rely on someone else — to rely on Stephen. There was no one else in the world I trusted. Not even the Old Man. Not anymore. Only Stephen.

The feeling no longer appeared to be mutual.

"We'll have to hurry," he said crisply. "I'm on call." And he glanced automatically at his wristwatch. The watch I had given him on the one birthday I'd been around for. An artifact of a relationship lost to time and distance; there seemed something ironic in my choice now.

"You needn't have come yourself," I said, hobbling along. "I could have grabbed a cab."

Wrong answer again. He gave me an austere look, his hand tightening wardenlike on my bicep, unconsciously lengthening his stride. He must have talked to one of his mates in the Justice Department. I hadn't expected him at the airport, and hadn't offered any flight info.

Sweat broke out along my back, my underarms. It was oppressively hot in the airport terminal — or maybe it was just me. Stephen looked as cool and poised as a marble statue in a crystal fountain — if marble statues wore jeans and black polo shirts. His profile was impassive as he steered me along, impersonal and efficient. Overhead the loudspeaker announced another arrival — or perhaps another departure. It was all starting to run together.

We stepped outside and the late May sun blasted down, shimmering off the pavement in waves. I swayed a little and Stephen's arm came around my waist, hard and reassuring.

"All right?"

I offered a crooked grin. "A bit tired…"

"The Jeep's just over here."

The "Jeep," which was in fact a black SUV, was parked in one of the lots adjacent to the general aviation terminal. The smell of asphalt and jet engine exhaust hung in the still, humid air as we walked across the parking lot.

Stephen unlocked the front passenger door, tossed my holdall into the rear seat, and helped me up. I dropped back in the seat and wiped my forehead.

He lowered the window a few centimeters. "Sit tight." The door slammed shut; Stephen locked me in using the remote key fob and was gone before I got myself together enough to tell him I didn't have any luggage.

I sat there, head back, feeling woozy with heat and exhaustion — the dregs of alcohol still moving sluggishly through my bloodstream. I stared up through the twin sunroof windows at the unmoving clouds in the blue sky. Blue as water. Deep water. For an instant I had the sensation of falling forward into it.

I shook my head, reached back for my holdall. Unzipping it, I fished out the steel and polymer pieces of my Glock 18, assembling them quickly. The grip felt right in my hand. Familiar. Reassuring. I slapped the magazine in.

Untrue about the Glock not setting off airport metal detectors. The metal barrel, slide, magazine — not to mention the ammo — could all be detected by X-ray machines. But my employers had a certain…licensing agreement with the US Government. And I'd taken advantage of that. These days I never traveled unarmed. Not that I was expecting trouble. No more than usual.

I let my head fall back again, pistol resting in my lap. Closed my eyes telling myself it would just be for a moment. Just to rest my eyes. Christ, I was so…*tired*…

The sound of the automatic locks flicking over jerked me awake. The door opened and I lunged across the console and shoved my pistol in Stephen's face before I realized it *was* Stephen.

"Jesus Christ! Are you *crazy?*" he said furiously, even as I brought the pistol down.

A legitimate question. I wasn't sure myself of the answer anymore. He was staring at me like I was from another planet

"Sorry," I got out. "Stephen, I'm...sorry. You startled me."

"It's mutual." He got in, slammed the door with barely restrained violence. He rested his hands on the steering wheel, not looking at me. "Maybe you'd better tell me what's going on."

A right rollicking cock-up from first to last, Mr. Hardwicke.

I'm sorry, sir.

Sorry? Sorry is for lovers and politicians. If the press gets wind of this...

"Can we have...the air?" I requested. I mopped my face with my sleeve. It was stifling — impossible to breathe in the close confines of the vehicle.

He did look at me then. A hard long look. He turned the key and cold air blasted out of the dashboard vents; it steadied me like a slap. I took a couple of deep breaths. ICBM. Instant Calm Breath Method. And I was okay again.

I realized that Stephen had made no move to start driving — still waiting for me to talk.

I wondered if he'd do it. If he was angry enough, disgusted enough to shove me out of the car and leave me. I found the idea funny, and I knew I had a weird smile on my face — could tell by the way his brows drew together. I said, "There's not a lot to tell, really. The job...went south. I had some leave coming..."

"And you wanted to spend it here? I'm honored." He didn't sound honored. He sounded acrid.

I wasn't sure what to say. That last had clearly been wrong — giving no clue to how much I'd missed him, how much I wanted to make it all up to him. I was so bad at this kind of thing. Always. Until Stephen made it easy. Probably because he had done all the work.

My vision blurred, and I rubbed my eyes, trying to focus on his face. But Stephens's profile didn't encourage further heartfelt confidences. He started the engine.

We pulled out of the airport car park without further discussion. I thought of the pain pills in my bag, decided they weren't worth the bother.

Stephen expertly negotiated the SUV's passage through pedestrians and other vehicles. Before long we were on the main motorway, picking up speed. I relaxed a fraction.

Signs flashed by, offering information, urging caution, spelling out the rules. So many rules in a civilized society. How did people remember them all? So many things to be careful of, cautious of.

Stephen turned on the radio.

"...stated in a press briefing, "US and coalition forces operating in Afghanistan are to continue to have the freedom of action required to conduct appropriate military operations based on consultations and pre-agreed procedures..."

He changed the channel, sliding through talk radio, adverts, static, and settling at last on a classical music station. Ballade no. 1 in G Minor.

I realized I'd been holding my breath, and I exhaled softly. Focused on the scenery sailing past. I'd forgotten how pretty it was here. "Daughter of the Stars," that was what the Indian word *Shenandoah* was supposed to mean. It was one of the loveliest places I'd ever been. Green as England, but a nicer climate. I remembered cool, crisp mornings and lazy, sunny afternoons — and the stars at night. A sky full of stars glittering like diamond dust. I had left before the first snowfall, but I could imagine how pretty it was in the winter. Like an old-fashioned greeting card. There were a lot of farms here, and we wove our way through a patchwork quilt of gold fields and green orchards.

To the east were the Blue Ridge Mountains, to the west, the Appalachians, and through the rich and fertile valley, the famous river itself glinted and tumbled along its rolling way. Compared to the ancient worm-holed history of Afghanistan, this part of the world seemed relatively young and untouched. But that was an illusion. The American War of Independence, the War Between the States — the valley had been a strategic target for both the South and North.

Most of Stephen's family had fought for the Confederacy — and their fortunes had fallen with it. But they had been lucky. The Thorpes had Northern relations and loyal, influential friends; picking up the pieces after the war had been easier for them than for most. The family had recovered its fortune within a generation. Now Stephen belonged to a committee dedicated to preserving Civil War battlefields in the Shenandoah Valley.

"What's wrong with your leg?"

I forced my attention back on Stephen. "Nothing really."

"Were you knifed or shot?" He sounded angry again.

I said vaguely. "A screwdriver, actually." Then, at the tension in his face, "Don't ask if you don't want to know."

"Has anyone looked at it?"

"Countless people. It was quite the topic of conversation on the plane."

He was unamused.

"It's fine," I reassured. "It's healing." It had stopped bleeding at least. I'd changed jeans on the airbus. I'd had to run to make the flight, and the wound had come open again. Stressful for the other passengers but nothing serious. I needed new stitches, but that was nothing that would keep me out of action for long. Not that I wouldn't have liked to play doctor with Stephen.

"That's right," he said. "You're a valuable commodity. Your employer will want you fighting fit again as soon as possible."

"Asset is the word you're looking for," I said.

"Is it?"

I hated that cool tone. I hated the fact that he didn't look at me. I realized for the first time that coming back here might have been a mistake. A worse mistake than leaving.

I said, half-joking — trying to sound like I was joking anyway, "Still. Good to know someone cares if I live or die."

"I don't want you dead, Mark," Stephen said. "I just want you out of my life." He didn't smile. I felt my own fading.

I gazed out the window at the fields of a vineyard. Rows and rows of green leaves glistening in the sun. An occasional billboard flew by. After a time I put my head back and slept.

Chapter Two

"We're home."

The words sounded hard, unwelcoming.

I opened my eyes. Stephen had the car door open and stood beside it, holding my bag.

I blinked at him, wiped my bleary eyes. "You what?"

"We're at the house."

"Right. Yes." Still half-asleep, I fumbled around with the seatbelt and then unfolded awkwardly from the car, reaching for the door to steady myself.

We were parked in the shady circular drive in front of a white mansion. Built back in the 1800s, the house was a blend of traditional Queen Anne architecture and stone and shingled New England cottage. Pretty. Prettier than I remembered. Inside it had high ceilings and hardwood floors and a lot of antique furniture. I recalled the huge old bed I'd shared with Stephen, the moonlit nights and the sound of the geese down by the lake, and lazy, sunny mornings with breakfast in bed — not that I recollected eating a lot of breakfast. Truthfully, I didn't remember much about the house — never thought of it really, beyond being where I could find Stephen. I realized now that it was lovely. And, unexpectedly, it looked like home.

My leg was stiff and uncooperative after the long drive; I staggered a little as I stepped away from the car. Stephen moved to steady me — reluctantly. I could feel that reluctance to touch me as though he'd said it aloud, and it hurt worse than my leg.

Strange, because his arm felt so familiar against my back. It was like my bones and muscles recognized his touch. I didn't understand how it could feel so right to me, but not to Stephen. I wanted to ask him about that, but it was hard to think of how to put it without further offending him. And yet he used to be the easiest person in the world to talk to. There was a time when I'd thought I could tell him anything.

"All right?" he asked.

I nodded vaguely, looking toward the house as a large chocolate-brown dog, a Chesapeake Bay retriever, rose from the long covered porch and came toward us barking and wagging his tail in an excess of nervous energy.

"Buck," Stephen warned the dog.

"Hullo, Buck," I said, putting my hand out. I was prepared for rejection here too; Buck was pretty much a one-man's dog. But he snuffled my hand with his cold snout, and made that funny growling that Chessies do when they're pleased to see you. "He remembers me," I said, foolishly pleased.

"Yes," Stephen said. "He never was much use as a guard dog."

I laughed, and then Stephen smiled too — wryly. Buck nuzzled my fingers, pushed past and thrust his nose in my crotch, and I jumped — which hurt the ribs and the leg...considerably.

"Goddamn it, Buck," Stephen said, shoving the dog away, still keeping hold of me.

There were several funny things I could have said but I just stood there stupidly, and something changed in Stephen's hold. Grew...kind.

"You *are* tired," he said from a distance.

"Yes," I agreed politely. My eyes kept closing although I wanted to look at him, explain — or just show him I was paying attention.

Very important that last bit. Very important.

"Mark?" Stephen said from the other end of the tunnel.

The next time I opened my eyes I was lying on an examining table in a doctor's office. Like one of those kinky dreams. Stephen leaned over me. I couldn't see his expression — there was a bright light blazing over his shoulder — but he was holding my cock. I smiled at him, encouraging him to do something besides hold me in that cool, clinical grip. Just that was making me hard though.

And then I realized that he was furious. Not just furious. There was something like fear in his shadowy face.

"What's wrong?" I asked, trying to sit up. I realized that I was naked — that I had no idea where my pistol was. That was like a totally different kind of dream.

I shoved Stephen's restraining hand aside, the tissue rustling loudly as I rolled off the table — and then crumpled to the cold tile floor as my leg gave way. The pain nearly blacked me out again; I balanced there on my hands and knees, taking deep breaths.

"What the hell is *wrong* with you?" Stephen said. He sounded almost distraught.

Bewildered, I raised my head to stare up at him. I gasped, "I thought something was wrong."

He was looking at me as though I'd shinnied down the bed sheets when the orderlies weren't watching.

"I thought you were in trouble," I said. The surge of adrenaline drained away, leaving me sick and shivering. My heart was still racing in fight-or-flight response. Could you have a heart attack at twenty-nine? Could you keel over from plain old exhaustion?

Incredulously, he said, "You thought *I*...?" Whatever he saw in my face must have convinced him I was speaking the simple truth. "Sweet Jesus," he muttered, bending over me. "Lovers and madmen." He half-lifted me up. I'd forgotten how strong he was. It was startling. I resisted the desire to wrap my arms around his neck and refuse to let him go, cooperating instead in getting to my feet and clambering onto the table again.

Stephen helped me lower myself to the crumpled tissue covering the padding. My ribs protested forcibly. An assortment of hitherto unacknowledged aches and pains announced their arrival, and I swore. Loudly.

Stephen swore right back. "Goddamn it, Mark. What the hell's the matter with you?"

It had a rhetorical ring to it. I said, "You're the doctor. You tell me."

"Well, let's start with the physical," he said. "At least we can fix that. You've got a bruise on your right cheekbone where someone punched you. You've got two cracked ribs where you were kicked. I can tell that from the boot-shaped bruises on your chest and back and hip. Assorted lacerations, scrapes, contusions. And a stab wound in your inner thigh — from a screwdriver, according to you — where someone tried to carve your dick off. There's a scrape…" He stroked a gentle finger along the length of my cock — which twitched wearily in response. "You look like a piece of carved meat."

I wished he'd keep brushing my cock with that delicate tracing touch. I wished he'd wrap those long, cool fingers around me and work me with that easy expertise I remembered so well — or, better yet, take me into his mouth. I used to dream about that minty-fresh mouth of his and the things it did to me.

"Garden parties," I said. "They do take it out of a bloke."

He shook his head, not seeing the humor. Which was sad because before we'd always managed to find something to laugh about.

All at once I felt very tired. Old. I closed my eyes, closed out the harsh lights and Stephen's grim face. If I lay very still, I'd be okay. It was only moving that hurt. And thinking. And breathing. And as much as this hurt, it was still better than the alternative. That was the rumor anyway.

"Can you manage to walk upstairs?"

I opened my eyes and caught his expression before it changed. And I thought then that perhaps the rumors were greatly exaggerated, because Stephen looked sorry for me, and I wasn't sure I could take that.

"Of course," I said. I wondered what he'd do if I said I couldn't manage it. Would he carry me? Sweep me up the stairs like Rhett Butler scooping up Scarlett O'Hara? The idea held a certain charm. He must have lugged me in from the front yard — and what a pity I'd missed it. Better not to try my luck or his patience again. He was liable to leave me here in the cold.

He moved away, returned with a little paper cup full of water. "Here. I know you don't like pain pills, but take these."

I sat up, peeled the tissue paper off my damp skin. I took the offered cup, popped the pills, and washed them down with lukewarm water.

He was saying briskly, "I've stitched up your thigh again, given you a tetanus booster and a vitamin B shot and pumped you full of antibiotics. I should retape your ribs."

"Nah. They feel wonderful," I assured him. I was wondering how long I'd been out. More than a minute or two, clearly. I touched the dressing on my thigh. "Did you stitch a secret message into the embroidery?"

His mouth twitched, but it wasn't really a smile. I moved gingerly off the examining table, and he steadied me. I couldn't help myself. I reached for him. Slung an arm around his shoulder and leaned into him, pressing my face in the curve of his neck — just holding him.

Stephen didn't move, neither rejecting nor accepting, just standing still, breathing quietly, steadily. His skin was warm and smooth against my face, and I could feel the pulse in his throat and hear his even exhalations. I could smell his aftershave, and that faint persistent hint of antiseptic and mouthwash, and the cottony-laundered scent of his polo shirt.

After a time he put his arm around me and stroked my back, the weight of his hand slow and soothing down the length of my spine. He didn't say anything, and neither did I; we just stood there.

Finally I pulled away. I could feel him searching my face, and I was glad that there was nothing to see.

"You just need a good night's sleep," he said.

I didn't remember the guestroom, although I don't suppose it had changed since J.E.B. Stuart last slept there. It was a large, sunny, second-floor suite with a view of the old magnolia trees and the little lake beyond. There was a lot of spindly cherrywood furniture and white wallpaper with tiny violets.

Stephen helped me into the bed, and I inched myself around trying to get comfortable. The feather mattress was like sinking into a cloud, and I couldn't help groaning my relief. I closed my eyes. *Heaven.*

"Yell if you need anything," he said.

I smiled, not bothering to open my eyes.

I thought he'd gone away but then he put his hand on my forehead. It felt nice. Cool. He brushed the back of his hand against my cheek. Pleasant to be on the receiving end of this attention, so I didn't bother to assure him that I was perfectly all right.

Perhaps he thought I was already asleep. He ran his hand lightly over my hair. A slow caressing sweep. And then again. I kept my eyes closed. I figured if I opened them he'd stop, and the feel of his cool dry hand stroking my skin and hair was wonderful. I thought of a line from *Little Dorrit*: "It came like magic in a pint bottle; it was not ecstasy but it was comfort."

I didn't make the mistake of making too much of this comfort. I recognized the impersonal kindness of it — like a vet might stroke a tranquilized tiger. But I kept still and soaked it up and the next thing I knew I was waking from what felt like a long, deep sleep.

The dying afternoon sun streamed through the window, bathing the room in the last rays of golden light. I turned my head on the feather pillow, feeling crisp linen beneath my scraped cheek, my battered body cushioned and comforted by the down duvet and the plump mattress. It was like being in a cocoon. It felt...safe.

For quite a while I lay there not thinking at all, simply enjoying that feeling of well-being, listening to the peaceful sounds of the coming evening in an elegant old house.

A long way from the fiery winds and dust storms of arid Kandahar. But I didn't want to think about Afghanistan now. Didn't want to think about Barry Shelton. Didn't want to think about cities in rubble or crying women — Afghan women, English women — didn't want to think about fields of bloodred poppies, or hand-held heat-seeking missiles, or ancient statues blasted into oblivion.

The world will not find rest by simply saying "Peace." Just like the bastard to quote an Afghan proverb at me. But I didn't want to think of the Old Man. Couldn't. I turned my head, relaxing as I spotted my Glock lying within easy reach on the nightstand. The magazine was beside it, and I smiled faintly despite the clear message of Stephen's disapproval.

I used to think about Stephen nearly every night before I fell asleep. I liked picturing him in this old, comfortable house in this quiet corner of the world. It was comforting somehow to think of him here, to think of how far removed he was, how safe he was, from everything I knew. From everything I was.

It had kept me centered, focused, believing that I could one day come back here and be part of this life — of Stephen's life. In a way it had given me the strength to keep doing what I had to do.

The lacy curtains across the windows stirred gently in the breeze. It was cool now. The humid heat of the day was only a fever memory. Outside the window, birds twittered in the trees, settling down for the night. Homely sounds floated up from the kitchen. The beams and rafters popped like cracking knuckles. The scent of magnolias drifted through the open window — and suddenly I was restless.

I tossed off the duvet, sat up wincing, favoring the ribs. The sight of my bruised, bandaged body in the oval mirror over the dresser was startling. I eased out of the bed and padded over to the mirror.

I spy with my little eye...

Something starting with "B." Broken? Bruises? Blood?

I looked like I'd been beaten within an inch of my life — which was not far from the truth. It was only seeing it through Stephen's eyes that made me realize...

And I was still a lot luckier than Barry Shelton. Or Arsullah Hakim. But I wasn't going to think about Barry. Or Mrs. Shelton throwing a peeler — and then the bowl of potato peelings — at me. I was out of it. I was safe. I was home.

Except...as Stephen pointed out, this wasn't my home.

I examined a foot-shaped bruise over my hip and then looked up into my mirrored eyes. My expression gave me pause. I looked...different...but I couldn't define how. I looked tired, of course. Black shadows under my eyes — and the beard looked alien now. The bruise on my cheekbone didn't help, but *British GQ* wouldn't have been pounding on my door in any case. I didn't remotely resemble Pierce Brosnan or Daniel Craig. Nor did I want to. In my line of work, the less memorable the better. Looking like everyone else was an advantage, and in Afghanistan dark-haired, dark-eyed, sharp-featured, slightly-built men of medium height were very much everyone else.

I turned from the mirror. My bag sat by the dresser, but the blood-soaked jeans were nowhere to be found. Nor were the clothes I had been wearing when I arrived. Probably still down in Stephen's examining room. I found a robe hanging in the antique wardrobe and pulled it on. It was too big for me, but I liked it. It smelled faintly of Stephen's soap, although I suppose that was really the scent of his laundry detergent.

Making my way downstairs, I found Stephen in the kitchen. He was grilling steaks with onions and tomatoes — British style, the way I liked them — and my heart lifted a little.

"Smells good," I said.

He glanced around quickly. "I didn't hear you."

No one ever heard me. That was the point. I said, "That's the best sleep I've had in a long time."

"It's the *only* sleep you've had in a long time," he said dryly. "I thought you'd be out for another hour at least. I was going to bring you something on a tray."

"Not necessary." I limped over to the table and sat down. I hadn't realized how hungry I was until I smelled food cooking. I tried to remember the last time I'd eaten. It was a little vague. Someone had given me an ORP on the military transport plane, and the Old Man had offered me tea during my debriefing. Tea. That still seemed comical. Scones and sandwiches and tea. I'd thrown them all up in the toilet on my way out of the building.

It occurred to me that by now everyone would be well aware I hadn't turned myself in for medical evaluation and treatment. But of course they'd have already known. They'd have known about my visit to Devon and Barry Shelton's mother within the hour.

I said, talking myself away from it, "I wasn't sure you'd be here. I thought you might have been called into the hospital."

"It's just a little community hospital," he said. "Twenty-five beds."

"You're not at Winchester Medical Center now?"

"No." His eyes were very green and very direct. "I decided it was time to make a few changes in my life."

"Ah." That would have been the last birthday. The milestone birthday where he turned fifty. I offered a smile, but he had turned back to the stove.

Stephen continued to prepare our supper; he could have been by himself for all the attention he paid me, and yet it was rather relaxing. I liked watching him. He was built well. Strong but not burly. He moved with a sort of easy, long-limbed grace. Comfortable in his skin. I liked his quiet and his calm. The mark of maturity, I thought. He had worked out what he wanted from life and he was at ease with his choices, with who he was. But then he had fought for that privilege. His family had wanted very different things for him.

The longing to put my arms around him, hold him was like a physical hunger. Worse than physical hunger, actually. I warned myself to be patient, to give him time. I said, "I appreciate your letting me stay, Stephen."

"You didn't leave me much choice."

I stared at the wooden tabletop, looking for answers in generations-worth of crackling veneer. "No. I suppose not. There aren't many people I can trust."

"Oh, it's about trust?" His tone was unpromising.

"It is rather."

Silence. Stephen turned the stove off, dished out food, set a plate in front of me, and sat down on the other side of the table. He speared a bite of steak, chewed ferociously, swallowed, and then said very quietly, "You've got a fucking nerve talking to me about trust."

As my own mouth was full. I had to chew fast, swallow — and he interrupted before I could speak.

"I don't know what happened to you. I'm sure you have no intention of telling me. But it's obvious you need a little breathing space. So I'll give you that. I'll give you time to rest and recover from whatever the hell is the latest disaster. But when you're back on your feet, I want you gone, Mark. You understand? You can stay here till then, but after that you're on your own."

I stared at his face, unfamiliar it its hardness. I had done that. I had I made him hard and bitter. But surely he realized I hadn't meant to. Hadn't meant to hurt him, to let him down, to betray the thing between us because I knew — yes, even *I* knew — how rare that thing between us was.

I said, "Don't I get to —"

"*No*, you don't." His eyes met mine with anger as black as the inside of an oil barrel.

"Right." It occurred to me that he was the only person on the planet I was afraid of. And he was the gentlest man I'd ever known.

Don't push him, I thought. *Don't crowd him.* I picked up my fork and made myself continue eating.

For a time there was nothing but the scrape of silverware on china, the creak of chairs and the heavy old table.

I put my fork down. "Look, Stephen. You're not —"

"Two fucking years, Mark." He was coming right back at me without skipping a step; and even I could hardly miss that this was a fury that had been building for months. "And I don't want to hear anything about having a chance to tell your side of it. I gave you every possible opportunity. You know what the last thing you said to me was? You said you couldn't talk."

The unfairness of that left me feeling winded, and for a flash I was back brawling in the sand with someone's boot in my guts. I barely remembered the phone conversation Stephen referred to. It had taken place four months ago. Right before I left for Afghanistan. I'd been distracted, preoccupied — naturally.

I said, "I was preparing for an OPO, for God's sake!"

He stared at me like I was mad. "You still don't get it, Mark. That wasn't the *opening* dialog, that was the closing. The end. That was your last chance."

"I don't —"

"Understand? I know. You really don't. The truth is there were two years before that last operation — or whatever OPO means — and you couldn't find time to talk then either. Two years. Two *years*."

Two years?

Had it really been two years? Yes, I suppose it must have been. And I suppose that did explain some of Stephen's anger.

He waited for me to say something. All at once I was very tired. Too tired to think of a good answer. Probably because there wasn't a good answer. And a bad answer might mean the loss of any last chance to save this thing. I picked up my fork and made myself continue eating.

The steak was cooked exactly the way I liked. It was good. My brain assured me of that. My mouth told me it was pencil shavings.

I could feel Stephen staring at me, could feel his disbelieving silence. But when I said nothing he gave a short, disbelieving laugh and also resumed eating.

We finished our meal without further conversation.

"Can I help with the dishes?" I asked, as he cleared my plate away.

He put the dishes in the sink and said brusquely, "Lena Roosevelt comes in tomorrow morning. She'll take care of it."

He glanced at me, and I knew he was waiting to see whether I remembered who Lena Roosevelt was.

"I remember Lena," I said. And I did. Sort of. She was a large, motherly black woman who had worked for Stephen's family since Stephen had been at school.

"Good. Because I'll be at the hospital all day tomorrow, and I don't want you pulling a gun on her and scaring her out of her wits."

"I rarely shoot the domestic staff," I assured him. "I know good help is hard to find." Truthfully, I thought it would take a lot more than a man with a gun to scare the wits out of Lena Roosevelt.

He turned back to the sink without comment. I stared at the long, unapproachable line of his back. Sometimes words merely complicated what was really quite a simple issue. I took a step forward and he said, "If you put your arms around me, I'll knock you down, so help me God."

I stopped.

Words then. I just needed to find the right words.

The sprinklers came on outside, filling the silence. And still Stephen didn't face me.

I was supposed to be a pretty good negotiator, and yet I couldn't think of any argument that would reach him in this mood. I was still too tired. That was the trouble. Once I'd caught up on my sleep I'd see the situation more clearly, find the right way to approach him.

He couldn't have changed in his feelings for me that fast.

Two years.

"I think I'll lie down for a bit," I said.

Stephen's hair was soft as silk, like spun silver threading through my fingers. I needed to touch, needed that connection because the pleasure of that mouth sucking strongly on my cock was almost frightening in its intensity. Hot wet delight of mouth on the pulsing heartbeat of my prick. Nothing should feel that good…sheer sensation sending me spinning out of control — overwhelming to feel this much. Dangerous. I gazed down into Stephen's smiling eyes. All the warmth, all the love, all the tenderness —

"Mark."

I opened my eyes at once. It was nearly dark, the twilight shadows lengthening into night. I was lying on a bed in a strange room. My pistol was…to the right of me within hand's reach. But I didn't move toward it; the voice in my dream had been Stephen's.

And then I realized that it was not a dream. At least…disappointment vibrated through my neurons like the tongue of a mournful bell…I was not alone in the room. A pale blur stood in the doorway of the bedroom — and I remembered everything that had happened in the past four days.

Unbelievably — against all odds — I was really here. In Stephen's home.

"Yes?" I moved to sit — and then put my hand to my side as my cracked ribs reminded me of recent events.

Stephen said, "Don't get up. I just wanted to make sure you don't need anything before I leave."

"Before you leave?" I repeated, trying to make sense of that.

"I'm going out for a few hours. I have plans for the evening."

"Plans?"

Simple English but I couldn't seem to translate. A note in his voice sent a warning prickle down my spine. There was no reason he shouldn't have plans. Stephen had a lot of friends — and a lot of responsibilities.

"Yes," he said in that elaborately casual tone. "I'll be back after midnight, and I'll probably be gone before you're awake in the morning, but I'll ring you tomorrow around lunch time."

"All right." But my sense of unease grew.

He turned to leave — then turned back. "Are you sure you're all right by yourself tonight?"

What on earth...?

I said gravely, "One night of my own company won't drive me to put a bullet in my brain."

"Not funny," he said.

Wasn't it? Probably not. I said, "I'm fine. I expect I'll sleep right through."

I could feel his hesitation. It was a little annoying, actually. Didn't he believe me? Did he not trust me with the mint julep glasses? What was the problem?

"I'll see you tomorrow," he said finally.

I murmured something, waiting until he had returned downstairs, waiting until I heard the front door close. Getting out of bed, ignoring my body's protest, I limped across the hall to the bedroom that looked down over the drive.

The porch light gleamed off the sterling of Stephen's hair as he walked down the steps. There was another man with him. They were talking in low voices, but I heard Stephen's husky laugh.

They crossed the drive to the sports car parked there. The second man, shorter and heavier than Stephen, unlocked the passenger side door, turning away. Stephen reached for him, and they kissed briefly.

The pain felt removed, almost distant. A little worse than the leg, a little less than the ribs. Bearable if I didn't think about it or move suddenly.

Stephen lowered himself into car. The other man crossed around to the driver's side. The car engine came on, the headlights illuminated a stone statue on the lawn. Pulling way quietly, the car disappeared down the drive.

I watched the red taillights till they disappeared from sight.

Two years was a long time. A very long time.

Chapter Three

The sound of a vacuum cleaner moving through the downstairs rooms...I opened my eyes to bright sunlight and the sound of birds outside the window. It was already warm but it was the gentle warmth of late spring in a civilized country — and for a few seconds I couldn't think where the hell I was — like one of those novels where the hero wakes up on a different planet or fifty years in the past. I blinked up at the old-fashioned ceiling fan whispering overhead.

Then it all came rushing back. We'd been rolled up. The operation had gone bad, Barry and I had been arrested. It played out in my memory like a film: the ambush, our capture, our escape — Barry's death.

I tried to put the pieces in order. The last four days seemed like a dream. A fever-dream. But two points were very clear: I had made straight for Stephen like a homing pigeon — and I was essentially AWOL. I had done a runner. I was playing E&E with my own team. I lay still absorbing it, dealing with it.

It took some absorbing.

Downstairs the vacuum turned off. I heard the back screen door bang open and shut, and then the dull thud of what sounded like someone beating a rug.

Shoving off the bedclothes, I hobbled over to the window and looked down on the yard below. I could see the top of Lena Roosevelt's gray head. She was whaling away with a broom on one of Stephen's antique Persian rugs. Buck pelted around her in a giant circle, apparently unable to contain his excitement. Divots of grass flew up beneath his feet as he rocketed around the yard. Lena directed an occasional acerbic comment his way.

For a time I watched her, watched the dog slow and eventually lose interest. He trotted down to the lake to harass the geese. It was peaceful. The sunlight flickering on the leaves of the hickory and magnolias had a soporific effect. But I'd slept plenty in the last twenty-four hours. It was time to pull myself together. Especially since my defection was unlikely to go unremarked. Interestingly, I cared less about what the Old Man would have to say than the fact that Stephen had promised to call around lunch time. The brass alarm clock on the dresser indicated it was nearly eleven o'clock.

I shrugged into the navy bathrobe and made my way down the hallway. The door to Stephen's room was closed. I hesitated, but continued on. I could find out what I needed to know without resorting to that. And if I couldn't...well, there was always that.

In the guest bathroom was a big, old-fashioned claw-foot bathtub and a bottle of tropical bubble bath on the windowsill. The "rain-flower scented" bubble bath — which didn't seem at all Stephen's kind of thing — proclaimed the merits of kukui nut oil and vitamin E. I poured a generous amount into a couple of inches of hot water and carefully lowered myself in.

I couldn't afford to get my stitches or the taping around my ribs wet, but no way was I going to settle for soap and flannel. Whatever rain-flower scent was, it had to be an improvement over sweat and blood and whatever else I stank of. I splashed around in the few inches of water, scrubbed up the best I could, then hauled myself out. It took a while to shave off the beard. When at last it was gone and I'd rinsed the last whiskery traces down the sink, I stared at myself. The pallor of my jaw and chin was in marked contrast to the rest of my face. But there was something else. I looked closer. What was it? Why did that man in the mirror not look like...me?

Uneasily, I re-donned the bathrobe. I headed downstairs.

I found Lena in the kitchen doing dishes. I knocked on the door frame in an effort not to startle her. She glanced over her shoulder and there was no particular pleasure in her face.

"Morning, Mr. Hardwicke. Dr. Thorpe said you were visiting."

She was a tall, big-boned black woman of about seventy. She had handsome, rather severe features — definitely severe at the moment — and iron gray hair in a tight bun. She wore wire spectacles, sensible shoes, and a cotton dress with blue flowers.

She didn't appear to have aged a day in two years. I, on the other hand, felt a lifetime had passed.

"Lovely to see you again too, Mrs. Roosevelt," I said, gently mocking that disapproving tone. "How's the family?"

Her mouth tightened. "My family is fine, Mr. Hardwicke. Dr. Thorpe said to make you a good breakfast when you woke up. What would you like?"

A time machine? Failing that, I'd have liked Lena as an ally, but that obviously wasn't going to happen. I said, "Anything is fine. You haven't seen my clothes by any chance?"

"Your jeans are in the dryer now. I believe I got all the bloodstains out." Her mouth compressed in further censure. "Dr. Thorpe left a shirt for you." She nodded to where a white shirt on a wire hanger hung on one of the kitchen cupboard doors. "I can fix you eggs, French toast, pancakes…"

"Anything, really. Tea would be nice, but I can —"

No, I couldn't. Her look stopped me cold. I was not a member of this family. I was a guest. An unwelcome guest at that.

I took the shirt, got my jeans from the dryer, and went upstairs to change. When I came back downstairs bacon was frying in a pan and Lena was dipping bread in a bowl. The kitchen was redolent with cinnamon and nutmeg and bacon. Pulling out a chair at the table, I said, "That smells good. I guess I'm hungrier than I thought."

She sniffed, unmollified.

I gave her just enough time to forget about me sitting quietly at the table. She turned the bacon, put the egg-soaked bread in another pan, turned the heat down on the whistling tea kettle.

"How is Stephen? Is he all right?" I asked neutrally.

There was a little pause. She said without looking at me, "Dr. Thorpe is just fine."

"Does he like working at the new hospital?"

Her profile softened minutely as she poured tea into a white china cup. "Yes, he does."

I watched without comment as she splashed milk in my tea and sugared it appropriately. How the hell could she have possibly remembered how I took my tea?

As she brought the cup to me, I asked, "Is he still on the Save the Battlefields Committee?"

"He's a member of the Battlefields Foundation, yes." Her mouth twitched a little. I'd always suspected that, like me, she appreciated the wry humor in that.

"And the Arts Council? And the Theater Guild?"

I was teasing, but she wasn't having any of the bonhomie stuff. "The Thorpes have lived in this valley for a long time. Mr. Stephen — Dr. Thorpe — is an important man to this community."

"Yes." I said, "He's important to me too."

She gave me a look then, but said nothing, turning back to the stove and flipping the toasting bread.

"I take it he's seeing someone now?"

I knew it was a difficult question. Stephen's sexual orientation had been a problem for his politically-connected family, and while Stephen didn't hide it, he didn't flaunt it. Lena had been very kind to me when I was with Stephen, which led me to believe her sympathies had always been with him, but now I was an outsider, and talking about such a sensitive topic presented a quandary for her.

I didn't think she was going to answer, but finally she said curtly, "Yes."

"Do you like him?"

That offended her sensibilities on so many levels she didn't know where to start. She finally spluttered, "Mr. Boxer is a very nice young gentleman. I *do* like him, not that my likes or dislikes amount to a hill of beans."

By which I gathered that if Lena'd had her druthers, I wouldn't be staying at Thorpe House. I didn't care about that. What interested me was that Mr. Boxer was not a doctor, and he was "young," which I took to mean younger than Stephen. But was he younger than me? Because Stephen had fretted a bit about the age difference between us.

I watched her flip the French toast onto a plate and sprinkle it with powdered sugar and cinnamon. She piled on the bacon and carried the plate to the table, positioning it perfectly on the lace placemat in front of me.

"I'm glad," I said. "Stephen's happiness matters to me."

And it did, but she was right to give me that that grim look over the top of her glasses.

"Stephen Bodean Thorpe." He was grinning.

"But that's nothing," I scoffed. "Try going through life with a last name like Hardwicke."

He laughed, and I leaned forward and kissed him hard. I loved the way he tasted, a little different from everyone else. Clean and cool with a hint of spearmint. He kissed me hard back, insinuating his tongue into my mouth, and I shuddered in his arms.

He laughed again — and I could taste that too — and withdrew. "That bad?"

"That good." And I covered his mouth once more.

The screen door banged and I was suddenly sitting on the back porch swing, throwing a tennis ball to Buck, and avoiding thinking about all the things I should have been thinking about.

"Doctor Thorpe calling for you," Lena said crisply. She brought the phone to me and I pushed the button. I took a deep breath, let it out. "Hullo," I said. "I believe I owe you an apology."

After a beat, Stephen said, "How are you feeling?"

I was astonished at the way my heart had sped up at the sound of his voice. A Pavlovian response if there ever was one. "Much better, thanks. Listen, Stephen, I'm sorry about yesterday. Sorry for forcing my company on you. I...haven't...been myself for a few days."

I read wariness and surprise in his silence. He said finally, "No, I realized that. You made it clear enough four months ago that this was the last place you wanted — or intended to be." He didn't sound angry...just stating a fact.

I said, "Maybe my subconscious knew something I didn't."

That time he barely paused, saying briskly, "I'll be home for supper, but I'll be out again this evening. Anything you'd like me to bring you? I can rent a movie or something."

I said over my disappointment, "Thanks, yes. A film would be terrific. Nothing with guns. Nothing set in the Middle East. Something from Merchant and Ivory, perhaps. I've got some catching up to do."

That was a little obvious on my part. We'd watched *Maurice* together the first night I had come to dinner here — started to watch it, anyway. We never did get through the film. The evening had ended upstairs in Stephen's bedroom. We'd fucked, slept, woke around midnight and ate the pecan pie and ice cream that we hadn't had for dessert. Then we'd fucked again — only by then we'd been making love.

"Got it," Stephen said. "Some kind of costume drama about a handsome Englishman fucking up his life and everyone else's. I'll see what I can find."

It was my turn to pause. Into my silence, he said — still crisp and businesslike, "Stay off the leg as much as possible. I'll see you tonight."

He rang off.

Lena insisted on fixing me lunch, although I'd only had breakfast a few hours earlier. I ate enough to avoid insulting her, and then realized I was dead tired again. My body craved sleep like a drug. I'd never experienced anything like it.

Hauling myself upstairs, I stretched out on the four-poster bed. I wondered how long it would take for our lads to track me down. Not long. The Old Man probably already knew where I was. I wondered what he would do — and why I wasn't more worried about it. I was still wondering when I drifted off.

"You're not seriously worried about the age difference?"

"I could be your father."

"I like older men. I like the fact that you're experienced." I kissed the bridge of his nose. *"I like the fact that you're wise."*

He snorted. "If I was wise I wouldn't —"

I didn't want to hear that. I cut him off, covering his lips with mine, distracting him and losing myself for a few seconds in that sweet mingling of breath and lips. "And bloody sexy," *I added.*

He was smiling, but ruefully. "Then again you've got a thing for older men, don't you?"

"Only you. I'm saving my thing for you." *I nipped his lower lip, and he sucked in a sharp breath.* "Want to see my thing, Stephen?"

It was after five when I woke again. The shadows in the room had lengthened, and I could smell something mouth-watering cooking downstairs. I realized that Stephen must be home, and I felt that mix of anticipation and anxiety as I rose and made my halting way downstairs.

He was in the kitchen pouring a glass of wine. He looked handsome and successful — and absolutely untouchable — in charcoal trousers and a pale blue shirt with sleeves pushed up to bare his tanned, muscular arms.

He glanced up as the floorboard squeaked, instantly on guard. But his voice was pleasant enough. "Well, you look about a hundred percent better."

"I feel about a hundred percent better." I took a chair at the table under his critical eye. A DVD lay next to the bowl of fruit: *The Fellowship of the Ring.*

"How's the leg?" he asked.

"Mending. The ribs hurt more, tell you the truth." I picked up the DVD. "*Lord of the Rings?*"

"Have you seen it?" He sipped his wine, observing me with those elven-green eyes.

"No."

"You'll enjoy it. There's a lot of dragon slaying."

"Sounds like my kind of thing."

"That was my thought."

"May I have a glass of wine?"

"You shouldn't." He went ahead and poured a glass for me. I sipped it while he returned to the stove.

"Dinner is just about ready," he said. "Beef stroganoff."

I wasn't hungry. I hadn't been hungry in months, although he was a very good cook — off-hand I couldn't think of anything he didn't do well. "I could have fixed myself something," I told him. "Since you've got plans."

He didn't respond.

"So do I get to meet him?"

"Who?" He was frowning.

I said lightly, "The new man in your life."

"Conducting a surveillance op on me now?"

I said, "Believe it or not —"

"I don't believe it," he cut across. "So let's not go there."

"I'm...trying to be civil." It was harder than it should have been to dredge up a smile. For someone who made a living dissembling I was having a hell of a time.

"I don't need you to be civil. I just need you to tell me exactly what your plans are."

It was a simple enough question but it felt as though someone had unplugged me from the mains. I could feel the life and energy draining away. Some of it must have shown in my face, because his brows drew together. When he spoke again, his tone was quite different. "Mark, what the hell has happened? It's obvious something has."

I shook my head. "It's nothing. I'm...burnt out, is all. Need a holiday. A rest cure." I smiled. "I already feel loads better. You noticed yourself."

To my surprise, he pulled out a chair and sat down cattycorner from me — close enough that our knees brushed. "You said you were in trouble on the phone. What kind of trouble?"

It wasn't fair. He was close enough to pull into my arms. I could see the reluctant concern on his face, the kindness there — despite his desire and intention to remain detached. And I was desperate enough to take kindness tonight — if it came from Stephen. I was acutely aware of the way his hair curled over the back of his collar, of the broad muscular shoulders and smooth chest beneath the tailored shirt, of the scent of faded aftershave and mint which on him was peculiarly erotic.

I swallowed down my yearning, my loneliness — and surprised myself by telling the truth. "I'm...not ready to talk about it yet. Can't. Not even to you. Is that all right?"

His face changed, and fleetingly there was something there that made my own heart light with hope. "Of course it's all right."

"Thank you." And there was no doubt I meant it. Embarrassing.

He nodded, squeezed the knee of my good leg, and rose.

The meal was good. Noodles and beef made a pleasant change from lamb and chicken and rice — you eat a lot of rice in Afghanistan. Rice and stews. Qormas, they call them. I did my best to eat because I knew Stephen was observing me with that professional eye. Inexplicably, telling him I couldn't talk to him was finally the right move because he was much more relaxed, almost friendly. He talked about his work at the hospital, and about his day. It was all very ordinary and normal, and it gave me a chance to pull myself together. I was realistic enough to know that that was probably why he was doing it, that he was now viewing me in a professional light, putting aside his personal antipathy for the time being.

And I played to that quite shamelessly. I let him win tired smiles from me, let him distract me from my preoccupied silences, made myself swallow food I didn't want when he glanced at my plate. Except...it wasn't really playing. The guile here was in deliberately lowering my guard to let him see...the truth. That I was worried and afraid. And I was...except that I couldn't feel it. But I knew how to act it, and so I did — for Stephen's benefit.

It seemed to work. After the meal he showed me how to operate the new VCR/DVD player in the den, got me settled on the wide sofa with extra pillows and a throw rug, and told me where to find the microwave popcorn or the ice cream should I be so inclined.

He wasn't warm, but he was more than the grudging host he'd been. It was nice for a change, although I couldn't help remembering the nights we'd cuddled on this same sofa watching films and talking about nothing. Nothing more important than what we were going to do with the rest of our lives. At that time it had seemed a joint decision.

I wondered what would have happened if I hadn't left. If I hadn't let the Old Man talk me into one last job. That was rather funny to think of two years later. One last job which had somehow turned into…eleven assignments. So in the end, Stephen had been right. I wonder if he got any satisfaction out of it. Maybe he'd convinced himself it was all for the best. Maybe he told himself there was no proof we'd have stayed together even if I hadn't left.

Having got me settled to his satisfaction, Stephen went upstairs to change, and I turned on the film I had no desire to see, and let my thoughts roam. They didn't roam far. They seemed knobbled these days.

"I'd pretty much given up on you ever showing up."

I shivered. He pulled me close, chuckling. I liked the fact that he was physically demonstrative, open about his feelings — just the opposite of me. Just the opposite of nearly every man I knew. I rested my head on his shoulder, lulled by the tenderness he offered so easily.

He murmured against my ear, "Of course it hadn't occurred to me that you were still growing up."

I sat up, punched his shoulder. "Leave off, Stephen. I'm not a bleeding toddler!"

And he'd laughed. We'd laughed a lot. More than I could remember laughing with anyone.

Stephen came back downstairs, but didn't come into the den. I heard him moving around in the kitchen, heard him go out the front. I wondered if he was slipping out without saying goodnight, but a few minutes later he was back — and he had company.

"Mark, this is Bryce," he introduced. "Bryce Boxer, Mark Hardwicke."

Bryce. Christ.

I got up fast from the sofa — ignoring the wrench of ribs and leg — and startling them both. Even before I saw

Stephen's expression or heard Bryce's, "Oh hey, we shouldn't have disturbed you, Mark!" I had myself back under control.

"A pleasure to meet you," I said, offering my hand.

Bryce was nice-looking. Attractive, not handsome. Thinning blond hair, blue eyes, about my height but stocky, midforties. He looked successful, assured, and happy. You don't see a lot of happy in my business.

Easy target, I summed him up.

His handshake was firm, his fingers and palm uncallused. So he didn't do a lot of driving or any manual labor. Stockbroker, teacher, architect — I could see him in any of those positions. I could see him face down in the dirt, too, with a hole blown through his back.

"Nice to meet you too," he said. "I've heard a lot about you."

What the fuck did that mean?

"You have the advantage of me," I said ruefully, and he laughed with me. Stephen did not laugh. Stephen watched me closely.

"So you're English," Bryce observed. "I love your accent. My college roommate was English." I waited for him to ask me if I knew a bloke named X, but he refrained. "Stevie said you had some kind of accident." There was curiosity in his eyes.

I cooled down a fraction. It was all right — that part of it anyway — Stephen wasn't going to say anything to compromise me. He'd grown up in Washington. He might not approve of what I did for a living, but he wasn't going to burn me. And of course he'd have had to say something to explain my presence.

"Yes," I said. And unobligingly left it at that.

Bryce's brows rose, but he was still smiling. "It's a shame you're not getting to see any of the sights."

Stephen had told him about me, and Bryce was relaxed, friendly, and unthreatened. He was confident of Stephen. Confident they had something I couldn't touch. It worried me like nothing else had.

"I've seen the best ones," I replied, and I smiled at Stephen.

"We should be going if we don't want to miss the start," Stephen said.

Bryce glanced at his watch. "You're right." To me he explained, "We're seeing the Smithsonian Jazz Masterworks Ensemble."

"Oh, jolly good!" I said.

"Okay, let's go," Stephen said, reading me correctly.

Bryce shrugged, untroubled at being hustled away. "Nice to have met you, Mark. Take care now."

"Always," I said.

Stephen was back a few moments later.

"He seems nice enough," I said, having resettled myself carefully on the sofa. "Does he know you hate jazz?"

He ignored that. "I'll see you tomorrow evening."

"Not planning on coming home?"

"If you've got any sense at all you'll be asleep before then."

"Oh, but I'll want to hear all about the Smithsonian Jazz Masterworks Ensemble."

He said flatly, "I knew this was a mistake. But Bryce wanted to meet you."

That brought me up short. "Of course. Why shouldn't we meet? Come on, Stephen, I'd like to think we were friends — at the very least."

He looked unconvinced.

"How long have you been seeing each other?" I asked

It was a perfectly reasonable question, and I asked in a perfectly friendly tone of voice, but apparently Stephen knew me pretty well.

"Mark." I could see him thinking of how he wanted to say it: how to make his point without destroying the fragile truce between us. "Let's get something clear. You don't...have any rights here. I let you come because you begged, because you're in some kind of trouble. For old time's sake, that's all."

I smiled. "How long?"

Irritably, he answered, "Seven weeks."

Seven weeks. Not long. Not...established. And practically on the rebound. Still vulnerable to attack whatever Brent — Bryce, whatever it was — though.

I smiled again — and, reading that smile, Stephen said, "Don't think it, Mark. You're the one who'll be hurt this time."

CHAPTER FOUR

Machine gun fire ripped through the night, I could hear it hitting the Jeep. Arsullah Hakim's face was illuminated in the headlamps, his blackened teeth, the scar through his eyebrow, flecks of spit in his beard as he cursed me. My fingers slipped in the blood from his broken nose as I tried to gouge his eye out. Dimly, I was aware of Arabic voices crying out and Shelton yelling, of the rocks jabbing into my back as the Taliban and I rolled around in the dirt, grappling for the screwdriver. The driver lay dead a few feet from us — his gaze fixed and staring. I didn't know about the third man. My leg pulsed with dull pain where Arsullah Hakim had stabbed me once already. I sank my fingers into the tendons and nerves of his wrist trying to force him to drop the screwdriver...

Someone was speaking to me. A calm, quiet voice cutting through the confusion and desperation, speaking right over the shots and screams — and the dream died away, faded out like someone turning down the volume.

The voice said clearly, "You're dreaming, Mark. Open your eyes."

I opened my eyes.

The reality was violet-sprigged wallpaper and soft-shaded lamplight and Stephen sitting on the edge of the bed, his silver hair ruffled, his green bathrobe gaping open to reveal the hard brown planes of his chest. Beyond him the window was open. Through the screen I could see the golden moon peeking over the sill, and beyond the gently stirring curtains, the sound of crickets and water and geese.

The hushed ordinariness of it was shattering after the violent chaos of the nightmare.

"All right now?" Stephen asked, and my gaze jerked back to him.

"Storming," I managed.

He rose from the bed, went into the bathroom. I heard the taps running. My heartbeat slowed. I wiped my face. It was wet with sweat.

"That was some dream," he said, coming back into the room carrying a glass and a hand towel. His low key acceptance made it easier.

I elbowed up, wincing, and he offered a corded forearm. I grabbed on, pulling myself the rest of the way upright, taking the towel and mopping the perspiration off my face and chest. "I don't dream."

He said dryly, "Then you've got some unpleasant memories."

I gave him a twitchy smile and relaxed against the pillows, handing back the towel. He exchanged it for the glass of water.

"How was the concert?" I asked when I'd drained the glass. The clock next to the bed read three twenty-two.

"Fine. What did you dream?"

I shook my head. "I never remember my dreams."

Stephen said, "I know that's what you always said. I don't think I ever believed it."

"It's true." I started to shrug but re-thought it. "Images, impressions. That's all." If I could have had my dreams made to order, I'd have dreamed of Stephen, but I didn't even dream of him. That I knew of. There were mornings I woke up rock-hard and rarin' to go, and I always figured Stephen had played a starring role in the night's brainwaves. I said, "Sorry I woke you."

Stephen sighed. He looked tired — and he badly needed his sleep. "It's okay. If you're all right now —"

He turned and I got out, "Don't go."

Immediately, his face closed. He said wearily, "Mark, I don't have the energy for games."

"No games," I said with an effort. "I just...don't want to be alone. If you could see your way to sleeping here tonight....I promise to stay on my side of the Mason-Dixon line."

I felt like an idiot, but even so I didn't look away. He scrubbed his face with his hand, then he studied me, hand over his mouth.

I grimaced. "I'd kip down with Lena if she were still about."

He snorted, but oddly enough, that seemed to decide him. "Okay, Mason. Scoot over."

I shifted gingerly to the other side of the bed, and he turned out the lamp. I watched him, silhouetted in moonlight, as he shrugged out of his robe, threw it to the foot of the bed, and pulled the covers back, slipping into the sheets beside me, stretching out. He was wearing pajama bottoms, but I could feel his heat. He smelled familiar, a subtle musky fragrance unique to him.

I inched down in the bed, levering myself onto my side facing him — happily the side where the ribs were not broken.

His breath was light and cool against my face. His eyes glinted in the moonlight.

"Thank you," I said softly.

"You're welcome," he said equally soft, and the words seemed to take on new meaning. He held my gaze. Then he closed his eyes.

If I reached my hand out — but if I reached my hand out, he would get up and leave the room. *I love you,* I thought. I closed my eyes and went to sleep.

"I'm not the villain here."

"You're sure as hell not one of the guys in the white hats."

"I've news for you, Stephen, not everyone wearing white is a good guy. I've seen burning crosses and women flogged. I've seen — homosexuality is a capital offense in most of the Muslim nations."

"And you think the end justifies the means."

"Sometimes. Yes. These things aren't settled by knights jousting each other in tournaments, for God's sake."

"There's a reason they shoot spies."

"Fuck you, Stephen."

But he grabbed my arm before I could walk away. "That's not what I meant. Of course I don't think you're a villain. And I'm not so naïve that

I can imagine a world where espionage doesn't play a major role in the balance of power. Listen, the truth is I'm scared. Scared to death every time I think about what could happen to you if you're caught and captured. You think I could survive seeing you beheaded or shot on the nightly news?"

"There's a call for you," Lena said from the back porch doorway.

I looked away from the hypnotic glitter of sunlight on the lake. "It's not Stephen?"

"It's not Doctor Thorpe. I'll bring the phone out here." She returned, handed me the phone, and eyed Buck — who was sleeping comfortably sprawled over my legs — a disapproving look.

"That dog's not supposed to be up on that swing."

I winked at her and took the phone. She gave me one of those severe looks and went back into the house.

"Yes?" I said into the receiver.

"What the hell is it you think you're up to, Mr. Hardwicke?" the Old Man snarled.

I hung up.

Then I stared in astonishment at the phone. Had I just done what I'd apparently done — or was I really losing it? Actually, in either case I appeared to be really losing it. Buck wriggled over onto his back, and balanced there braced against my jeans-clad legs, paws raised in sleeping surrender.

The phone rang again.

I answered. "Yes?"

"Don't hang up again," came the distinctly unlilting Irish accent of my employer.

I could picture the Old Man clearly. A tall, rawboned man in his sixties — fighting a valiant rearguard action against mandatory retirement — a hawkish face and a shock of unruly white hair. I always thought he looked a little like those pictures of the traitorous Anthony Blunt, but I'd never been suicidal enough to say so.

"What do you want?" I added belatedly, "Sir."

"What d'you suppose I want? Would you like to be explaining to me what the hell you're doing in the States when I expressly ordered you into hospital for rest and observation?"

I was silent trying to marshal my arguments, but in the end all I came up with was a short, "I want out."

"Out? *Out?* What the hell do you mean, you want *out?*"

"I want out. I want to retire. I told you two years ago I wanted out, and you told me that you needed me for one more job. No one else had the skills, the experience, that's what you said. And two years and eleven operations later, I'm still working for you."

There was an electric silence, and the Old Man said silkily, "That, boyo, would be because you never mentioned leaving again. There was never a word out of you when I gave you an assignment. Never a murmur."

Lunch hadn't agreed with me. Ice tea and cold chicken salad. I wasn't used to rich things like that. I was used to…rice. And yoghurt. And fruit. I felt queasy. And the heat was giving me a headache. My head pounded with it.

I focused with effort. "Well, I'm saying the word now. Two words. I'm through."

"Nonsense."

"*Nonsense?* It's not nonsense. I'm resigning."

"It is nonsense. Resigning from a job you enjoy? A job you excel at? Why?"

Because I'm tired of lying and being lied to, of betraying people and being betrayed. Tired of risking life and limb. Tired of running. Tired…

Because it cost me Stephen.

But I couldn't accept that. I said, "I'm…tired."

"Of course you're tired. That's why you're on sick leave."

"This isn't something that can be cured by sleeping tablets or a couple of weeks in Spain. I need to make a break."

"You do important work for which you are very well paid —"

"I'm not going to change my mind."

"I see." I could practically hear the gears changing. "Very well. We'll discuss it when you return."

"I'm not coming back." I closed my eyes, absently tugged Buck's silky ear. I desperately needed to lie down and sleep. Sleep away the churning in my guts, the throbbing in my head.

"You're not...?" For the first time in all the years I'd known him, the Old Man seemed truly at a loss for words. "Are you mad? What do you mean you're not coming back? Not at all? Not *ever*? What kind of childish talk is that? What about your family?"

Well, there was a silly question. My great-uncle was dead. There remained only a few scattered cousins I never heard from beyond the occasional Christmas card — received usually a month or two late when I returned from wherever I'd been last posted.

The Old Man moved on quickly, "Your friends?"

Friends? Like Barry Shelton?

"What friends? I don't have any friends. I have colleagues. I have contacts."

Next he would ask about lovers. But no. The Old Man was unlikely to make that mistake. Instead he made a sound of impatience. "What about your flat? Your car? Your book collection?"

I said nothing. What was there to say? *My book collection?* Why didn't I simply eat my pistol now?

"There are procedures, Mr. Hardwicke. You've got to follow the prescribed course of action for this kind of thing. You can't just bloody well walk out like — like someone on the television!"

Did the Old Man watch telly? I tried to picture that. Had he seen *Lord of the Rings*? He wouldn't make a half-bad wizard.

"I realize that." I said. And I did realize it. I would have to return home eventually. I had a change of jeans, a toothbrush, and a service-issued pistol. Hardly enough to build a new life on. But I didn't want a new life. I wanted my old life. The life I had passed up when I chose to go back to work instead of staying with Stephen as we'd planned.

The only problem with that plan was that Stephen no longer wanted me in his life. Which meant I had zero reason for remaining in the States. I might as well go back. Why didn't I?

"You realize what?" he said sharply when I said nothing else.

"I realize that I need to come back for a final debriefing. And I will." I rested my forehead on my hand. "But I need…"

He said nothing as my voice trailed off. When I didn't pick up the thread again, he said, "Very well. Given the injuries you sustained on your last assignment, I'll give you a little time. Forty-eight hours. But I warn you —"

I thought of the old television series with Patrick McGoohan. What was it called? *The Prisoner*, that was it.

"What?" I asked. "What will you do if I don't come back?"

He said, precise and cold as an ice pick, "I hope you never have cause to find out, Mr. Hardwicke."

Stephen's mouth on my nipple. Suckling, nibbling the tight nub. I moaned, arching up against him, and he paused in that teasing pull of teeth and lips to offer a sexy little laugh. Could you laugh with an accent? Stephen's chuckle had a soft Virginia drawl to it.

Hands sliding over his sleek hard body, stroking him, running my fingernails — such as they were — down his broad back, I tried to draw him down while my cock jutted up against his belly. Even I wasn't clear what I was urging him to do, so it was a relief when he took me in hand — literally — pumping me once, and then a second time.

I said dizzily, "Again? But what about you?"

"I'm an old man. Twice in one night is my limit."

My breath caught in my throat as his teeth closed delicately on my nipple, and I pushed into his hand.

The book slipped out of my hands and I started awake. There was a shadow standing over me, but before I could react, Stephen said, "Sorry. I didn't mean to wake you."

I relaxed into the chair, hoping he hadn't noticed that I'd been about to spring on him and knock him to the floor. I expelled a long breath. "That's all right. I don't know why I'm sleeping so much."

"It's called recovery."

"Yeah? Funny. I don't remember sleeping this much when I was shot."

He'd left for the hospital before I woke that morning, so I'd had no chance to see him since last night's dramatics. To my surprise he sat down on the footstool next to my feet and said, "We should probably go downstairs and change the dressing on your leg."

I grimaced. Then, eying the copy of the *Rubaiyat of Omar Khayyam* in his hands, I nodded at the book and said, "I'm glad you kept it."

"It's a beautiful book. And it was a gift. There's no reason not to keep it."

The inscription on the flyleaf read: *One thing is certain, and the Rest is Lies.*

At the time I hadn't believed there was any relevance in the rest of the quotation: *The Flower that has blown for ever dies.*

Stephen studied the blue leather cover with its gold lettering and design — and I studied Stephen: from the disarming way his hair fell soft and pale over his forehead, to that intractable square jaw. He had a sexy mouth and short, thick, dark eyelashes like a doll's. His hands were beautiful and well-cared for: long, tapered fingers equally adept at healing and giving pleasure.

He looked up, catching my gaze, and I reddened as though he could see my thoughts in a cartoon bubble over my head.

"I brought Chinese takeout for you," he said. "I have dinner plans tonight."

Disappointment closed my throat. It was ridiculous. I really was too old to feel like this. I said calmly, "Three nights in a row. Well, you've never been one to drag your feet when you see something you like."

He said tersely, "I'm not seeing Bryce. I'm having dinner with friends and then I'm attending a scholarship committee meeting at the university."

Well, that was a little relief. Not much. I urgently wanted — needed — to spend time with him. I felt sure that if we had more than a few moments on our own I might manage to open my mouth without putting my foot in. But I could see that he just as urgently wanted to avoid that very thing.

"You're very hard to say no to, did you know that?" That wry smile creasing his tanned cheek.

"The fact is, you don't really want to say no to me."

"Unfortunately you're right."

"Unfortunately?"

Even then the self-mockery in his eyes had given me pause.

I followed him downstairs to the little office and examination room where Stephen occasionally saw a few local elderly and impoverished patients. He washed his hands and dried them with a paper towel while I studied the botanical sketches on the wall.

"Is the leg giving you a lot of trouble?" His voice sounded absent.

I glanced around. "Nothing to speak of."

"And you wouldn't speak of it if it was."

"Oh well. Whinging never won wars."

"I know who that sounds like."

"Who?" I met his gaze and felt a funny flare of awareness. "The Old Man? Yes, I suppose it is one of his greatest hits."

Pulling down my jeans, I climbed carefully onto the examining table.

Stephen removed the bandage from my thigh and studied the wound. His hands were cool and dry and very gentle. I distracted myself from his touch with an effort. The injury looked all right to me. Still a little puffy and pink around the sewing but clearly healing. The tiny black stitches were so perfect a machine might have done them.

"Will I ever dance again, doctor?" I inquired as he opened a tube of antibiotic cream.

"Mercifully, no."

I laughed, and Stephen's cheek tugged into a grin. Our eyes met briefly. It was hard to look away — for me anyway. And it was hard to ignore the fact that in his effort to smear my torn thigh with antibiotic cream he was inadvertently brushing my cock with his hand.

Inevitably this began to produce results.

"Look who's awake," I remarked, since there was little hope of ignoring the tent pole in my briefs.

"Yep," Stephen agreed, glancing and then away. He continued pasting the cool cream over my sensitive inner thigh, brushing his knuckles against the hard length poking the soft cotton of my briefs — it would have been hard to miss at that point.

"That's actually a relief," I said — feeling that I had to say something. And at his blank look, I clarified, "He hasn't shown much sign of life lately."

"He hasn't?" He sounded disinterested, but his fingers lingered, his touch more caressing than medicinal. "That's common with trauma. You'll be back to normal fast enough."

"Normal" apparently not a good thing where I was concerned. I put my hand over his, holding him still against the hard large muscle of my thigh.

"Thank you for taking care of me. I don't know what I'd have —"

"Don't." He slid his hand out from under mine, and the fine hair along my thigh stood up as though brushed by static electricity.

His eyes were angry. I nodded.

Neither of us spoke as he placed a new bandage over the stitches and taped it neatly. His breath was cool and light against me, his eyelashes flickering against his cheeks as his kept his gaze on what he was doing.

"You're so goddamn lucky it didn't hit the femoral artery." His voice was low when he finally did speak.

"I know. Thanks. It does feel better." I jumped off the table — which was a mistake — and pulled my jeans back on with unsteady hands while he washed up again at the little sink.

We walked back upstairs with neither of us saying anything. Shortly afterward Stephen left for his dinner, and I ate Chinese takeaway and watched the news. As usual the news was mostly bad — and that was just the surface coverage offered by the American news programs.

Inevitably pictures of Afghanistan filled the flat screen.

The bookish-looking female correspondent reported, "One person is dead and several others were wounded in Afghanistan Saturday when, according to witnesses, police opened fire on protesters accusing US-led soldiers of killing civilians."

I stared at the brown stuff in the white carton. Mongolian beef. I supposed I should be flattered that Stephen remembered I liked it, but I was no longer hungry. I headed back into the kitchen, dumped the food into Buck's dish, and put the dish out on the back porch. Opening the fridge to see what beer Stephen had, I discovered he'd got in Guinness. Tall cans of it. Not as good as at home, of course, but better than the pale ales Stephen preferred. I had a can — ignoring the little voice that sounded strangely like Stephen saying "Antibiotics and alcohol? You know better." — staring out the window over the sink at the scarlet and black-streaked skies.

The evening was long and dull. For a time I tried to read *Little Dorrit*, but for once Dickens failed to work his comfortable magic. I was too restless to concentrate, finding no pleasure in the slyly humorous but sentimental depiction of Victorian England.

"The Artful Dodger, that's you." But there was no sting in it. His hand rested warmly on the small of my back guiding me through the door he held open with the other.

"No. I'm David Copperfield searching for true love. I'm a romantic."

"I've never met anyone less romantic than you." He let the door to the restaurant close behind us. I glanced at his face but he was amused, slanting a knowing green look my way.

"Hey, that's very wounding. I'll have you kn —" I broke off as he leaned in and kissed me, his lips soft and deliberate as they pressed mine. When he released me, I said, "You don't really care if I hold off meeting your friends for a bit, do you? Because if it really matters..."

"It doesn't matter."

"I'm not awfully good at small talk."

"You're not awfully good at big talk." But he was laughing.

I gave up on *Little Dorrit*, got another can of Guinness from the fridge, and wandered out onto the back porch to enjoy the cool breeze and scent of magnolias. Buck had cleaned his dish of all traces of Mongolian beef. There was no sign of him, but I could hear his tags jingling in the darkness.

I had probably irretrievably bungled this from the moment I'd phoned from that drafty Devon phone box. Begging for help. Not very romantic, that. In my imagined reunions with Stephen I always showed up on his doorstep with flowers and gifts — I believe I usually wore formal evening dress — and somewhere in the distance music was playing. Lynyrd Skynrd probably. And I always managed to say all the right things. Starting with the fact that I was sorry for letting him down so badly and that I knew he was too good for me — but that if he was willing to make allowances for abysmal stupidity, I'd spend the rest of my life making it up to him.

This imaginary Stephen was occasionally tearful and occasionally angry, but he was always forgiving. Where the hell was that bloke? Why couldn't he have a word with the real Stephen?

The truth was as the weeks — months — *years* had passed I'd exchanged the real Stephen for this dream Stephen who would always be patiently waiting for me to pull myself together and come home. The real Stephen was an intelligent, strong, sensitive man who had got tired waiting…and had found someone else. That was the simple truth, and I needed to face it. Accept it. And move on myself.

I knew it. I believed it. And yet I couldn't make myself do it.

Instead I was hanging around like some mournful ghost of love lost — one of those confused old shades who didn't yet realize he was dead.

I smothered a yawn, wondering how Stephen's meeting was going and if he would be home before I fell asleep. I usually healed quickly; even taking jet lag into consideration, my current need for so much sleep felt odd. Granted, it was a long time since I'd felt safe enough to really sleep. Maybe I was making up for lost time.

Sometime after eleven I heard Stephen's SUV in the drive. Buck came flying across the grass and up the porch steps. He stood at the porch door and whined. He looked back at me beseechingly, and I said, "He'll come. Give him a minute."

The dog and I listened to the faint vibration of the front door opening and closing — Stephen being quiet, no doubt thinking that I was tucked up in bed upstairs sleeping the deep sleep of the unjust. He moved quietly through the house, and then walked into the kitchen.

Quivering with eagerness, Buck whined at him through the screen.

You and me both, mate, I thought wryly.

"Hey, boy," Stephen said, pushing wide the screen. Buck went past him into the kitchen. Stephen stood there, his eyes searching the darkness and finding me on the old swing.

"Mark?"

"Right here."

He stepped out onto the porch, letting the door swing shut behind him, Buck hurtling back out before the door closed all the way. To my surprise, Stephen crossed to the swing and sat down beside me.

"Everything okay?"

"I just stepped out for a breath of fresh air."

I could feel him searching my face in the gloom. "Makes a change from Afghanistan, I guess."

I gave a short laugh.

He had an apple. He bit into it, chewed. The scent of apple mingled with the fragrance of the night flowers.

He handed the apple to me, and I took a bite, the taste sweet and tart on my tongue. I handed the apple back, and his fingers brushed mine, warm and familiar.

For a time we sat there watching the moonlight on the lake, listening to the lap of water. I thought of asking him how his meeting went, but it was peaceful like this and I had the illogical feeling that we were saying more in the silence than we usually managed in words — although that was probably wishful thinking.

He stirred at last, tossed the apple core over the railing into the flowerbed, and said, "You should be in bed."

"I do agree."

"Sleeping," he added dryly.

"I sleep better when you're with me."

Nothing.

I said lightly, "I suppose you wouldn't…?"

"No. I wouldn't." Was that regret I heard in his voice?

I sighed. "Oh well. I suppose I can sleep when I'm dead."

Apparently unmoved by thoughts of my mortality, he said, "The life you lead, that probably won't be long."

I wished I could read his expression. He was just a pale blur in the shadows. I said carefully, "What if I told you I don't want to lead that life anymore."

After a pause, he said, "You told me that once before, remember? It turned out you were mistaken."

"Maybe I was just…afraid."

"I don't think so. I don't think you're afraid of much," he said.

"You'd be surprised."

"I would. Yes."

I wasn't sure what to say, but I wasn't likely to have more than one shot at this. I needed to take it. I said, "It's all I know." It was easier like this, in the darkness with Stephen just a shapeless silence on the gently creaking swing. "I've been in this game since the Old Man recruited me right out of university." I'd grown up in the service. Grown old in some ways.

"Game," he said without inflexion.

I turned my head to stare at his silhouette. "It *was* a game at first. I was nineteen. Everything's a game at nineteen. I thought it would be adventurous. Romantic. I thought it would be better than teaching history or working as a translator. The pay was certainly better."

"I know," he said. "We talked about that quite a bit as I recall." He added coolly, with that southern gentleman's drawl,

"No arguing there's damn all excitement living with a country doctor."

"That's not why I went back, Stephen. It wasn't because I craved the excitement."

"No? What was it about? You needed the money?"

"It was my job." I didn't quite know what else to say. I knew how pathetic an excuse that was. "I couldn't just…quit. Not without…" Saying good-bye? Giving notice? I said, "I owed him that much."

"You owed *him?* Do you know what's weird? You never say his name. Never. It's always "the Old Man" like he's a character in a Dickens novel. Or you are."

"His name is John Holohan." No one ever referred to him as anything but the Old Man except perhaps in the Halls of Power. Granted, we were the agency everyone pretended didn't exist, so perhaps there too he went unnamed.

Stephen said, "Then you do know it. I used to wonder. I used to wonder what the hell you called him in bed."

I went very still. "That was years ago," I said finally.

"How many? Because we were years ago too."

"It was over long before I met you. Seven years ago."

He gave a short laugh.

"I'm not lying."

"I'd have to take your word for it."

I'm not sure why that hurt so much. We were both aware that I lied for a living. I guess what stung was the implication that I also lied for recreation. I took my lying rather more seriously than that.

When the time for me to answer had come and gone, Stephen said, "Do you remember how we met?"

"Of course."

I'd accompanied the Old Man to Langley to take part in a weeklong counterterrorism and integrated intelligence strategy training session for the CIA and several other intelligence agencies. I'd met Stephen at a State Department dinner. His father was a retired senator and Stephen, who had worked for a time at Walter Reed Army Medical Center, had accompanied him. I'd first spotted him across a particularly ugly centerpiece — and I thought he was beautiful in a sophisticated Cary Grant kind of way. He wore a tuxedo like it was meant to be worn, handsome and suave as he sat there listening to the speeches with that faint cynical smile. Feeling my gaze, he'd looked my way. After a long moment he smiled at me through the bonfire of candles and the forest of miniature American and British flags.

Stephen said patiently, "No, I mean, do you remember why you were there acting as liaison instead of a more senior officer?"

To some extent because I was one of the Old Man's favorites and that had been a plum assignment, but what I answered was, "I was recovering from a shooting."

"Right."

I started to get angry despite my best intentions. "I don't know what your point is, Stephen. People get hurt in my business. That wasn't why I wanted to leave the service — because I was afraid."

"That's not what I'm saying."

"What the hell *are* you saying, then? Look," I said, "I don't run out on my obligations."

"No?" He had me there. I heard the bitter satisfaction in his voice. "Were you planning on coming home this year? Next year?"

I opened my mouth but the words didn't come in time. "I —"

"That's what I thought." He rose and went into the house, letting the screen door whack shut behind him.

CHAPTER FIVE

I found him in the study putting the copy of the *Rubaiyat* back on its shelf.

"Yes," I said. "I was coming back."

Stephen looked at me appraisingly. "Well, you think you were, so I guess that's something."

"I *did* come back," I said. "I'm here. Why doesn't that count for anything with you?"

He shook his head like it was too tiring to try and explain.

"It was all — it *is* all — I'm trained to do." I said again, needing him to understand, "It's all I know."

"I realize that," he said.

Yes. He realized that. We'd talked about all this. Talked about everything. Stephen knew more about me than anyone — up to and including the agency I worked for.

"It's what you're trained for, and you're very good at it. And, assuming you don't get your head blown off, you'll probably have a long and illustrious career. The impression I received in the one real conversation I ever had with the man, was that Holohan plans on eventually grooming you for his position. Assuming you survive that long."

The thought had quite literally never occurred to me. I was struck silent.

He must have seen the surprise on my face, because he said, "Why do you think he pulled out all the stops getting you to come back?"

"I'm valuable to him."

"Yes, you are. Not only are you one of his top operatives, you're one of the only people in the world he trusts. He wasn't about to let you go without a fight." He shrugged. "And he won."

"No, he didn't," I said. "I've left the agency."

He was closing the glass-fronted bookshelf, but that got his attention. "What are you talking about?"

I hadn't intended to tell him that, but there was no turning back now. "Except...I didn't do it the way we — I'd — originally planned. I just...walked away. I'm technically AWOL, I suppose."

"You're *what?*"

"Absent Without Leave."

"I know what it means!"

"I wanted to see you. I...needed to see you."

He didn't look pleased or flattered, he looked stone-faced. "And you? What did you do?"

"After I was debriefed, after this...last time, I was supposed to report to hospital for rest and ob — treatment."

His eyes flickered.

"Instead I...I...just kept going." Clutching my Glock and my copy of *Little Dorrit*. Maybe locking me up wasn't such a bad idea.

"Why didn't you tell me this?" Definitely stone-faced. Granite.

"I was waiting for the right moment."

His brows drew together in a silver line; he opened his mouth, then closed it.

Finally he said, "What will happen to you?"

"I...Honestly? I don't know."

"What do you mean, you don't *know?*" He was angry again. Nothing used to ruffle him, now he was angry all the time. With me. "Are they going to come after you?"

"You mean like in the films? Or a le Carré novel? Because I know too much?" I was smiling because I thought that just *maybe* he did care a little. He didn't want to, he had convinced himself that he didn't, but on some level he still had feelings for me. Of course being Stephen he'd probably be concerned for a stranger in my position too. "I'm a field agent. I know next to nothing useful. Not in the larger scheme of things."

He made an impatient gesture. We both knew that wasn't how it worked.

"I suppose I'll go on the dole with the other ex-spies."

"Christ Almighty. I don't see anything funny about this!"

It occurred to me suddenly what might really be worrying him. I said, "There won't be any trouble, Stephen. I promise you. I'll leave if things look like getting awkward."

"I'm not worried about the social scandal for God's sake." He looked like he wanted to say something else but whatever it was, he stopped himself. "I've still got political connections. I can make a few phone calls if necessary."

On my behalf or his own? I wasn't sure. I said, "I don't think it's necessary."

He didn't have an answer.

"Anyway," I said turning to leave the room — because knowing when to walk away is crucial in successful negotiation, "I wanted you to know. I was always coming back. I *did* come back."

I hoped he'd call to me, but he didn't. I left him staring after me and went upstairs

§§§§

Someone was in the house.

I opened my eyes staring into the darkness.

The dreams receded to a quiet distance but the conviction remained. Someone was in the house.

Rolling out of bed, I reached for the Glock and eased the magazine into the frame. I was across the floor in two steps, back pressed to the wall next to the door. I listened, took a quick glance around the door frame, and moved into the hall, taking shelter behind the antique steamer trunk along the wall. The door to Stephen's room was closed.

Good. I wanted him well out of the action. Safe.

I listened. Someone was moving downstairs — someone was going through papers. I could hear the faint scrape and rustle…

Slowly, softly, I pulled the slide back on the Glock, chambering a bullet. I rose from my crouch behind the trunk and moved down the hallway. As I soft-footed toward the head of the stairs, a rug rose up out of the darkness at my feet — a rug that turned out to be twenty-four inches tall, furry, warm and alive. I tripped and went sprawling, my finger instinctively tightened on the Glock's trigger and I heard the oval mirror on the first landing shatter as a shot blasted through the night.

Buck began to bark. Stephen's door flew open and the landing light came on as I was pulling myself to my feet with the help of the banister railing.

"*Mark?* Jesus Christ! What the hell is going on now?" He strode down the hallway toward me — barefoot, navy pajama bottoms, unarmed — shocked eyes taking in the shattered glass, the barking dog, and me.

"I think there's someone in the house." I started hobbling down the staircase, and nearly fell over Buck again as he charged down ahead of me.

That kind of thing just didn't happen in the field. Frankly, nothing like this had happened to me in a decade worth of field work. I caught myself from tumbling headlong once again, and then Stephen grabbed my other arm.

"What are you trying to do? Where do you think you're going?"

I yanked away and, for an incredible third time, nearly fell over the bloody damned dog galloping back *up* the stairs. The only thing that saved me from pitching forward that time was Stephen's hasty grab for my shoulder.

And all at once the adrenaline drained away, leaving me weaving slightly with bewilderment and fatigue. The dog would not be racing up and down the staircase if someone was actually in the house. Despite Buck's poor taste in liking me, he actually was a pretty good watchdog, and belatedly it dawned on me that he would not have slept through a break-in that was loud enough to wake me.

Steven was staring at me like he suspected I might detonate. He still had my shoulder in that hard, restraining hold. All at once my various aches and pains — and a few new ones — came rushing back.

"Sit down for a second," he ordered, and I did, folding up on the stairs, resting my arms on my knees and my head on my arms. Stephen loosened the Glock from my hand, and I didn't even care.

Was I going insane? What the fuck was the matter with me?

The dog's breath was hot on my arms. He snuffled my hair.

"Get away, Buck," Stephen said, resting his hand on the back of my neck.

I jumped, then relaxed as he absently probed the knotted muscles with his long, strong fingers.

"I thought someone was in the house," I said, muffled.

"Yes, I...er...gathered that." There was no anger in his voice now.

"I could hear them going through your papers..."

We were both silent, and into the silence came the scrape of fluttering papers. I raised my head, and Stephen said — a little guiltily — "I probably left the fans on downstairs. I do that sometimes. It's moving the newspaper around."

I nodded, pressed the heels of my hands to my eyes. He continued to stroke and knead my neck.

"Sorry about the mirror."

He actually sounded amused as he said, "I never liked it anyway. It always emphasized the bags under my eyes."

Neither of us said anything for a time.

"What do you think is the matter with me?" I asked. I didn't dare take my hands down, didn't dare look at him.

"I think you're suffering from nervous exhaustion. Maybe traumatic stress," he said calmly. "What do you think is wrong with you?"

I thought that over. Could it be something that simple?

"I'm afraid I'm one of those people who can't adjust to...civilian life."

"Do you really want to?"

I nodded, risked a look at him.

He sounded indulgent, like he was humoring me. "Yeah? What would you like to do with the rest of your life?"

I managed to joke, "Besides spend it with you?"

And he actually smiled back. "Besides that."

"I don't know. Write a big, bestselling roman á clef based on my brilliant career."

He was quiet for a moment. "You talked about teaching. Before."

Before. Two years before when we had been planning to build a life together.

"I'd like to teach, yeah."

"Why don't you think about how you could make that happen?" His hand stroked down my spine and I shivered.

If I had never met the Old Man, if I hadn't allowed myself to be lured away from the dull safety of academia by the promise of adventure and romance like a right prat in the *Oxford Book of Adventure Stories* I'd have followed in my great-uncle's footsteps with a fellowship at some quiet little university. I wouldn't have been shot or stabbed. I wouldn't have watched a woman immolate herself in a market square or seen children blown to pieces by a car bomb.

I'd never have met Stephen.

"Let's get you back in bed," he said, and obediently I rose and climbed back up the stairs with his help.

§ § § §

He ejected the magazine and laid the Glock back on the stand. I met his eyes. His mouth quirked into a reluctant half-smile.

"I am sorry about the mirror. I know it was an antique." I climbed painfully into bed. "I'll pay for it, naturally."

He had stepped into the bathroom. He returned with a glass of water and a couple of pain pills — at least I thought they were pain pills. I wouldn't have blamed him for knocking me out for the rest of the night. He said, "Forget about the mirror. Everything in this place is an antique. Including me."

I snorted. Tossed the pills back, washed them down, and got over onto my good side, pausing as a spasm caught me off guard.

"All right?"

I nodded quickly. The little thrill of anguish faded and I eased down. It was better once I was lying flat. I said tentatively, "Will you stay for a bit? Just till I drop off?"

He barely hesitated. "If you'd like."

"I'd like." I sighed. "I'd like it every night for the rest of my life."

He didn't respond to that, but he went ahead and climbed into bed and I reached for him. He gathered me against him and it felt easy and natural — and right. He held me for a bit and then said, "How are the ribs?"

"Hurting like hell."

I felt him smiling against my hair. "I bet. We could try lying —"

"I don't care. It's worth it." And it *was* worth the ache of knitting bones and muscles to lie like this, to have the freedom to rest my head on the warmth of his bare shoulder, feeling the steady thump of his heart against my own, feeling his breath warm and even against my face. His arms were hard and muscular but they seemed to cradle me.

He said quite kindly, "You'll get over it, Mark."

I thought about not answering, but I said finally, "You may be right about my ribs, but you don't know a damn thing about my heart."

He didn't say anything.

After a time the pain pills kicked in and my ribs didn't hurt so much despite the awkward position. Stephen's body was relaxed but I could feel him awake, feel him thinking. I wondered what his thoughts were, but it no longer seemed crucial to know. Somehow in the long stretch of silence I felt we had reached some kind of truce, even a sort of understanding.

I said softly, "I think I might be losing it."

He considered it. Said equally soft, "You might have temporarily mislaid it. I don't think you've lost it." The smile in his voice was reassuring. I believed him.

Then Buck, curled up on the floor somewhere beyond the foot of the bed, suddenly groaned in that exasperated way dogs do, and we both chuckled.

Dawn was scented of the lilacs that grew along the back of the house. For a time I lay there watching the first fingers of sunlight reach through the curtains, stretch across the ceiling. I listened to Stephen breathing softly beside me. The soft rosy light reminded me of the artwork in the copy of the *Rubaiyat of Omar Khayyam* — the first gift I had given him.

He had hated what I did for a living. He didn't pretend for the sake of politeness — not even in the very beginning. But I liked that about him. I liked his blunt honesty. It was unknown in my trade. With Stephen it wasn't about politics — although it bothered him that it wasn't about politics for me either — he was a doctor and he saw what was happening in the Middle East purely from the humanitarian standpoint. He saw war — all war — as a terrible tragedy.

And he was right, of course. But it did seem a little beside the point.

Even once I had decided to leave the service we still argued about it. About war, about espionage, about the Middle East itself.

I wasn't sure where my own fascination with the Middle East stemmed from. One too many readings of the *Jungle Book*? I vividly remembered flipping through the lush illustrations of my great-uncle's copy of the *Rubaiyat*. I had been nine — not long after the death of my parents in a plane crash. My great-uncle David, a Fellow at Grey College, was my only close relative, and I had gone to live with him.

"Two old confirmed bachelors, that's us, my boy," he'd used to say cheerfully.

He died when I was eighteen.

He had a sumptuous collection of Asian and Middle Eastern art books and literature. But it was the *Rubaiyat* with those astonishing watercolors by Edmund Dulac that had first caught my attention, opening a doorway into another world. A world of romance and adventure and mysticism. A land of white peacocks and moonlit temples and secret gardens and princely men in turbans. Granted, by the time I'd been recruited by the Old Man I wasn't stupid enough to imagine that was the way it really was, but combined with my adolescent fondness for Ian Fleming, I suppose I was a natural recruit for the latest version of The Great Game — and an eventual posting in the Land of Light.

And some of it had been just as I imagined. The land — the part that wasn't blasted to bits — was starkly beautiful and strange like any fairytale landscape, the people were as alien as characters in ancient legends, and the history fascinated me — but that was where the magic ended. Violence, deceit, betrayal…that was the coin of the realm.

And yet…

Until Stephen it had not seriously entered my mind that I could walk away from it. Not even after I'd been shot in a botched operation in Calcutta. What was there to walk away for?

I was distracted by the feel of Stephen's morning erection prodding my belly; I'd been up and awake — literally — for some little while. I smiled to myself, nestling still closer, fitting my hips to his, moving carefully against him. I could feel his heat through the thin cotton of his pajama bottoms.

His breathing changed as his cock swelled and filled, shoving its way through the fly of the constraining pajamas. I bumped my hips against his in soft, stealthy movements that might weave themselves into his dream — or not.

He mumbled something sleepy and opened his eyes.

I smiled into his sleep-hazed green eyes, and he smiled back — and it was just like old times. There was happiness in his eyes and his mouth found mine in a sweet, sleepy kiss. He tasted smoky, like a darker version of himself. I fingered the mussed silver of his hair, running my hand down his bristling cheek, a cheek flushed and pink as a boy's.

He closed his eyes again. Maybe he thought he was dreaming. If so, I didn't want to spoil it by saying a wrong word. I kissed him again and slipped my tongue into his mouth, touching his tongue delicately with my own. He made an approving noise. His tongue swirled lazily around mine.

It was killing my ribs to hold my arm up, but I stroked the silky soft hair on the nape, resting my hand on the back of his neck, drawing him closer, deepening the kiss. I slipped my other hand inside his pajama fly, finding and holding the velvety softness of his balls. He touched me back, and I sighed my pleasure as he ran a slow hand down my torso, light as a feather over the taping on my ribs, then smoothing his palm over my abdomen.

"Rub my belly for good luck," I whispered.

He smiled, not opening his eyes, and gently rubbed his hand across my navel.

"Now make a wish," I told him inaudibly, and kissed him.

His hand slowly slid down till his fingers tangled in the pubic hair where my cock nested. I murmured encouragingly into his mouth.

Languidly, we caressed and stroked each other. So drowsily intimate, smelling pleasurably of the clean linen and our warm bodies. Reaching beneath the bedclothes, he freed himself from his pajama bottoms. And I hurried to follow suit, painfully wriggling out of my briefs — and that was lovely: bare naked skin finding bare naked skin.

He slid his hands beneath me easing me over onto my back, and I liked his strength and his carefulness, though I didn't need him to be careful. I felt fine. Better than fine. I smiled up at him and his eyes were open. He wasn't smiling; his lashes shadowed his gaze, but there was something tender in the serious line of his mouth.

I let my legs fall open as he leaned over me, hands planted on either side of my shoulders, cock brushing mine but his weight off my body, the sheets and cover tenting over us.

"It's okay," I whispered, running my hands down the smooth skin of his ribcage and flanks. I reached up, cupping his taut buttocks with my hands, inviting him to settle on top of me. He resisted. "I want you to."

"Shhh," he said, and I shhhhshed as his warm mouth found my throat, trailing moist kisses down to my collarbone and finally closing over my nipple right above the stiff taping around my ribs.

I sucked in a sharp breath, half pleasure, half pain as I made the mistake of arching against the feel of that mouth on puckered skin. Our cocks rubbed against each other, stiff and velvety and slick all at the same time.

The moving finger writes, I thought as Stephen's prick inked a salty message against my abdomen and groin. My own cock slid against his, penning an urgent answer. I thrust up against him, biting back frustration as the reminding twinges of various cuts and bruises and breaks made themselves felt.

"Shush now," he murmured.

And despite wanting his weight on me, pressing me down into the pillowy softness of the feather mattress, despite wanting our bodies locked together in heat and hunger, I sealed my lips. This felt very good, that delicious friction as he rocked against me, our cocks thrusting and scraping against each other despite the fact that it had a distant dreamy quality to it. I found it hard to believe that Stephen and I were really lying there fucking, and yet at the same time it had a sense of inevitability.

Slowly, relentlessly, tension built to that unbearable peak and then suddenly that spurt of wet warmth, a fountain of delight spilling out of me in dulcet pulses. Splashing his groin and belly, splashing my thighs. Lovely, loose release murmuring through my nerves and muscles and bones.

Poised above me, Stephen shivered down the length of his body, hips freezing. He bit off a sound, shot thick cream across my belly and chest, sharply pungent with his essence.

His left arm gave way, then his right, and his body lowered solidly onto mine. He panted into my ear and hair, and I wrapped my arms around him, holding him in place when he'd have lifted off me. My heart thudded in slow, happy time with the beat of his. I closed my eyes savoring it, treasuring that moment, wanting it to last forever. I hoped he wouldn't regret it.

And having writ, moves on. Nor all your Piety nor Wit shall lure it back to cancel half a line...

"I'm hurting you," he muttered after a bit, trying to lift off again. I hung on, knowing he would have to permit it. He wouldn't risk wrestling with me.

"Then we're even," I whispered. I felt the tension in his body but couldn't have stopped the words if my life had depended on it. After a heartbeat or two he relaxed.

We drifted while the sunshine spread across the floorboards. After a time I came back to alertness and realized Stephen was easing off me. I let him go reluctantly, relieved when he lowered himself beside me, wrapped his arm around my middle, and went to sleep. I closed my eyes and drowsed, content — even confident that everything would be okay.

Nor all your Tears wash out a Word of it.

Lulled, I closed my eyes. I felt him rise an hour later, easing off the mattress. The dog followed him out of the room, nails clicking on the hardwood floor. I heard the old plumbing rattle, and a short time later the house settled back into sleep.

Chapter Six

I was having breakfast — French toast with red raspberry sauce — when the phone rang. I watched Lena answer it, watched her eyes slide my way. I felt certain it was something I wasn't going to like — although after the start my morning had had, I felt it would take a lot to ruin it.

"It's a Mr. Holohan for you," she said at last, holding the phone up.

For a beat I couldn't think who Mr. Holohan was. Then I said, "Tell him I'm not here."

She was shaking her head — not entirely regretful to give me bad news. "He said you would say that. He said he has to talk to you. It's urgent."

I rose, taking the phone with a sound of impatience, and went out on the back porch.

"You said I had forty-eight hours."

The Old Man snarled, "Oh for God's sake, man. Forty-eight hours is nearly up!"

"No it's not. I've still got..." I looked at my wristwatch, calculating.

He snapped, "Mr. Hardwicke, our prior arrangement is rescinded. You're to come in now."

"You can't arbitrarily rescind —" He could of course, and frequently did, but my rage was chilled by his next words.

"Listen very carefully. This morning the Cousins raided an illegal embassy in Kunar. Your name was discovered on a hit list of enemies of the Taliban."

In the following silence, I could hear Buck in the distance barking at something in that mechanical, repetitious way dogs do when they can't remember what got them started in the first place.

I said when I could think clearly, "*My* name? My actual name? Why the hell should my name be on anything? I'm just —"

"Think, man. Use your head. Arsullah Hakim was the younger brother of Mullah Arsullah."

It rocked me. Mullah Arsullah was a senior Taliban commander. I said after some rapid thinking, "Still. What are the odds? I've left Afghanistan and I won't be back. And even if they're hunting me, why should they look for me here? And if they did..."

They had my real name. It was a shock, admittedly.

"The Istakhbarat has operatives looking for you. There's a price on your head. One million rupees."

"There is no Istakhbarat," I argued. The Istakhbarat was Afghanistan's former intelligence agency under the Taliban regime. Officially there was no Istakhbarat. Unofficially... "Anyway," I swallowed hard. "A million rupees. What's that work out to, about fifty quid?"

He said flatly, "It's over two hundred thousand American dollars. But that's merely added incentive. Killing you is a matter of honor. A matter of pride. You must come in now."

"I've still got twenty hours," I said.

"Oh, for God's sake, Mark," the Old Man said. "Is it worth your life?"

"It might be." I heard the words and realized I meant them.

He argued of course, but even he had to admit the odds were against terrorists tracking me to this small corner of the Shenandoah Valley.

"Are you willing to take the chance with Thorpe's life?" the Old Man asked finally, unanswerably.

"You've said yourself the chances of my being found here are practically nonexistent."

"Then you're willing to take that chance? You're willing to risk his life?"

I was silent. If I left now, I knew it would be over. Stephen wouldn't believe such a melodramatic reason for my pulling out, and even if he did, it wouldn't matter because I had screwed up too many times. I was out of chances. I might not even have a chance now, although it had certainly felt this morning that I did.

"You know damn well I'm not," I said bitterly. "I'll call you this evening and set up when I'm coming in."

§ § § §

Despite the phone call, I felt better that morning than I had for days. I was finally able to stay awake for more than an hour or two, and I spent the morning checking out teaching programs at local universities. I told myself I was just curious. Then I told myself that even if I did have to leave for a time I could convince Stephen to…

To what?

Each time my thoughts sheered off like a low flying plane narrowly avoiding treetops. I concentrated instead on the different websites and the wealth of information offered.

The University of Shenandoah had something called a Career Switcher Program for individuals who hadn't completed teacher training curriculum but had "considerable life experiences, career achievements, and academic backgrounds that are relevant." I had considerable life experiences, and a decade of survival in my business was quite a career achievement, but was any of it relevant?

I was well paid and I'd saved a considerable amount over the years. Other than having acquired a number of first editions of Dickens, I didn't spend a lot — even on the rare occasions I'd been home for any length of time. I could afford to go back to university and get a proper teaching degree. And I liked the idea of teaching, especially of teaching history. It hadn't been something I'd said because I thought Stephen wanted to hear it.

If I could find some place local…

There were all kinds of colleges and universities. Blue Ridge Community College, Southern Virginia University, James Madison University. I studied pictures of brick buildings and smiling young faces and tried to tell myself it wasn't too late. I could still do this. People went back to school all the time.

I could start school in the fall — if Stephen liked the idea. If Stephen was willing to give me another chance.

A little before lunch time I had a surprise visitor: Bryce Boxer.

"Stephen's not here," I said after Lena showed him into the study where I was surfing the Web on Stephen's desktop and making copious notes on courses of study and prerequisites, tuition, and fees.

Bryce approached the desk, and I clicked to reduce the screen. His blue eyes met mine, and I could read the suspicion there. What did he imagine? Credit card fraud? Chat room scams with underage boys? It was obvious he didn't have the details of why Stephen and I had broken up, but he saw me as the bad guy.

Granted, I *was* the bad guy.

He said, gaze returning to my face, "Yeah, I know. I wanted to...speak frankly to you. Man-to-man."

Queen, I thought. I said politely, "Go ahead."

He picked up the Civil War cast iron rifle piece that Stephen used as a paperweight and then put it down again. He seemed to have trouble coming to it. I pushed back in the chair, folded my arms, waiting.

He said abruptly, "I know exactly four things about you, Mark. You like Dickens, Guinness, dogs, and French toast."

I raised my brows.

He said, "Make that five. You broke Stevie's heart. What else should I know?"

I could tell you but I'd have to kill you.

Why would Stephen want to be with someone like this? I said, "I like classical music and I took a first in oriental studies at Cambridge. What else do you think you need to know?"

"How long did you plan on staying?" he asked bluntly.

"That's up to Stephen. I'd like to stay permanently. Why?"

Apparently the man-to-man thing wasn't supposed to be quite that frank. "S-s-stay?" he stuttered. "You can't *stay!*"

"Why?"

"*Why?* Because...because it's over between you. It's ended. Finished."

I shrugged. "Things change."

"Those things don't change. And you know why? Very honestly? Because your being here makes Stevie unhappy."

Stevie.

My lip curled. "Unhappier than when I'm away?"

"Yes! These days, yes."

I smiled, deliberately provoking. "I shall have to work on that."

"You arrogant shit!"

I raised an eyebrow. I wanted him to come after me. Try to hit me with the Civil War relic or take a swing at me. Something. I hadn't quite decided what I would do if he did. The best thing would be to let him knock me down. That would put him squarely in the wrong with *Stevie*. But I wasn't sure I had the discipline to do it. I so dearly wanted to smash his face in.

But either his self-control was better than mine or I didn't look nearly as unthreatening as I believed. He didn't make a move my way — choosing instead to keep flapping his mouth.

"Do you care about Stephen at all? Or are you just using him again?"

I consciously forced my hands to unknot, relax. It didn't matter what this prick thought. I didn't need to justify myself to him. Stephen's opinion was the only one that mattered. Stephen didn't think I had used him. He couldn't think that. Stephen knew I had loved him. This was all Brent. I said coolly, "What do you care?"

Brent's mouth worked. I thought he might even cry. He said, "Because I love him. Because he's starting to love me back. Because we could have something good together if you don't destroy it — just because you can."

In two steps I could be out of that chair and across the floor. In two steps — approximately four seconds — I could snap his neck. It would be easy. A pleasure. But I wouldn't. I wouldn't harm even one of the remaining hairs on his head.

Because without meaning to he'd told me what I most wanted to hear.

§ § § §

But of course, proof of how little I understand the way these things work, in the end I won the battle and lost the war.

Stephen arrived home early as I was e-mailing off requests for information and school brochures. My smile faded as I saw his face. Back to square one, apparently. He had looked more pleased to see me the day I arrived bloodstained and dazed at the airport — it felt like a very long time ago.

He said furiously, "What the hell did you say to Bryce?"

I admit I hadn't thought Bryce would run straight to him. Not only did it indicate a level of trust and understanding between them that I hadn't been counting on, it was embarrassing to be caught squabbling over him like a pair of adolescent queens.

I said slowly, confusedly absorbing just how angry he was, "But Brent attacked me."

"*Bryce*," he shot back. "And *what* in God's name can *possibly* be going on in that scrambled brain of yours? He *attacked* you? How the hell did he attack you? Do you know what an attack is? Do you understand the concept of disagreeing with someone without having to destroy them? *Jesus Christ*, Mark. You don't…you don't use nuclear weapons on white mice."

I had never seen him like this. He looked like he hated me. I tried to think back to the scene with Brent — Bryce. Surely he was the aggressor there? I had gone for his weak spot, yes, but…he had gone for mine, hadn't he? And wasn't the deck already stacked in his favor?

With a sick pang of shock I realized what Stephen was saying. He loved Bryce. When I hurt Bryce I hurt Stephen because…Bryce was the one Stephen wanted. Not me.

I blinked, trying to comprehend this as Stephen went on in that low, ferocious voice. "I didn't want you here. I let you come against my better judgment. I specifically told you that you had no rights here. That there was no longer anything between us." That was a little harsh even for Stephen. He must have heard it — or perhaps read it in my face. He qualified tersely, "Other than friendship. And this is not the way friends behave. You've deeply hurt someone I care about."

Well that was plain enough, even for me. I said unemotionally, "He wanted to know when I was leaving — as I seem to be getting in his way."

His eyes narrowed. "And what did you tell him?"

"That it wasn't any of his business."

He paused, possibly to consider his words, and then he said quietly — no room for misunderstanding, "And when exactly *are* you leaving, Mark?"

I considered the possibility that he was asking because he was actually afraid of my going, but reluctantly let the idea go. It was clear from his expression that he wasn't anything but impatient to see the last of me.

It took a second to face it, but then I was all right again. I hadn't really believed this was going to work out, had I? Surely I wasn't that naïve? That…romantic? That goddamned, bloody stupid? I pressed "cancel" on the email I had been about to send.

I said, "It seems I'm leaving tonight."

And it made perfect sense. Better for me, really. And not most because I might have one or two representatives from the psychopath community hunting me — not to mention the embarrassing possibility of the Old Man arranging a courtesy call from the Cousins on my behalf. Wouldn't Stephen love that? The CIA showing up on his front porch?

"Would you like me to talk to Bryce?" I offered. "I could…" I could what? Explain that I wasn't quite sane when it came to Stephen? Maybe not quite sane period.

He stared at me in disbelief. "You must be joking. You've said plenty already."

I nodded.

Stephen's anger seemed to fade away. He said more calmly, "I'm not saying you need to leave tonight. Or even tomorrow. So long as we're clear —"

"Crystal," I assured him. I dredged up what I hoped was a reassuring smile. "And don't worry. I didn't say anything to Bre…Bryce about last night — this morning, rather."

He winced. "Mark, that was —"

I couldn't bear hearing him say it was a mistake. I said quickly, "No, I realize that. I'm not such a fool that I think it was anything but what it was. Sex. Lovely sex at that."

He didn't return my smile. He looked like he was in pain. Well, that would be his oversensitive conscience. He'd have to work that one out on his own. I nodded at the computer and said, "I should have asked first. Is it all right if I use this to look up flights?"

"Of course." He said a little irritably, "But you don't need to worry about it for a day or two."

"No worries," I said vaguely, turning back to the screen and clicking automatically. British Airways came up filling the screen.

I could feel him hesitating. I wished he would go away. What did he want from me? I kept tapping the keyboard and at last he turned and left me to it.

Once his footsteps had died away down the hall, I let my hands fall to my lap and I closed my eyes. I was so…tired…

"I love you." His green eyes were soft and serious.

I opened my mouth, but nothing came out.

"Too soon?" And he was actually smiling — smiling — as though he understood completely. And of course he didn't. How could he?

My eyes stung. I blinked hard and said gruffly, "God no." I put my arms around him so he couldn't see what a fool I was. I said against his ear, "I love you too. I always will."

Lena's voice said crisply, shattering my numb solitude, "Personally? I don't care if you go drown yourself in that big old Atlantic Ocean. I think Mr. St — Dr. Thorpe could do a lot better than you. I think he deserves a lot better than someone like you."

I opened my eyes and looked at her. "Are you just saying this to cheer me up?" I inquired. "Or do you really mean it?"

Her mouth tightened, but she went on anyway. "But for two years that man hung on — *two years* — waiting for you to pull your head out of —"

She caught herself. I said politely, "The clouds?"

"And when it ended — when you told him whatever it was you told him — I thought he would die of grief."

It must be catching, I thought. I said, "People don't die of grief."

"Honey, when you've been around as long as me, you can tell me what people do and don't do." She studied me. "I've known Dr. Thorpe since he was a boy, and he's always known who he was and what he wanted. When the Senator tried to pressure him to go into politics, he stuck to his guns. And that took some doing. And when his mother, bless her heart, wanted him to marry and give her a grandchild, he was just as gentle as he could be, but he told her the truth."

I said, "Yes, he's very good at saying no. No room for misunderstanding."

She made a noise…it sounded something like *Tchaw!* "You feel mighty sorry for yourself, don't you?"

I thought it over. "Not yet. It's not real to me yet. Mostly I feel blank."

She blinked. Her next words were brisk, but there was something different in her tone. "I've known that man his entire adult life, and the happiest he ever was, was with you. It's not over for him. I heard some of what he said, and I guess he wishes it were true, but he still —" She took a deep breath. "He still loves you, honey. And I don't think, whatever he says, that he really wants you to leave."

There wasn't much to pack. There never was. I traveled light. Always. He travels fastest who travels alone — and I preferred traveling alone, really. It was much safer that way. Safer for everyone. I stuffed my copy of *Little Dorrit* into my bag and thought about Barry Shelton. We'd entered Afghanistan four months ago traveling mostly on foot from the

Pakistani border city of Quetta across the straight and rigid white mountains that lined the frontier and, sticking to tracks too rough and remote for anything but mountains goats and bandits, journeying far into the rugged hills of the central Oruzgan province — and from there to Khandahar.

I'd liked Barry. I hadn't loved him. We were partners. Mates. It had nothing to do with the way I felt about Stephen. I'd never felt for anyone the way I felt for Stephen. But we'd made a good team, Barry and I. And there had been a few nights that we'd offered each other affection and comfort, and it had been good. It had kept us strong. Kept us sane.

It hadn't felt like a betrayal, because...at that point there was nothing left to betray. Stephen had broken it off with me. Although, if I was honest with myself, I never believed for an instant that I couldn't mend that bridge. Needed to believe it. Because Stephen was my talisman, and his love for me was the dreamcatcher — the shining bit of improbability that kept away the darkest moments. When the job was over I planned to find him, apologize, explain, woo and win him back. I had it all planned. That was all right with Barry. Not that we talked about it. But he had a girl waiting for him. *Chloe Scratchett.* I didn't think I would ever forget her name. It sounded so Dickensian. Or perhaps like a porn star. He used to ramble on about her all the time.

I packed my bag and sat on the edge of the bed in Stephen's guestroom, and a wave of tiredness hit me. I wanted to lie down and close my eyes, close everything out. But now I knew what it was. Nervous exhaustion. And what was that except being afraid to face facts?

So I forced myself off the bed and went downstairs.

I found him in the kitchen staring out the window over the sink. I made sure he heard me coming, stepped on the third floorboard from the doorframe, the board that always squeaked, but he didn't move, didn't turn.

I said, wanting to make this easy for him, "My flight from Dulles is scheduled for tomorrow at fourteen hundred which means I had to book a flight from Norfolk for nine —" His expression, as he turned from staring out the kitchen window, gave me pause. I said, "If you'd like me to get a taxi —"

Stephen said, "I don't want you to get a taxi. I'll take you to the airport."

"You don't have to. It means getting up at the crack of dawn. I'd just as soon —"

"I said I would take you." He stared back out the window.

"All right. Thank you."

Nothing.

I studied the tense line of his back, and then I thought…what the hell? May as well be hanged for a sheep as a lamb. I moved behind him, slipped my arms around his waist. He stiffened instantly. I rested my head against the back of his. His hair was silk against my face.

For a moment he let me stay like that. I felt the fast, steady thump of his heart next to mine. Excited. Not angry, not alarmed. He liked this too. But he didn't want to, and that made all the difference.

"I love you," I said quietly.

He shook his head.

I kept talking. What did I have to lose now? Nothing. And I owed him this much. Owed him for those two years when he had hung on, holding the door open for me, offering me safe passage if I'd just been able to see it. "I know you don't want to hear it. I know it's too late."

"It *is* too late." There was regret in his tone, but certainty.

"The mistakes I made — they didn't have to do with anything but being afraid. I did love you. I do love you."

"Don't." He pulled away. Not roughly — but without haste or reluctance. "There is no point to this now." His eyes were very green — brilliant — but the tears were for the waste of it.

"Can I just say it anyway? For the record?"

"What's the point?"

"I don't know. Confession is good for the soul? And mine needs all the help it can get?"

His expression turned sardonic. "So it's really about you."

"This part is."

He waited.

I said, "It's the oldest story in the world. I got scared. You offered me everything I ever wanted — just like that. Mine for the taking. And it frightened the hell out of me. I didn't see how it could be...true."

"You should have stayed long enough to find out."

"I should have. Yes. I always meant to come back, but — this is the part that's hard to explain, the part you won't understand — after a time the dream of it, the promise of it became too important to...test."

Zero comprehension on his face.

I took a deep breath. I was so very bad at this kind of thing, but if I was ever going to explain myself properly, now was the time. "These last few days have given me time to think it through. My life, personally, professionally...it's about lies and deceit and betrayal and treachery. Since I was nineteen. It's my job to persuade people to trust me, and then I use them. Sometimes I betray them. Even if I don't personally betray them, I know that they will be betrayed. I lie to people. I trick them. I get them to turn on each other, sell each other out. I've always believed it was for a good cause, but mostly...it's my job." At his expression, I said, "I'm not excusing it, just trying to explain. So you'll understand that it wasn't...you."

"I know damn well it wasn't me."

"Right. Well." I shrugged. "It sounds feeble, I realize. I don't have...a great opinion of human nature."

"Are you trying to say you didn't trust me?" Stephen inquired.

"I'm trying to say I was too afraid to find out. That having the dream of you and this place was better — seemed safer, anyway — than finding out that it wasn't true."

He shook his head. "That's sad. I don't know what else to tell you. It's one of the saddest things I ever heard. Because it was all here for you. All you ever had to do was reach for it."

"I know." And I knew I could never make him understand how terrifying it was to be offered your dream.

Stephen said, "I waited two years for you to make up your mind. There was always one last job, one last crisis, one final commitment, and you kept drifting further and further away. The last time we talked — before you went to Afghanistan — I was talking to a stranger."

I thought of all the times he had needed me, wanted me: his father's death, his fiftieth birthday, changing jobs — and all the long days and lonely nights in between.

I said, "Maybe it seemed that way, but I was coming back. I knew after we talked the last time, after you broke it off, that I'd made a mistake. That I couldn't lose you. I told Barry —"

"Barry?" he interjected politely.

I hesitated. I didn't want secrets between us, but now was not the time to try and explain about Barry. "A fellow agent — a friend. I told him, right before things went...wrong...that I'd worked out what I wanted."

"How nice for you."

Once again I'd managed to say the wrong thing. I stared at Stephen's impassive face, saw the coolness in his eyes, and knew that I'd managed to confirm his decision that I was not someone he wanted or needed in his life.

I said, "I'm no good at this. I realize that it's over for you. That for you it's been over for some time. All I wanted to say was that I did love you. Still do love you. Can't imagine ever not loving you. And I'm sorry. Truly sorry. And I hope you'll forgive me for wasting two years of your life."

A muscle moved in his jaw. I could see him weighing it, deciding whether he would accept it at face value or not. He said finally, "Thank you. I know that wasn't easy for you."

And that was it. What had I expected? It was over.

Chapter Seven

"I'll be gone for about an hour, but I'll be home for supper," Stephen said from the porch.

I tossed the ball one last time to Buck and glanced back. I'd heard the phone jangle a few minutes before, and I knew who he going to see. Bryce would, not unnaturally, want a full accounting.

"Not to worry," I replied. "And no need to rush home. I'll probably have an early night." And I probably would. Tomorrow was going to be a long day.

"Up to you," he said indifferently.

When I looked back he was gone from the porch.

I threw the ball a few more times to Buck, but even he found my efforts disappointing and eventually wandered off to harass the waterfowl.

I watched the sunset for a time, then went inside the house. It seemed unnaturally quiet. Lena had left for the day shortly after her pep talk to me — kindly meant but clearly off-mark. I made myself tea, found some oatmeal biscuits in the cupboard, and went into Stephen's study to call the Old Man.

I caught him on his way out for a late supper for some Minister or another. I told him I was coming in, and gave him the details. He was surprisingly cordial — but then he was always gracious in victory and relentless in defeat.

"I'll be letting our associates at Langley know," he said.

"I don't need a babysitter," I said. "I can get myself home without an escort."

"All the same," he said. And I shut up. Of course I would have a CIA escort — certainly until I got on the plane, and maybe all the way across the shining sea. That was mere professional courtesy. I had broken protocol, violated a dozen policies. Having my flight changed to one of the chartered CIA specials was the least of it. I was looking at a psych evaluation and a probable sanction. I might even be out of a job, but that was probably too much to hope for.

I said, "Then can we set the pick up for Dulles?" I didn't want to be taken into custody in front of Stephen.

The Old Man hesitated, but he was a shrewd old bird and I think he knew exactly what my problem was — and of course the more I cooperated, the happier everyone would be.

He agreed, told me urbanely he looked forward to seeing me, and rang off. I turned on the TV, watched for a time. Was there anywhere in the world that wasn't a mess?

An hour went by.

Then another.

It was dark outside and the crickets were chirping — and there was still no sign of Stephen.

Not totally unexpected. In Bryce's shoes I'd have been equally reluctant to trust me. Nor would Stephen be looking forward to an evening of my company should I not be tactful enough to take myself off to bed early.

Another hour passed.

I must have dozed. When I opened my eyes I heard Buck barking, and I knew that bark. I'd heard it outside mountain villages and inside the walls of a private estate. I knew it because I was usually the cause of it. The barking grew louder and then I heard Stephen's SUV in the front drive, tires crunching on gravel.

The floorboard near the kitchen creaked.

And all at once I knew we were in a hell of a mess.

I turned out the lamp next to me. I rolled off the sofa onto the floor. Footsteps vibrated down the hall toward the study. I skittered over to the rifle cabinet, but it was locked. Probably no one had opened it since the Senator died.

Diving behind Stephen's desk, I grabbed the heavy cast iron paperweight. The overhead light went on, the fan whirring softly into life. I stayed still. Depending on where the intruder was in the house when the light had gone out, he might think — assume — I had turned out the lamp and gone upstairs. Or maybe not.

He stood inside the doorway listening for me. I could feel him in the strained silence.

Except that it wasn't silent. Buck was barking hysterically, and then the barking cut off on a screech.

"Buck?" Stephen called from the front of the house.

And we were out of time. The footsteps started back down the hallway toward the front door. I scrambled up from behind the desk and followed him — a bulky figure in black wearing a dark ski mask. He was not fast on his feet. I caught him up in three steps. He spun around, and I slammed him over the head with the paperweight. He slumped to the floor, and I stepped over him and picked up his fallen pistol — a Heckler & Koch SOCOM specially fitted with a sound and flash suppressor. Fitted with an infrared laser sight as well, but the would-be assassin wasn't wearing goggles — which was the first good news I'd had in twenty-four hours.

A second man was coming through the back porch door. I shot him in the chest with the silenced gun and he fell back out the door, the porch door swinging back with a bang against the house. I turned out the kitchen light. Turned out the porch light as I reached the back door — just in time to see Stephen coming around the corner of the house.

"Get down!" I yelled, stepping over the dying man feebly waving a pistol my way. I kicked him hard in the head, plucking the pistol from his hand. Putting the safety on, I wedged it in my back waistband.

About half a second later a Micro Uzi raked the side of the house, stitching bullets through the walls and windows. Glass shattered, wood splintered from inside the house. I was already scrambling to the end of the porch, peering down through the railing.

"Stephen? Jesus. *Stephen?*"

To my relief he was crouched in the flowerbed. He looked up, unhurt, his face a pale glimmer.

I felt almost dizzy with relief. I hissed, "Are you all right? You're not hurt?"

"What the fuck is going on?" He sounded shaken but there was no panic in his voice. Anger, yes. Outrage. Fear. But all of it under control.

"It's another long story." I wished he wasn't wearing a white shirt.

"I heard Buck squeal," he said. "They shot him, didn't they?"

"I'm sorry."

"*Goddamn you*," he said quietly and intensely, and I flinched.

There was another burst of machine gun fire. Bullets tore through the wood of the porch posts, the swing's canvas, hitting stone and wood and glass.

I whispered into the silence that followed, "I'll lay down a covering fire. If you could climb up here?"

He nodded curtly.

I slid across the wood flooring to one of the stone and wood pillars, stood — making myself as narrow a target as possible, and began methodically firing in the direction of the lake. I could hear the ducks and geese in a panic, saw them taking wing against the night sky.

Behind me I heard Stephen climb onto the porch.

The gunman by the lake answered back with bullets. They gouged the stone pillar in front of me, took chunks out of the wooden overhang. I watched for the muzzle flash, holding my fire.

Behind me Stephen was speaking rapidly in a low steady voice — though apparently not to me.

There was a pause in the festivities. I glanced around. He was on his cell phone calling for help. And I was proud of how cool he sounded. His father would have been proud too. And all those generations of Johnny Rebs.

He closed his cell phone. I squatted, offering him the pistol I'd taken off the second assassin, but he shook his head.

"For God's sake, Stephen. You've handled a gun before."

"I haven't shot a rifle in over a decade. And I sure as hell never shot at anything capable of firing back. I'd be worse than useless with that," he said.

I gnawed my lip, thinking. Maybe he was right. I said, "I'll cover you again. Get inside the house and barricade yourself in the cellar."

"What are you going to do?"

"What I'm trained to do."

"No." He was shaking his head. "Help is on the way. We just need to wait it out."

"That's exactly what we're going to do. Only I'm waiting out here. And you're waiting inside."

"I'm not hiding in the goddamn cellar while you're up here getting shot at!"

There was another short burst of machine gun fire. Stephen pressed down lower to the wooden planks. I ducked against the stone pillar. I thought the gunman was angling around for better position. Into the pause that followed, I said, "We don't have a lot of time to debate this."

He said furiously, "I'm not leaving you under fire!"

"Goddamn it. Do I tell you how to fix a broken leg? Do what I ask before you get us both killed."

He was shaking his head stubbornly, and I said desperately, "Please. All right? Stephen, *please* go to the fucking cellar so I can go after this son of a bitch without having to worry about you."

And to my bewilderment, he laughed, a breathless gust of sound and scooted over to the post where I crouched. "The magic word? Is that what you think I'm waiting for?" He grabbed me by my shoulders. "Listen to me. There's a magic word all right. It's love."

I gaped at him. "Stephen —"

"Listen to me."

I threw a look over my shoulder. Beyond the trees I could see the black glitter of the lake. The third gunman was out there somewhere, moving through the reeds, coming toward the house. And there might be more of them as well.

"Listen to me," Stephen repeated, and I switched my attention distractedly back to him. "I can't take it if something happens to you. I've spent the last two years living in fear every time the news reported a British citizen arrested for spying. Or a British soldier captured. Or killed."

"I'll be all right. And — anyway, there's nothing to blame yourself for. I brought this on."

His fingers dug in painfully. "No. You're not paying attention. I've spent the last four hours trying to convince Bryce — and myself — that I don't still love you."

I admit that did get my attention. "Come again?"

He took my face in both his hands and kissed my mouth — and it was all there in that hard warm press of lips. I felt shaken as I pulled away.

"Don't throw your life away," Stephen said.

"I...don't intend to." I swallowed.

He stared at me, and I was almost grateful for the shadows that hid our expressions from each other. It went through my mind that he might be saying this — saying anything to keep me from further harm — but I dismissed the thought. This was Stephen and he wouldn't lie about this. Not even to keep me from throwing my life away.

"I won't let you down again," I said.

To my relief he nodded once, curtly, and turned away. I rose and began firing at the reeds moving in the distance. Stephen dashed for the door, jumping over the dead man, disappearing inside the darkened house.

The Heckler & Koch clicked on empty. I set it aside and pulled out the pistol I'd taken from the second assassin. A Beretta M92F. Fifteen rounds in the magazine, so I needed to make every shot count. I called softly, "Stephen?"

He answered from inside the kitchen, equally softly.

I said, "Watch yourself. There could still be someone inside."

If he answered, I didn't hear it. I dropped down and scooted across the porch to the railing, letting myself over the side and landing on the grass in a crouch.

Silence. I could hear the weathervane high above moving rustily in the breeze. A rose trellis knocking against the side of the house. Down by the water, the ducks and geese were still having fits. Light shone from the front room, casting a yellow oblong across the grass and flowerbed.

As I watched, I saw the red fiber-optic beam of a laser slide along the front of the porch, probing the shadows — and I smiled. *I spy with my little eye…* Eleven to eighteen yards away. That put him on the edge of the reeds toward the west end of the house. Better yet, he believed I was still somewhere on the porch.

I sprinted to the nearest magnolia, rested my spine against it.

The geese continued to cackle and honk near the water's edge. I looked back at the house. The living room light had gone out. The house appeared quiet and still. I turned my attention to the lake.

I wondered how long till we got reinforcements. Better — much better — if this ended here and now. Arrest meant a trial. Trial meant publicity. Publicity would be very bad news. For me. For Stephen.

I waited.

The red laser dot disappeared.

What now?

I darted to the next tree.

Nothing.

I slid down on my haunches, back against the trunk, waiting. The stitches in my thigh throbbed in time to my heartbeat. The good old femoral artery pulsing away next to all those careful little stitches. My ribs ached as I tried to draw a deep breath. I wiped my forehead. Waited.

Just as the would-be assassin appeared to be doing.

I risked another look around the tree trunk. I could see the pinpoints of starlight like tiny candles drifting on the water, and strangely a line from *Little Dorrit* came into my mind: *While the flowers, pale and unreal in the moonlight, floated away upon the river; and thus do greater things that once were in our breasts, and near our hearts, flow from us to the eternal seas.*

I could still taste Stephen's kiss on my lips. Somewhere to my left I could hear a funny, low whining. My eyes raked the darkness, picking out a long black shadow within the other shadows. Buck. He lay in the deep grass beneath the tall trees.

I considered him. "Lie still, Buck," I said keeping my voice low.

He whined and lifted his head a little.

Bullets thunked into wood above my head as the Uzi opened up again. I yelled like I'd been hit, threw myself in the grass, flat as I could get, head raised just enough to see over my hands as I steadied the Beretta.

Such an old trick. But then one reason it had been around forever was because it worked so well. He stood up out of the reeds, machinegun at ready, striding up the embankment toward where I lay motionless.

I took careful sight. The light was poor and my hands were not quite steady. I had to wait longer than I wanted to be sure I had him. I fired. The bullet hit him low in his left shoulder. He screamed and fired. Grass chewed up next to me in great gobs of mud and green. I rolled away and fired again, this time hitting him dead center.

He went down, still firing, bullets plowing into the ground until he slumped forward.

For a time I lay there panting, heart hammering, watching him. He didn't move.

I got up, bracing myself with my free hand, walked over to him, pistol trained. I planted one foot on the machine gun barrel, rolled him over with my other. His eyes stared frozenly through the holes in the ski mask.

Kneeling, I felt him over quickly, took a pistol off him, pulled the machine gun out of his hand, and walked back up the slope. I stopped beside Buck, knelt painfully. He whined again, thumped his tail feebly.

"Good dog," I muttered. His fur was sticky with blood, but the bullet had taken him in the shoulder. I stroked his coat. Considered trying to carry him, but there was no way with my ribs, and dropping him was not going to be beneficial.

"Stay, Buck," I ordered, as he thrashed around, trying to get up. He subsided, whining. I gave him a final pat and rose.

The house stood dark and silent as I approached. I brought the pistol up, moving quietly onto the porch. The dead assassin still sprawled in the doorway. I stepped over him, moved across the kitchen, picking my way through glass and pottery, pulped fruit, and splintered wood.

The fridge was silent, mortally wounded. The clock ticked peacefully on the wall. The door leading down to the cellar was closed.

I moved into the hall. The lack of light made it nearly impossible to see. I moved forward silently.

Moonlight spilled onto the floorboards outside the study door. The first assassin was gone.

Jesus fucking Christ. That was my fault for not wanting to soak Stephen's floorboards with blood. I prayed my carelessness hadn't resulted in harm —

Harm. I couldn't consider anything beyond that.

Maybe the assassin had fled when he regained consciousness.

Maybe Stephen had hauled him downstairs to his office to patch him up. Just like Stephen, that.

Or maybe he had taken Stephen hostage.

Maybe he'd slit his throat.

My stomach roiled in sick panic. *Shut it,* I thought fiercely.

I stepped back into the kitchen, finding my way through the utility room with the washer and dryer to the cellar door. It swung open silently.

Flattening myself against the wall, I whispered, "Stephen?"

Nothing.

It was a struggle to control my growing dread. I couldn't think beyond the fact that Stephen might already be dead and it was my fault.

I felt for the wall switch, found it. Light flared on illuminating the cellar. Wine racks neatly lined one side, and on the other, shelves with canned goods, bottled water, tins, Christmas decorations. No sign of Stephen — but no sign of violence either.

Then something hit me from behind and I went crashing down the staircase with someone on top of me.

I landed at the bottom, half-stunned, my crushed ribs screaming protest. Wriggling, I tried to get out from under the weight pinning me to the floor. My right shoulder felt dislocated, and I felt frantically with my left hand for the pistol I'd dropped.

Hands locked around my throat. I stared up into black eyes behind a glistening, blood-soaked ski mask. The weight on my damaged ribs was red agony, making it difficult to think and nearly impossible to breathe. I grabbed for his hands, trying to secure one of his arms, but my right arm still wasn't cooperating. I threw my foot over his same side foot — and tried to buck him off.

He nearly toppled, but managed to keep his hold on my throat, sinking his fingers in deeper, and I wheezed for breath. One-handed, I couldn't break his grip and I was beginning to see stars shooting through the red tide.

Stone fragments stung my face. The rifle shot was deafening, echoing around the stone walls as the bullet plowed into the cement floor next to me. The hands around my throat stiffened — then loosened. Blood spilled out of the hole in my attacker's chest. He pitched forward, landing half on top of me, half beside me.

I gulped for air, dragging sweet oxygen into my laboring lungs, and the dark receded from the edges of my vision.

Staring past the meaty shoulder pressing into me, I saw Stephen coming down the cellar stairs fast, rifle in hand. I wanted to tell him to be careful, to take no chances, but my bruised throat wouldn't work.

He rolled my attacker off me.

"Were you hit? I had to take the shot. I was afraid he'd break your neck." He was talking to me, but his voice sounded odd and his face was the face of a stranger as he knelt and checked the man he'd shot.

Checked to see if he was still alive. If he could be saved. Because that's what Stephen did. Healed people. Saved lives.

Until tonight.

I tried to push up, and the pain nearly blacked me out again. He laid the rifle down, turning to me. "Don't try to move. Just tell me where you're hurt."

I shook my head, reaching for him — needing to see, verify by touch, that he was really all right, really unhurt. I'd been so sure he was dead. That I'd caused his death.

He was shaking as he took me into his arms but his hands were gentle and professional as he felt me over, checking for injuries.

I croaked, "I'm all right. Are you sure you're not...?" I saw his face then. Saw beyond the quiet control. Saw the shock and the horror. Saw the depth of heartsickness in his eyes and understood a little of what this blooding had cost him. What *I* had cost him. And finally, too late, I grasped how deluded I'd been, convincing myself that coming back was the way to make everything right, was the best thing for all concerned. Arrogant and stupid and selfish from start to finish. What the hell was there left to say? *Sorry? Forgive me?* Requiring still more from him, this time his absolution for my own sins.

"What is it?" he said, alarmed. "Mark?"

I managed to get my battered vocal cords to cooperate. "Thank you...for..."

For my life.

His face twisted. "I'd never let anyone hurt you, you know that," he said.

I lost it. Suddenly I was sobbing. I couldn't stop.

Quite calmly, he gathered me to him, and astonishingly what he said was, "That's right. Let go. Let it out. That's just what you need."

It was the last thing on earth I needed. I shook my head but the tears wouldn't stop.

And Stephen held me through it all, as though this were perfectly normal behavior, nothing to be ashamed of. In my whole life no one ever gave me permission to fall apart, to let go. He was the only person in the world who thought I needed taking care of, protecting.

"Is any of this blood yours?" he asked, his hand still moving carefully over my gore-soaked shirt.

I pulled back a little. Wiped my face with my hand, then my sleeve. My eyes were still leaking, but the worst was over. "Literally or metaphorically?" I got out.

"What kind of talk is that?" he muttered, pulling me against him, and he kissed my wet eyes.

It was...something inside me melted away, and I leaned against him. I said helplessly, "I thought you were dead. That I'd killed you. I shouldn't have come back. I knew it but I —"

"Stop it." His vehemence stopped me. "Don't say that again."

I nodded, wiped my face in his shirt. It was embarrassing to have fallen apart with him like that, and yet...it was liberating. Cleansing.

"Can you stand?"

I nodded tiredly, sat up. Remembered something, clutching at him with my good hand. "Buck! He's not dead. At least he wasn't fifteen minutes ago."

"Okay. Let's get you on your feet. Hold your right arm against your chest."

I obeyed. He hooked an arm around my waist and lifted me to my feet, and I managed not to throw up or black out. He walked me over the dead terrorist, and then got me up the stairs. As we reached the kitchen I heard the sound of sirens in the distance.

That reminded me that I had phone calls to make as well. My brain just didn't seem to be working. I wiped a hand across my wet lashes.

"Go get Buck," I said, pulling away. "I can handle this."

§ § § §

The mattress dipped. I came to groggily, lifting my head. In the dawn's early light, I could see Stephen climbing into bed beside me.

"It's just me," he said.

Which somehow seemed like the understatement of the year. We had only finished talking with law enforcement an hour or so earlier. Stephen had finished patching up the wounded — me — and the bodies had been carted away.

"How's Buck?" I asked. My voice was still raspy from the bruising on my throat.

I had crashed not long after the vet had arrived. Stephen said, "I think he's going to be all right. John's hopeful that because of his age and his general condition, he'll pull through."

"That's good."

"How are you?" He stretched out beside me, and I moved awkwardly into his arms. He hugged me, careful of my shoulder — and ribs — and leg.

"I'm all right." And I realized I was. I studied his drawn face. "How are you?"

He met my eyes. "I'll be all right."

I swallowed over the blockage in my throat. "I'm sorry, Stephen. I can't tell you how sorry."

"I know. And you've got plenty to be sorry for." His smile was faint. "But not that. You're lying here next to me, alive, and that makes all the difference in the world."

My eyes prickled again, and I closed them. I couldn't remember crying since I was a little kid, but apparently I was making up for lost time.

He said gently, "If those tears are for me, they're not necessary."

I nodded. Took a deep breath and managed to get control. I opened my eyes again. "What changed?" I asked. "Last night you sounded pretty sure it was over."

"Then you're the one person I managed to convince." He nuzzled my face, finding my mouth with his — about the only part of my body that didn't hurt. I put my good arm around him, ignoring the pain of my ribs. He kissed me softly, mouth, nose, eyes.

He said, "I guess I finally faced the fact that by sending you away I was just hurrying up the thing I was afraid of all along."

"I know what I want now. And I won't leave you ever again."

He smiled, not entirely convinced. It didn't matter because I knew I was telling the truth, and convincing him in the days to come would be its own reward.

He asked at last, "Can you tell me now what happened to you?"

I lay quietly, watching his face. "I've told you most of it." Dawn cast an uncertain watery light, like the tints in Dulac's illustrations of the *Rubaiyat*. Stephen's eyes looked gray and unreadable. I said, "I was in Kandahar with another agent."

"Barry," he said.

"Barry Shelton, yes." I closed my eyes. It was easier like that. "Taliban resistance is very strong in that part of the country. Ostensibly we were there on a fact-finding mission, but we were actually there to shore up wavering support from local tribes for the US and UK efforts."

He brushed the knuckles of his hand against the lower part of my jaw — where the skin was paler from the beard I had worn for months. "Go on."

I opened my eyes. I found I wanted to watch his face, after all. "We were sold out. Betrayed. I don't know by whom. Or why. It doesn't matter. It's nothing new. Nothing that hasn't happened before. Nothing that won't happen again. To someone else."

"What happened?"

"We went to meet with a local warlord, and we were taken prisoner." I swallowed, seeing it all again, feeling the fists, the boots, seeing the naked hate in the faces that had smiled a few minutes before. Reliving the sick helplessness, the brutal buzz of fear, knowing what was ahead for us. "They were transporting us across the border. Our allies attacked. Created enough of a diversion that we were able to get free. I managed to escape. Barry was killed. Shot."

"And you decided you'd finally had enough."

It was important that he understand this. I said, "I'd decided I'd had enough before I ever went. The last time we talked…when you said it was over — I decided then that if, *when*, I got home — I was packing it in. That if you'd still have me, I'd try and make it up to you. I know you don't believe that."

He interrupted. "I was angry and disappointed. I thought for my own sake, I needed to move on. We'd lost two years together, and I didn't know if you'd ever see your way to settling down. I thought you'd changed your mind — and I didn't blame you because, frankly, about the most excitement we see around here is when Buck corners a possum."

"I suppose it depends on your definition of excitement. Personally…"

He said, "I'm not saying it doesn't have its moments."

He tried to be careful with me, but as much as I craved his tenderness, I needed something more, needed to reassure myself that he was really mine, that it wasn't just kindness or self-sacrifice. He took it with bemused, heavy-lidded calm, kissing my face, my bruised throat as I clutched him, nuzzled his hair and thrust awkwardly into his taut, aroused body.

"Easy, easy. You're going to break something," he murmured, his mouth finding my lips. He rubbed his cheek against mine, his beard rasping teasingly against my sensitized skin.

"Sorry." I tried to slow myself down, catching my breath in pained little gulps. "Am I hurting you?" It felt so good sheathed deep inside his body, the dark velvet grip that owned me even as I tried to possess him. I stilled my movements with an effort.

"Not me." His hands slid down my sides, trying to ease my position. "You." His hands settled on my arse, stroking with feathering fingertips.

And I chuckled, surprising him, because broken bones notwithstanding, for the first time in my life I felt completely whole.

§ § § §

"Now what in the world is that?" remarked Lena, staring out the window over the sink as we had breakfast in the kitchen alcove the following day. "As if we haven't had enough trouble around here."

"Well, what do you know," Stephen said grimly. "I think the mountain has decided it would be faster to visit Mohammed."

I looked up sharply from my blueberry French toast in time to watch a helicopter rocking slowly down behind the trees to settle by the lake.

The geese, who had finally returned after the excitement of thirty-six hours earlier, took flight once more. The reeds around the lake whipped in the wind from the helicopter blades.

"Goddamn it," I said, and Lena made a disapproving noise.

As we stared, the door to the helicopter opened and a young man hopped out. He turned to help a tall and familiar figure disembark. Even from where we sat I recognized the shock of white hair and stooped shoulders. "It's the Old Man himself," I said in disbelief.

Stephen swore quietly.

I rose and went out onto the porch. Stephen followed me down the hill, past the yellow crime scene tape marking off the gun battle of two nights earlier.

The old man, impeccably tailored as always, strode toward us, moving with that characteristic decisiveness and dispatch. He held an official-looking manila envelop.

"Well, Mr. Hardwicke," he said as he reached us, his eyes taking in Stephen standing calmly at my shoulder. "It's nice to see you looking so well. I was led to believe your health was in a far more precarious state."

"Just seeing you again is a tonic, sir," I said gravely.

The wind whipped his long white hair over his forehead and he raked it back impatiently, glaring at us with his pale blue eyes. Then his shoulders slumped and he sighed. "I shall miss you, Mark. I had you earmarked for bigger and better things. However, ours is an organization that does not thrive in the limelight, and events of the past few days have brought undue and unwelcome attention your way — and thus our way."

He handed me the envelope.

Stephen snorted. "You're giving him his pink slip?"

The Old Man said haughtily, "I think Mr. Hardwicke will agree the terms are quite generous — provided he agrees to all our terms."

"Terms?" Stephen inquired warily, looking from me to my employer. "What are we talking about here? A no compete?"

I felt my mouth twitching into an inappropriate smile, but catching the Old Man's glare, I bit it back. "I have to agree to keep my mouth shut." As Stephen's eyes narrowed, I added, "I hope I can find work teaching because I won't be able to write that bestselling roman á clef after all."

"You won't starve," the Old Man said.

"Thank you, sir," I said, and I meant it. I didn't care about my pension. He was letting me go without a fuss, and that was all that mattered to me now.

The Old Man nodded curtly, and started to turn away. I realized that I would probably never see him again.

I said, "Sir, would you care for some breakfast before you head back?" Stephen threw me a look of disbelief.

The Old Man fastened that pale gaze on me. "No, thank you, Mr. Hardwicke. I must be away. I merely happened to be in the neighborhood."

"Ah."

He turned, then paused. "There is one final thing. You may hear on the news tonight that several high ranking Taliban were killed in a missile attack in Kandahar yesterday. One of the dead has been confirmed as Mullah Arsullah."

I stared at him. It seemed too much to hope for, but I couldn't see any point in his lying about it.

"There's no mistake?"

"There's no mistake." Just for an instant there was something I had rarely seen in his eyes — something I'd used to crave — an emotion dangerously akin to affection. "Let us hope, Mr. Hardwicke, that you don't grow bored with what seems destined to be a very long and uneventful retirement."

"Not much chance of that, sir."

In silence we watched as he made his way swiftly down the hill, climbed back into the helicopter. The blades picked up speed, the helicopter lifted and whirled away. In a few moments it was a tiny speck in the distance.

Stephen's hand rested warmly on my shoulder, and I turned to him.

"Welcome home," he said.

A Limited Engagement

This was my contribution to Torquere Press's donation to Lambda's Legal Fund in support of gay marriage. Basically it's a little story about the desperate things love can drive you to — or doing the wrong things for the right reasons. *Do not attempt this in your own home!*

I heard the key in the lock, switched on the porch light, and opened the door.

The rain poured off the roof of the cabin in a shining fall of silver needles, bouncing and splashing off the redwood deck. Ross stood there, blue eyes blacker than the night, the amber porch light giving his skin a jaundiced cast.

"You're here," he said in disbelief. The disbelief gave way instantly to the rage he'd been banking down for — well, probably since the newspapers came out that morning. Even in the unwholesome porch light I could see his face flush dark and his eyes change.

I stepped back — partly to let him in, because really what choice did I have? Even if I'd wanted to keep him out, it was his cabin. Partly because...it was Ross and I had no walls and no doors and no defenses against him.

He followed me inside, shaking his wet, black hair out of his eyes. He wasn't wearing gloves, and his hands were red from the cold. His Joseph Abboud overcoat dripped in a silent puddle around his expensively shod feet. "I am going to kill you," he said carefully and quietly, and he launched himself at me.

I jumped back, my foot slipped on the little oriental throw rug, and I went down, crashing into the walnut side table, knocking it — and the globe lamp atop it — over. The lamp smashed on the wooden floor, shards of painted flowers scattering down the hallway.

Ross's cold hands locked around my throat. Big hands, powerful hands — hands that could stroke and soothe and tease and tantalize — tightened, choking me. I clawed at his wrists, squirming, wriggling, trying to break his hold.

Til death do you part...

"R-R-ogh —" I tried to choke out his name as he squeezed.

The blood beat in my ears with the thunder of the rain on the roof. The lights swirled and dimmed, the black edges swept forward and washed me out with the drum of the rain on the roof.

§ § § §

I could hear the rain pounding down. I opened my eyes. I was lying on the floor in the entrance hall of the cabin, the rug scrunched beneath me. The lights were out but the flickering from the fireplace in the front room sent shadows dancing across the open beamed ceiling. I could make out broken glass winking and twinkling in the firelight like bits of broken stars fallen around me. My back hurt, my head buzzed, my throat throbbed.

There was no sign of Ross.

Levering myself up, I got to my feet, leaned dizzily against the wall while I found my bearings, then picked my way over the fallen table and through the broken glass into the front room.

Ross sat in front of the fireplace, head in his hands, unmoving.

I felt my way over to the sofa and sat down across from him.

He didn't look up. I could see that his hands were shaking a little.

Mine were shaking a lot.

I croaked, "Rawh." Tried again. "Ross...will you listen to me?" It came out in a hoarse boy demon voice.

I guess Demon Boy was about right. He looked at me then, and even in the uncertain lighting the pain in his eyes was almost more than I could take.

He said tonelessly, "Why did you do it?"

I had to struggle to get the words, and not just because of my bruised throat.

He said, "I did everything you wanted. I paid every penny of your goddamned blackmail. Why the hell did you do it?" I could tell he'd been asking himself this all the long drive, all the long day. Six hours from New York City to this little cabin in the Vermont woods. He must have left not long after the news broke.

"I —" my voice gave out on another squawk.

His eyes shone in the firelight as they turned my way. I shook my head.

"Do you have any idea what you've done to me?" he asked. "You've destroyed me. *Why?*"

I couldn't answer. The burn in the back of my throat moved to my eyes and dazzled me. I could just make him out in a kind of prism — as though he were trapped in crystal.

"You don't think you owe me that much?" He got up fast. I flinched. He stopped.

"I'm...sorry," I got out.

"Sorry?"

I nodded.

"You're...sorry?" The bewilderment was painful. "You outed me to the press. You've ruined my career, my marriage —"

"Engagement," I said quickly.

There was a little pause. Ross said, "You've ruined my life...and you're sorry?"

I said, "I'm sorry you're suffering. I'm not sorry I did it."

I thought he really would kill me then. Fists clenched, he took a step toward me, and I straightened, squaring my shoulders. For a long moment he stared down at me, then, sharply, he turned away. I could hear the harshness of his breathing as he fought for control.

"Ross —"

"Don't say anything, Adam." His voice was muffled. "Don't speak. I'm not —"

Neither of us said a word as the rain thundered down on the roof. I could see it glinting outside the windows like grains of polished rice — like a shower of rice outside a church. But they didn't throw rice at weddings anymore, did they?

Finally Ross gave a long sigh. His shoulders relaxed. He moved away to the liquor cart and poured two brandies. Brandy in the wrong glasses: he really was upset. Handing me a tumbler, he down on the other sofa, and said conversationally, "That's twice tonight I've almost killed you." He met my eyes. "You shouldn't have come here, Adam. I can't believe you did."

"I'm not running from you," I said.

He raised his brows. "You should be running from me. Because I'm going to return the favor and wreck your life."

"All right." I tossed my drink back and then stared down at the empty glass sparkling in the firelight.

He gave me that dark, unfathomable look. "You don't believe me?"

I actually managed a crooked smile. "I think I beat you to it, yeah?"

Yeah. Because of the two of us, my career was less likely to survive. Ross was a playwright. A brilliant, respected playwright, at that. I was an actor. A mostly out-of-work and previously not very well-known actor. Not many openly gay actors find leading man roles on or off Broadway. Especially the ones who indulge in kiss and tell with powerful playwrights and producers. I was going to be a pariah, the Ann Heche of the *theatah, dahling*.

There also was the fact that I loved Ross — as much as he now hated me.

He swallowed a mouthful of brandy slowly, thoughtfully. "Not a smart move from a career standpoint," he agreed. "Either of your careers. You know, you're not going to get far as a blackmailer if you betray your paying customers."

"Why did you pay me?" I asked.

He said as though explaining the facts of life to a numbskull, "Because you threatened to out me to the press."

"You could have gone to the police."

"How the hell would that have helped? It would just have outed me faster."

"You preferred to keep sleeping with me even though I was blackmailing you."

"You're not hard to sleep with," he said dryly. "Far from it. And as we — and now everyone — know, I like to sleep with men. And I'm not that choosy."

I ignored that last comment, although it stung. I pointed out, "And then when I demanded money, you handed that over too."

"That's my point," Ross said. "I gave you what you wanted. Everything you wanted, you got."

I said bitterly, "Right."

"What the hell did you not get? You asked for a part in the new play, and I got that for you too. Jesus Christ. I did everything I could think of —"

"That's right," I said, and suddenly I was on my feet and furious. "You're so goddamned *afraid* that you let me blackmail you into a part in the new play. Was there anything you wouldn't have done to keep my mouth shut? To keep yourself —"

He was staring at me, mouth slightly parted — not a look I'd ever seen on Ross's face before. Ross Marlowe was the living personification of Man About Town. The suave sophisticate who knew what to do in every social situation. But I guess confronting your blackmailing ex-lover wasn't covered in *Debrett's Etiquette and Modern Manners*.

"What the hell are *you* crying about?" he asked.

I wiped my face on my sleeve. "Oh go to hell," I said. "If you don't know by now, there's no point me spelling it out."

He was very still.

It took some effort, but I got myself under control while he stared at me with those midnight-blue eyes.

"Look," I said finally. "You asked why. So here's why. Part of why. All these plays you write about characters finding their true selves and owning up to who they really are, and making difficult choices and standing behind them — *two* plays about gay men being true to themselves against the odds — and all the time you're hiding behind this…façade of Ross Marlowe the brilliant heterosexual playwright." Tears and my injured vocal cords closed off my words.

He said slowly, "I see. This was for my own good?"

I nodded, not looking at him, mopping again at my runny nose, leaking eyes. "I don't expect you to understand," I got out.

"Lucky for both of us." Watching me, he shuddered and pulled out a pristine hanky — and who the hell carries hankies?

Wasn't that proof to the entire civilized world right then and there that Ross was gay? He tossed it my way. "Jesus, mop your face."

I took it with muttered thanks.

"So basically," he said, watching me scrub my face, "You had some idealistic image of me and I disappointed you, and this is your revenge?"

Horrifically the tears started again. It took effort to stop them. I managed. "You never disappointed me."

"No." His gaze was intent. "What then?"

I said — and I tried to be matter of fact, "I don't believe you would have been happy like that, Ross. I don't believe you —"

"Christ, you're young," he said, but he sounded weary, not angry. He set down his glass, rose, and came over to me, taking me in his arms. "Okay, listen, Adam. You're twenty-three. I'm forty. I think I've got the edge in experience here. I believe in the things I write about, but I don't want to live my life as some kind of gay poster boy for the arts, all right? I like my privacy."

His arms felt very good around me, strong and kind and familiar. He smelled good too: a mix of rain and pipe tobacco and some overpriced herbal aftershave you probably couldn't buy in Vermont. I put my head on his shoulder. I was very tired. I hadn't slept since I'd done the interview with the reporter from the *New York Times* Theater section.

Playing Desdemona to Ross's Othello hadn't helped much either.

"This isn't privacy," I said. "This is...a lie. You're marrying someone you don't love."

I felt the steady, even pulse in his throat against my face. He was past his anger now; Ross was the most civilized man I knew — and maybe that was part of the problem. He said levelly, "I like Anne. I do care about her, whether it meets your...naïve definition of love. It's a good working partnership — or it would have been before you blasted it to Kingdom Come with your exclusive to the papers."

Well, Kingdom Come was where I reigned. I didn't think he'd find that funny though — I didn't — and instead I said,

"Marriage should be about more than friendship and respect, Ross."

"Respect and friendship — companionship, shared interests — that's a good basis."

I shook my head. "It's not enough."

"You're the expert now?" His tone was dry. "What's the longest steady relationship you've had?"

"We've been together one year, eight months and twenty-seven days," I said.

He didn't have an answer. After a moment he couldn't even meet my eyes.

I added, "Depending on how you use the word 'together.'" I pulled out of his arms.

After several minutes Ross said quite gently, "Did you feel I used you? Is that why?"

I shook my head.

I could feel his gaze on my profile. "It was never my intent. From the moment I saw you I…wanted you," he said honestly.

Yeah. No question. I still remembered looking up from reading for the part of George Deever in *All My Sons* and meeting those smiling, blue eyes. Ross, who was good friends with the show's producer, had been sitting in on the auditions that day. Every time I'd glanced up from the script I'd seen him watching me from the almost empty sea of chairs.

I hadn't got the role. Apparently I didn't look like either a lawyer or a veteran. But as I'd left the audition, Ross had followed me out of the theater. He'd offered to buy me a drink. And, as consolation prizes went, I'd have taken a drink with Ross over eating for the next three months easy.

We had cocktails at the M Bar in the Mansfield Hotel. Mahogany bookshelves, and a domed skylight. It had been raining that night too, glittering down like a fake downpour on a stage set. We drank and talked and then he took me upstairs to a luxurious suite and fucked me in the clouds of down comforter and pillow-topped mattress. In the morning he fed me cappuccino and croissants and put me in a taxi. I never expected to see him again.

I figured he did that kind of thing all the time.

Two nights later he had called me, and after a painfully stilted and painfully brief conversation, he'd asked me out. We'd had dinner at 21, and he'd taken me back to the Mansfield. And in the morning Ross had let me fuck him.

After that I'd seen him a couple of days almost every week. Stolen hours. Borrowed time.

The best had been the week we'd spent here at his cabin in Vermont just on our own.

That had been four months ago — in the summer. We'd swum in the lake and fished and sunned ourselves. We'd barbecued the rainbow trout we caught and drank too much and watched the stars blazing overhead as it got later and later. We'd talked and laughed and fucked and laughed some more. He'd let me read his new play. I told him I'd been offered a job in Los Angeles, and he told me not to go.

That was the happiest I could ever remember being — because I'd been sure Ross was falling in love with me. But the next week he'd announced his engagement to Anne Cassidy. I read it in the Theater section of the New York Times. Anne was an entertainment columnist for the *Daily News*.

Ross apologized for that, and said he had planned to tell me himself, but Anne had got a little overexcited about the upcoming nuptials. I told Ross that if he broke it off with me I'd go to the papers too. He'd laughed, but he'd kept seeing me — though not as frequently.

Their formal engagement party, a month later, received quite a bit of coverage in the local papers. I was still reading about it when Ross called and asked if I was free for the evening. I told him I wasn't free, and that if he didn't want me to tell his fiancée he was queerer than a postmodern production of *Not about Nightingales*, he would have to pay me a hundred dollars a week. He had been less amused but he'd given the money and he'd kept sleeping with me, and the wedding plans sailed smoothly along.

A month ago I'd told Ross that if he didn't get me a part in his new play, *God's Geography*, I'd go to the papers. He'd given into that too — granted, a very minor role — although he didn't sleep with me for two weeks after that escalation of hostilities.

He'd finally called me late one night, sounding faintly sloshed. I'd insisted that he come to my place, for once, and he actually had. He'd actually shown up at my battered apartment door with a bottle of Napoleon brandy, and fucked me long and hard in my blue and white striped Sears sheets while we listened to my next-door neighbors quarrel with each other to the musical accompaniment of their kid wailing in the background.

"I even want you now," he'd said, when he had rolled off me. It wasn't a compliment.

So as I stared at him in the shadowy firelight, I said, "I know. You never made any secret about it."

He said — not looking at me, "I wasn't going to dump you. You must know that. I didn't intend to stop seeing you."

"Is that supposed to make it better?"

His eyes widened at my anger. "I didn't mean to…tried not to…take advantage of you. Of your…youth, your generosity." The words seemed difficult for him. "Did you feel used? Is that why?"

The playwright always wanting the loose ends neatly tied up. Living in fear of the critics, apparently.

I said, "I don't think you used me. I think you fell in love with me."

He was silent for a long time. I thought my heart would shatter into pieces like an asteroid waiting for him to say something. In the end all he said was, "And for that —?"

I stood up, hugging myself against the cold, although between the brandy and the fireplace, the room was warm enough. "And I fell in love with you," I said. I wanted to sound strong and convincing, but I just sounded pained. "The second morning at the Mansfield, the first time you let me fuck you. I made some stupid joke, and you laughed, and you kissed my nose. I've never wanted anyone or anything as much as I want you. I would give anything —"

He looked away at the fire and a muscle moved in his jaw.

"And I couldn't stand there and watch you marry Anne Cassidy. It's not right. It's not fair to any of us. Not even to her."

He said impatiently, "Anne knows exactly what she wants. And so do I."

"Then why are you settling for companionship and respect when you could have all that and love and passion as well?"

"Because you're twenty-three years old and queer — and what the hell does that make me?"

"Older and queer!"

He put his head in his hands.

I stared at him. "Well, that's that," I said. "Anyway, you'll be okay. It's New York. It'll be a nine days wonder and then no one will even remember."

He looked at me with something close to dislike. "You don't think so?"

"Hell, I don't know." I rubbed my face. "I'm sorry. Sorry to hurt you, but not sorry to have stopped it." I added, "If it is stopped."

"Oh, it's stopped." He sounded sour.

And that really was that. All at once I was out of ideas — and energy. I said, "I can't keep saying I'm sorry. I guess…you know where to find me."

I started for the door and he said harshly, "Adam, if you thought you were in love with me, why didn't you say so?"

At that, I had to smile. "I did Ross. I said it in every way I knew. If I'd actually said the words, you'd have broken it off. You didn't want to know."

"You think I do now?"

I shook my head. "No. You'd still prefer to think it was just sex."

Ross said slowly, "But you came here anyway. Drove all the way up here on the chance that this is where I would come."

"Yeah."

"Knowing how I would feel about you after this."

I admitted, "I couldn't stay away."

Neither of us said anything. The fire popped sending sparks showering.

His voice was very low as he said, "I could have hurt you very badly; you know that."

"You could have killed me," I said, "And it wouldn't have hurt as much as watching you marry someone you don't love just because it fits your image or whatever the hell it is with you."

It wouldn't hurt as much as watching him marry anyone who wasn't me.

"You're so sure it's you I love?"

"I am, yeah." I said it with a sturdy confidence I was a long way from feeling — but that's what acting is all about. "I think that's why you kept giving into my demands, because you didn't want to break it off either. I don't think you're that afraid of me."

"I wasn't, no." Astonishingly, there was a thread of humor in his voice. "But then I didn't fully grasp what you were capable of."

To my surprise he held out a hand. I took it, and he drew me down onto the sofa. For a moment he sat there, absently playing with the fingers of my ring hand. My fingers looked thin and brown and callused next to his own manicured ones. When I didn't have a paying acting gig — which was usually — I worked as a bicycle messenger for a courier service. Yeah, safe to say eHarmony probably wouldn't have set us up as the perfect match.

He said, "Has it occurred to you that if I did love you, you destroyed it with your actions?"

I swallowed painfully. Nodded.

"And you still don't regret it?"

"Maybe I will." I met his eyes and tried to smile. "Right now I'm sort of numb."

"That's two of us." He leaned forward, finding my mouth, kissing me. I slid back into the cushions, surrendering to whatever he wanted. He kissed me softly, and then harder. His mouth bruised mine, a punishing grind of lips and teeth, but I opened to it, opened to him, and almost immediately he gentled. His hands moved under my sweater, pushing it up.

His touch was warm and sent a tingle spreading beneath my skin. I murmured approval.

"I have never known anyone like you," he said.

"But that's good, right?"

He snorted and sat up, but his fingers went to the buttons of his tailored shirt.

I yanked my sweater up, banging my head on the arm of the sofa as I pulled it over my head, dropped it. I humped up, wriggling out of my jeans.

Ross was hurrying to undress too, and it was a relief to know that the desire between us remained intact. It was always like this, hungry and hurried — and then sweet and satisfied. It was…nourishing.

Because, regardless of what Ross told himself, it wasn't just sex — and it hadn't been for a very long time.

I kicked my legs free, kicked my jeans away. Ross stood up, unzipped, and stepped out of his trousers. I brushed his long, lightly furred thigh with my hand.

Naked, he lowered himself to me and I ran my fingers through his hair that was drying in soft silky black strands smelling of rain and firelight. I pressed my face to his throat and licked him, licked at the little pulse beating there. He exhaled a long breath. Relief? Resignation?

I said, "It wasn't easy. Just so you know — it —"

He pulled back a little. "No. I know. When you opened the door you looked…" He considered it and then said, "Terrified and sick and hopeful all at the same time."

"That pretty much sums it up." I wanted to make a joke of it, but it wasn't funny.

Everything that mattered to me was going to be settled in the next few hours. Maybe minutes. I didn't know if this was a hello fuck or a goodbye fuck. Maybe even Ross didn't know.

"I love you so much," I said, and my voice shook.

"I know." He sounded pained. So…good-bye then?

I kissed the underside of his jaw, and he tipped his face to mine and found my mouth in hot, moist pressure. Something as sweet and simple as kissing: mouths moving against each other, opening to each other, the sweet exchange of breath.

His tongue slipped into my mouth, a teasing little thrust, and I sucked back. He tasted like Ross with a brandy chaser.

I kissed him, and he whispered, "You're fearless, aren't you? Going to the papers, coming here tonight, opening up to me now. I don't think I've ever known anyone as fearless as you."

I moved my head in denial. "I'm scared," I said. "All the time. I'm just stuck in drive. When it comes to you, I don't know how to stop or how to reverse."

He shook his head a little, his mouth found mine again, nibbling my lower lip, moving his mouth against mine in feathery, teasing brush. I nuzzled him back and his kiss deepened. I liked his weight lowering on me, warm and solid, I liked the roughness of his jaw against my own, I liked his taste and scent, and the feel of his fingers against my cheek — and the insistent prod of his cock in my belly.

I put my hands on either side of his face and said, "Can you just tell me if this hello or good-bye? I just want to know, so I can stop…hoping." The alcohol and exhaustion made it easy to be honest, to accept whatever the truth was going to be. If the answer was no, then in the morning I would deal with it but tonight we were going to make love.

A little grimly, he said, "What if it's good-bye? Are you planning to write a book about me next?"

I shook my head. "If it really is good-bye, I'm all out of ideas."

Ross raised one eyebrow. "No ideas at all?"

"Other than the obvious: make this a night you won't forget."

His face softened. He said, "There isn't one night with you that I've forgotten. Nor a single day. You must know that much."

"I know how it is for me."

And then we said nothing for a time, communicating by touch. I thought he does love me, he does — even if he hasn't realized it, hasn't accepted it — he does — hissing a little breath of pleasured surprise as he pinched my nipples, making them stand up in tiny buds.

"You do like that," he whispered, his mouth tugging into another of those sexy little smiles.

"I like it when you lick them too," I whispered, tugging him closer, smoothing my hands over the hard flesh of his back and shoulders. Hard muscle and soft skin — the musculature of a normal healthy adult man, not a movie star, not an iron man. Our naked bodies rubbed against each other, starting to find that rhythm, my own cock rock hard and requiring attention, jutting up, nestling against his.

Ross groaned, and his mouth drifted down my throat and over my shoulder, stopping to lick and kiss, to bite and linger. I groaned and my throat protested squeakily, and he kissed me there too, tenderly.

"Thank God," he said. "Thank God, I didn't…"

I stopped that with more kisses.

"I could make you happy," I told him. "I'd do everything in my power to make you happy."

He looked up, surprised. "You do make me happy."

"Sometimes."

He bent his head; his tongue lapped across one nipple, drawing it firm and upright instantly. I sucked in a sharp breath. Moaned. He liked that. I felt his smile as his mouth ghosted across my chest. I moaned again, and soon the rasp of his tongue wet my other nipple. I pushed against him, loving that feel, loving that lave of tongue on teat. My heart was pounding dizzily in my chest. I worked my hand down through the fissures between our bodies, slipping past his groin, cupping his balls in my palm.

He grunted, closed his eyes briefly. I caressed him languidly.

"What do you want?" he asked.

Something old, something new, something borrowed, something blue, something to have and to hold from this day forward. I got out, "Will you fuck me? I need it. Need to feel like I belong to you."

His bit his lip. "I don't know if I can walk."

I chuckled, squeezed his balls, lightly.

"Hold on," he jerked out.

I did, stroking myself leisurely until he was back. He knelt over me, his cock long and thick and beautiful as it rose out of the dark nest of his groin. He rested his hand against my cheek.

"You're beautiful, Adam."

"So are you."

I started to get up, but he pushed me back, smiling. I looked my inquiry and then whimpered as he knelt and took the head of my shaft into his mouth. Oh my God how I loved this. Was there anyone who didn't? But especially I loved it from Ross. *His* elegant, clever mouth doing those unspeakably erotic things to me: *his* wide and warm and wet hole for me to bury myself in. I began to jerk my hips in response to that slow slide. Sensation shivered through me, stripping my thoughts away, and the trembling started.

You lovely, lovely boy, Ross said, without saying a word. His tongue and lips said precious, loving things instead.

I arched my back, crying out.

He began to suck hard. I groped for him — needing something to ground me with pleasure taking me that high. My fingers dug into Ross's broad shoulder, watching through slitted eyes, watching how beautiful he was with his mouth wrapped around my dick. I wanted to tell him so, but the sounds coming out of me were not particularly intelligent. An electrical buzz seemed to crackle up my spine, bright lights flared behind my eyelids, I wondered if I might just short circuit entirely in a kind of sensory overload.

Ross let me feel his teeth and I whimpered, and then he was sucking again so very softly, sweetly. He varied the pressure, sucking me hard and long. My balls drew tight and I began to come in hot wet spurts, crying out his name.

And Ross swallowed it. I felt tears start in my eyes, but I blinked them back. It was not like he had never done that before, it just…meant more tonight. He swallowed my cum and licked the head of my cock clean, while I lay there panting and trying not to embarrass myself.

When I finally lifted my lashes Ross was smiling. He bent his head to mine. His mouth brushed my mouth and I tasted myself on him — salty and sort of sweet.

He said, "You've gambled everything, haven't you? What are you hoping for?"

I answered with a question of my own. "Did you think I might be here when you decided to come to the cabin?"

A strange expression crossed his face. "It went through my mind. I…didn't think you really would. I didn't think you'd have the nerve."

It was hard to ask, but I made myself. "Did you…hope I would be here?"

He seemed to look inside himself. "I think I did." He added ruefully, "But not necessarily for the reason you hope."

"But you did want me?"

"I always want you. That doesn't mean…"

"What?"

And he said, "It's easy to be brave when you're young."

"No, it's not."

Maybe he read something in my face because he seemed to draw on something within himself. "No. It's not always," he agreed. "And you want me to be as brave as you, don't you? Idealistic youth expects no less."

I nodded. "There is recompense, though." I slipped from the sofa and got on my hands and knees on the rug before the fireplace. I glanced back and he was already settling on his knees behind me.

"Recompense." He sounded amused. "That's a good old fashioned word." I heard the unlovely sound of something squirting, followed by the delicate scent of oranges and honey.

"Orange blossom?" I suggested.

"Dear God," he said, and his laugh had a choky sound. Still, his eyes were smoky with desire as his thighs brushed mine, and his finger pushed against my body.

Always so cautious and gentle with this, although we both knew I had three times his experience. One finger insinuating a long, slender length through that tiny puckered mouth, soothing with oil and honeyed oranges, then two slick fingers.

"I love this part," I admitted, pushing back against his hand.

He pushed the third finger in. Always, always three fingers with Ross. Such a careful circumspect man. I liked the little rituals. I reached out my hand and he squirted oil on my fingers, and I smeared the oil the full length of my cock, stroking myself, enjoying the pull while his silky fingers slid in and out, knowing exactly where and how to touch.

"Now," I managed. "Please."

"You do have nice manners," he admitted. "Usually."

He withdrew his fingers, positioning himself at the entrance of my body, nudging slowly, slowly inside. He pushed smoothly in past the ring of muscle, joining us, wedding us. I drew back on my knees, resting against Ross's broad chest and belly. I turned and kissed the side of his throat. He stroked his hand slowly down the length of my torso, stroking my belly.

I shifted in his lap, Ross's hips pushing against me. His voice was warm against my ear, "I'll give you this much, Adam. I do love you. Nothing changes that. Nothing could."

Tears blinded me for an instant as we rocked together in gentle lullaby motion, that seesaw of give and take, the balancing act…and that was love, right? That was marriage? For richer for poorer, for better for worse, in sickness and in health, push pull, an irresistible force meeting an immovable object…and somehow finding a way to make it work?

The heat built like a fever, like joy…

Ross's hand stroked my hip as he steadied into that rhythm, and then faster and sweeter, and I thrust back at him trying to take him deeper, further, gasping with each hard stroke, shivering with the sweetness of it, the cycle, the circle, beginning and the end of us that was hopefully just another beginning.

I pressed my back and spine against Ross and his fingers laced within mine across my chest, and then he surged up into me and held very still and emptied out all the heat and hunger and heartache.

Then, another couple of tight jerks, and he was slumping forward and taking me with him in a heavy boneless sprawl on the soft fur of the carpet.

We lay there panting for a long time, unmoving. Ross lifted my hand to his lips and kissed the palm.

When his cock finally slipped from my body, he rolled off me, and the loss felt too familiar — like it could get to be a habit. But he put his arm around me, pulling me close, and we lay for a time on the rug. The rain beat on the roof in steady soothing rhythm, and the fire crackled in counterpoint, and our breathing slowed and steadied and evened out.

After a time he said, "And you think love is enough?"

"Sex helps." He didn't laugh and I said, "I think love is the point. Because anything else is just a business contract."

He said wearily, "I had my life all planned out."

"I know."

"You're not a very good actor," he said. "I've known from the first that you were in love with me."

"You're not a very good actor, either," I said.

The firelight moved across the ceiling beams in lazy, flickering shadow.

He said, "There's a justice of the peace in Greensboro."

"Is there?"

He turned his head and pressed his face into my hair. I felt his lips move against my forehead as he said, "Do you have any idea of what I should do with an unused marriage license?"

"I do," I said.

DARK HORSE

Dark Horse is the first story I wrote specifically for the m/m romance market. I wanted to try my hand at a character less normal and well-balanced than Adrien English — a man who was not only younger, but perhaps a little emotionally fragile, insecure. And then I thought of the old film *Gaslight*...

Dedication:
To all those for whom
The Charioteer made a difference

"But I should have come back, anyway. I should have had to come back."

The Charioteer, Mary Renault

Chapter One

The post card was nestled between *Variety* and the Edison bill.

Just an ordinary picture postcard. White font proclaimed *MALIBU!* across the mai tai-colored sunset. I turned the card over, and there was the spidery black writing I had thought I would never see again.

Miss me?

No signature. No signature needed. I looked at the postmark. Pacific Coast Highway. Yesterday's date.

I stared for a long time while Dan's deep voice receded into the cries of the gulls overhead and the pound of the waves on the beach a few yards away, until those too faded to a kind of white noise.

No. God.

Then Dan stretched across and took the card from my unresisting hand, and I was abruptly returned to the present.

The wooden chair creaked as he leaned back, his long muscular body at ease. His dark brows drew together. Absently, he raked his still-wet hair back. It wasn't like there was a lot to read. One simple sentence.

Miss me?

A rhetorical question if there ever was one.

Water glistened on Dan's broad sun-browned shoulders, one drop trickling down between his rock-hard pecs, sparkling through the dusting of dark hair across his flat abdomen. The tiny flicker of irritation I'd felt at his arrogance faded in the wake of lust. After he'd spent nearly a month playing Bodyguard to the Stars, I couldn't blame him if he still occasionally reacted like he was getting paid for overtime.

"It's not Hammond," he said, and tossed the card to the table. It landed face up in a blob of crabapple jelly.

"The writing is the same."

"Superficially. We'd have to get it analyzed. Anyway, it doesn't matter. Say one of his cards *was* delayed for a few days; it doesn't change the fact that he's dead."

"If he is dead."

His eyes, blue as the surf behind him, met mine levelly. "Sean, he's dead. I saw the car. No one could have survived that crash."

"Then why wasn't his body recovered?"

"It's somewhere in the aqueduct. I don't know. It must have been swept away or lodged somehow."

I nodded tightly. It's not like there's high tide in the California Aqueduct.

Dan's large hand slid under my fingers nervously fiddling with a teaspoon. "It's over, chief. Trust me."

"I do." It came out more husky than I'd intended.

He turned my hand palm up, lightly kissing it. The warmth of his lips against my surf-chilled skin made me shiver. I dropped the teaspoon. It hit the edge of my saucer with a silvery chime. He grinned.

You only ever hear about closeted cops, so Dan's relaxed attitude still caught me off guard. He was probably more at ease with his sexuality than half the "civilians" I knew. He sure as hell was more relaxed than me.

I pulled my hand away at the familiar yap-yapping of the four-legged hairball belonging to our nearest neighbor, Mrs. Wilgi. Sure enough, a moment later "Mrs. Wiggly" came around the cairn of rocks, armed with her usual binoculars and police whistle.

I caught Dan's eye. His grin was wry. He was getting to read me pretty well.

I said, "Hey, for all I know Mrs. Wiggly has a spy cam concealed in her muumuu."

He forked another waffle off the plate. "I don't even want to think about what that muumuu conceals."

I laughed. My glance fell on the jam-stained postcard, and I made myself look away. If Dan said it was over, it was over. He was the expert here.

All the same, after a year of being stalked, it wasn't so easy to drop my guard. One week after Paul Hammond lost control of his car during a police chase on Highway 138 and crashed into the California Aqueduct, I still tensed when the phone rang, waiting for that familiar whisper. I still sorted through my mail fast, trying to get it over with in case, like today, something ugly fell out of the mix. I still watched the rearview mirror everywhere I drove, although for the past three weeks Lt. Daniel Moran of the LAPD had been riding shotgun with me — when he didn't insist on doing the actual driving.

I said, talking myself away from my anxiety, "I just don't want to turn up in the *National Inquirer* as the gay Bennifer or something."

"Dansean?" Dan suggested, playing along.

"I'm the celebrity," I pointed out. "My name gets top billing. Maybe…Seandan."

"You can be the top anything you like." Dan's eyes were very blue. "Just say the word."

Heat rose in my face.

I mean, how ridiculous was that? You'd think I was a blushing virgin of seventeen, instead of being a reasonably experienced twenty-five year old veteran of the Hollywood party scene. True, most seventeen-year-olds probably saw more action than me — although things were definitely looking up these days.

Automatically, I returned Mrs. Wilgi's wave as she tromped along the shoreline, her red and yellow dress puffing out and flattening against her ungainly body. The dog, barking hysterically, veered off, galloping toward the deck where we sat, as though he'd just noticed this house on the otherwise empty beach.

"Doesn't that thing have an off button?" I murmured.

Mrs. Wilgi began clapping frantically and calling to the dog.

"Binky! Binky!"

"Speaking of off buttons," Dan remarked, "I'm supposed to start back at work tomorrow."

"Oh."

I tried to hide it, but I knew he could see my disappointment.

He said, his tone very casual, "Were you planning to stay out at the beach for a few days or should I drop some things off at the house?"

"The House" being my place in the Hollywood Hills. My place and now, maybe, Dan's place, too. It was still so new this relationship, so unexpected. We were both tentative, feeling our way along. Trying not to take too much for granted. Or spoil it by not taking *enough* for granted.

I said, going for the same off-hand note, "I was thinking of staying out until next weekend. What do you think? Malibu too far to drive every evening?"

"Not if I'm waking up next to you every morning."

My heart skipped a beat. How the hell could he say this stuff and not sound corny? Practice, I guess. Dan was ten years older than me — and they had been an active ten years.

I said, "That can be arranged."

We'd been sleeping together for one week, starting with the night Dan had returned home to tell me Hammond had crashed into the aqueduct. But the attraction had been immediate. My manager, Steve Kreiger, kept saying what a great screenplay it would make. Gay cop falls for the gay actor he's assigned to protect from a crazed stalker. And it was true: for once real life was every bit as satisfying as the movies. Dan was a decorated officer frequently held up as the poster boy for the new and improved (read "sensitive and diverse") LAPD. It didn't hurt that he was articulate, smart, and old-fashioned movie-star handsome. A straight arrow in every way but one — and that one way got him assigned to my bodyguard detail.

So now we were finding out what happened after the screen faded to black and the final credits rolled.

Mrs. Wiggly was blowing her police whistle like a crime was in progress. The fur ball ignored her, barking shrilly, plumy tail waving frantically as he stood at the steps of the deck.

I tossed a sausage link, just missing Binky's indignant nose. Both Dan and the mutt disapproved of this — the mutt vocally,

Dan silently. I was getting to know him well enough to translate his silences. I smiled at him, and he shook his head a little.

"I'm trying to win him over," I said.

"I don't think he appreciates your cooking the way I do."

"I guess not."

I was going to miss our early morning swims followed by these lazy breakfasts. I was going to miss having Dan around all day. Hopefully, I'd be going back to work myself before long. But what happened if the next film I got required a location shoot? Dan and I were way too new to survive extended long distance. I knew, without asking, that he would not be willing to hang up his career in law enforcement to keep me company in New Zealand or Romania for twelve weeks. And I was at a place in my own career where I had to pick my projects carefully.

He pushed his chair back and said, "I think I'll have a quick shower and drive into town. I want to pick up a few things."

"Okay." My gaze wandered back to the postcard.

"Want to help me try out my new back-scrubber?"

I laughed. He made it so easy. I rose, dismissing the card, but as I followed Dan indoors, I couldn't help wondering…if Paul Hammond hadn't sent that card, who had?

§ § § §

"Gotta admit, I had my doubts about you when I saw the pink bubble bath." Dan squirted pastel gel into the ramie mitt and slid it over my shoulders. Scented steam rose from the granite floor of the large shower stall.

"Mm. That feels good." I bent my head, and he smoothed the mitt down the nape of my neck. "It's not bubble bath. It's shampoo slash shower gel. There's a difference."

"You'd know. I've never seen so many grooming aids in one bathroom." The rough cotton felt good on my wet skin, and Dan applied just the right amount of pressure. I relaxed — only recognizing at that moment how wound up I'd been.

"Tools of the trade," I informed him. "I'm a commodity. I'm in business, and I am my product."

"That attitude and a pair of tight jeans will get you arrested on Hollywood Boulevard."

"They tell me attitude is everything."

He pulled me back against his wet, hard body. I arched my neck for his kiss and his mouth closed on mine, warm and male, and with a hint of the tart-sweetness of crabapple. Our tongues slid together, twined. My heart started that heavy slow beat that matched the throb in my groin.

"You are so beautiful..."

"I bet you say that to all th —" His hands slid over my slick body, flicking my nipples. I moaned into his mouth, words failing me. If felt so good. Everything he did felt good. He never made a wrong move; that was the advantage of having so much experience. Of course, that kind of expertise was a little intimidating sometimes.

Putting my hands over his, I held them against my chest. He palmed the nipples, back and forth, just the right amount of teasing abrasion.

I turned to face him — wrapped my arms around him.

Smoothing the mitt over my ass, Dan gave one cheek a playful squeeze before sweeping the mitt up my spine. My dick came up like a divining rod, nudging his already hard thickness. Heart pounding, I pressed against him, wanting more, wanting closer. I was surprised the shower drops didn't sizzle on my skin; I was so hot for him. Dan shook off the mitt and his hands closed on my ass, urging me closer. I groaned, feeling for his cock.

"Yeah, Sean, just like that," he muttered.

His fingers slid down the crevice between my butt cheeks, intimate and familiar, finding the mouth of the secret passage. He delicately circled my opening, then slipped the tip of one finger inside: a sweet and slow piercing. I caught my breath.

Just a fingertip, like the press of a button — a button I badly wanted him to push. That weird clawing ache started in my belly. I made a sound in the back of my throat; even I wasn't sure what I meant.

Dan's kiss gentled. He kissed the underside of my jaw, his finger simply holding its place, like a book he meant to read later.

Let go, I instructed myself, impatiently. *What the hell is the hold up? You want him. He wants you. Act, if you have to.*

Act like…a porn star.

I found his mouth, kissed him back hard, surging up against him. I could feel his surprise. His mouth covered mine hungrily. He pushed his finger into me deeply; I started, my foot slipping out from under me in the sudsy warm water.

He steadied me, both hands on my arms, smiling. "Easy, chief."

"Yeah." I laughed, but after a week of this I wasn't fooling anybody, including myself. "I'm just not sure about that yet," I said, feeling like a fool. I still felt the memory of his finger in my body — an erotic fingerprint.

"I know." He sounded easy and a little amused.

"I mean, I want to," I said. "I'm just…" Why did I have to say anything? The last thing I wanted was for this to turn into an *issue*. Why couldn't I just have let it happen, naturally, spontaneously?

"We don't have to rush it."

Was six days rushing it? Probably not. His dick poked into my belly like an elbow in the ribs reminding me that he had places to go and things to do, and so far this morning he wasn't getting anything but talk.

Porn star, remember? Act. It's what you're good at.

"Let me tell you a little secret," I said and slid to my knees to take the head of his cock into my mouth.

"Oh, my God," Dan said, closing his eyes. His fingers brushed my cheek. "What you do to me."

Yeah, this I knew how to do, sucking him with soft wet heat and then hard. I murmured encouragingly — not really an act, come to think of it — and tugged with my lips. Sweet and soft. Tight and hard.

Dan's breathing went slow and deep, fingers fluttered over my ears, the base of my skull, urging me closer, but not forcing — never forcing.

The water sluiced over his shoulders and rained down on me. I tasted shower gel and clean skin and the salty tang of pre-cum. His swollen cock throbbed between my lips; he pushed deeper into my mouth. I relaxed my throat muscles and took more of him. A muscle in Dan's cheek jumped. He looked down at me, and his eyes seemed dazed.

I made soft sounds, inciting him to riot.

Groaning, Dan braced his hands on the granite tiles. His legs trembled.

I backed off a little, laved the cleft in the head of his cock with my tongue, took him back in and sucked hard.

"I'm going to come," he warned throatily.

His cock jumped and he began to come. Hard.

Not a problem for me. I liked this part. I swallowed enough to show I cared, then buried my head in his belly, nuzzling his genitals. He twitched and shivered. Petted my wet head, stroking the hair back from my face.

I smiled, watching him. After a few moments he shook his head like a wet dog and gave a shaky laugh.

"You are one crazy guy."

"Hey."

"Hey, you." He reached up and turned off the tap, drawing me to my feet. Energized. And how the hell *that* worked, I had yet to figure out.

There were dents in my knees from the granite floor, and my legs felt wobbly with my own need. He pulled me against his long strong body, one hand cupping my balls. I rested my head on his shoulder, breathing in the scent of his clean wet skin. The hair on his chest tickled my nose. Just the feel of those steely fingers handling me...

I guided his hand to where I needed it to be. He wrapped his fingers around my cock

"I like that little sound you make," he whispered.

The bedroom phone rang.

"What the hell!" I opened my eyes.

"The machine will get it."

I nodded absently, listening. Dan's heart was settling back into its normal rhythm. The phone rang again. Dan's hand slowed. I rested my hand on his, urging him on. He tightened up a bit, and I caught my breath. Big brown capable hands. Good for all kinds of things: gripping a gun or shaking cocktails or…driving me to total distraction.

The phone rang a third time, and then the answering machine picked up.

"Dude!" the tinny voice of Steve Kreiger, my manager, drifted from the other room. For an eerie minute it was like he stood in the doorway watching us; I could picture him scraping the lank red hair out of those mournful basset-hound brown eyes. "You there? T.J. Hooker got you handcuffed to the bed or what?"

"Damn! I've got to take it." I popped open the shower door and abandoned that sweet steamy warmth, sprinting for the bed and the night stand beyond. I heard the shower door close behind me.

I bounced on the white duvet and stretched, grabbing the phone off the receiver. Reached across to pick up the phone. "Hey."

"Hey. So you *are* still alive."

"Yep. Alive and…uh…kicking." I sucked in my breath as two hard hands wrapped in a plush bath sheet closed around my waist. Dan toweled me down with hard efficiency, blotting shoulders and ribs and butt through the folds of the oversized towel. He rubbed my head briskly. I put the phone against my ear, listening through the fluffy cotton.

"I got a copy of *The Charioteer* script. I was planning to drop it by this afternoon," Steve said.

"Roll over," Dan ordered quietly.

I rolled over, the Naturlatex mattress molding to the contours of my body. The duvet felt damp beneath my back. I stared into Dan's blue eyes.

He smoothed the towel over my chest, sliding down to my groin. My dwindling erection made a pup tent of white towel.

I closed my eyes and expelled a shaky breath as Dan's fingers wrapped around my dick once more. "Er...great." And it *was* great. I'd been hounding Steve to get me a look at the script for weeks. You wouldn't think that the screen adaptation of a minor gay classic would require security clearances worthy of the Pentagon — especially given the typical indie film production budget.

Dan's hand slid up the length of my cock. Slowly slid down. I gritted my teeth to keep from moaning.

From a long, long way away Steve said, "Yeah. But there's a problem. Lenny Norman is directing and he doesn't want you."

I sat up, dislodging Dan's hand. "You're kidding!"

"Nope."

"I've never even worked with him. Why doesn't he want me?"

"For one thing he thinks you're too good looking for the part of Laurie."

I glanced across at the reflection of myself in the mirror hanging over the bureau dresser: tall, lanky, brown eyes, brown hair. "I'm not that good looking," I protested.

"I agree. I don't think you're so good looking. In fact, I think you're butt ugly. This is his opinion."

I gnawed my lip, ignoring these witticisms. "That's it? He doesn't want me because of my looks?"

Steve said, a little more serious now, "That, and he thinks you're not gay enough."

"What? What the hell does *that* mean?"

"Hey, I'm just telling you what was said."

"But what does that even mean? I'm gay. I'm out. What more does he want?" Dan's hand closed around the nape of my neck, his fingers knowledgeably prodding the muscles knotting up. I felt a spark of annoyance; I could practically hear him telling me to take a deep breath, relax. I didn't feel like relaxing. This was business. This was my career.

"It's not like we had an in-depth discussion. I think it's a political thing with him. He feels like you're walking a line with straight audiences, that you're not openly gay. 'You play it too straight,' that's what he said."

"Well, so does Laurie! So does Ralph. I mean, it's historical drama. It's World War Two. Nobody was out. What's this idiot planning to do, portray them as a couple of flaming queens?"

"Chill, dude. Don't kill the messenger. I'm just letting you know what you're up against. He went ahead and FedExed me a copy of the script, so you're not totally out of the running."

I was silent. Dan scraped the back of my neck with his fingernails and I shivered. Never mind the P-Spot. Apparently I had an N-Spot.

I made myself focus.

"Do they have someone else in mind?"

"For Laurie, no. For Ralph I think they're looking at Peter Grady."

I swore. The last film I'd done with Peter Grady had earned us the title of "The Gay Tracy and Hepburn" in the queer press. I loved working with the guy; we had major league screen chemistry — one more reason I so wanted to do this project.

Steve soothed, "You haven't read it yet. Maybe you won't like the adaptation. Maybe you won't want to do the film. Let's not worry about it anymore 'til you've seen the script. Okay?"

"Okay."

"I'll see you around two."

"See you." I hung up and flung myself back against the mountain of pillows.

"So who's the bastard with the bad taste not to want you?" Dan inquired. He was sitting on the edge of the bed, putting his watch on, so apparently we had lost our window of opportunity.

"Oh." I grimaced. "Lenny Norman. He's directing that film I told you about. The adaptation of *The Charioteer*. He doesn't want me. He thinks I'm too good looking."

"The guy must be blind."

It barely registered. "It's that goddamned *People* magazine article. "*People*'s 50 Most Beautiful People." I was number 49 or something." I brooded over this for a moment. "And he thinks I'm not gay enough."

Dan's brows rose. "You seemed gay enough to me five minutes ago."

I grinned reluctantly. "Maybe you could vouch for me."

He got off the bed, the squeak of floorboards giving voice to my inner protest. "I'd have preferred to do something else for you, but now I'm running late."

I shot him a quick look. He sounded regretful, not annoyed; his smile was rueful. "Sorry," I said. "I kind of had to take that call."

"Yeah, I know."

I had the uncomfortable feeling that he did. Well, hell. I was out of practice at having relationships. Actually, who was I kidding? I'd never had a real relationship. Not like this. Not living together twenty-four/seven with a for-richer, for-poorer, in-sickness, and in-health option. The closest I'd come was when Steve and I roomed together for about a year after college. That was when Steve had still been trying to make it as a comic. Before he'd decided that managing my career would be easier and more lucrative than having his own.

I watched Dan move around the room dressing. Casual wear: khakis and a black T-shirt. Not the beautifully tailored suits and expensive ties he wore on duty. You couldn't afford suits like that on a cop's salary, but Dan supplemented his salary by working as a consultant for the film industry — which was the other reason he had snagged the bodyguard gig with me.

I tried to think what I would do all day. Now that I didn't have to worry about being taken out by a potentially homicidal fan I'd have to find a new hobby.

Maybe I'd go for another swim after I worked out in the weight room. No problem going by myself now. Just like a big boy. Maybe I'd see if I had a copy of Renault's *The Charioteer* here at the beach house and reread it. Or no, maybe that would interfere with my reading the script. Maybe I'd just put on some music and catch some rays. Sunshine was supposed to be good for depression — not that I was depressed. Exactly.

"What time will you be back?"

"About five." Dan slid the leather badge-wallet into his pocket, double-checked the fit of his khakis in the bureau mirror. "You want me to bring something home for dinner?"

Home. That was kind of nice. I gave his question the careful deliberation it deserved. "I'll cook. Could you pick up some scallops?"

"I'll do that, chief." He bent down over the bed and gave me a quick, hard kiss. "Have a good day. And don't worry about anything."

I answered with one of Steve's favorite lines. "What, me worry?"

"You're right," said Dan. "That's my job."

Chapter Two

As usual Steve was late.

He showed up at a quarter to three, trudging around the back of the house to the deck where I sat sunning myself and flipping through the latest issue of *Food and Wine*. Duke Ellington's "New Mood Indigo" floated through the open sliding door, floating up to where the gulls wheeled overhead.

"Dude, you changed the lock on your front door," he announced, tossing a powder blue-bound screenplay onto the patio table. "You never even used to close the windows. Was that Dan the Man's idea?"

"Sort of." The truth was I'd changed the locks after the first time Paul Hammond showed up uninvited in my living room. Steve had to be thinking of the old days — back when I'd believed I was the only crazy person to worry about.

He went into the house and reappeared a few moments later with a Corona. Pulling out one of the wooden chairs, he sat down.

"Where is he?"

I didn't need to ask who. "He went into town to pick a few things up."

He nodded noncommittally, took a long swig from his beer. "So how are you doing?"

"Good."

"Yeah?"

I grinned. Steve's answering grin was lopsided. He was my age, medium height, compact build, and an attractive freckled face. We'd been friends since college, practically as long as we'd been business partners.

He reached for the ring I wore on a silver chain around my neck. I put up a protective hand.

"Isn't this moving kind of fast?"

I shrugged. "Feels right to me." I could have explained the ring. It wasn't what Steve thought. Dan and I had been in an antique shop. I'd seen the ring and said it was pretty, which it was: old-fashioned setting and "chocolate" diamonds. Dan had bought it for a couple of dollars. Mostly as a joke. It didn't fit me or anything.

"So he's moved in?"

"Not officially," I admitted. "But we haven't spent a night under separate roofs since he took the bodyguard gig."

Steve's smile was wry. "Well, you're the happiest I've seen you in a long time."

"I am."

"Just...fuck, I don't know."

I studied him curiously. "You don't like Dan, do you?"

He reached over and shifted the screenplay next to his elbow a fraction to the left. "I don't know. He's okay. I mean, he's a great looking guy and he seems to really care about you. He makes you laugh, which is good." He grimaced. "Maybe I'm jealous."

"Nah. Come on. What is it?"

Steve's brown eyes met mine. "He seems a little controlling. Possessive."

I considered this. "He does?"

Steve raised a shoulder. "Yeah. Maybe it's a cop thing."

"Yeah," I said slowly.

Steve drank more beer. "Hey, listen. I know you're hot on doing this role, and I respect that. It's a good script and a great role, I have no doubt. Just remember, it's the kind of part that's liable to get you typecast, which until now you've avoided. And that's a good thing, regardless of what that asshole Lenny Norman thinks or says."

"Duly noted," I said.

"Peter Grady has already expressed interest in working with you again."

"He has?"

"His people called your people."

"You mean his agent called you?"

"Yep. And Winston Marshall, who is producing the film, is definitely interested in you — which I think is how we managed to score a copy of the script. I think he put pressure on Norman."

It was all I could do not to grab for the screenplay then and there.

"Just keep in mind that working with a director who didn't want you wouldn't be a good thing. Especially for you."

"Come on, Steve," I said.

"Hey. I'm just saying. There are other considerations."

"Like the fact that I wouldn't get my usual fee? Such as it is."

"Bingo."

"Money isn't everything."

"It is when you need it."

We talked a while longer and I invited Steve to dinner. He declined on the grounds that he had previous plans, and took off not long after. I wondered if he really had plans or if this was about Dan. It would be awkward as hell if Steve really disliked Dan.

I wondered what Dan thought about Steve. Or if he thought about him at all.

Rising, I got myself another beer from the fridge, changed the record to Frank Sinatra's *Only the Lonely* and settled back in the lounge chair with the screenplay for *The Charioteer*.

FADE IN

EXT. DUNKIRK — DAY

The sea air worked its way into the script as I pictured the chaos of Dunkirk: the sprawl of the dead and dying beneath the black pall of smoke in the windless sky; the makeshift armada of ships and boats and skiffs and rafts and anything that could float; the exhausted and shamed British troops. Ice cold water, the whistle of shells overhead, the smell of guns and brine and blood and death — Laurie Odell with his kneecap blown off, out of his skull with morphia and pain and seasickness.

Sort of put my own problems into perspective. How the hell did anyone hold it together under those conditions? And how the hell were they going to convey the magnitude of the disaster of Dunkirk on a shoestring budget?

I had just reached the part where Ralph Lanyon realizes that the blood-drenched soldier he is asked to pronounce dead is Laurie Odell, a man who holds a special place in his boyhood memories, when I got that prickly feeling you get when you know you're being watched.

Looking up, I expected to see Mrs. Wiggly on patrol. Nothing. The white beach was blindingly empty in the afternoon sun. A few boats dotted the distant blue glitter of the water.

I caught movement out of the corner of my eye. I turned my head, staring up at the hillside behind the house. A man stood on the flat-topped rock that overlooked this private stretch of beach.

He was too far away to make out his face, but I recognized the shaggy blond hair, the baggy Hawaiian shirt, the black sunglasses.

Paul Hammond.

My mouth went dry. My heart started slugging hard against my ribcage.

It can't be, I thought. Don't flip out over a coincidence. This is a beach town. Half the guys around here have shaggy hair. Half the guys out here wear sunglasses and Hawaiian shirts.

I blinked. The guy on the rock was still looking my way. Or maybe he was just facing my way. *Don't start imagining things*, I told myself.

Shading my eyes with my hand, I tried to get a better look, and as I stared — trying not to be too obvious about it — he waved to me.

I short-circuited, incapable for several long seconds of thinking what my next move should be. Finally, shakily, I stood and walked into the house. From inside the doorway I stared back at the hillside.

The man was gone.

He couldn't be gone, gone. He must have moved on down the hillside where I couldn't see him from where I stood.

"Maria?"

Maria Martinez, my housekeeper, withdrew from the oven, holding up her inky-stained orange plastic gloves. "*Sí?*" She gazed at me with her beautiful, solemn olive eyes.

"When you cleaned up the breakfast dishes, what did you do with the postcard that was on the table?"

"I didn't see no postcard, Mr. Fairchild."

"There was a picture postcard on the table. Right next to the jam pot." I could hear the agitation rising in my voice despite the silliness of the words.

Maria was staring at me, slowly shaking her head. "No."

"Yes." I made a little square with my hands as though that might refresh her memory. "There was a postcard."

Somehow her expression managed to look both polite and like she thought I was losing it. Then she brightened. "Oh, *sí*. Mr. Moran. He take something off the table. You ask heem, Mr. Fairchild." She smiled to show me there were no hard feelings and returned to scrubbing the inside of the stove.

I walked over to the sliding door and stared out through the screen. Chaparral stirred in the wind. The hillside was bare of anyone.

Dan was late getting home — and that was not usual.

I told myself to get used to it. I'd done enough cop shows to know that detectives keep irregular hours — even when they're not working.

It was nearly five-thirty when the screen door suddenly slid open. I nearly jumped out of my skin, but Dan didn't seem to notice, walking out on the deck and kissing me hello.

"Sorry, I'm late. Traffic was a bitch down PCH." He handed me a bottle of wine and a flat brown-wrapped parcel.

"It's okay." I glanced at the wine — a very nice chardonnay — and took the parcel. "Are we celebrating?"

"Aren't we?" Just for a moment his smile was unsure.

"I guess we are." I picked at the string of the package. "What's this?"

"Something for you."

"Yeah?" I couldn't remember the last time somebody bought me a gift Just Because. When you're the guy with the money, people just assume you're picking up the tab.

I tore open the wrapping and studied the indigo-blue cover: Ella Fitzgerald's profile faced the New York nightscape. The original 1957 Verve recording of *Ella Fitzgerald Sings the Gershwin Song Book*.

"My God, where did you find this?"

"That little place in Santa Monica where you buy the phonograph needles."

"I...thank you." I turned the cover over and studied the play list. "'The Man I Love,'" I read aloud. "'Nice Work if You Can Get It.'" I smiled at him.

"Ain't that the truth." He leaned forward and kissed me again. Fresh male with a hint of mint. If this kept up I would soon be addicted to the flavor of him "Want me to put it on?"

I nodded, handing it over and following him inside to unwrap the scallops sitting on the counter. Looking through to the living room I could see Dan's suitcases sitting by the staircase.

I was smiling as Ella launched into "But Not for Me." *Wrong this time, Ella.*

I washed the scallops while the chopped onion and garlic sautéed. Dan poured himself a martini and refilled my glass.

"So what did you do today?"

I shrugged. "Relaxed mostly."

"Good. That's what you need."

I bit back my first response. He didn't mean anything; he was thinking of the last couple of weeks, that was all. And I couldn't really blame him. By the time Steve had persuaded me to go to the police, panic attacks were becoming part of my daily routine — right there with all the grooming aids.

I replied, "Then I got what I needed. I worked out. Read. Steve brought the script by."

I measured out white wine and chicken stock, poured them in to the frying pan, turned the heat down to a "smiling boil." I love that phrase: smiling boil. The aroma of the cooking garlic, onion, and wine worked their magic. Cooking as therapy.

"How's old Steve?" Dan settled on the bar stool across the counter, sipped his martini. Not that many guys can carry off a martini glass, but he had that kind of '50s cool that enabled him to drink martinis and still look tough.

Adding the Pernod to the pan, I reduced the heat. "Okay. Like usual."

I hesitated. I wanted to tell him about the guy that looked like Paul Hammond, but I knew what he would think. And I knew that Paul Hammond was dead.

I did know that, it was just…

"So what did you think of the script?"

"I've only started reading it. I like the choices they've made so far."

He picked up the plate of scallops. "You want me to start these?"

I nodded. He went outside and I added more Pernod to the sauce and took the rice off the burner. The asparagus had been perfect ten minutes earlier, but there was no way of fixing that.

When I stepped outside Dan was seated on the railing, staring out at the sunset. The water looked dark and purple, the sun orange, like a Malibu postcard. I didn't want to think about postcards.

He glanced my way and asked, "So you think you'll want to do it?"

I knew what he meant. "I think so, yeah. Assuming Lenny Norman can stomach the idea of me playing the lead in one of his films."

He held his glass out and we clicked rims.

"You get restless not working," he observed. "Cooking is not much of a diversion. And God help you if your metabolism ever slows down."

"I'll become the forty-ninth most beautiful character actor in Hollywood." My metabolism would never slow down. No one in my family was fat.

Or gay.

"Those are ready," I said, nodding to the scallops sizzling away on the grill.

According to Dan, any cooking that didn't involve charcoal or a spatula was out of his class. He claimed he had two dishes he served for dates: his secret recipe spareribs and his eggs Benedict special. I had the impression these usually followed one another closely in his social calendar. He hadn't fixed either of them for me yet; I wasn't sure if that was a promising sign or not.

He rescued the scallops, handing the plate over to me. "Are we eating inside or out?"

Evenings were chilly here on the coast, but I liked being outside, liked the sound of the waves a few yards away, liked looking up at the stars. It felt like we were a million miles from town — just about far enough.

"Out."

Dan brought down sweaters and we ate by the flickering candlelight, listening to Ella through the open glass door.

I talked to him about the script. In one of my rare pauses for breath it occurred to me that he didn't have much to say tonight — but then Dan chose his words carefully. I wondered if he liked it this way or if I needed to give him more chances to get a word in edgewise.

In a way it had been easier a week ago when we were just dealing with being attracted to each other — now that we were embarking on a relationship — and we *were* embarking, the luggage in my front room made it official — it was suddenly much harder. I found myself worrying about stuff I'd never previously considered — like was he liable to suddenly notice that I was boring and self-absorbed?

I mean, I played make-believe for a living — and earned (when I did manage to get paid) a ridiculous amount of money for it. Dan was a real-life hero. He had saved lives. His job made a difference — *he* made a difference.

"You're quiet all at once," he observed.

"Makes a nice change, doesn't it?"

He shook his head a little as though that wasn't worth answering. "So what's the deal with this movie? Why do you want to do it so much?"

I shrugged. "It's hard to explain. The book was a big influence on me. You've never read it?"

"No."

"It's beautiful. It's by Mary Renault, the one who did all those historical novels about ancient Greece. This one is contemporary — well, it was when she wrote it. Kind of a wartime romance. I probably can't explain it without making it sound trite."

"What's it about?"

"It's about a wounded English soldier who falls in love with a conscientious objector during World War II."

"Sounds like fun."

"Telling you the plot doesn't really explain it properly."

"I'm guessing they're both gay?"

"That's kind of the point of the novel. Coming to terms with their sexuality. Laurie knows he's —"

"Laurie?"

I had the sinking feeling that if he kept interrupting, or worse, if he mocked the book, it was going to change the way I saw him, the hopes I had for what was happening between us.

I took a deep breath. Tried again. "Short for Lawrence. Mostly he's called Spud. Anyway, he knows he's gay, but the kid, Andrew, who is a Quaker as well as a CO, doesn't. Doesn't know that *he's* gay. Actually, he doesn't know that Laurie's gay either."

I hesitated, expecting another interruption. Dan said nothing.

"And then there's also Ralph who was Laurie's house master or whatever they called it when he was at school. Public school — which in Britain is private school. Laurie was sort of in love with Ralph, without realizing it. Because back then, he was like Andrew. Laurie, I mean, not Ralph. So his feelings for Andrew mirror his own relationship with Ralph, but they aren't realistic. They aren't real life love, see? And the book is really about *that*, about balancing the needs of the soul between the earthy and the ideal — and about living your life with honor and dignity. It's based on one of Plato's dialogs, *Phaedo*, and Renault refers back to the metaphor of a charioteer trying to control two horses, a white one and a black one."

I was babbling. But Dan nodded as though I was making great sense.

"So, anyway, Ralph comes back into his life and Laurie has to choose between Ralph and Andrew."

"Who does he choose?"

"He chooses the dark horse. He chooses life with all its complexities and contradictions and disappointments and...delights." I half-swallowed on the last word, surprising myself by my own intensity. I tried to explain, "I read it when I was...ill."

I met Dan's eyes. In the wavering candlelight his gaze was attentive, understanding. I had to look away. Maybe it would have been easier if he had just laughed.

Hurriedly, I said, "I don't know how good a film it will make because it's a lot of talk and a lot of Laurie thinking. And it's a period piece. And it's a gay romance."

"But you want to do it anyway."

I nodded. "It...helped. The book, I mean. It helped a lot. It convinced me that there were people out there like me. Men like me. And that they were decent and honorable and courageous, not the warped diseased things that my parents believed in."

God, how much had I drunk? I couldn't believe I'd told him that. I wished he would say something. I felt naked; I had said too much. I shrugged. "I can't put it into words. It struck a chord with me. It struck a chord with a lot of people. It's considered a classic."

"I'll have to read it one of these days." He covered my hand with his.

"Or maybe you can just see the movie." Belatedly I was the one trying for lightness.

"I'll be in the front row." He lifted my hand and kissed the inside of my wrist, his lips sending little frissons over the sensitive scar tissue.

§ § § §

Later, when we were undressing for bed, I said impulsively, "I thought I saw Paul Hammond today."

Dan, mid-shooting his boxers into the dirty clothes hamper, halted and turned my way. "Where?"

"On the hill behind the house."

I knew immediately it had been a mistake to tell him. He continued to study me for a long moment, not saying anything, just assessing the situation like a good detective.

I said quickly, "I know it couldn't have been him. It just…spooked me. It looked like him from a distance."

"What was he doing?" I knew that neutral tone.

"Nothing. I mean, I guess he was looking out at the ocean. He waved to me." Dan's face changed. Before he could say anything I qualified, "I mean, I was staring his way and he waved to me, so obviously he couldn't have been Paul Hammond. Especially since he's dead."

Okay. Shut up now.

Dan said, "It's natural after a year of that bullshit that you're still keeping an eye out for him. And it's natural that somebody with Hammond's build or coloring would remind you of him."

I nodded. Was he trying to reassure me or himself?

Chapter Three

There was another postcard in the mail the next day.

Vintage colored pencil drawing of the old "movie star colony" on Roosevelt Highway. I stared at the little white houses with their red and green roofs as though I could see my poison penpal sitting inside plotting his next move.

The message on the back was in Hammond's writing.

Soon ...

I rang Dan at work.

He listened in silence as I finished, "If it's not Hammond, then who's sending these? The postmark is Malibu."

He said quietly, "It's probably some nutcase who read about you and Hammond in the papers."

"How would he get the beach house address?"

"It might be someone local. Malibu has its share of whack jobs like anywhere else."

"Great. So now what? I have another psycho after me? Have they found Hammond's body?"

"It's not Hammond."

I clamped my jaw on a lot of things that I knew I would regret saying later.

"Fine. It's not Hammond. So who is it? And, by the way, what did you do with the postcard from yesterday?"

I heard him draw in a breath. He said very patiently, "Okay. Look, do you want me to come home?"

I did, but hearing him say it brought me back to Earth fast. Maybe it was the word "home."

"No."

"Are you sure? I know this is the last thing you needed right now."

Maybe he meant because I was in the middle of reading a script for a movie no one wanted me to do. Or maybe he meant because I wasn't bouncing back as quickly as he'd hoped from my last psycho-stalker bout.

"I'm okay. I just don't understand why this is happening again." What the hell were the odds of attracting two stalkers within a year? Was it my aftershave?

"I promise you, if I thought this was a genuine threat —"

"What *did* you do with yesterday's postcard?"

Did he hesitate? I couldn't tell. He said, "I'm having it analyzed."

So was that reassuring or not? He obviously thought the threat was real enough to investigate — or maybe he was just being careful. He was a very careful guy.

"Well, how long will it take before you know anything?"

"It's not like TV or the movies. It takes time."

"I know that. How long do you think?"

"A couple of weeks maybe."

"Weeks?"

He said matter-of-factly, "It's not high priority, Sean. I'm doing it for confirmation, that's all."

Into my silence, he asked again, "Are you okay or do you need me to leave work early?"

There was only one appropriate answer. I said, "I'm fine. I'll see you this evening."

Swimming makes me ravenous. I was raiding the fridge after a late morning dip when the phone rang. I poured OJ into the glass Maria handed me, and passed her the plate with zucchini-walnut muffins to heat in the microwave.

"Dude, you're not going to believe this," Steve began as I picked up. "I think someone shot at me yesterday afternoon!"

"You're kidding me."

"No shit. There's what looks like a little bullet hole in the Sebring's windshield."

"When did it happen?"

"I don't know. Sometime after I left your place yesterday afternoon."

"Have you called the cops?"

"Dude. What would I tell them? I don't know when it happened, let alone where or who might have done it. It's probably kids screwing around. It looks like a BB hole to me, to tell you the truth."

"You should probably report it, though."

"Uh, yeah. Sure."

On impulse, I said, "Are you doing anything this afternoon?"

"Yeah. I'm taking a meeting at Warner Bros and then I'm driving down to Santa Anita Park."

"On a weekday?"

"You're kidding, right? The Oak Tree meet runs all this month."

"Could you postpone the race track and meet me for lunch?"

I thought for a moment Steve's cell phone had cut out, then he said with unusual seriousness, "What's up? Something with Dan?"

"Dan? No. No, it's complicated."

"Okay. Yeah. I can meet you. At the house?"

"No, I want to get out of here for a little while. Maybe Pt. Dume? We could eat at Coral Beach Cantina. I like the crab enchiladas."

"Yeah," said Steve. "'Cause nothing goes with crisis like crab enchiladas. Okay, but I can't be there before two thirty."

"That's fine. It's past Heathercliffe on PCH. Down the big hill."

"I remember," Steve said. "I'll call you if I'm running late."

I said, "You're already running late. I'll wait."

§ § § §

Sitting on the tree-shaded patio of the Coral Beach Cantina, I ordered a micro brew and nachos. The juke box was playing "Boys of Summer" by Don Henley, and I was counting the disproportionate number of blonds, both male and female, filling the seats around me, when Steve dropped into the chair across the table.

"Dude, you're so mysterious. It must come from living with a cop."

I summoned a weak smile.

"So what's up?" He reached for a tortilla chip. Gooey strings of cheese stretched a foot from the platter.

"You want to order first?"

Steve grimaced and waved the waitress over. We ordered and then Steve sat back in his chair. "Okay, come on, Sean. You're starting to make me nervous. Are you looking to change representation?"

"Of course not."

"So what's the deal?"

I said, "I think Paul Hammond is still alive."

Steve swallowed his beer the wrong way. He set the mug down shakily, coughing into his bare arm. When he had his voice back, he questioned, "Why the hell would you think that?"

"Because they still haven't found his body."

"Because his car crashed into the aqueduct."

"So what? There should still be a body."

"It washed down the aqueduct."

"It's not like there's a riptide in the aqueduct. They had divers looking and they couldn't find the body."

"Yeah, but Sean, there's no way he could have survived that crash. I saw the photos in the newspaper. No way he walked away from that."

"What if he wasn't in the car when it went into the aqueduct?"

"It was a high speed pursuit. It's not like he had time to stop, get out and push the car in and then hide behind some bushes. He was under police surveillance for another thing."

"It was night. Someone might have missed something."

"Sean —"

"I got a postcard from him yesterday. And another one today."

Steve's brows drew together. "What are you talking about?"

"The postcards have started again. Yesterday's card said, 'Miss me?' Today's said, 'Soon.'"

"Was the handwriting —?"

"Dan's having it analyzed to be sure, but I know his writing. It's Hammond."

"So Dan knows about this?"

I nodded. "He was there when I got the first card, but he doesn't believe Hammond is alive."

"Then who's sending the cards?"

"He thinks it's a copycat stalker. Someone who read about Hammond and me and decided to pick up where Hammond left off."

"He's the expert, I guess."

"There's more," I said. I lowered my voice as though afraid somebody — Dan? — might hear this part. "I think I saw Hammond yesterday."

Steve had a weird expression. "You are shitting me. Where?"

"On the hillside behind the house. I couldn't be sure, but from a distance it looked a hell of a lot like him: same build, same shaggy blond hair, same baggy Hawaiian print shirt, black shades."

"But that was from a distance," Steve pointed out.

"I know. But I did see someone. Dan thinks —" I bit the rest of it off.

"Dan thinks what?"

Reluctantly, I said, "I feel like maybe he wonders whether I'm imagining things. Or that I'm making too much of a coincidence."

Steve said slowly, "He knows about your breakdown, right?"

I nodded.

Steve thought it over. "But you didn't imagine the postcards."

"True."

Two tanned twenty-somethings stopped by our table. A chubby blonde handed me a damp cocktail napkin to autograph.

"You were *so* great in *Winchester 2010*," she said. "I was so, like, *totally* pissed when they killed you off."

"Thanks." I ignored Steve's snickers.

"Told you so," he remarked to no one in particular.

"Are you really gay?" the red-haired one said. She offered a Sharpie and her bare shoulder for me to sign.

"Nah," I replied. "It's just something I say to meet girls."

They giggled then moved off whispering and looking back.

Steve drained his beer, and leaned forward on his elbows.

"Look, why don't you come down to Santa Anita with me? Spend the weekend kicking back. I think it would do you good to get away."

I studied him, liking the broad freckled planes of his face and his wide wry mouth. I remembered kissing that mouth. And how weird to think of that now.

I shook my head. "I don't like crowds. And I'm tired of relaxing. I want to get back to work."

His gaze dropped down to my chest, as though making note of the ring on the chain. "Okay. Well...what do you want me to do?"

"I don't know. Obviously we can't go to the cops again, since the cop I live with doesn't believe there's a problem."

"Dude."

The waitress brought our lunches. I waited for her to depart before I offered a lopsided smile. "I don't know that there's anything to do at this point. I needed to talk to someone, that's all."

"Hey," Steve said, "I'm still here for you, you know that. Besides, I remember how long it took to convince you to go to the cops over Hammond. You don't panic that easily. If you say something's going down, I believe you."

"Thanks, Steve."

"One thing I can do," he said, "is talk to LAPD myself. Find out where they are in recovering Hammond's body."

I said, "That would help."

"Not if Hammond's still alive," he said with an odd laugh.

What I like about cooking is that, so long as you follow the recipe exactly, everything always turns out perfect. It's too bad there's no recipe for happiness. Happiness is more like pastry — which is to say that you can take pains to keep cool and not overwork the dough, but if you don't have that certain light touch, your best efforts still fall flat.

The work-around is to buy what you need. I'm talking about pastry, not happiness, although money does make things easier all around.

There are a number of café bakeries in Malibu, but I mostly satisfy my sweet tooth at Cooke's Family Market, which is where I headed after saying goodbye to Steve. I felt better having shared my fears with someone who didn't instantly suspect I was cracking up, and I spent a pleasant half an hour selecting pastries for Saturday morning breakfast, lingering over the varieties of cheese and the amazing selection of olives.

I wasn't allowing myself to think about Paul Hammond. I focused my thoughts on *The Charioteer* screenplay, and while I shopped I thought about what it would be like to lose a knee cap. Now they could probably reconstruct the joint — maybe do something bionic — but back in the '40s? You'd be crippled, no doubt about it. And any injury to a kneecap was going to be excruciatingly painful. Laurie Odell was younger than me; what would it be like to face years of pain? To face the rest of my life as a disabled man? I tried to think of all the things I took for granted: swimming, running — having sex. The film-Laurie was going to wear a leg brace. I felt that was gimmicky and heavy-handed, but it would make it easier to play. No having to remember which leg or faking a limp.

Pushing the cart, I turned into the arctic produce department and froze — literally. Paul Hammond stood a few feet away. He held a cantaloupe, weighing it in his hand.

I couldn't seem to move. He was so close I could have rammed my cart into him. It was him: blue Hawaiian shirt, bushy blond hair that looked like a fright wig, deeply tanned pock-marked skin, black sunglasses...

He had to feel me staring at him, had to have followed me into the market, but he just stood there, ignoring me, fondling melons.

His cheap aftershave filled my nostrils. I felt cold to the bone, shaking on the inside and out. I opened my mouth, but I couldn't think of what to say. If he had spoken to me — even looked at me — but he did nothing. We were alone here. Why didn't he acknowledge me?

I couldn't think of what to do. It was surely something obvious.

Hammond replaced one melon on the pyramid and chose another. He stepped a foot closer as he reached for a plastic tear-off bag.

I abandoned my cart and fled.

"Hi!" I said brightly as Dan walked into the kitchen.

Dan pulled off his sunglasses and studied the countertops crowded with plates of food: baked ham, scalloped potatoes, cheese macaroni, cauliflower-broccoli salad, applesauce, and pineapple cottage cheese. "Are we having a dinner party?" he asked.

I dumped a pan of corn muffins into a basket, wrapping a tea towel around them to keep them warm. "I just thought I would do something special for supper."

Dan's brows rose. He tilted my chin up to kiss me hello; a nice leisurely kiss that told me he had missed me and was glad to be home. I resisted the impulse to plaster myself to him and pour out my latest trauma.

"Catch any bad guys today?"

I thought my tone was just right but he was frowning a little, still watching me. "Not today."

"Slow day for crime? Everything is ready. Why don't you get changed?"

He ran an absent hand up and down my back. "Okay. You want me to open a bottle of wine?"

I nodded.

"Let's see. What goes with everything in the pantry?"

I considered. "Martinis?"

§ § § §

Despite some really fabulous culinary exertions on my part, dinner was not a success. I wasn't hungry and Dan seemed preoccupied, although he listened without interrupting as I chattered on about this and that and the other. Mostly the other.

It wasn't until the third time I reached for the pitcher containing the blueberry vodka martinis, that he stirred.

"That's your fifth, chief."

"Third, but who's counting?"

He didn't bother to argue.

I was irritated, but I tried to keep my tone easy. "Does it matter?"

"It doesn't so long as you're not planning on going for a swim or getting behind the wheel. But you're going to have a hell of a morning."

"Promise?" I batted my eyelashes at him.

His lips twitched. "Now *that* is definitely the liquor talking."

What did that mean? I thought I knew and opened my mouth to object, but Dan had apparently more to get off his chest.

"A couple of things I've noticed," he said. "When you're stressed-out you cook for a cast of thousands. And you stop eating."

"I'm eating," I protested.

"You've had one bite of ham and three bites of salad."

"And five drinks. Jesus, am I under surveillance?"

"Hey." His smile was crooked. "Naturally I notice what you do."

"You notice what everyone does. It's how you make your living. I don't like it when you turn it on me."

As usual he did not allow himself to be distracted from his point. "So far I've heard about the seasoning in the crab enchiladas at Coral Beach Cantina, I've heard that you're not sure you approve of the sex scene in this new script, I've heard that damn dog crapped on our deck, and I've heard that the weather was perfect this afternoon. When do I hear what's really on your mind?"

I laughed. And I knew I had it exactly right: lazy, untroubled. "Dan, relax. I'm just making after dinner conversation."

There was a funny silence. He said, "You're acting."

Which I guess was better than being told I was lying, except he sounded like it really bothered him.

I stared at him. He stared back. It felt unpleasantly close to being emotionally strip searched.

I blurted out, "I think I saw Paul Hammond again."

He didn't move a muscle. At last he said, "Where?"

"At the market in Point Dume. I went grocery shopping after Steve and I had lunch." Surprisingly, this did distract him. "You didn't tell me you were with Steve."

"It was an impulse. Why do you care?"

"I find it odd. This morning you were freaking over postcards from the grave and in the afternoon you're having a lunch date with Steve."

"It wasn't a date and it's not like I tried to hide it." But as I said it, I realized I had been avoiding telling him that I'd been with Steve; I wasn't sure why exactly — or maybe this was why: the instant interrogation.

"Is that the issue?"

"Do we have to make an issue of it? You're not on the job now. According to you there's no danger, right? Hammond is dead."

"I'm not talking about my job," Dan said curtly. "I'm talking about the fact that we're supposed to be a couple."

Something in the way he said it caught me off guard. He was so cool and self-assured that it never occurred to me that he might not be secure about his place in my world.

For the first time it occurred to me that if I had decided to go to Santa Anita with Steve I would have to — should, at least — run it past Dan first.

I opened my mouth but before I could explain, Dan asked, "Did Steve see Hammond?"

"No. This was at the market afterwards."

"Did anyone see him?"

"I don't know. I didn't point him out to anyone. He…" I stopped, knowing how it would sound.

"He what?"

"He was picking out melons. Or at least pretending to."

"I see."

His expression couldn't have been more impassive.

"I know you think I'm imagining this. I know —"

"Did this guy who may or may not be Hammond make any attempt to speak to you?"

I shook my head.

"Did he do anything that could be construed as threatening?"

"He was avoiding looking at me." I couldn't hold Dan's gaze. I knew how it sounded — which is why I hadn't told him.

"That doesn't sound like Hammond, does it?"

I shook my head.

A little more gently, he asked, "Are you sure it was Hammond?"

"It looked like him."

"You're not sure."

"No." I said, "What about the postcard that came this morning?"

"I'll have it analyzed." My relief was short-lived as he added carefully, "Sean, maybe it would help if you talked to someone."

I felt like my stomach dropped to my feet. I stared at him. "You mean a psychiatrist?"

"Yeah."

"Dan," I said desperately, "I'm not cracking up. I did see Hammond. I'm not crazy!"

"I don't think you're crazy." He reached for me, resting his hands on my shoulders, kneading my knotted muscles. "I think you've been under a lot of strain. First the thing with Hammond, now this business with the postcards."

"So you agree there is something to these postcards! Or do you think I'm sending them to myself?"

I saw by his expression that the idea had crossed his mind.

I struck his hands away. "Jesus, Dan! I'm not crazy!"

"I know that. I know you're not sending yourself postcards, okay? But what's wrong with talking to someone? Cops do it. Hell, I've been through it."

I pushed away from the table. "I am talking to someone. I'm talking to *you*. I don't need a shrink. So stop using that careful tone with me. Say what's on your mind."

"Okay," he said evenly. "Then here it is. I want you to talk to me, and I will help you in whatever way I can and in whatever way you need. But I'm not a doctor and we both know you have a history of..." He changed his mind about finishing that. "I think this kind of prolonged emotional strain would not be good for anyone, and it is especially not good for you."

I stared at him. When I could speak I said huskily, "I had a breakdown when I was a kid. Yes, I tried to kill myself. That was nine years ago. It had nothing to do with — you *know* why. You know it was about trying to come to terms with who I was. With realizing I was gay and knowing how my family felt. How my friends saw me. How everyone saw me — thought of me. How they would take it once they found out the truth..."

I couldn't finish it. I got up and went to the railing to stare out at the path of moonlight across the black sea. The hurt and betrayal were almost more than I could deal with. I had told Dan about this in confidence, and he was using it against me now.

"You had a second breakdown when you were twenty," he said quietly.

Hurt gave way to indignation. Obviously he had run some kind of background check on me. Probably when he was first assigned the bodyguard gig, but maybe it was since then. Like this week when I appeared to be losing it.

I wheeled back to face him. "I was depressed. I got help. *Voluntarily.* It was nothing like the other time. And I've been fine ever since. I'm not unstable mentally or emotionally. Yes, I push myself hard, and I'm under strain — that isn't anything new —"

"This isn't a normal amount of strain," he interrupted. "You had some freak stalking you for nearly a year and now you've got some other asshole harassing you. Anyone would need a little help dealing with that — and, listen, the last thing I want to do is hurt you, which I can see I'm doing."

I knew I couldn't speak without my voice cracking, so I said nothing.

"I think it would help you to talk to someone neutral. Someone who could help you put this…experience into perspective. Will you at least consider it?"

He was right about drinking so much. My head was already pounding. And that much alcohol on an empty stomach was not good.

I pushed away from the railing and headed for the glass door.

"I'm going to bed."

"Sean —"

I slid the door shut.

§ § § §

Scratchy beard, warm soft lips on my bare back. One velvety kiss for each link of vertebra in my spine. Kiss by kiss across the little mountains of bone and nerve to the small valley above my ass. I opened my eyes blearily.

"How are you feeling this morning?" Dan murmured.

"Great," I muttered.

"You feel great to me, that's for sure." His mouth moistly nuzzled the sensitive hollow; I sucked in a breath, trying not to wriggle. Closed my eyes. My head throbbed and my gut felt like it was filled with boiling acid, but it wasn't the hangover that made me shiver. How the hell could you be irritated with someone and still crave their touch?

I burrowed my head in my folded arms and asked muffledly, "How was the couch?"

"Lonely."

I considered this silently while he slowly rubbed his bristly cheek against my ass — cheek to cheek. "You know, insanity is not contagious," I said. I thought I was joking, but I sounded sour to my own ears. I didn't think I was still angry or even wounded. I could see how this all looked from Dan's viewpoint. He didn't know me really. I didn't know him.

"I don't know about that," he said, his breath warm on my bare skin. "I'm pretty crazy about you."

I gave a short laugh. Never at a loss for words, was he?

The mattress shifted underneath as he sat up. "I wasn't sure I was welcome in here," he admitted.

I raised my head and eyed him skeptically. He wasn't smiling, in fact, just for a moment he looked younger, unguarded.

I shrugged noncommittally and buried my head in my arms again. "It was lonely here too," I told the sheets.

"Yeah?" I felt him relax. He stroked my flank lazily. I loosened up, rested there, trying to ignore the pounding in my head, just enjoying the feel of his hand on my skin. I wondered if it would be possible to ever get tired of being touched and petted. I wondered how I'd managed to go years without it. Wondered how I would survive if I had to go back to it.

Dan's hand stilled. He shifted around on the mattress, nudging my legs apart. I didn't have time to do more than register this when, to my shock, I felt him spread my cheeks and lick the tender flesh like you'd taste a peach. I bucked, and he gave a low laugh.

"Jeeeeesus," I whispered.

He licked my balls, then behind my balls, working his way back up. I couldn't believe it — this rude kiss. He was such a fastidious and careful guy — and with the papers to prove it. I could not believe this was Dan nuzzling my ass. Maybe I *was* delusional.

It took all my willpower to lie still as his tongue did those shattering things: delicate, wicked, teasing tracery as he worked the sensitive skin around my hole.

Rim job. That's what they called this. Ugly phrase for something that felt so…ravishing. Now there was a good old fashioned word — a Biblical word — and this obviously was not Dan's first time at ravishing someone, and if he kept this up I was most definitely going to come —

Slippery heat slowly pressed in.

I whimpered, squirmed, humped. He caught my hips, holding me fast. He kept pressing, pressing.

"D-Danny…" I wondered if I would simply dissolve; my insides felt like hot liquid. My mind felt gray and blank and shaken like the magic screen on an Etch A Sketch.

Dan's tongue circled and then pushed right in. Deep. I could hear myself mewling, inarticulate and helpless, as his hot slick tongue thrust in and out of my clenched-tight hole. And, right on cue, I began to come.

And all those words flitting around in my brain flew away and left me spiraling into some sweet and silent space where the only thing real was Dan's strong arms holding me close.

Chapter Four

When I woke the next time it was hours later and I had the vague memory of hearing the front door close. I rolled over and checked the clock on the other side of the bed. Nearly one o'clock.

I sat up cautiously. I felt a hell of a lot better than I had that morning, that was for sure. I rubbed my eyes, listened to the sound of the sea a few yards away and the wind whispering at the window casements. Beyond that…silence. A safe silence. The security system would be on. Dan was meticulous about that.

My ring glinted on the nightstand. I didn't remember pulling it off, but I must have when I'd come in last night. That had been childish. I picked up the chain and fastened it around my neck.

The floorboard in the doorway creaked and I glanced around. Dan stood there filling the doorway, and I felt the hair at the nape of my neck prickle. He was so quiet. I was sure he'd gone out.

"Did I wake you? I just stepped out to check the mail," he said.

The mail.

Not easy to speak around the knot in my throat.

What would today's postcard read? *I'm on the first step…*

Before I could form the question, Dan said, "There was nothing for you."

"There…wasn't?"

He shook his head.

The wave of relief was so fierce it caught me off balance; I had to look away so that he didn't see the effort it took to control my face. I leaned forward, pretended to feel under the bed — like, what was I looking for? My dignity?

The mattress sank. I stiffened as he sat down next to me on the edge of the bed. Then he put his arm around me, and I surrendered to the desire to be held, to be comforted, turning to him, resting my face against his throat. I could feel the warmth of his skin against my mouth and eyes, feel the pulse beating at the base of his neck, slow and steady and calm. His words vibrated against my face. "Did you have a good sleep?"

I nodded. Raised my head. Pretended I was wiping sleep out of my eyes. "Yeah. I did."

"Your cheeks are pink." He brushed his knuckles against the bristle on my jaw. "What were you dreaming?"

I thought of what had preceded that deep, deep sleep and felt my face warm. I had dreamed about him but in the dream we had been arguing. I was glad that it had only been a dream, that we were okay again.

"I don't remember. Remind me not to drink that much on an empty stomach."

"You want me to fix you something to eat?"

Spareribs or eggs Benedict? I shuddered.

"I think I'm going to work out."

He smoothed his hand over my back. "Okay, chief. If you're going for a swim or a run, give me a shout. I need the exercise."

§ § § §

I was staring out the window watching the surfers when the phone rang.

"I can guess who that is," Dan commented. He closed the dishwasher and turned the dial. Maria only came in on weekdays and Dan couldn't tolerate clutter for more than a few hours. My eyes lingered on the broad shoulders beneath the plain white undershirt, lean hips and long legs encased in faded blue Levis. All this and housework, too.

"Dude!" called the answering machine over the rumble of the dishwasher.

I gave Dan an apologetic look and picked up the phone.

"Hey."

"So…" Steve asked cautiously. "Any more special deliveries?"

"No."

"No?" He sounded as surprised as I had.

"Nothing since Friday." I glanced Dan's way. His back was to me, but I knew he was listening. It gave me an uncomfortable feeling.

Next to my ear, Steve said, "Wow. Maybe…maybe it was just that Hammond's last few cards got delayed somehow."

That startled me. "What do you mean? Why would you say that?"

"Dude, chill. I mean cards he sent before he died were delayed by the mail. Not that he's still out there picking picture postcards. And try saying that three times fast."

"Oh. Right." I tried to inject a smile in my voice, but I must not have been successful.

"You okay?" Steve asked. "You sound…off."

"Fine."

"No more panic attacks, right?"

I flicked a look Dan's way. He was watching me openly now. "Nope."

I wanted to ask Steve if he'd had a chance to talk to anyone at LAPD about the recovery of Hammond's body, but I couldn't do it with Dan standing there. I knew that would not go over well.

"Well, groovy. Nothing to worry about, because it's all over, right? Hey, listen, I've got some good news."

"About *The Charioteer*?"

"Huh? Oh. No. Have you finished reading the screenplay?"

"Yes. I want to do it."

He sighed. "All right. I'll see what I can do. In the meantime, what do you think about doing a voice-over for the new StarCatz series?"

"What the hell is StarCatz?"

"A very hot kid's show that NBC plans to use as a mid-season replacement. The creator and producer, Dick Dexa, saw you in *Winchester 2010* and he's expressed an interest in you for Captain Starbuckle's teenage son Jason."

"I hope you're kidding." Sometimes it seemed like I'd gotten more damn attention from a bit part as a smart-ass strung-out hired gun in a big-budget action adventure flick, than I'd received in my entire film career.

"I'm not kidding you. NBC anticipates a mega hit with this show."

"With a cartoon show?"

"I know. Unbelievable, huh? Even more unbelievable, they want you."

"But...there's nothing distinctive about my voice."

"What can I say? Dick Dexa thinks you sound like a spunky space cadet."

"Spunky? Funny."

"I thought you'd like that." He grew serious. "Sean, listen for a sec. I know this isn't really your kind of thing, but it's an easy gig and...we need it. The artsy fartsy stuff is fine and it wins awards, but you've got to balance it with something that pays. If it wasn't for your Uncle Sean's trust fund you'd be living on pasta salad and oatmeal these days instead of whatever it is you and The Rock eat for supper."

I said, "I understand. Twenty percent of zero is still zero."

"Since you put it like that, yes. The decisions you make affect my income too — or lack thereof. I don't have any rich dead relatives."

He had a point, but...cartoon voice-overs?

I hated to disappoint him. I could hear how keen he was on this project. And I did have a responsibility to take jobs that would be good for both of us. I said reluctantly, "The thing is, what happens when the word gets around that a gay man is playing a teenage boy on a children's show?"

"Who cares if there's some kind of lunatic right-wing fundie boycott! All publicity is good publicity."

"Tell it to Pee Wee Herman. You think I was anxious before, wait till I've been the victim of a blacklisting campaign."

He laughed. "Hey, come on. You don't want Lenny Norman to hear you talking like that. He'll think you're not Proud and Out."

Now *that* bothered me. "It's Out and Proud, and I don't have to prove anything to Lenny Norman. He should be casting roles based on talent and ability."

"Yeah, well, it's not a perfect world," Steve said with unexpected bitterness. "So are you willing to read for the StarCatz pilot?"

"I'm not comfortable with it, Steve. I'll have to think about it."

Silence. At last he said, "Okay, dude, it's your life."

I replaced the phone and went to join Dan, who had gone out on the deck. He lay on one of the wooden lounges, reading the paper, which he put aside as I hopped onto the railing, staring up at the cloudless blue sky. It was a truly beautiful day. The most beautiful day I'd seen in a long time.

"You're sure old Steve doesn't still have a thing for you?" His smile was quizzical.

"I'm sure. It's just business."

"What is?"

"The fact that he calls all the time. He's my manager. And, unofficially, my agent. We have to stay in touch."

"Out of curiosity, are you his only client?"

"I'm his main client."

He nodded as though this confirmed something.

"Do you not…like him?"

"It doesn't matter what I think about Steve. I respect your relationship."

I realized that was the truth. I didn't have to defend or explain — and the fact that Dan didn't demand it somehow made it easy to talk about it.

"The romantic thing only lasted about a year. We really didn't have a lot in common besides my career. I think I got on his nerves and —"

"He got on yours?"

"Not exactly. His insecurity makes him unkind sometimes. His humor, I mean. He makes these little digs; they're supposed to be funny, but there's an edge. It was…tiring. Distancing."

"That is one hell of an observation, chief."

I grinned at his obvious surprise. "Crazy like a fox," I said, and tapped the side of my head. "But he's been a good friend and a great manager. He's gone to bat for me again and again. Personally and professionally. The fact that the other thing didn't work out...well, that was probably just as well."

"I think so." He held out an arm and I slid off the railing and went to join him on the lounge.

"We survived our first argument."

"You sound surprised. Did you think we wouldn't?" Dan speared one of the shrimps out of the salad I had made for his lunch, chewed, his blue eyes thoughtful on mine.

"It's still a milestone." I selected a cherry tomato from his plate and popped it in my mouth. A little burst of sweet tangy juice on my tongue.

"I guess it is."

"Have you ever done this before? Lived with someone?"

"No."

"Why?"

He lifted a shoulder. "Maybe I have a few trust issues of my own."

I frowned. "You think I have trust issues?"

His smile was quizzical; he didn't actually answer me. I remembered the subject was supposed to be him.

"So what kind of trust issues do you have?"

"Maybe that's not the right term. It's probably a cop thing. People can get a little weird when they find out you're a cop."

"But it's probably a turn on for a lot of guys, right?"

He seemed to be looking inward at some unpleasant memory. "Sometimes. A lot of times, the opposite." He impaled another shrimp, chewed, swallowed. "There's a reason cops have a high divorce rate. The hours are brutal, it's a high stress job, and you can't talk about it most of the time."

I opened my mouth, and he said, "I mean it's the kind of stuff you don't want to bring into your own home, not that someone wouldn't be willing to listen." There was something in his eyes that made me feel young and naïve.

I said slowly, "And I guess it takes a toll being afraid the person won't come home."

He didn't say anything, just looked at me. I felt my breathing go funny like I was about to have one of my famous panic attacks. He said, "I'm careful, Sean. There are no guarantees in life, but I'll do my best to come home to you."

I nodded.

He hadn't really explained the trust thing. Or had he? I guess he was saying that he needed to be trusted as much as he needed to be able to trust. Which was pretty much the same way I defined trust.

I opened my mouth to make another brilliant comment, but Mrs. Wilgi's four-footed feather duster came hurtling across the sands toward us, barking hysterically.

"Jail break," Dan remarked.

"I keep hoping he's going to run away."

"He has. To you."

The dog planted itself at the foot of the stairs to the deck, yapping thinly.

"I was hoping for something further from home. Like Mars."

"I told you not to feed him."

"What happens if you shoot him? You have to fill out a lot of paperwork?"

"Yep."

"It's your lucky day," I informed Binky. He barked all the harder.

It was my lucky day, too. Dan and I had survived our first real argument and somehow come out of it a little stronger than we had been. We walked on the beach and talked, cuddled on the couch and talked some more. Casual talk. Nothing life or death — no mention of loony stalkers, dead or alive — no reflection on where we stood as a couple. Just…talk. Like real couples do.

Late in the afternoon Dan went out to rent a couple of DVDs and bring back my favorite guilty food pleasure — Taco Bell. I think my Friday night culinary binge had unnerved him. Or maybe he was just getting tired of my cooking. We settled on the sofa with bags of tacos and burritos to watch *Cool Hand Luke*, one of Dan's favorite flicks — and one I'd never seen.

We'd just got to the famous, "What we've got here is failure to communicate," line when the phone rang.

I stopped crunching. Dan sighed and hit the pause button.

"It might not be Steve," I pointed out. "I do know other people."

"None of them seem to have this number."

"True." The beach house was my get-away. I liked the fact that when I was there I was basically inaccessible — or had been before Paul Hammond had somehow found out about this place.

The phone rang the third time, the machine picked up, and Steve called, "Dude! Are you there?"

"I'll make it quick," I promised.

"I'm not going anywhere." He smacked my butt as I crawled over him and off the couch.

I picked the phone up in the middle of Steve's imperious, "Sean? Are you there?"

"I'm here."

"Dick Dexa called again. Have you thought about the StarCatz role?"

"How is this going to work if I land *The Charioteer*? When would they need me in the studio?"

An awkward pause.

"Look, Sean, Lenny Norman hasn't returned my calls. I don't think you're going to get *The Charioteer*."

My Taco Supremes began to churn. "Can I try calling him?"

"No, you can't try calling him!"

"I just mean —"

"I know what you mean. Do you trust me to handle your career or not?"

"Of course I trust you — barring the sudden passion for cartoon cats."

I was teasing, but he said shortly, "Do you want the part of Jason or not?"

"Doesn't Dexa want me to read first?"

"Sean, it's a fucking cartoon, not Ibsen. Dexa wants you. Can I tell him you'll take the role?"

My pulse sped up. I hated arguing, especially with Steve.

I said haltingly, "No. I'm not comfortable with it."

"Okay! Shit. Was it that hard to give me a straight answer?"

"No. I just know you think I should take the part."

"Yes, I do. I think you need to start working pretty soon. I was right about *Winchester 2010*, wasn't I? But whatever. If you're not comfortable, that's cool. We'll find something else."

I opened my mouth, but before I could speak, he added, "And, yes, I will try Lenny Norman one more time."

"Thanks, Steve."

I hung up and returned to the couch, climbed back over Dan's legs. He caught my hand and pulled me down half on top of him scattering taco wrappers and shredded cheese and lettuce.

"Everything okay?"

"Fine." I shifted onto my side and stretched out beside him, resting my head against his chest. He smelled like suntan oil and tacos and himself. Heady stuff. He put his arm around me and started the film again. I thought that maybe this was the best part of being a couple — just relaxing together, spending time with someone you could be yourself with. To my surprise I realized that I was starting to be myself with Dan. Little by little I was letting my guard down and worrying less about who he might want me to be versus who I was — I thought something in his easy acceptance of my...vulnerabilities made that possible. Of course, he hadn't had to put up with my ticks — quirks — for very long. He hadn't had more than a taste of life in the fish bowl, and we hadn't had to deal with *my* irregular hours or my being away for weeks on end.

There had to be some reason he wasn't already taken. It couldn't be for lack of offers. Maybe he really did have trust issues.

The movie ended and Dan said he had some paperwork to catch up before bed, heading for the spare room, which he had turned into his makeshift office. Through the wall I could hear the indistinct rumble of his voice on the phone while I did Pilates in the weight room next door. Kind of late for phone calls, I reflected, but cops don't work regular hours.

I finished working out, took a quick shower and retreated to the bedroom to watch some TV and make notes on the *Charioteer* screenplay. I refused to think that I wouldn't get the part. I knew how persuasive Steve could be when he wanted, and if Paul Grady was pushing for me to co-star, I knew I still had a shot.

Dan joined me in the bedroom as I was idly surfing through the channels.

"One thing I never noticed about *The Charioteer*," I told him. "A lot of the misunderstandings between Laurie and Ralph and even Laurie and Andrew could have been so easily resolved if they'd just *talked.*"

"That's true of most relationships, isn't it?"

"I guess so."

Of course, Laurie hadn't asked questions because he hadn't been ready to hear the answers. He had been afraid of the answers.

"Hey, go back," Dan ordered, pulling on a pair of plaid sleep pants, and staring at the TV.

I groaned.

"Turn it back."

I flipped back to the cheesy horror film.

He bounced down beside me on the bed. "That's you!"

"Don't remind me."

We studied the on-screen mayhem in silence.

"Your hair," Dan remarked finally.

"Yes, it's the scariest thing in the film."

We watched for a few more minutes.

"So…you're actually the star of this? Do you get the girl in the end?"

"Please, Dan," I said, "This is heterosexual romance. The girl does not 'get it in the end.'"

His laugh sounded surprised — and I could guess why. I slanted a look his way and he shook his head. "You're asking for trouble, chief."

"How many times do I have to ask before I get some?"

He raised his brows and then lunged. I fell back in the nest of pillows, bringing my knee up — but watching where I put it because the last thing I wanted to do was really put him out of action. I planted my foot in his chest and he rolled over, taking me with him. We wrestled around, laughing. I liked the fact that though I was tall — six feet — Dan was taller. And I liked the fact that — although I was strong and worked out regularly — Dan was stronger. It didn't threaten me and I didn't feel any of the competitiveness I usually would have.

He got one arm around my waist and the other around my thigh and managed to flip me over onto my back. The Swedish mattress swallowed my frame a few obliging inches.

"The bed is having me for dinner," I said, laughing up at him.

"And I'm having you for dessert," Dan said, his voice deep and velvety. He was braced over me, knee between my thighs, one hand keeping both my wrists pinned above my head — not easy to do to another healthy adult male.

I didn't have to glance at his crotch to know he was as excited as I was — though admittedly neither of us was as excited as the guy on TV behind us selling cleaning products at the top of his voice.

I said, in a very bad imitation of James Cagney, "Okay, copper. You got me fair and square."

His lean cheek creased in amusement. "Oh? You're going to come quietly?"

"I always do," I whispered.

His eyes darkened and he shifted his weight back onto his knees. The hand formerly holding me prisoner was now stroking me, feathering down from the outside of my wrists to the insides of my elbows. I generally didn't like anyone to see — let alone touch — the scars on my arms. "No hesitation marks," Dan had said the first time his fingertips had brushed over the ugly tracks of scars. "You weren't kidding around."

Now my arms went relaxed and heavy under that delicate touch. I murmured my pleasure. His free hand slipped inside my boxers.

I sucked in a breath, arching blindly into his caress, reached up and yanked the soft flannel pants down, running my hands down his lean flanks. His skin felt warm and smooth.

"Open your eyes," he ordered huskily.

I lifted my lashes. Every muscular inch of him was brown and supple; his black hair, thick and glossy, fell boyishly into his eyes as he gazed down so seriously at me.

I raised my head and kissed him, a little nip of a kiss. He kissed back, wanting more as usual, wanting it slow and deep and sexy. His lips were so soft. I stilled, opened to him. Our tongues slid together, sweet and spicy. Dan groaned in the back of his throat as though it were too good to bear, sending a little shiver down my spine.

I pulled him down on top of me and we settled into each other, his hand fastening on my hip, tugging me into that fierce bulge against my belly. My own cock throbbed in time to the pound of my heart as his hand found the elastic of my boxers and I raised my hips enough for him to hitch them off. The feel of bare skin lowering on bare skin was satisfying. Our dicks scraped up against each other, old friends and good neighbors, rubbing shoulders.

"What do you want?" he said breathlessly, his breath hot against my ear.

I shook my head. Too hard to form the words when I was having trouble forming the thoughts. "You," I got out.

"How?"

"Suck me?" It came as a little plea. I was a lot more comfortable giving than receiving, but tonight I craved the idea of burying myself in that wet heat. "Please."

He chuckled at the "please." Maybe it *was* funny. He lifted off me, resettled and ran a light possessive hand down my tummy, fastening on my shaft. I murmured encouragement. He bent, kissed the head of my cock and took it into his mouth.

Unbelievable.

It was like stepping into a golden bath — whatever the hell that means. Wet and hot and intense. Was it the warmth or the wetness or the pressure that felt so good? Maybe the mind-blowing combination of all three? This was where all that experience came in handy. He'd obviously been on the receiving end enough to know the little things that made all the difference. Where I offered style, he gave substance and the wonder was I didn't shoot my load in the first five seconds.

"Oh, my *God*," I groaned, and it did indeed feel like a religious experience.

That crazy mix of glib tongue and soft lips and the graze of teeth: sucking, nibbling, licking — but it was mostly the sucking that felt so shatteringly good — hard and then easy and then hard. I couldn't help making abject sounds as he brought me to the edge, then tilted me back, then tipped me forward into the moment.

I spilled over into pleasure, moaning and tossing my head on the pillow like I was in a high fever.

Afterwards I just lay there spent and a little stunned, and he lapped up my cream, the rough rasp of his tongue reminding me of a cat — a big eat-you-alive cat — like a panther. He braced himself over me and when his mouth took mine, I could taste myself. "Fuck me, Danny," I begged him huskily.

"Yeah?" He kissed me again, hungrily. "Sure?"

I nodded, moving against him restlessly, blindly. "I want it. I do."

I could feel him hesitating. I didn't want him hesitating; I didn't want to have time to think. I wanted to ride this wave of sensation all the way out. Eyes closed, nerves still quivering in the pleasure ringing through my body, I urged, "Fuck me. Please fuck me."

There was a dreadful little delay, cold air over my body, the slide of a drawer, a liquidy squirt. I opened my eyes. He was solemnly rubbing gel over his fingers. Lashes flickering on his cheek as he studied his slimy fingers. Oh, right. Preparation F. I closed my eyes hastily.

He moved next to me again, his hand brushing my dick. Just that accidental touch had my breath rushing in and out of my lungs, my heart pumping like mad. I scooted over to give him easy access.

He stroked and feathered, and then his well-lubed finger pushed into my tightly puckered hole. My eyes opened wide, breath catching. *"Oh."*

I tried to make it sound pleased because if there's one thing I've learned both from therapy and from acting, if you pretend strongly enough and consistently enough, eventually the thing you project will become real.

He smiled, but there was a little frown between his brows. "You're trembling."

I gave him a twitchy smile. Not so bad. I could do this. It almost felt good in a too-much- sensation-crawling-through-my-guts kind of way. He slid his finger in and out in a tame parody of fucking and my breath quivered in my chest.

It wasn't hurting. It felt...exciting. Alarming, but exciting.

He finger fucked me gently awhile, and then said, "You want to take it to two?"

I nodded jerkily. I did. He wasn't pushing for anything more than I wanted myself.

He pressed his other finger in slowly. Sweat broke out all over my body. I bit my lip against a yelp. It wasn't that bad really, my body was accommodating him, it was just strange. So intense. So...familiar.

"Relax. Try not to tense."

I laughed unsteadily. Yeah, right. I had what felt like a steel pipe jammed up my ass and I was supposed to relax? Then he did something with his fingers and I stopped laughing. A thrill of pleasure rippled through my body. What was he doing?

"How's that?"

I grunted.

He did that thing with his fingers again. I moaned — even I could tell it was an encouraging moan.

"This is nothing," he said softly. "It gets a lot better than this."

I risked opening my eyes again. He was smiling, enjoying my reaction.

He knelt into the mattress, guiding my legs up to my stomach. I tucked my legs up — not a really comfortable position. I felt awkward and exposed, my butt hanging out. I didn't know what to do with my hands. I couldn't reach him at this angle. I couldn't read his face. My heart started pounding hard with anxiety. My breath caught in my chest. His hands were big, like fetters around my ankles. His dick swung around like a cudgel, sweeping against my ass and thighs. He positioned himself, the head of his prick nudging against my anus like a torpedo lining up to fire. He prodded. A flare of pain went through me. He was too damn big.

The bigger the better, if you were a chick. Not so great for a tight-ass like me.

"Wait!" I got out.

Dan waited, expressionless. A wave of cold sick panic flooded my gut. I brought my legs down and rolled away from him.

"I can't do it," I said. Way melodramatic, crouching on the edge of the bed in this flight- or-fight response, but I was aware that by now he must be ready to throttle me.

He sat back on his haunches. No need to fight. No need for flight. He was frowning but his body was at ease. He wasn't coming after me. His voice was dispassionate.

"We don't have to."

"I'm sorry."

He shook his head. Sorry was not necessary. "Not everyone likes it."

"You do, though."

Instead of answering, he said slowly, "We could try it the other way around."

"God, no!"

He gave a funny laugh. "Or not." He reached out, touched my cheek. "It really is okay, you know."

"It's not that I don't want to..."

He got that speculative look — the very thing I wanted to avoid. "It can be painful the first few times. Especially if your partner isn't experienced."

I shook my head. "There was no first time. No one hurt me. There's no drama here. I just — I can't explain it."

Maybe not totally accurate. I closed my mind to the memory of my father's enraged face. The memory of spit-flecked words screamed in my face. "*Gay?* There's nothing *gay* about queers. There's nothing gay about taking it in the ass, getting butt-fucked by another queer. Men don't take it in the ass. Queers do. Are you telling me that's what you are? My only son is a *queer?*"

Dan said quietly, "Whatever is making you look like that, let it go. This isn't a problem for me, and I don't want it to be a problem for you."

I nodded.

A smile tugged at his mouth. "It's not like we can't find other ways to amuse ourselves."

Sunday started out every bit as beautiful a day as Saturday. Dan and I woke up early, made love, went for a swim — although it was starting to get too chilly for swimming. Summer was truly over and autumn was in the air. I could smell the wood smoke down the beach from Mrs. Wilgi's cottage.

Dan suggested we have brunch at the Chart House, which, despite being the place in Malibu where all the tourists go, has good food, a spectacular view of the ocean and a casually romantic atmosphere. I admit I hesitated. I was a little wary about my personal life getting into the tabloids. I thought a person's private life should be exactly that, even if you were a "celebrity." And the idea of photos of me and my gay lover in the *National Enquirer* or the *Star* took my appetite away. But I didn't want Dan to think I didn't want to be seen with him in public. More, I didn't want him to think that being with me meant he couldn't have a normal life, so I said, sure.

To my relief none of the dogs from the "Hollywood Hunt Club" lurked in the crowded parking lot. Inside, the restaurant was packed, but one of the perks of being a celebrity is that we were seated right away. People at the crowded tables looked up and leaned over to each other as we wound our way to the table by the window. To my amusement, I realized that they were looking at Dan, wondering who he was, what they'd seen him in. Even in jeans and a sports shirt he had presence, style — not to mention striking good looks.

He would never make it as an undercover cop, I thought.

"What's so funny?" he asked, glancing at me over the top of his menu.

I shook my head, smiling. He raised his brows and went back to his menu.

We ordered our meals, and the waitress brought our wine and warm sourdough bread crusty with garlic, thyme, and butter.

I looked across the table at Dan and he was smiling.

"Happy?" he asked.

And I realized I was. Very. And if that fullness in my chest meant anything, I was pretty close to falling in love.

He held his wine glass out and we clinked rims — and I didn't give a damn who saw.

"Excuse me."

I glanced up. There was a scarlet-faced kid with terrible skin hulking beside my chair.

He threw a nervous look over his shoulder at a crowded table taking up the center of the room. "Hi, my name is Sam Bowers. You came and spoke at my school last year and I just wanted to say thank you. It…meant a lot to me to…" His voice cracked nervously. "To hear about how it was for you."

I said, "You're welcome, Sam. I'm glad I could help."

"I want to be an actor too. I've been in some school plays. This year I played Judd in *Oklahoma* and Iago in *Othello*."

"That's great."

"I got great reviews in our local paper. Well, for Judd."

I said, "That's excellent. Hang onto those clippings."

"Everybody makes fun of me, but I don't care. They make jokes about the way I look. They call me queer bait. They're all a bunch of pricks."

I wasn't sure what I could tell him. I hadn't been out in high school; I'd thought being dead was preferable. His courage awed me.

"It gets easier as you get older. You won't care what people think."

As much.

"I don't care what they think now!" His face got redder, his eyes were too bright. He glanced at Dan and seemed to recollect himself. "Anyway, I just wanted to thank you. You're my hero."

"You're...welcome."

He suddenly reached down and hugged me awkwardly, meaty arms clutching fiercely. I patted his back. Sam let me go and walked quickly back to his table, which was now staring our way and whispering.

I glanced at Dan and was startled at his grim expression. "What's wrong?"

"Nothing."

I couldn't understand his tension. He couldn't be jealous. Did he view Sam as a potential threat? According to him there was no real threat — not anymore. "He's just a kid," I said.

"I know. It's cool." He gave me a quick smile that didn't quite soften the blue steel of his eyes.

The waitress brought our meals, sea bass for Dan and swordfish for me. We drank more wine. Sam Bowers and his family left, Sam glancing back at me several times — which did not go unnoticed by Dan.

"You can't think that kid's a threat."

"I don't." He said, in answer to my obvious puzzlement, "It's just...you're very...accessible. Even after what you've been through this last year, you're not..."

He didn't finish it, and I realized he didn't want to make me self-conscious. Or afraid. He said instead, "You were great with him. Patient, kind. You're good with everyone. No star tripping with you; that's one of the things I noticed right off the bat."

"I'm not exactly A-List."

"The biggest assholes in this town are not the A-Listers." He smiled. "You'd be the same regardless of the roles or the money. You don't take it seriously."

That troubled me. "I take it seriously."

"I don't mean the work. You're a professional. You don't take the celebrity thing seriously."

"Oh. Right." That was true. I wasn't that crazy about being a "celebrity." I liked my privacy.

The waitress arrived with a dessert tray. Dan went for coffee. I chose café glacé.

Dipping my spoon into the coffee-flavored ice cream, I asked, "What did you mean Friday night when you said you had been through therapy?"

Dan's eyes followed my tongue as I licked the whipped cream from the spoon. "I had counseling after I made the decision to be open about my sexual orientation on the job. Law enforcement is still a conservative and fairly homophobic profession; it wasn't an easy decision."

"What made you decide to come out?"

"It wasn't that I wasn't out, but I was very careful to keep the boundaries distinct between my personal and professional life."

That sounded uncomfortably familiar. "Don't ask, don't tell?"

"Right. Which to a degree I still believe in. I don't feel like it's anyone's business who I sleep with." He sighed. "And…law enforcement is, in general, kind of a macho gig. We've got more than our share of assholes on the force, so I guess I was glad to not have to take a stand. But I had a situation come up: a homicide suspect recognized me from a gay bar and tried to…let's call it 'negotiate' with me."

"You could have been undercover," I pointed out.

He smiled faintly. "I could have, but I was a regular at that bar, and we both knew it. I realized I had to come clean to my superiors — had to put it all out on the table."

I wondered what I'd have chosen in that same situation. "Were you tempted to go along with the blackmail?"

"No." He met my eyes levelly. "I knew once I started down that slope there would be no stopping. I wasn't about to endanger a job I love. I was never ashamed of being gay."

"And what happened after you came out?"

"A few guys were assholes and a few guys were stand up, but mostly nobody really gave a damn. Except the brass. They saw an opportunity to reverse some of the bad press and capitalize on how diverse and sensitive the new LAPD was."

"Did the counseling help?"

"It did." His gaze was curious. "You do all those public service announcements advising teens to seek counseling. You don't have faith in the process yourself?"

"It's not that. If I had been able to talk to someone when I was sixteen…things might have gone differently. Now I don't need someone helping me understand what I'm afraid of." I was no longer talking about being gay, and we both knew it. I added, "And I don't think my fears are unreasonable."

He was smart enough to leave it at that.

When we got back to the house I turned on the phonograph and put on the 1954 recording of Louis Armstrong playing W.C. Handy. I carried a stack of prospective screenplays Steve had sent over earlier in the week onto the deck and settled into the lounge chair, smearing suntan oil over my shoulders while the music wafted out through the open sliding door.

It was cooler today, the sun slipping in and out of clouds; the salty wind off the water had a nip to it. I wiped my hands together and leaned back in the chair, reaching for the first screenplay: *Favored to Place*. My eyes focused on the brown rag hooked to the deck railing.

Not a rag.

More like…a large toupee or something…furry.

I dropped the script from nerveless fingers. The pages fluttered in the breeze.

Far overhead I could a seagull crying. What a weird sound that was. Like mewing. Like a cat. Like a fluffy brown cat. Or a fluffy brown dog.

I stood up fast, but my foot hooked and I tipped the lounge chair over, sprawling on the deck. I felt like I'd had the wind knocked out of me.

"Dan," I yelled breathlessly. "Dan! *Dan!*"

In the distance I could hear a jaunty trumpet sashaying into the opening notes of "Loveless Love."

Along with the sudden lack of oxygen, I couldn't seem to get my footing. I kicked away the cushions and chair — unable to tear my eyes away from the thing nailed to the deck railing. Nailed by its tail...

The screen door opened and Dan stepped out. "What the hell —?"

I scrambled to my knees. "It's the dog," I gasped. "Mrs. Wiggly's dog." I pointed, hand shaking.

The consternation on Dan's face changed to something else. Something dangerous.

"Get up," he said. He reached down and hauled me to my feet. "Inside."

He thrust me through the half open door, stepped in behind me and locked it. Guiding me by the arm, he edged me back a few steps. "Stay away from the door, stay away from the window."

"He k-killed it," I chattered. "While we were at brunch. He's watching the house. Why would he do that? That stupid little dog. How c-could he know — But I didn't want *that!*"

Dan brushed past, lifted a gun the size of a small cannon out of the clutter on the middle bookshelf, and I realized in a distant sort of way that although he had seemed to dismiss my fears he was, in fact, on high alert.

Moving past me, he unlatched the door. "Don't open for anyone but me. Understand?"

I stared at him.

"Sean," he said sharply. "Do you understand what I'm saying?"

I sucked in a quavery breath. "I understand."

"I'll be right back. Lock the door behind me."

He stepped out. Gestured to the lock. I moved to the door and fumbled it locked. He motioned to me again, and I backed out of sight of the door.

Hearing his footsteps on the deck, I went to the window and, staying to the side, watched him cross the deck fast and jump down to the sand below.

He disappeared from sight.

Chapter Five

The scrape of a key in the lock brought me to my feet. Dan stepped inside, caught sight of me and stuck the gun in his back waistband, walking across to me.

"He's long gone."

"It's Hammond," I said. "I know it."

"Shhh." He took me in his arms. "Sean." He held me tightly; I couldn't have moved if I'd wanted to. I didn't want to.

"He's alive. I know it." I spoke into his chest, the words vibrating against the strong thud of his heart.

"It's not Hammond." He stroked my back calmingly. "This isn't Hammond's MO."

I raised my head. Met his eyes. "It *has* to be."

"Sean, over a dozen witnesses confirm that he went into the aqueduct. He couldn't have survived that crash. It's not possible."

"Then where's the body? Why hasn't the body shown up yet?"

He said patiently, "It washed down the aqueduct and lodged somewhere. I don't know. But I do know that whoever is doing this, it's not Hammond."

I was struggling against a riptide of emotions: fear, frustration, bewilderment all dragging me further and further from shore, from safety, from sanity.

"Then who?" I cried, trembling. "Nothing else makes sense!"

"You've got to calm down."

"How can I be calm when you can't — or won't — see what's happening? What does it take to convince you? He's *out there*. He's coming for me."

His hands clamped on my shoulders, anchoring me fast. "He's not getting you. *No one* is getting to you. I'm not going to let anything happen to you. I stopped Hammond, I'll stop this freak too. He's not getting near you."

"He's already near me!" I couldn't help it. My control was slipping. I heard my voice shaking and wild. "He's out there now. How could he know about what a pest that damn dog was? Tell me that? He had to have heard us. He could be listening to us now. This place could be bugged."

"Jesus, Sean." He pulled me close, holding me against him like he wanted to smother the words spilling out. "Stop it. Sweetheart. Stop. You're making yourself sick."

He kept murmuring words I couldn't comprehend, but I understood that he was petting me, quieting me, and after a while I stopped ranting, stopped trembling, finally managing to slow those panicked shallow breaths that were making me lightheaded.

We moved over to the sofa. He left me for a moment or two. I scrubbed my face, wiping away tears I didn't remember crying. I rested my head in my hands and tried to think. Nothing made sense. The postcards had stopped but Hammond had escalated to violence. It had been all threats up until this point. What had changed?

Dan sat down beside me. Set a glass of water on the table. He held a small brown vial that I recognized from my bathroom cabinet. I had news for him; those pills were well past their expiration date — like me apparently. I watched him shake two tablets into his palm.

"I don't want those."

"I know. But you need them."

I gave him a hostile look. Anything I said now would be put down to my irrational state of mind. I held out my hand. He dropped the pills in my palm, I popped them in to my mouth, took the glass of water he handed over. I washed the pills down, handed him back the glass, stretched out on the sofa and closed my eyes.

Dan brushed my hair from my forehead. I kept my eyes closed, rejecting that light, tender touch.

"Just relax."

Yeah. Right.

"Everything will be okay, I promise you."

I swallowed. Didn't answer. Kept my eyes closed. He said that a lot: "I promise you." But what did that mean? He couldn't promise me anything. Not when he didn't even believe me — when his main concern was to shut me up.

He kept stroking my hair. I didn't want him to. I didn't want to be comforted by him. I didn't like the fact that his touch seemed to find a way through my defenses, that he seemed to be able to converse with me through his fingertips and my nerve endings. I tried to shut out my response, but my scalp seemed to tingle beneath the deft fingers threading my hair. The tears stopped leaking beneath my lashes. The torpidity lurking at the edge of my consciousness eddied around and sucked me down.

§ § § §

When I opened my eyes it was dark. I was lying on the sofa in the living room. Someone — Dan — had tossed the lambswool throw over me. The lights were off, but there was a fire in the fireplace. The shadows changed against the walls, flickering and indistinct. Never two the same — like Rorschach plates.

I turned my head. Dan was sitting in one of the chairs before the fireplace. His profile looked flushed in the firelight. He was staring at nothing in particular. I wondered where the gun was now. On TV and in the movies cops shoot people all the time. Dan told me he had only drawn his weapon a dozen times — and he'd only fired once. That was when he had shot and wounded a robbery suspect. He had been off-duty at the time. He had earned a citation for bravery, but there had also been an Internal Affairs audit.

"What time is it?" I asked.

His head snapped my way and he stood up. I didn't want that. It was hard to keep the walls in place with him near me, and I wanted the walls up. It was safer behind the walls.

"How are you feeling?" He started to sit on the edge of the sofa, but I sat up, moving away from him.

"Groggy. Sorry for the…hysterics."

"Sean."

I cut across his compassion. "What happened — while I was out?"

"I called the sheriffs and filed a report. Then I walked down to Mrs. Wilgi and told her what happened." He added, before I did more than look at him, "A deputy stayed here at the house until I got back."

I nodded. I wasn't thinking about who had been watching over me; I was thinking about poor Mrs. Wilgi who had loved that ugly little dog as though it had been her child.

"No one is taking this threat lightly, Sean."

I refused to look at him. "I know."

"I've been thinking that it might be a good time to move back to the house."

I shrugged. "What's the difference? He knows where I live."

He didn't speak for a moment, then he said, choosing his words, "If this is not Hammond, then he may not know that you have a home in the Hollywood Hills."

I laughed derisively. "*If?* You mean you're willing to consider the idea that Hammond may not be dead?"

"Yes."

That surprised me, and I did look at him then, trying to read his expression in the gloom. His eyes glittered in the glow from the fireplace — a little spooky.

"Are you humoring me?"

"No."

Some of my tension drained away.

"What changed your mind?"

"I don't know that my mind has changed — but I'm keeping it open. I agree with you that it is highly unlikely you would attract two aggressive stalkers in this space of time."

Tiredly, I thought this over. He didn't think I was crazy; that was good, right? The fact that someone was out to get me: not so good. "When you said it wasn't Hammond's MO, what did you mean?"

"Hammond was what we call an Attachment Seeker. Killing the dog is more the action of a Rejection-based stalker — except the dog wasn't yours. You didn't even like the dog, so as threatening as the action seems, it could be perceived as a service to you." Wearily, he added, "Which still doesn't make sense psychologically."

"It makes sense," I said. I'd done plenty of reading on stalkers all on my own. "He sees himself as rejected. He didn't get what he wanted from me and he's moved from simple stalking to intimidation and threats. Rejection-based stalkers are the most likely to turn to violence. Isn't that true?"

"Yes," he said reluctantly.

"If he's watching me, he knows that you and I are involved now. That could be the catalyst."

"Hammond wasn't gay."

"Maybe he was a closet case."

"Either way," Dan said, "We need to think about how best to ensure your safety. I think moving back —"

"I don't think the locale matters. We've got a great security system here and I can see anyone coming from a mile away."

He looked unconvinced but didn't argue, and I guessed that he didn't want to pressure me when I was already emotionally distressed. That's one of the perks of having a history of breakdown. People don't like to upset you unnecessarily.

"All right. We'll leave it for now. I've already spoken to my captain and we'll have someone from Special Investigations here tomorrow on security duty."

"Who? I don't want some stranger in my —"

"Listen," Dan said crisply, "We've got to have someone here during the day, and it can't be me."

"Why? I don't understand."

"Because we're involved now, chief. There are protocols that have to be followed in order to authorize protection for you. We're dealing with a government bureaucracy, among other things."

"What other things? If you were the best person for the job before —"

He drew a deep breath. "It's...like a doctor operating on a family member. I can't be objective about your safety; I don't have any emotional distance, which means I'm not the best person for the job now."

I opened my mouth to argue and he said, "I don't tell you what roles to take in your career; how about you don't try to tell me the roles to take in mine?"

His tone was even and he was still sort of smiling, but he was dead serious. I stared at him. Finally lifted a shoulder.

Sergeant Jack Markowitz had apparently transferred in from a neighboring police state — to his iron-jawed dismay. Tall, trim and no-nonsense, he showed up at the beach house at the crack of dawn on Monday before Dan left to drive into Hollywood. They greeted each other tersely, stepped out front briefly to discuss "the case," before Dan came out to the deck to tell me goodbye.

"Stick close to the house today — and stick close to Markowitz."

I raised an eyebrow and he said, "Not that close."

Markowitz watched stonily from the doorway as we kissed.

"Can I fix you some breakfast?" I asked my new bodyguard after Dan drove off.

"No. Thanks." Markowitz managed, looking like breaking bread with me would choke him.

I spent an uneventful morning working out and reading through the stack of screenplays Steve had sent over. Most of them seemed to consist of roles for strung out smart asses; I began to think being typecast as a gay man wouldn't be so bad after all.

At ten o'clock Maria let herself in the back door, like usual, and Markowitz scared the shit out of all of us by throwing down on her. Once we got that sorted out, Maria, with a lot of muttering under her breath, got busy vacuuming, and Markowitz amused himself "checking out the perimeter" for the nth time.

By eleven o'clock I knew it was going to be a very long day.

Steve called after lunch. "I've got good news and bad news. What do you want to hear first?"

I didn't know if I could take any bad news at the moment. "What's the good news?"

"Winston Marshall, the guy producing *The Charioteer*, has invited you to dinner tomorrow night."

I felt like someone turned the lights on inside me. "For real? Where?"

I expected to hear Spago or Musso & Frank Grill, but Steve said, "At his place in Bel Air. Lenny Norman will be there too."

"Does that mean —?"

"I don't know what it means," Steve admitted. "I can tell you that Marshall likes your work. He was very interested when I said you were hooked on the idea of playing Laurie. The bad news is he didn't know you were hooked before because Lenny Norman hadn't mentioned it to him — and that's because Norman doesn't want you. They're looking at David Cort for the role."

"David Cort," I echoed. Davie Cort would be perfect for Laurie Odell. I could see him already in the khaki wool Battle Dress uniform of the period. He was the right age, casually attractive, a decent actor — and English. I felt nauseous.

"So is that the bad news: they're pretty much decided on Davie Cort?"

"No." Steve paused and I could feel my already wrenched nerves strrrrrreeetch another foot on the rack. "Um...have there been any more postcards?"

"No."

Silence.

I said, "But someone killed my neighbor's dog and hung it on our deck."

"Jesus fucking Christ!"

"You said it." I glanced at Markowitz who was out on the deck using binoculars to check out the bikini-clad women far down the beach. A real security threat, those teeny little swimsuits.

"Okay, well, I did some checking, like you asked. This is totally unofficial, but according to my source at Hollywood Division, there's more than a little doubt as to whether Hammond was even driving the car when it went into the aqueduct."

It was like he was speaking a foreign language; I heard him but the words didn't make sense. "What?" I said at last.

"Hammond may not be dead."

Wasn't this exactly what I'd been saying the whole time? Why had Dan tried so hard to convince me otherwise when it was obvious his colleagues thought there was a good chance Hammond was still out there?

"Why didn't anyone bother to share this before?" I asked.

Steve said carefully, "I think they did. I think Dan…didn't want to alarm you."

I bit down on my anger at Dan. "Do the cops have any leads on Hammond?"

"They're watching his apartment and the motorcycle shop where he used to work. Nothing's turned up. I mean, he *could* be dead. They're not ruling that out."

My brain seemed to have stalled. Steve was still talking. I tuned back in to hear him query, "You coming to this premiere at the Chinese?"

"What?"

"Are you getting hard of hearing? The premiere party for this new Peter Jackson flick. You plan on making an appearance?"

"I don't think so."

"*Why?* Sean, you need to get out and be seen. You know how this business is. Not to mention the fact that sitting around brooding is not healthy."

"I don't know how healthy it is for me to set myself up like a sitting duck at some big Hollywood party."

"What are you talking about? What could be safer than a tent filled with bodyguards, security, and cameras? It's called hiding in plain sight."

"I just don't feel up to it."

Mistake. I knew what he was going to say before he said a word. "Are you having…trouble again?" Which was his diplomatic way of asking if I was headed for another stay in the loony bin.

"I'm okay."

"For real? I mean, you're eating and sleeping and taking your meds?"

"I'm not on meds, Steve. I'm fine."

"Hey, panic attacks are not fine."

"I'm not having panic attacks." Well, not many.

"Whatever you want to call not being able to function."

I was used to Steve, so I'm not sure why that stung. "I can function just fine."

"Really? Well, then explain to me what's going on? You don't want to work; you don't want to do the publicity. You do remember that acting is a job, right? That we're in business here?"

"Yeah, I remember," I snapped, because I was feeling guilty. Playing the publicity game is a big part of the acting biz.

"You're hiding out there in the sand dunes. I mean, if by some miracle you did land *The Charioteer*, would you be ready to take it on?"

"Of course!"

"Is this recluse shtick Dan's influence?"

"It's nothing to do with Dan. It would be easier for Dan if we moved back to Hollywood. He wouldn't have to drive so far to work."

"Then what the hell is going on?"

"I don't know. I'm just…enjoying my Indian summer, I guess. I feel safer here." I hadn't meant to say that last bit aloud; it just slipped out.

"*Safer?* Is Dan telling you you're safer out there? Is it his idea to keep you so isolated?"

"Why do you keep coming back to Dan?"

"Because you've changed since you've been with him. You seem afraid to make decisions on your own. I don't know. Less confident. More dependent. More like...before."

By "before" he meant when we had first met in college, when I was not that long out of the hospital, and still shaky. I had been less confident back then. I'd had trouble making my own decisions. No, that wasn't true; I'd made my own decisions, but I'd agonized over the consequences. It had half-killed me to know I was disappointing people, hurting people, failing. Steve had been my only friend during that period, and I had depended on him a lot. And he'd been there for me, which is what now kept me from giving into the blaze of anger his words sparked.

I worked to keep my voice neutral. "What are you talking about?"

"I'm just worried about you, dude. I've known you a long time."

I had to wonder if some of my anger wasn't partly due to unease that Steve might be getting close to the truth. Was I starting to rely on Dan too much? Was I slipping back into unhealthy habits? I mean, as much as I wanted to believe that I'd be the first person to know if I wasn't okay, that's not usually how it works.

But I *was* okay. Anyone would be a little freaked with what I'd been through this past year. Even Dan agreed with that.

Although Dan had also suggested I might need to start seeing a shrink again.

Slowly, I absorbed what Steve was really getting at. I said, "Have you heard something about Dan? When you were asking about Hammond, did someone say something that gave you a bad impression?"

He hesitated, and I felt the hair on the back of my neck prickle. "Steve?"

"No," he said quickly. "I mean, cops are sort of a different breed. Sort of above the law, right? He's never...I don't know...gotten rough with you or anything, right?"

"Dan?"

He gave an uneasy laugh. "Yeah. No, I mean, that's what I mean. He's not that kind of cop."

"What kind of cop? What are you talking about?"

"Nothing. The kind of cop you hear about on TV. I watch the news. Cops get indicted for shit all the time. Bribery, corruption, murder. They've got really high rates of domestic violence… "

My throat went so tight I could hardly wedge the words out. "Dan's been nothing but wonderful to me. From day one, he's looked out for me in every way." Now I was angry with myself for having started this line of conversation with Steve.

He returned with unexpected bitterness, "Dan's the man, that I do get. Unlike Dan, who I guess, gets it all."

That caught me off guard. I didn't know what to say. It never occurred to me that Steve truly had a moment's regret for the past.

Into my disconcerted pause, he said, "Forget I said that. I'm sure he's a great guy off-duty. Okay? Put it down to jealousy. Mine and maybe some other folks." He tried to sound light. "Besides, you haven't changed your will or anything, right? Left him your record collection and your subscription to *Food and Wine*?"

"No, I haven't changed my will. And what the hell is that supposed to mean?"

"Chill. It was just a joke."

"Good thing you kept your day job."

"Okay, so it was a bad joke. Listen, Sean, don't get pissed off because I still care about you. I understand the guy won a medal, and he treats you great, but just go slow, okay? You haven't known him that long. You've only spent a couple of weeks together. Basically the dude is an unknown quantity. He's a…a dark horse."

I laughed — sort of.

"I'm serious, dude."

"I know you are, and it's fucking ridiculous."

The glass door slid open and Markowitz gave me a narrow look. I realized I didn't sound nearly as relaxed and humorous as I'd hoped. I lowered my voice. "I don't want to talk about this anymore."

"Everything okay?" Markowitz growled.

I nodded.

Steve was saying, "Fine. I don't want to talk about it either. I'm sorry I ever brought it up. So, since everything is wonderful, do you feel up to taking this dinner with Marshall?"

"Hell, yes."

Stiffly, he gave me the details, and I wrote them down while Markowitz held an undervoiced conversation with Maria that apparently had to do with what he wanted for lunch.

"Are you going to be there?"

"No," Steve said shortly. "You're going to have to sell yourself to them. And let me tell you now, Lenny Norman is a tough audience."

§ § § §

Dan got home about six for a changing of the guard with Markowitz. Once again they went outside for their powwow, which I found annoying. I watched Markowitz get in to his car and drive away.

"No postcards," I informed Dan when he came back inside.

"That's what I hear," he said, dropping a kiss on my mouth.

"What else did you hear?"

He gave me a curious look. "I didn't ask him for a report. Is there something I should know?"

I knew I was being a jerk and shook my head.

It was too cold to eat outside even if dining al fresco had been approved by my security team. I had the dining room table set and Dean Martin playing on the stereo. Hard to be down with Dino lounging around the room.

We had dinner and chatted about his day and mine. Dan had been called to the scene of an officer-involved shooting and was dealing with the fallout, and I'd read a bunch of scripts, so I wasn't sure why, as usual, I seemed to be doing most of the talking.

The record player needle moved to the brassy opening of "Ain't That a Kick in the Head." As much as I had tried all day to block out Steve's comments, they'd worked like burrs into my consciousness. I broke off what I was saying to ask, "Have you ever had any complaints about the way you do your job?"

Dan, in the process of cutting off a bite of pork chop, paused. "What are you talking about?"

"I mean did anyone ever accuse you of excessive force or anything?"

He didn't say anything for a moment, and I couldn't read his expression at all. At last, he said, "I'm a lieutenant now; it's not like I'm out there rousting suspects. But yeah, I've had a few complaints over the years."

"Like what?"

Reluctantly, he said, "Police put people in jail for breaking the law. That doesn't win you popularity contests. I've had suspects claim I violated their rights or that I used unnecessary force. I've had female suspects accuse me of sexual harassment." His smile was wry. "I guess that one was kind of funny, although I didn't think so at the time."

I wasn't quite sure what to make of his admission; I'd been hoping he would just categorically deny it.

"Why?" he asked.

Which was a perfectly reasonable question. But for obvious reasons, I couldn't give him a good answer. I already knew how he'd view my discussing him with Steve: pretty much the same way I'd view him discussing me with anyone else.

"I just wondered," I said.

"You must have had some reason for wondering."

I said vaguely, "It's just the cop thing, I guess."

I wasn't really thinking about the implications of that comment, so it caught me off my mark when he responded seriously, "Is that a problem for you? Because that is who I am."

"No, it's not a problem." But into the pause that followed my words, I wondered if that was totally true. When I felt vulnerable and threatened, I appreciated the fact that Dan totally took charge. I felt safe with him in a way I'd never felt as an adult. Maybe it was the gun. Or maybe it was the fact that he had an air of being able to handle anything. But was I still going to feel that way once the danger was passed? I didn't want or need someone taking charge of me in my normal day-to-day life. It wasn't reasonable, but there was a little part of me that resented how closely Dan watched me, and — a little — how he tried to protect me. I guess it reminded me, uncomfortably, of being ill. Of needing to be protected, of needing someone to take charge. I never wanted to be that person again.

But I didn't see how I could tell that to Dan without sounding like I was pushing him away, so I did what I always did when in doubt. I started babbling. And Dan did what he always did, which was let me blab until I had to stop for breath.

"So what is it about this role that makes you want it so bad?" he asked after I'd told him about the invitation to dinner with Lenny Norman and Winston Marshall.

I shrugged. "I guess because I identified with Laurie so strongly when I was a kid. Now that I've read the screenplay I see how blind Laurie is. The role with teeth is Ralph. He's the real hero of the thing. Even from the way Renault describes him in the book you can tell that it's his story. There's a psychological depth there that would be a real challenge to capture."

"But you want the Laurie part?"

"Well, I don't have the physical presence to carry off Ralph. And Laurie's not bad. He's smart and sensitive, and he's got a sense of humor. He sees the stupidity of war, but he never wavers about doing his duty, and once he's crippled, he never whines about it. He's not afraid to face up to things. Well, except the one thing. But he's still got a lot of courage despite his blind streak."

"He sounds a lot like you. No wonder you identify."

I laughed nervously. "Oh, right!"

Dan's brows drew together, and to keep him from drawing any more ridiculous comparisons, I said quickly, "I guess it's his ordinariness that appeals to me — appeals to most guys who read the book. Although I'm a little more impatient with him now that I'm reading as an adult. I don't know if he's afraid to face the reality of who he is — *what* he is. Maybe he's just afraid to lose himself by loving someone completely."

Dan's expression was odd.

Changing the subject, I said, "I don't know what to do about tomorrow night. I can't show up with a bodyguard. It'll confirm everything Lenny Norman thinks about me."

"I don't give a damn about what Lenny Norman thinks," Dan said. "Until we've figured out who's harassing you, I don't want you out there on your own."

Once again I felt a flare of antagonism at what was, after all, pretty much common sense. I guess it was the authority — verging on arrogance — in Dan's voice. Like there was no room for discussion. What was especially unreasonable was that I'd been resentful before because he hadn't seemed to take my fears seriously, and now that he was taking them very seriously, I was equally offended. What did I want?

"Yeah, well, I care what Lenny Norman thinks," I said. "I want this role and I don't want to do anything that confirms his image of me as some stereotypical Hollywood himbo."

"A stereotypical Hollywood himbo wouldn't want that role," Dan pointed out.

Somehow everything he was saying tonight irritated me. I said shortly, "He thinks I'm gutless, personally and professionally, and showing up with a cop escort tends to reinforce that idea."

"When is the dinner?" Dan asked. "I'll get off early and drive you."

"It's the same thing!"

I heard the hostility in my voice before it registered in Dan's eyes. There was an uncomfortable silence — long enough for me to try and take the words back, but I didn't. Steve was right. I was getting way too dependent on Dan. I needed to set a few boundaries.

After a moment Dan said, "I wasn't inviting myself to dinner. I'll drop you off and you can ring me when you're ready to go."

I almost couldn't stop myself from saying, "How is that going to look?" but sanity prevailed — a limited engagement. I said, "I'm supposed to be there at seven."

"I'll be home by five."

"Great. Thanks." If my tone had been any chillier we'd have had to throw another log on the fire.

Later that evening I stood in front of the bathroom mirror frowning at my reflection, trying to decide if there was anything I could do that might make me look more like whatever Lenny Norman imagined Laurie Odell looked like. I could skip shaving. Would chic-scruffy be more appropriate for an invalided soldier? Probably not for a guy in a World War II military hospital. Being tanned wasn't a good idea either. I was probably too tall as well — although Peter Grady and I looked pretty good on screen together.

Davie Cort was shorter than me and a bit stockier. And a lot paler. Better shoulders. He had one of those appealing boney intelligent English faces — saved from effeteness by a broken nose.

And he had that damned accent.

Not that I couldn't do an English accent. I was pretty good at accents, actually.

"I say, old chap," I said to my mirrored self.

There was a quiet laugh behind me. I turned. Dan stood in the doorway, smiling. Our eyes met in the glass. He unbuttoned his collar.

"What number were you again?"

It took me a second to remember *People* magazine. I bit back a laugh, although I wished he hadn't reminded me of that. "Go to hell."

He chuckled.

"You look more like a movie star than me."

"No need to be nasty."

It was true, though. For old fashioned good looks, Dan was the guy. My face was all bones, sharps and angles. I photographed well, but in real life there was nothing remarkable about me. Tall and lanky, brown hair, brown eyes (okay, "sherry-colored eyes" and "sun-kissed chestnut hair" if you wanted to quote *People* magazine).

"You'll do fine, Laurie," he said, turning away.

I caught my own wide-eyed look in the glass. It occurred to me that one of the things irritating me tonight was the very thing that bothered Laurie about Ralph: his take-charge attitude when no one was asking him to take charge; the protectiveness that verged on domineering; the assumption that, because he didn't see a problem, it didn't exist. The funny thing was that Laurie's attitude in the book had always bothered me. He didn't seem to fully appreciate Ralph. Now I sort of understood his point.

By lunchtime on Tuesday I was getting a little tired of Sergeant Markowitz. He had all the personality of one of those Easter Island statues. He ate about as much, too. Maybe he thought I'd sprinkled gay powder in the roast beef sandwiches. The only time he livened up was when he went out on the deck and checked out the beach bunnies — and the beach bunnies were few and far between now that the weather had turned. He even made Maria nervous — not an easy thing to do.

It was obvious he felt like he was wasting his time, and maybe he was right. There were no more postcards, no phone calls, nothing but the horrible memory of the dead dog. Maybe someone else had disliked that damned dog and got rid of it thinking it was mine. It spent so much time at my cottage I could see how the mistake might be made.

The morning dragged. The afternoon wasn't much better. I was freaking myself out thinking about dinner that evening, wondering what I could say or do to convince Lenny Norman that I was the right guy for the job.

About two o'clock I worked out in the weight room, showered and came downstairs for a snack. As I reached the ground floor I could hear Steve's excited and tinny voice echoing through the dining room.

"Sean. Fuck. Sean, pick up. Fuck, *pick up!*"

Through the glass door I could see Markowitz and Maria out on the deck in deep discussion. About what? I stretched across the counter for the phone.

"What's up?"

"Sean! Someone shot Lenny Norman!"

I said stupidly, "When?"

"I don't know. His gardener found him this morning."

"Is he —?"

"Yes, he's dead! He was shot to death. Somebody blew a couple of holes through his chest."

Behind me I heard a key in the front door. Too early for Dan. I turned, automatically dropping the handset into the cradle, cutting Steve's shocked voice off.

I stared across the wasteland of counter and table tops, the stretch of carpet and wooden floor. The sunlight lancing through the blinds and bouncing off the wooden floor was so bright it hurt my eyes. Hurt my head...

The front door opened and Dan stepped in, his face hard and unfamiliar behind dark sunglasses. He looked like a movie hit man, well-dressed and ruthless.

I said, "Lenny Norman's dead. Hammond shot him."

My voice was quiet and tired in the big empty rooms. Not strong enough to carry through the rush of noisy sunshine, but maybe he already knew what I was going to say.

I couldn't read his face behind those dark glasses, but his mouth opened. From a long way away he said, "Sean..."

Chapter Six

I opened my eyes.

I was lying on the sofa. The ceiling fan whispered above me, the blades swirling in a hypnotic blur. It threw a black shadow flower against the plaster, the petals whirring into a smear.

"Hey, sweetheart." Dan leaned over me, his face white. Even his lips looked pale. There were little lines around his eyes I didn't remember seeing before. Poor Dan. Just what he needed after a hard day of chasing bad guys: scraping his crazy boyfriend off the carpet.

I whispered, "Sorry about that."

He stroked my hair back from my forehead. "There's nothing to be sorry for."

There was, though. Lenny Norman.

I covered my eyes with my arm.

"Don't, Sean. It's not your fault."

Funny how easily he could read my mind.

"No?"

"Christ, no."

"He thinks he's helping me."

But how could Hammond possibly know that I was trying for a role in *The Charioteer*? How could he know that Lenny Norman stood in the way of what I wanted?

"Whoever is behind this doesn't think he's helping you."

I lowered my arm. "We know who's behind it. Jesus, tell me we aren't going to go through this again. You know Hammond did this. He killed the dog and now —"

"Listen to me," he said, and something in his tone caught my attention. "They found Hammond's body."

"They..." I felt winded, like he'd punched me.

"There's no mistake. Paul Hammond is dead."

I blinked. I had been so *sure*.

Dan said, "He must have been thrown from the car when it went off the road. From what the ME could tell, he crawled several yards away from the crash site before he died from internal injuries. They found him in a small gully. Apparently, because the car wound up in the aqueduct, no one thought to canvass the surrounding area."

I put a hand to my head trying to make sense of this. "There's no doubt?"

Grimly, Dan said, "I visited the morgue myself to make sure."

I gathered from his expression that the trip to the morgue had been pretty ghastly; I recognized that this had been done as a favor to me, something I should be grateful for. Instead I felt bewildered.

"Then who shot Lenny Norman?"

"We can't assume that Norman's murder is connected to whoever is harassing you. It could have been a jealous boyfriend, a drug deal gone bad; he was not a popular guy. It could have been someone he fired or someone he turned down for a role."

"You don't believe that, do you?"

"I know that you believe Norman's death is too much of a coincidence, but I'm here to tell you that coincidences happen."

I barely heard him. It was like someone had dumped water on the circuit board of my brain; my thoughts kept shorting out. Norman's death *couldn't* be a coincidence, but how could anyone outside my immediate circle know that I feared he would stop me from getting *The Charioteer*? Only a handful of people could possibly know I was interested in the role. And killing Norman wasn't doing me any favors. Most likely the entire production would be cancelled now; the adaptation had been his baby, his project, he had been the one fueling it. So if someone was trying to do me a favor, it was someone who didn't understand how the film industry ran.

Watching me, Dan asked, "Feel ready to sit up?"

I assented.

He slipped an arm behind me and I sat up, surprised to find that I really needed his help. I felt weak. Shattered.

I stared around the room like I'd never seen it. It was so white. White carpets and white upholstery, white walls — so clinical. Medicinal. Had I picked all this stuff? The seascape over the fireplace, the dark wood furniture and bookshelves. The books themselves. They all looked like they belonged to someone else, someone who lived a long, long way away from me — maybe on another planet.

The only thing that felt real was Dan's arm around me. Was he afraid I was going to keel over again?

I said, "I need a drink."

He hesitated. "You don't want to mix pills and booze."

"I don't plan on taking any pills."

Another pause while he searched for a way to say what he wanted to without antagonizing me. "You might want something to help you sleep. Later."

I shook my head. He squeezed my shoulder and rose. He was back in a minute with two fingers of brandy in a tumbler. I knocked it back, barely registering the burn down my throat, the heat pooling in my belly. Dan's hand absently stroked up and down my spine.

"Where's Markowitz?" I asked, then nearly dropped the glass as the phone rang. "I can't talk to anyone," I told Dan.

"I've got it." He rose, and I instantly missed his warmth and strength. Too much.

From that detached distance I listened to him talk. Quiet and clipped. Cop talk. I remembered that I had hung up on Steve. I needed to talk to him. Later. He'd understand that it had to be later.

Dan came back and sat down beside me again. "Norman had an argument with his neighbor last night — and not the first."

"I don't believe —"

"Just for the sake of argument, look at these things separately for a minute."

A thought popped into my head. I interrupted him, asking, "When did you find out Hammond was dead?"

"Yesterday."

"Yesterday?"

No apology, no explanation. Just the facts, ma'am.

Something else didn't make sense, but I couldn't put my finger on it. I said, "Where did you say Markowitz was?"

Dan nodded toward the front room. "Did you need him for something?"

"No. I don't need him."

I woke up with the confused memory of the phone ringing.

The room was in darkness, the shutters closed, drapes drawn. Dan's side of the bed — he had a side now — was empty. I rolled over in a twist of sheet, checked the clock on the nightstand. Seven-thirty. *At night?* What the hell was I doing in bed? I was supposed to be at dinner with Winston Marshall and Lenny Norman.

It all came flooding back. Steve's phone call and the news Lenny Norman had been murdered. My faint. Then talking with Dan until the alcohol had hit and I'd gone up to lie down. Had I taken pills after that? I didn't remember, but I felt groggy, doped.

I hadn't dreamed that single aborted ring, had I?

I picked the phone up and heard Dan talking. "... shock. I don't want to wake him."

Steve replied, "I understand, but I think he'll want to take this call."

"I'll tell him you rang as soon as he wakes up."

Still only half awake, I dropped the handset, had to feel around in the coverlet for it. I put it back against my ear in time to hear Steve saying, "You mean, what *you* think is best for Sean. Maybe Sean wouldn't agree."

"In this five seconds Sean isn't the best judge of what he needs."

I blinked at this from a great distance. Did Dan mean that the way it sounded? Because what *did* that mean? And whatever it meant, it was pretty damn high-handed.

And apparently Steve agreed. He said in a tone I'd never heard before, "But I guess you are?"

I waited for Dan's answer. He didn't say anything, which I guess was his answer.

I replaced the phone carefully on the hook. I didn't feel up to talking to Steve right now, I didn't feel ready to deal with whatever this new piece of news was, but Steve was right. Dan didn't have a right to screen my calls. I should be a lot more angry, right? It couldn't be a good sign that I felt so apathetic; that all I wanted to do was roll over and go back to sleep.

Maybe Dan wasn't so far off base. Maybe I wasn't as well as I believed. My stomach twisted into knots of anxiety.

But anyone would be shocked about murder, right? And death threats, that would take a toll on anyone.

Wasn't I basically stressing over how stressed I was? In fact, this was really sort of funny if I looked at it in just the right way.

Yep, hysterical. And if I started laughing, I'd never stop.

Say I did crack up again, what would happen with Dan and me? Nobody was going to hang in there for that. You couldn't expect it. I tried to picture Dan driving down on visiting days to have lunch with me in my bathrobe.

I hugged the pillow and buried my face in the cool cotton. It smelled good. Like Dan.

§ § § §

I jerked awake to furtive rustling sounds.

"It's me." Dan spoke from near the window. "I didn't want to startle you with the light."

Right, because creepy sounds in the darkness were a lot less alarming.

"What time is it?"

"About three in the morning." His shadow passed through the bars of moonlight. The mattress dipped on his side of the bed. I could hear the fatigue in his voice. "Do you need anything? You didn't eat dinner. Do you want some scrambled eggs?"

"No."

"A hot drink?"

I had a sudden and totally inexplicable longing for the hot cocoa and plain animal cookies my mom used to fix me when I a little kid and feeling sick or sad. I hadn't seen or spoken to my mother in five years. Not since the memorable lunch where she'd spent the first half reassuring me that there were doctors and clinics and therapies to help me get over being gay, and the second half crying about what she and my father could have done to deserve a son like me.

Two days later I'd checked myself into the hospital for a few weeks of R&R. But, it only took a day for me to realize that being depressed or nervous didn't mean I wasn't safe with the cutlery. The first step had been learning to trust myself. The second step had been putting a healthy distance between me and my family.

"Nothing," I told Dan. And then belatedly, "Thanks."

He lay back with a sigh. "Jesus, what a fucked up day," he muttered. I don't think he meant to say it aloud. I'd never heard him sound so drained.

I lifted my head. "Are you okay? Can I get *you* something?"

He said huskily, "I could really use a hug right about now."

For a sec I didn't think I'd heard him right. I was so used to him being the caretaker that it didn't occur to me that he might occasionally need solace — or that I'd be the person best qualified to offer it.

"Hey," I whispered, and reached for him. His arms locked around me. I wasn't exactly sure who was hugging whom. I rested my cheek against the soft crispness of his hair, kissed him lightly. His breath was warm against my ear. Toothpaste and a hint of the coffee he'd had earlier. He inhaled sharply. Held me even tighter.

"I love the way you smell," he whispered.

I smiled a little. Gave him another of those tiny stray kisses. After a few minutes, I felt his body relaxing against mine, growing heavy and drowsy. It was unexpectedly comforting. I held him until I too gave into sleep.

I slept late the next morning. Dan was gone by the time I wandered into the front room.

Markowitz sat on the couch reading *Variety*. Maria was scouring the granite countertops. She looked up, smiling with false brightness when I walked into the kitchen.

"Buenos días!"

"Morning." I opened the fridge. Took out the jug of orange juice.

"I make you breakfast, Mr. Fairchild," Maria said, handing me a glass. Her soft brown eyes looked worried. Why was she worried?

"How about if I make you breakfast," I said. "Markowitz, would you like breakfast?"

"I had a couple of Pop Tarts before I left the house," Markowitz said from behind the newspaper.

"Me, I'm dieting," Maria said.

That made it unanimous. I drank my orange juice watching Mrs. Wilgi walking the beach. A little speck danced in front of her. A puppy.

I sat down and turned on the TV, flipping channels 'til I found a local station. I sat through two morning talk shows with celebrity guests — all of them much younger and prettier than me — cartoons I didn't recognize, and finally a news update on Lenny Norman.

Police were questioning a neighbor with whom he'd had a long-running feud. And that was about it. Norman had been shot to death late Monday night. His bullet-riddled body had been found by his gardener Tuesday morning.

News at eleven. Eleven *a.m.* because it wasn't very important news, the murder of one small-time indie director. Few, if any, of the at home viewers were going to recognize his film credits.

"The victim was killed by three shots from a nine mm semiautomatic," announced the perky blond reporter in her faux trench coat.

I said to Markowitz, who had lowered the paper for this news flash, "That's the old police issue, isn't it?" I knew Dan still carried a Beretta M9, though a lot of cops had switched to Glocks.

"I prefer the grip of a Beretta," Markowitz said quite civilly. "They've been having problems with the Glock 21s."

From the kitchen, Maria made clucking noises. "You don't want feel your head with that bad stuff, Mr. Fairchild!"

The phone rang. My keepers exchanged looks.

I uncurled out of the overstuffed chair. "I've got it," I said. I picked up before the answering machine.

"Dude, is that you?" Steve sounded unusually subdued.

"Yes." I glanced at Maria. "I'll take this upstairs."

She nodded.

I ran upstairs, picked up, and said into the phone, "You can hang up now, Maria." I waited for the clatter of the phone settling back on the hook, and then said, "What's up?"

"Is everything okay?"

"Of course."

"I tried to call last night."

"I know. I'm sorry. I was kind of out of it last night."

"Yeah. I heard."

Awkward pause.

"Well, listen," Steve said finally, "I've got some news. I think it's good news. Winston Marshall called me this morning. He's going ahead with *The Charioteer*. He's already talked to Bruce Watts about replacing Lenny Norman as director, and the first person Bruce mentioned when he heard the Laurie role hadn't been cast yet was you."

"Bruce is going to direct?" Bruce Watts had directed my last two films. He was wonderful to work with, an actor's director.

"The part's yours if you still want it."

"If I still want it? Of course I still want it!"

"Are you sure, Sean? Because there are other films and other parts."

"What are you talking about? I want this part. I want this film."

Steve, sounding totally unlike himself, said, "Okay, but are you...sure you're up to it?"

"Hell, yes, I'm up to it." The realization of what he was really saying hit me in the gut. "Why don't you just say what's on your mind, Steve?"

Clearly uncomfortable, he forged on. "Yeah, well, Dan and I talked last night. He said that you might not be…strong enough to go back to work so soon."

I was holding the receiver so hard I thought it might crack. "He said *what?*"

"Well, with all this shit going on. First Hammond and then this other lunatic and then thinking Hammond *was* this other lunatic. You have to admit you have been under a lot of strain. I mean, no wonder if you're emotionally fragile."

I felt like I couldn't get my breath. "Dan said I was emotionally fragile?"

Silence.

"Steve? Is that what Dan said? That I'm emotionally fragile?"

Steve said in an uncomfortable rush, "I think he's worried, Sean. I mean, we all are. But… Dan especially."

"What else did he say?" I had hung the phone up too quickly last night. No wonder Maria and Markowitz were giving me funny looks this morning.

"That you —" He bit it off.

"That I *what?* Jesus! Tell me what the fuck he said!"

Steve spoke like the words were being dragged out of him one at a time. "He thought that maybe we should talk to you together. Convince you to get yourself admitted to UCLA's Neuropsychiatric Hospital."

I felt like gravity suddenly slipped and I was about to float off into space.

The Neuropsychiatric Hospital at UCLA is a facility for patients who require medical assistance in stabilizing acute emotional psychiatric crisis. Residential treatment. Supervised activity from eight a.m. to eight p.m. Deck time and occupational therapy and exercise and medication. It's a great hospital. I know. I once spent nine months there.

There was a weird humming in my ears. I wondered if I was going to make a habit of fainting.

My mouth was so dry I could hardly get the words out. "He wants to have me committed?"

"No! God, no. He wants it to be voluntary. Voluntary hospitalization, you know. Just for rest and observation."

I swallowed so hard he must have heard it all the way in West Hollywood because he said quickly, "Like before. The second time, I mean, when you went in yourself for a—a rest."

"I don't need a rest. I need to get back to work."

"We all want what's best for you, Sean."

I wanted to scream at that kind, noncommittal tone. He sounded like Dan at his most aggravating. I said as calmly as I could, "You've known me a long time, Steve. Do you think I need to be hospitalized? Do I seem irrational?" I had to fight to keep my voice even, in case I sounded as irrational as Dan apparently thought I was. "Do I seem like a danger to myself or anyone else?"

"Shit, no!" he said quickly and loyally. But then he said, "But I'm not living with you, Sean. Dan sees a different side, I guess."

I said tightly, "If anyone is crazy, it's Dan."

He said, "Hey, he never used the C-word."

"Yeah, they're not supposed to," I retorted. "It's not politically correct."

He did laugh at that, an unwilling snort of a laugh. "Well, you sound normal enough. Normal for you, anyway."

"I'm going to have this out with Dan," I said. "I'm tired of his —" I bit the rest of it off. Despite Dan's betrayal whatever happened between us was still none of Steve's business. "You can tell Bruce that he's got his Laurie," I said.

"Is Dan going to go for that?"

"Dan doesn't have a say in this."

"Okay," Steve said doubtfully. "Maybe I'll wait to tell Bruce 'til you talk to Dan, though."

"Tell Bruce I'm in," I said tersely. "I'll deal with Dan."

"Uh, sure, sure. But call me after you talk to him. I just…want to make sure you're — well, just call me."

"I'll call you."

I hung up and went downstairs. "I need some fresh air," I told Markowitz. "I want to go for a run on the beach."

"Not a good idea," he said.

"You'll be with me. I'll be fine. I can't stay cooped up here all day."

"Easiest thing in the world for someone to take you out with a scope and a high-powered rifle."

Maria dropped a cup on the granite countertop.

The smash of china barely registered. I said, "This guy doesn't want to take me out long-distance, or he'd have done it days ago. Whatever he's planning, it's going to be personal delivery."

I waited for Markowitz to deliver his verdict. Waited to see if I was, in fact, already in protective custody.

Markowitz considered. He shrugged. "You're the boss."

Wobbly with relief, I went upstairs, changed into running shoes, met Markowitz on the deck.

"Here's the deal," he said. "If anything happens — and I mean *anything* — you go into the water. You go out as far as you safely can, and you stay there until I give the all clear."

I nodded, doing a few warming lunges, while I listened.

"If you hear me whistle —" He paused to whistle once, sharply. "Same deal. You go into the water and wait there."

I nodded and took off running.

It felt good to give my anger this physical release. I needed time and I needed distance before I confronted Dan. I didn't want to overreact. I realized that whatever he had said to Steve had been said out of concern for me. He cared for me; I didn't doubt that for a moment.

He wanted to shield me — whether from a bullet or a breakdown. He had been *hired* to protect me. So it would be a little ungrateful to be angry at him for doing that very thing now, especially since he felt he had a personal stake in my well-being.

My feet pounded the sand, my muscles burned. I ran faster, stretching out, trying to out- distance the thing I couldn't possibly outrun.

I was afraid I was losing it; so why did Dan's fear feel like such a betrayal?

Why did I expect him to have faith in me when I didn't have faith in myself?

Sweat stung my eyes. I slowed, stopped. Wiped my face with my sweatshirt front.

Markowitz was huffing and puffing a few yards behind, keeping an unhappy eye on the hillside above us. I realized that I was making his job a lot harder than it had to be.

I could imagine what Dan would have to stay about this stunt. He'd probably program the guys in the white coats into speed dial.

"I'm starting back," I called. Markowitz nodded, his relief plain, although I thought that was more about his heart exploding than my safety.

Turning, I started back toward the house at a lope.

Why the hell did I care so much what Dan thought? Dan had been wrong. Twice. He had been wrong about there being no threat to my safety, and he was wrong about me. Maybe I wasn't as calm and courageous as he'd be if someone was stalking him, but I wasn't losing my grip on reality. I was still operational, still firing on most of my cylinders.

For the first time I considered what would happen if I did collapse again. Would my parents be made my legal guardians? God help me. Or would I be placed in some kind of conservatorship? I'd been focused for so long on staying well and strong that the possibility had never occurred to me. I remembered Steve's joke about my will.

Not so funny, really.

I took the steps to the deck fast, went inside, not hearing whatever Maria said to me, and headed upstairs to Dan's office.

I told myself it was my house and I had a right to search for anything I felt I needed to search for — but it still felt about one step lower than Bunny spiking Ralph's drinks in *The*

Charioteer. I opened the top drawer of Dan's desk; it wasn't locked and I felt another stab of shame. Either he had nothing to hide or he trusted me to respect his privacy.

What had he said about having a few trust issues of his own? I guess the soup du jour was betrayal all around.

I shuffled briefly through his mail. A couple of utility bills and a credit card statement. I scanned the charges. Nothing ominous — although I winced at the small fortune he'd paid for that Ella Fitzgerald record.

I told myself I should drop it right then and there.

Instead I opened the deep side drawer and hit pay dirt. Inside the drawer was a large clear plastic bag containing postcards. My hand shook as I lifted it out. Three postcards. I turned the bag over. In Paul Hammond's spidery writing were the usual threats: *You'll be sorry; I haven't forgotten;* and, chillingly, *Time is up.*

Paul Hammond's hand and this week's postmark. But Hammond was dead. Had been dead for over two weeks now.

Cold sweat broke out over my body.

Dan could have shot Lenny Norman believing he was helping me out, removing an obstacle from my path. Norman had been killed by a 9 mm and Dan carried a 9 mm.

Nausea welled in my throat.

But then reason reasserted itself.

Dan had been home with me Monday night.

And if Dan was my stalker, he would certainly have locked this drawer. And more to the point, if he was stalking me, he'd have made sure I got the cards. Not much point in hiding them from me if he were the one trying to terrorize me.

In this five seconds Sean isn't the best judge of what he needs.

Sick horror gave way to rage. He had hidden these cards from me, and whatever his reason had been, he'd no right to do such a thing. He had lied to me. Pretended there was no threat. Allowed me to believe that it was all in my head.

He had withheld evidence.

I sat down at his desk and picked up the phone. I dialed his cell. He answered right away.

"Chief."

He sounded so normal. Like he was simply glad to hear from me and hadn't a secret in the world.

I had to steady my voice before I could get the words out.

"Can you come home?"

"What's wrong?"

"I need to talk to you."

"Where's Markowitz? Is everything all right?"

"Everything's fine. When can you get here?"

He did some mental calculations. "It'll take me about an hour."

"I'll see you in an hour," I said and hung up.

§ § § §

He was home in fifty-five minutes.

Lost in thought, I was startled when I heard the front door. Heard Dan's deep tones and Maria's lighter ones. Heard his footsteps on the stairs, coming down the hall. He started to walk past his office, then looked inside. He seemed puzzled to find me sitting at his desk.

"What are you doing in here? What's going on?"

"You tell me."

He looked confused. Not guilty. Not wary. Just confused. "What's wrong?"

"I had a talk with Steve. He said they've found a new director for *The Charioteer*, and if I want the part of Laurie, it's mine."

Dan's blue eyes studied my face. "So that's good news, right?"

"Yeah, I guess. Do you think I'm well enough to take the part?"

He said slowly, "Do you think you're well enough?"

"Yes. I do."

He considered me for a long moment. "Then what's the problem?"

"Did you tell Steve that I wasn't well enough to work?"

"Hell, no."

That caught me off guard. I didn't expect him to lie about it. I expected him to simply say what he obviously thought, that I needed to be locked up in a psych ward as soon as conveniently possible.

"You didn't tell him that I was emotionally fragile?"

His face changed. "I might have asked him to go easy on fanning your fears about Paul Hammond."

"You used the term 'emotionally fragile'?"

"I may have," his tone was guarded — obviously not wanting to rile the maniac too much.

"Did you tell Steve that the two of you should try to convince me to check myself into UCLA's Neuropsychiatric Hospital?"

"Huh?" He looked utterly taken aback. "Of course not."

"You didn't try to get Steve to pull an intervention with you?"

"Are you serious?"

"Yes, I'm serious. Steve said that you told him that I was ill and needed to be hospitalized. Voluntarily if possible."

"I don't know what the hell Steve is playing at, but I never said anything like that. Ever."

"Are you saying Steve lied?"

"Are you saying I would?"

I'd expected him to waffle a bit; claim that maybe Steve had misunderstood, although as far as I could tell Steve had got it right in every way that counted.

"*Steve* has no reason to lie."

I could see that hurt him; his face went stony.

"Come on, Sean. Steve is jealous as hell of you — and he plays you like a pro." And as though that weren't enough of a red flag flapping in my face, he added flatly, "And for the record, if I thought you needed to be hospitalized, I wouldn't waste time calling Steve for back up or trying to talk you into it."

I was so mad I could hardly get the words out without stuttering. "Now *that* I believe, you arrogant son of a bitch!" Dan's eyes turned arctic-blue. Hard to believe I'd ever seen them warm with tenderness or alight with laughter. "You want to explain this?" I hurled the plastic bag of post cards at him. He caught them one-handed, barely glancing at the bag.

"You went through my desk?"

His contempt made me defiant. "Hey, it's *my* house. And technically it's *my* desk."

He went so still he didn't appear to be breathing, and yet, despite the silence I heard something shatter. I didn't let myself stop to consider what I was doing; that I was deliberately destroying something that might be irreplaceable. I just kept sweeping the counters and letting the valuables smash on the floor.

"Saturday, Monday and Tuesday, but I never saw them. You want to explain that to me?"

All at once he was totally calm. "Why don't you tell me what you think it means?"

I said, "I think you had Maria take them out of the mail when you weren't here to grab them first."

"That's right." Zero apology or guilt.

"How the hell dare you?"

He snorted. "'How the hell *dare* I?' You sound like a B-movie. I'll tell you how the hell I dared. You were coming apart at the seams. I tried to protect you — if only from yourself."

Well, there was pretty much the confirmation I was looking for. He might not have phrased things exactly the way Steve remembered, but the intent seemed to be the same.

"I didn't ask you to protect me!"

"What are you talking about? It's my job to protect you!"

"Then," I cried. "Before we were together. Not *now*. Not once we —" I couldn't finish it because whatever we had been, it was ending now. Even if I'd wanted to pull out of this tailspin, it was too late. Our relationship was crashing and burning in front of us.

"Kid, you've got some weird ideas of what happens when people get together."

He had developed a knack for pushing all the wrong buttons.

"Like you're an expert on relationships?"

He opened his mouth and then bit back whatever he started to say. Unreasonably, his restraint further goaded me.

I sneered, "I don't have your experience, that's for sure. And I don't want it."

"Yeah, that came through loud and clear."

Not like I hadn't asked for that one, but all at once the heat went out of my anger. I felt numb. I said, "What else did you lie about? Obviously Hammond isn't dead, is he? I'm still getting postcards from him."

"The postcards aren't from Hammond," he said with acrid satisfaction. "I didn't lie about him being dead or about getting the cards analyzed. The writing isn't his. It's not even that good of a forgery."

"Then who sent them?"

"I'm not sure. Yet."

It took a second for that to register. He didn't say he didn't *know*, he said he wasn't *sure*. So he thought he knew. He had a suspect. Another piece of information he wouldn't be sharing because he didn't trust me with the truth. The arrogant son of a bitch actually believed that "protecting" me meant keeping me in a state of blissful ignorance. Only ignorance wasn't bliss. It was dangerous.

"Really? I thought you had all the answers."

Dan said wearily, "I thought I had one or two of them figured out. I guess not."

I understood that we were no longer talking about Steve or Hammond. My chest rose and fell as though I'd raced to get to this moment with Dan, and now here we stood with a chasm growing wider and wider between us. I could feel the ring he'd bought me resting on my breast bone like a weight on my heart.

I heard myself say, "I guess it's over."

I waited for him to say something. Anything.

He said nothing. His eyes never wavered from mine.

"I can't be with someone I don't trust. And I can't trust someone who doesn't trust me."

To my amazement he laughed. Not a very pleasant laugh, granted.

His gaze moved deliberately from the plastic bag of postcards to the desk I had searched. "I can see that might be a problem."

Heat flooded my face.

Dan shrugged. "You got one thing right. It's over."

Chapter Seven

I watched the Sebring crest the hilltop and wind down the road leading to the beach house. The car disappeared from sight.

I checked my watch. Four-thirty. Steve was late as usual. He'd be late to his own funeral.

Over the distant crash of waves I heard the faint slam of a car door and my nerves tightened. Show time.

I caught a glimpse of a blue shirt and the top of his head as he hurried along the side of the deck. He started up the stairs, checking when he noticed me sitting at the patio table.

"Dude! What are you doing out here?"

"Waiting for you."

"Yeah? Well, I got here as soon as I could." He glanced past me toward the open glass door. "So where is everybody?"

"Maria's gone for the day. Markowitz was recalled." I shrugged. "With Hammond dead, the cops didn't want to waste anymore of the taxpayer's money."

"How weird is that?" Steve shook his head. "I mean, to think he was dead the whole time." He eyed me speculatively. "But what about Lenny Norman's murder?"

"It wasn't connected. The cops are holding his neighbor."

"So it's just us? Dan really is gone?"

"Yep. That's over." I drained my glass. My hand shook a little and I watched him note it. The pain was real and raw; I couldn't hide it, but I couldn't let myself think about it for even a moment.

"Is he going to be stopping by later to pick his junk up?"

I shook my head. It had seemed like Dan's stuff was everywhere, but it had taken him exactly seventeen efficient minutes to collect his things. He'd left nothing but his fingerprints. He sure as hell hadn't left any excuse for coming back.

Straddling the bench across from me, Steve smiled that guileless smile I knew so well. The smile he wore when things had gone well at the race track.

"Shit, man. Just like that? True, I can't pretend I ever liked the guy, but I know you…" Despite the smile he couldn't bite back, his mournful brown eyes looked sadder than ever. "How are you doing?"

"Not good." He rose, reaching for my empty glass, and I added, "Not bad enough to do a Norman Maine."

He laughed at the *A Star is Born* reference and went inside the house. It took him about four minutes. When he came back he had refilled my glass and poured himself a beer.

"So…what happened?" He handed me my glass.

I took it and set it down on the table. "I asked him whether he had talked to you about getting me committed."

"He never used the word 'committed,'" Steve said, as though — in fairness to Dan — it was really important to keep this point straight.

"Yeah, that's what he said. In fact, he said he never had any such discussion with you at all."

"What's he going to say?" Steve asked reasonably.

"True."

"So he just denied everything?"

"Pretty much. He admitted he asked you to stop encouraging me to believe Hammond was still out there."

"Threatened me is more like it," Steve said.

"Really?"

"He wanted to keep you in a bubble," Steve said. "Like it was just you two and nobody else existed. That's not healthy."

He glanced at my untouched glass.

I said, "He also admitted he was having Maria pick up the threatening postcards each day before I could see them."

"Ah," Steve said. "Makes sense."

"Does it?" I grinned twistedly. "I thought for sure you were going to suggest that he might be the one sending them."

He met my eyes. "So you have considered that possibility?"

"For about three seconds. It wouldn't make a lot of sense for him to head off his own death threats."

"Oh. Right. But I don't know if he was exactly *balanced* in his feelings for you. I mean, think about how possessive he was. And controlling. And way over-protective."

I reached up, automatically touching the ring on the chain around my neck. Steve's eyes followed my hand.

"I guess I just never trusted the guy," he said.

"I guess it was mutual."

He stared. "What do you mean?"

"You said he threatened you."

"Oh. Yeah."

He glanced at my drink again.

I asked, "So when do I start work on the film?"

"The...film?"

"*The Charioteer*. What did Bruce say when you told him I was in?"

"Well, actually, I didn't get a chance to call him yet. I'll phone him tomorrow."

I said, "It's almost funny. I see this direct parallel between the characters in *The Charioteer* and what happened with Dan and me.

Steve blinked. "Yeah?"

"Yeah. In the book, Laurie keeps getting angry because Ralph keeps trying to fix things for him, but the truth is, Laurie is the one who sets that dynamic up. He turns to Ralph every time he has a problem. He knows how Ralph is. So why does he get so angry when Ralph tries to protect him?"

"Uh, dude, I have no clue what you're talking about." His eyes traveled to the lounge chair and the marked-up copy of *The Charioteer* script. "So which one offs himself?"

"What?"

"I read the scene in the script where the one guy is reading the other guy's suicide note."

"Oh." My smile felt like it was on crooked. "Things aren't always what they seem."

"You got that right." He held his beer out to me, and said, "Well, here's to not looking back." He nodded at my moisture-beaded glass, and I picked it up. He clinked the rim of his mug against my glass, and drank.

I watched the muscles in his throat move as he swallowed. I could remember kissing his throat — he had this way of throwing his head back when he laughed. I could vaguely recall what his mouth felt like on me, although those memories faded next to the vividness of my memories of Dan.

I said, "Like, for example, I can pretty much tell when someone is acting. Dan wasn't acting. You are."

Steve lowered his mug. Beer slopped out the top. "What's that supposed to mean?"

I thought I had myself pretty well under control, but heat suffused my body and my heart began to slug against my ribs in hard measured punches; I felt breathless with something akin to stage fright. "Can we just cut the bullshit?" I requested.

His eyes narrowed.

"You want to know where you first slipped?" I didn't wait for his answer. He didn't look like he would have one anytime soon. "It was that crack about changing my will. I haven't thought about my will since I first made it out — back when we were living together."

Steve gave a strange laugh. Hey, dude, don't go psycho on *me*, okay?"

"Up until the bit with the will you'd been pretty subtle."

"You really are losing it, Sean. Dan's right."

"Dan was right about one thing," I said. "You do know how to play me. You know just what buttons to push, what triggers my self-doubt. And there was always just enough truth in what you said. But you way overshot the mark with that story about Dan wanting me to check into UCLA."

Steve seemed to struggle with himself. Apparently the desire to show me how smart he was, won out. "You wouldn't take a hint," he said. "You hardly knew the guy but you were so goddamn stubborn about him."

I stared. I knew Steve so well. I knew everything from how he took his coffee to the sounds he made during sex. And it turned out that I didn't know him at all.

"You had to know he was going to deny it."

"So?" He smiled, spreading his arms. "He denied it, but here we are. I guess you believed it on some level. Maybe not for long, but long enough."

I swallowed hard. The truth was a bitter pill.

"How did he take it, by the way? You didn't really say. Was he iron-jawed and dignified, or did he cry?"

Stern and silent, actually, but I wasn't going to discuss Dan with Steve. Not now, not ever. I said, "Once I finally accepted that Hammond had been dead the whole time, I started thinking about who had a reason to want me out of the way. I remembered your comment about the will — and then I remembered that the will was still in your favor."

"I guess the fact that you never changed it says something," he said lightly.

We were silent for a moment.

"Why, Steve?" I asked finally.

He didn't speak, didn't look at me.

"Is it just for the money? Because I would have given you the goddamn money."

He rose then, shaking the table. He walked over to the railing, bracing both hands on it, staring out at the blue dazzle of the water. "No. It wasn't just the money. Not like you think. I got in deep. Too deep. I owe over four hundred grand in gambling debts — to people who don't understand installment plans."

"F-four *hundred* grand?" I said. "You owe almost half a million in gambling debts? How the hell did you manage that?"

"Easier than you think. I convinced people I was good for it. Actually, I convinced them that *you* were good for it."

"Why didn't you stop? When you were like...I don't know...eighty grand in? Why didn't you come to me for help?"

"How could I? Besides, I thought I could win it back. I thought my luck would change. It always changes sooner or later."

"Jesus Christ, Steve!"

"Don't be so self-righteous," he said hotly. "It's an illness — compulsive gambling. Like alcoholism. It's not like I could control it. You of anybody ought to understand about that kind of illness."

Was I supposed to feel sorry for him? Because it was hard to feel much of anything other than bewilderment.

"And one of the symptoms was you planned to kill me and inherit my trust fund?"

He looked me right in the eyes and said, "I never wanted that. Never. You're all I've got. I love you. I do. But...it's you or me, Sean. And I don't want to die."

I said, "I know the feeling."

He reached behind himself and pulled out a gun. I was willing to bet it was a 9 mm semiautomatic. He came back to the table and sat down. Meeting my gaze, he gave me a sad lopsided smile.

Bitterly, I said, "Why the big charade? Why the postcards and killing my neighbor's dog? Why not just shoot me on the deck one afternoon?"

"Because as soon as your will was read I'd have been the cop's number one suspect."

"You got the idea when Hammond's body didn't turn up."

"That's right. That was what originally gave me the idea. I realized that if Hammond had killed you, my problems would have been over. And when they couldn't find his body, I thought maybe if something happened to you, it would be blamed on Hammond."

"So you created the illusion that Hammond was still out there."

"It was easier than I expected. I still had copies of those first letters he sent you. So I just faked the postcards."

The idea he wanted me dead was bad enough, but the deliberate cruelty of sending those cards shook me.

"What did you do, hire some asshole who looked like Hammond to follow me around? Yeah, you did. And that's why the fake Hammond never really did or said anything to threaten me."

He got a weird look on his face. He didn't reply.

"Or was that *you?*"

"No."

I stared at him, and then I realized what I was seeing in his eyes.

"Did you… " I swallowed hard. "Jesus. He's dead, isn't he? That's why he disappeared again."

He said with macabre cheerfulness, "He asked one too many questions."

I absorbed this and realized that I was going to have to give up any hope of talking Steve out of killing me.

"So what was Plan B?" I asked. "If you pushed hard enough I might have another breakdown and hopefully do the job myself."

"If you had another breakdown and…did yourself, that would be like your choice." He was reasoning with me as though he believed he could somehow make me see it from his point of view. "I mean, you could have a breakdown a few years from now and off yourself and it wouldn't help anyone — whereas this way you'd be saving my life."

"But Dan kept running interference."

"Yep."

I owed Dan an apology.

I glanced down at my drink, the ice melted in the glass. "So what happens if I drink this?"

"You just go to sleep," he said earnestly. "Very peacefully and naturally. There's no pain or anything. Your heart just stops. That would be the best way. I don't want to…" he glanced down at the gun lying between us, and swallowed.

"Why not? You shot Hammond's double. You killed Lenny Norman, right?"

His eyes did this queer little flickery thing, like his brain was short-circuiting. But before I had time to react, he smiled, once more in control. "Lenny Norman was an asshole. I thought you might actually appreciate that one."

Years of training, but I couldn't quite control my expression, and reading my face, Steve said thickly, "I thought for sure that would be the end of that damned film. And I figured that might tip you over the edge — you were so obsessed about that role. But it was...bad. He begged me..."

"My God, Steve." I put my hand over my eyes, and then remembered I needed to keep watch on him. "Think about what you've done."

"I know exactly what I've done, and we both know I can't go back now. Look, I don't want to hurt you, Sean. Just drink the stuff and...go to sleep."

I stared into his eyes. This was *Steve*. Steve whom I had known forever. My partner, my friend, my former lover. I just couldn't seem to wrap my mind around it. Maybe because I didn't want to. I picked up the glass. "You know what? You're right. Living is overrated. Between you and Dan — I am a little tired." I put the glass to my lips and his eyes flared with — surprise? Excitement? Fear? Maybe he didn't know himself.

Wet touched my lips and I paused. "But you do know, Dan isn't going to believe this suicide scenario. Not unless I leave some kind of a note."

He hesitated, glanced toward the house, and I chucked the glass with all my strength at his head. It connected with a satisfying thunk and he fell out of his chair, nearly taking the table with him. As he collapsed, he grabbed for the gun, which went off with a bang, taking a chunk out of the railing a few inches to my left. *Jeeeeesus.*

I hopped up from my chair, wiping my mouth with my arm. I hadn't swallowed anything but who knew what the hell he'd laced my drink with.

"God damn you, Sean!"

His fury triggered a hysterical laugh. He was angry because I was trying to stay alive. And *I* was the crazy one?

Jumping from the deck, I hit the sand and sprinted for the side of the house, yelling, "Markowitz, where the hell are you?"

I slammed into a wall. A wall of hard muscle and bone and warm flesh. The wall reached out and steadied me. Dan. I blinked up at him dazedly. With his free hand he was holding a gun. Definitely not a movie prop.

Without a change of expression he put me behind him and trained the gun on Steve who had paused at the stairs of the deck.

"Freeze, Krieger."

Steve stared down in disbelief. Blood trickled from a cut in his hairline.

"What are *you* doing here?"

"Drop the gun." Dan ordered, adding, "Or I'll blow your fucking head off." Which was probably not LAPD-approved script.

Steve hesitated. I could see him running his options, weighing the risk, figuring his odds: always the gambler.

Dan was like a statue; he didn't flick an eyelash, didn't move a muscle. He was ready and waiting — and despite the fact that Steve had wanted me dead, had cold-bloodedly plotted and planned for that very thing — I couldn't take the idea of seeing his head blown off. I croaked, "Please, Steve…"

I spotted Markowitz edging behind the railing on the other side of the deck, his own weapon drawn.

Steve's eyes met mine over Dan's shoulder. He laughed the old Steve laugh and dropped his gun. It landed on the sand with a dull sound.

"Hey, what the hell." He held his hands out. "Book 'em, Danno!"

Dan went up the stairs, shoved Steve back into the table hard, and while Steve was picking himself back up, jammed his gun in his back waistband and took out a pair of handcuffs. Markowitz joined him a moment later.

"So it was a trap," Steve said, trying to look over his shoulder at me. "You knew and you set me up?"

"It's called acting," I said.

Dan's eyes met mine briefly. Blue and bleak. I had no idea what he was doing there — I had set my "trap" with Markowitz's assistance — but I was glad to see him.

The wail of sirens floated in the distance.

Steve was still trying to make eye contact. He said urgently, "Hey, Sean. I'm sorry, man. If there had been another way…"

My throat closed up, choking off anything I could have said — if I'd had anything to left to say.

"Very touching, asshole," Dan growled.

§ § § §

"When did you know?" I asked Dan.

The sheriffs had come and gone, taking Steve with them. Markowitz had followed shortly after, and it was just Dan and me now. Past that adrenaline overdrive, I felt a little numb and a lot shaky. I'd have given anything for a hug from Dan, but there were no hugs forthcoming. Dan looked like Dan, but there was a force field around him that even the Starcatz would have trouble neutralizing.

"That Steve was planning to kill you?" His smile was humorless. "I knew for sure this afternoon. That bullshit story of his — the only possible reason for that was to play on your insecurities and distrust. To drive enough of a wedge between us that either you would send me away or I'd get fed up and leave."

"He was running out of time," I said. "It made him desperate."

"And stupid."

"I need a drink," I said, and went to the bar. I poured myself a Bushmills. Dan's whiskey. Apparently the one and only reminder of his brief stay in my life. "Did you want something?"

Anything?

"No."

I could see the tiny lines of weariness around his blue eyes and unsmiling mouth, but he didn't sit down, and he didn't take his jacket off. He wasn't staying. He didn't want anything I had to offer.

I tossed back the whiskey, welcoming the burn in the back of my throat. It distracted me from the burn at the back of my eyes. That wasn't going to get me anywhere. It would just embarrass us both.

Refilling my glass, I said, "But you already suspected Steve, didn't you? That's what you meant today when you said you weren't sure who was sending the postcards."

Eyes on my glass, he said, "You were right about the odds of attracting two aggressive stalkers in such a short space of time; so I knew after Hammond's body turned up that I needed to look for someone with another motive for getting rid of you. Steve fit the bill."

I forced myself to meet his gaze. It was hard because, as I feared, there was nothing in his eyes. No emotion. "Thank you," I said. "You saved my life."

He shook his head. "I was just tagging along. It was Markowitz's show — and yours."

"Markowitz told you —?"

"He thought I'd be interested. He thought I had a right to know."

There was no accusation in his voice, but I knew that he was sore about that. I took a deep breath.

"Dan, I owe you an apology."

"You don't owe me anything," he said flatly. He looked at his watch. "If you're okay now, I've got some place to be."

"I'm okay."

If he walked out that door I was never going to be okay again.

I set my glass down and followed him through the rooms to the front door. Hand on the door knob, he paused.

"That reminds me." He pulled his keys out and began to work one off the ring.

"Don't." The word startled me. Startled him. I said, trying for lightness, trying to hide the desperation, "There's no hurry, right?"

"And no reason to stall, right?" He smiled — and he was either a better actor than me or he really didn't give a damn. He handed the key to me, and like a little kid I put my hands behind my back.

"I don't want it."

He reached around me, took my hand and pulled it forward. Not roughly, but not playing. He pressed the key into my palm.

"The truth is, I never had this." He folded my fingers around the bite of cool metal. "You were never open to me. Not really."

He turned, opened the door and I reached past him, slamming it shut.

"So...saving my life...that wasn't anything personal. That's just your job, right?"

I couldn't read the expression in his eyes, but his voice was level. "Right. It's my job. And wrong. Of course it's personal. Of course I still have feelings for you. But the bottom line is, it didn't work between us." He shrugged.

The shrug hurt more than the words — and the words hurt plenty. Mouth dry, I said, "I want to be open to you. If you'll show me how."

He said very gently, "You're still acting, Sean."

It was like taking a hard and unexpected fall. The air seemed to slam out of my lungs. "I'm not."

"Sean..." He sighed.

I said quickly, "You're going to say it won't change anything. And I guess that's true, but I want to make love to you. One last time. And for the first time."

He said, still trying to be kind, "It wasn't about sex, Sean. It was about intimacy."

"And intimacy is about trust. I do get that, Dan." I controlled my voice. "I still want my first time to be with you."

His eyes flickered.

We were close enough that I could feel his heat, feel the warmth of his breath fanning my face. I held his gaze with mine and I could see the darkness there, the hunger.

Into his silence, I whispered, "Isn't ex sex supposed to be the best?"

He put his hand behind my head and pulled me forward, his mouth hard on my own. It was a grinding kiss, an angry kiss, the bump of teeth and the smear of lips. I closed my eyes and opened to him, and almost at once he gentled. We breathed in balmy moist unison until at last he broke contact.

He said softly, "You're too good an actor, Sean."

"You're not being fair to either of us." I found his hand and put it on my crotch. "I'm not that good. I want you." He felt me over, and I strained against his hand, craving his touch through the stiff material of my jeans. "Do I have to beg? I will."

Sick, shameless pervert, said my father's contemptuous voice next to my ear. I closed my ears to that memory, focused on Dan's face. It was a handsome face, but I loved the strength and caring and intelligence more than the trick of bone structure and coloring.

I loved *him*.

My hands went to my fly, and then I rethought that and reached for his. And Dan bit off a sound that could have been a laugh or maybe just impatience, and undid the button at my waist. He pulled, and the buttons popped through the denim, one by one. His big hands, warm and knowledgeable, slid inside my jeans, fastened on my hips.

I pulled his Levis down and his boxers, and his dick sprang free, ready and willing, regardless of whatever his brain was telling him.

"You don't have to beg," Dan said, acknowledging what we both knew to be true.

"Bedroom?" I asked hopefully.

He nodded, and then he was pulling his shirt over his head. I stepped out of my jeans, kicked off my boxers, and preceded him into the soft gloom of the bedroom, bouncing down on the bed.

I reached for him and he lowered himself beside me.

I was braced for his resentment to play out in roughness or haste, but Dan took his time kissing and caressing every inch of my body: His tongue scraped my nipple in pleasurable chafing, a fingertip lightly scratching the back of my knee; he brushed his nose against mine in a child's Eskimo kiss. I smiled and sighed and relaxed, kissing him back when he'd let me, stroking his lean hard flanks and sides.

"Please..." I whispered. I didn't finish it. Even I wasn't sure what I was really asking. His leaving had left me empty, aching. I wanted to fill that emptiness with memories if nothing else.

At last he helped me over onto my belly. I ignored the tightening in my gut — partly anxiety but mostly desire — and spread my legs. There was no going back now, and I wouldn't if I could have. This was as much for me as for him.

The slide of the drawer, the squirt of the lube. I shivered convulsively as he worked warm lube between my ass cheeks. His finger delicately pierced me. I moaned at the strangely familiar invasion.

He paused. "It's not necessary, Sean. You don't have to prove anything."

"Want to..." I wriggled back against his hand, trying to force him to action.

"Why?" He didn't so much as twitch his finger.

I groaned. "Dan, why are we *talking?*"

"Because I need to understand what's really happening here." I heard the pain in his voice, and it startled me. If I could still hurt him, then on some plane he still cared for me.

I swallowed hard. "I'm trying to tell you. Trying to show you. I love you. I want to share this with you. Even if it's...too late for you." I pushed back against finger. "Please give me this."

He moved his finger again, and I caught my breath. His oily thumb lightly stroked across the sensitive mouth of my hole.

"Keep breathing," he said.

I whimpered as his thumb pressed in. He massaged, pushed a little deeper, rubbed some more.

"Relax."

I tried. I concentrated on loosening my muscles. The tip of his other thumb slid in and he used both to massage me strongly, widening my entrance. My breaths came in shallow pants as he prepared me. He was tender, but very thorough; I'd said I'd wanted it, and he was taking me at my word. It was intense and invasive, and seemed to go on forever.

My stomach muscles were quivering, and my legs felt like jelly by the time he withdrew.

"That didn't hurt, did it?"

I shook my head. I didn't think I could manage my voice. I rolled over onto my back, and tucked my legs up neatly.

He leaned over me, and his mouth found one of my nipples. He tongued it, wet heat turning the tip to a hard point. Distantly I felt the pressure from the blunt head of his shaft building at the entrance of my body, but more immediate was the tease of his lips as he moved to my other nipple. His teeth closed delicately on the bud, and I writhed beneath him, aching for more.

It was almost a relief when the pressure on my hole built to a distracting pain — and then, staggeringly, I felt my body's resistance give.

Dan's cock slipped past the tight ring of muscle. Nerves and muscles spasmed. He was inside me.

"Okay?" He seemed to have trouble squeezing even that one word out.

I gulped and nodded. And I *was* okay. My shivering body was already adjusting to that thickness. I wasn't tearing apart. I was still whole. Still me. I could still breathe. I could still move...

Dan's thighs tightened in response, and he thrust against me, just once. "Don't move yet," he gasped. His hands continued to stroke and smooth my belly, my ass.

Wonderingly I reached down and touched where our bodies were joined. We were like some astonishing mythological creature — not the monster my parents pictured, but something very old and powerful. I felt wrapped in the wings of an unexpectedly sweet revelation.

"How's that?" Dan's voice sounded strained.

"H-hey, it's not bad," I said.

He laughed shakily at the wonder in my voice and cautiously began to rock his hips against me. It was a relief to give up all control and just feel, just let it happen, just ride it out.

Not bad? It was actually pretty damn good.

"That's it," he breathed. "Just let go."

I looked into his face. It was too dark to read his eyes, and I wanted to watch his eyes while he took me. He was pounding me harder now. I began to move too. Awkwardly. My fists clenched on the comforter. Dan's hands slid under my ass and he lifted me up, shoving a pillow beneath my hips.

The changed angle sent a jolt of sheer exquisite feeling surging through me.

What the hell was *that?*

I found my own rhythm, straining into the push and pull cadence of our bodies. I jerked out, "Dan…"

He pegged me over and over, deep, powerful thrusts. It went on and on, lightning strikes of pleasure — and who was it said lightning didn't strike the same place twice?

My fists relaxed back into hands, and I reached for Dan, stroking his sides, running my fingertips down his back, fondling whatever I could reach. Trying to tell him with touch that this wasn't an act, that there was no pretense here.

He murmured encouragement. His face bumped my face, his mouth closed over mine, hot and wet and urgent.

Dazed, I realized that he was going to make me come just like this. I didn't think that was possible.

At the same time Dan yelled my name, and I felt liquid seed pouring into me. I began to come, white hot waves shivering through my bones and muscles and nerves. It went on and on, like a supernova.

Then, from a long way away I felt Dan gathering me up against him, saying comforting things — like I would need to be reassured after that. I kissed him back dizzily. *Lights out*, I thought.

Fade to black — although it was more of a soft and restful gray.

"Was it everything you expected?" Dan asked when he got his breath back. His voice was a little dry, but his callused hand was warm on my bare skin, lazy and caressing.

Was it what I had expected? I felt wrung out, used up, boneless. I felt sated. Complete. And at the same time I felt naked and unprotected. But it was okay to be vulnerable with Dan's arms around me. I felt closer to him than I ever felt to anyone in my life.

I shook my head. I didn't begin to know how to answer him. I said, "Are you going to leave me, Dan?"

He licked his lips, like this was going to be a difficult thing to say.

I reached for him, and his arms came about me, loving and strong. "I'm sorry for not trusting you, for the stupid things I said, for everything," I said into his shoulder.

"Shhh. Listen, Sean, I let *you* down. I screwed up. I should have listened to you. I did think you were letting your fears get the better of you." He took a deep breath. "I did believe the strain was too much for you."

It was painful to hear; clearly it was equally painful for him to say.

"I guess it was," I admitted.

"No. You're second-guessing yourself now, but the fact is, your instincts were correct. I let my own fear affect my judgment — and ultimately put you at risk."

I could hear the guilt and regret in his voice. And what was the point of that? We had both made mistakes, both let each other down. Was the important stuff where we had failed each other or the parts where we had got it right? It felt to me like we had got a lot of it right a lot of the time.

I was afraid to ask, but I had to know. "Is it too late for us?"

After what felt like the longest moment of my life, he said almost inaudibly, "It's not too late."

I closed my eyes and pressed my face into his throat. I could barely hear him, but I felt the words against my mouth.

"It's not that easy to turn it on and off."

I said, "I don't have a lot of experience."

"Neither do I." He must have caught my surprise because he said, "Oh, I have experience at this —" He ran a light hand down my back, leaving goose bumps of sensation. "Not with loving someone. I've never even used the word before."

My throat closed up and I had to struggle against the bubble of emotion threatening to tear out of my chest. *Love.* He was right. That's what this was about.

I managed to get the words out. "So this was your first time too?"

"Yeah, I guess it was."

"Was it everything you expected?"

He turned his head on the pillow, and I saw the glimmer of his smile in the darkness.

Ghost of a Chance

I love ghost stories and tales of haunted houses — and I love studying the mystical and spiritualist movements of the early nineteenth century — so I was trying to find a way to combine those things. It didn't quite go the way I expected, but I like this story. I like the mood of it. It's just…for fun.

Chapter One

Like the philosophers say, the line between genius and stupidity is a fine one.

Actually, it wasn't the philosophers, it was Nigel in *Spinal Tap*, but the point is still a valid one. Which is why what seemed like a perfectly good idea at the time—namely, prying off the screen and crawling through the open window of Oliver de la Motte's front parlor —turned out to be a really bad decision.

It's not like I hadn't *tried* to use the key Oliver sent. I'd tried for about two minutes, turning the damn thing every possible way — not easy in the dark of three a.m., and not pleasant either with that clammy sea breeze on the back of my neck — and rustling the overgrown shrubs. Not that I'm the nervous type or I wouldn't hunt ghosts for a living — well, for a hobby. No one hunts ghosts for a living.

When I couldn't get the key to work I jumped off the porch and walked around the side of the house till I found an open window. Pulling out my pocket knife, I pried loose the screen, hoisted myself up and climbed through...

And that's when all hell broke loose.

Something rushed out of the darkness and tackled me around the waist, hurling me to the hardwood floor. The very hard wood floor. My tailbone, elbows and skull all connected painfully. My glasses went flying.

"Christ!" I yelped, trying to get away.

"Guess again," growled a deep voice.

Human.

Definitely human. And male. Definitely male. I was wrestling six feet or so of hard, lean male. *Naked* hard, lean male. Definitely not Oliver who is sixty-something and built like the Stay Puft Marshmallow Man. And no one else was supposed to be here. Was my assailant a burglar? A naked burglar? The guy had muscles like rocks — speaking of which: I brought my knee up hard.

His breath went out in an infuriated whoosh. His weight rolled off me. I rolled over and tried to crawl away, but the rug beneath me bunched up and slid my way. A small table crashed down just missing my head, and I heard glass smash on the floor.

"You little son of a bitch," said the burglar who was probably not a burglar, looming over me.

I tried to scoot away, but a knee jammed into my spine pinning me flat. He grabbed my right arm and yanked it back so hard I thought he'd dislocated it. The pain was unreal. I stopped fighting.

For a minute there was nothing but the ragged sound of our breathing in the darkness. Then he reached past me and turned on the table lamp.

I had a blurred view of a forest of scratched claw-foot furniture, miles of parquet floors and a herd of dust bunnies. I could make out my glasses a few feet away beneath a wide ottoman.

"I don't understand what's happening here." I got out.

"What part do you not understand?" he inquired grimly.

"Who *are* you?"

It must not have been the question he expected. "Who the hell are *you?*" He didn't ease up on my spine, but there was something in his tone…a hint of doubt beneath the hostility.

"Rhys Davies. I'm a…a friend of Oliver's."

He made a disgusted sound. "Yeah, you and every other cheap hustler in the greater metropolitan area—"

"Cheap hustler!" I'm sorry to say that came out sounding way too much like a squeak. The squeak factor was partly due to the fact that with every shallow breath I inhaled his hot-off-the-sheets scent. He'd had a shower before bed, and that sleepy soapy skin smell was even more alarming than the fear he was going to crack my vertebrae.

"Oh, sorry," he said, not sounding sorry at all. "Cheap is the wrong word. These things are never cheap."

"Things?" I repeated. "I'm not…you've got this all wrong."

"Is that right?" He seemed unimpressed.

I requested with an effort, "Could you ease up on my arm?"

He let go of my arm. It flopped weakly down. I flexed my fingers, surprised that they still seemed to work.

"What are you doing here?" he asked. "Oliver's out of town for the next month."

"I could ask you the same question."

"Yeah, but I asked first." He patted me down with brisk, impersonal efficiency. "If you're not one of Oliver's boy toys, what are you? Reporter? You're not a burglar, that's for sure."

And neither, obviously, was he. So who the hell was he?

"I told you who I am," I bit out. "I'm a friend of Oliver's. He invited me to stay."

His weight shifted off my back, and he ran his hands along the outside of my legs — then the inside. He seemed to know what he was doing, but it was invasive to say the least. "Ever hear of knocking?"

"I didn't know there was anyone to hear me knock. I tried my key — the key Oliver sent. It didn't work."

"*Your* key?" He felt over my crotch with what felt like unnecessary familiarity. And in a tone I didn't like, he said, "I see."

"Hey! Then what's with the Braille!" I recoiled as much as you can with two hundred plus pounds of beef pinning you to the floor.

He hesitated, but only an instant, before pulling my wallet out of my back pocket. He thumbed through it, taking his time.

"Rice Davies," he said.

"It's pronounced Reece," I retorted, muffledly. "Like in Reese's Pieces."

Now why had I said that?

Amusement threaded his voice as he continued, "Ten forty-five Oakmont Street in West Hollywood. You're a long way from home, *Reece*."

Yes, apparently I had turned left after The Outer Limits. "Can I get up?"

"Slowly."

He stepped out of range as I sat up, wincing. I looked up — a long way up. He was a big blur, I had an impression of dark hair, big shoulders narrowing to more darkness, and miles of long brown legs.

"Can I get my glasses?"

The blur stepped away, bent, retrieved my glasses and handed them to me.

I moved onto the settee and put them on. My hands were a little unsteady. I haven't been in many fights. Not that academia isn't a jungle, but generally we don't end up brawling on the floor.

The man now sitting on the giant ottoman across from me came into sharp focus. He was not entirely naked after all. He wore cotton boxers with little red and blue boating flags, thin cotton very white against the deep brown of his tanned skin.

He stared back at me with equal curiosity.

His black hair was unruly — which could have been the result of an impromptu wrestling match. His eyes were very green in his tanned face. His features were too harsh to be good-looking. He looked…mean. But he wasn't quite as burly as he'd seemed in the dark. About six feet of strong bones and hard muscle.

"You're Oliver's nephew," I guessed, rubbing my wrenched shoulder. "The cop."

Something changed in his expression, shuttered.

"Bright boy. That's right. Sam Devlin."

I didn't know what to say. This was an unwelcome development, to say the least.

"I didn't know you were staying here."

He cocked a dark brow. "I didn't know I needed your permission."

"It's just…I'm here to work."

"What did you have in mind?" he asked dryly.

I remembered the leisurely way he'd groped me earlier and felt an uncharacteristic heat in my face.

"I teach a course in paranormal studies at UCLA," I said. "I'm working on a book about ghost hunting along the

California coast. Oliver invited me to stay here for a few days while I researched Berkeley House."

I'm guessing most people never saw that particular expression on Sam Devlin's face. After a moment he closed his jaw sharply. He studied me with narrowed green eyes.

"Well, well," he said mildly. "A ghost buster."

I hate that term. I hate that movie. Well, okay, there are funny bits: Rick Moranis as Louis Tully is a scream — but really. Not good for the image.

"Parapsychology is a science," I said firmly.

"Yeah, weird science." He considered me without pleasure. "This oughta be cozy," he said finally. Planting his hands on his muscular thighs, he pushed up to his feet. "Okay, Mr. Pieces. I can't see anyone making up a story that dumb. Help yourself to one of the bedrooms. I'm upstairs on the left. There are clean sheets and towels in the cupboard at the end of the hall."

I stopped massaging my shoulder, gazing up at him doubtfully. "That's it? You're going to bed?"

"Did you have other plans, Professor?"

That was going to get old fast. I said a little sarcastically, "I thought you'd demand to see my teaching credential at the least."

He said through a yawn, "Is that what they call it these days? I think it can wait 'til morning." Heading for the hallway, he tossed over his shoulder, "Impressive though it may be."

I was treated to a final glimpse of his long brown legs vanishing up the staircase.

Chapter Two

A cheap hustler?

Now *that* was a first. Pretty funny, too. Sort of. C.K. — my ex — would have thought it was a riot.

After a moment or two, I pulled myself together and went outside to get my bags from my car.

The distant moon hung soft and fuzzy above the sharp tips of stiff and silent pine trees. I cut across the lawn, unlocked my car and hauled my laptop and suitcase out of the back of the Volvo, setting them on the gravel drive. I was re-locking the trunk when I caught a flicker of light out of the corner of my eye. I turned.

Beyond the tall wall of pine trees stood the cliffs overlooking the ocean. And on the cliffs perched Berkeley House. It looked like the illustration on the cover of a Hardy Boy's novel — or a smaller version of Cliff House near Ocean Beach, which was where C.K. and I had been dining when I first got the idea to write the book.

As I stared, light drifted across one of the upstairs windows.

I removed my glasses, wiped them, and looked again.

The house sat in total darkness. But as I watched, that eerie glow appeared once more in the corner room window on the second floor.

Interesting.

In ten years of researching the paranormal I'd never yet come across something that couldn't be explained by natural causes or human intervention. I had to admit, though, this looked pretty authentic. Not Marfa Lights; this illumination really did seem to be inside the house, hovering from window to window. Probably too powerful to be a flashlight beam — the house was about half a mile away. Maybe a reflection off the sea below, or some trick of moonlight? I was pretty damned tired, maybe I was dreaming....

Fascinated, I started walking toward Berkeley House, watching for that mysterious light. It seemed to float from window to window, then disappear — only to reappear on the other end of the house.

I rounded a bend in the road and the house vanished from view. I kept walking. The night smelled of the pines and the sea. It was quiet except for the sound of my footsteps on the dirt road; I was a city kid, and not used to that kind of quiet. It should have been nice. People always talk about the peace and quiet of the country, but it made me a little uneasy.

I looked back and Oliver's house was now lost to sight. The woods crowded in on me.

I shook off my disquiet, focused on my destination.

It couldn't be a coincidence — a physical manifestation practically the moment I arrived? But who, besides Oliver, knew I was coming to investigate Berkeley House? Not even the nephew, apparently.

Just supposing the ghost lights *were* for real? As unlikely as that was, I decided I couldn't wait for morning. I needed to check this out now.

I hurried along the dirt road as quickly as I could safely go without risking a sprain or a fall.

When at last I emerged from the copse, I found myself on the edge of what must have once been a formal sunken garden. The hedges were overgrown with brambles and berries, an oblong pool filmed over with scum. A couple of wind-bent eucalyptus dotted the grounds as though placed there by Salvador Dali. Broken statuary littered the weeds like bone fragments.

I stared across the ruins of the garden to the house. The upstairs windows were unlit. Nothing moved. It could have been a painting – maybe one of those gloomy efforts by Atkinson Grimshaw.

I continued to wait for...something.

But nothing happened. The woolly moon sank further down the sky.

Something swooped over head and I ducked. A bird? A bat? Or — the way my night was going — a flying squirrel?

I peered at the luminous dial of my watch. Four-fifteen. The sun would be up soon. I rubbed the grit from my eyes and decided to call it a night.

Starting back for Oliver's place, the woods were even darker and creepier, pine needles whispering underfoot, the sea breeze sighing through the tree branches. My night vision was never great and it was especially bad when my eyes were tired. The shadows seemed to shift and slide. I kept my attention on the mostly overgrown road, having zero desire to spend the night in the woods with a sprained ankle.

Rounding the bend that took Berkeley House from view, I realized that someone stood in the road ahead of me.

I stopped dead thinking — hoping — the shadowy figure was just a trick of my tired eyes. The hair rose on the nape of my neck. It — he — was so still. I blinked a couple of times and willed him to disappear. No luck. There he stood: tall, dark and alarming.

Could it be a manifestation? I preferred to think it was a manifestation and not a transient. I waited for him to move or speak.

"Hi," I offered.

Bushes rustled to my left. I turned instinctively. When I looked back, the figure was gone.

Granted, I might not be the best judge, but I didn't think that was normal behavior.

Was he lying in wait for me? I stared at the empty road.

Abruptly, I decided to take the shortest distance back to Oliver's house even though it meant cutting through the woods. I slipped into the bushes to my right, hoping like hell this wasn't the right time of year for poison oak or lively rattlesnakes.

I was caught between feeling foolish and genuine unease; all the same I stayed low, sticking to the shadows. I moved as quietly as I could, pushing through the branches. Every few feet, I stopped and listened. There was no sound to indicate anyone was following me. I could imagine what C.K. would say if he could only see me now. I was probably going to end up with a tick down my collar and broken glasses.

Except…when I remembered that still silent figure blocking my way, I wasn't so sure I was overreacting. There had been something weird about the way he stood there. Something…menacing.

It took about fifteen minutes before I stepped out of the woods, brushing myself down, feeling my clothes sticky with pine sap and God knows what. By then I was too tired to care if Barnabas Collins himself was after me. I wanted a bath and bed. Actually, I just mostly wanted bed.

Oliver's house looked peaceful in the moonlight. I started across the lawn, belatedly remembered the whole reason I'd come outside, reversed, and headed for my car and the bags still sitting where I'd left them on the gravel drive.

Some sixth sense caused me to glance over my shoulder.

I froze.

The blunt outline of a man stood unmoving near the woodline. What the hell? Was this guy *following* me?

He sure as hell was watching me.

Okay. Enough was enough. I diverted my flight pattern from the car and redirected to the front porch. The peacock blue door, which I'd left propped open with an umbrella stand from inside the hallway, was now closed. The umbrella stand rolled gently in the night breeze.

I crossed the porch and tried the door.

Locked.

Again.

I could have howled my rage and disbelief to the now-nonexistent moon.

Once more I tried the handle. Still locked. I shoved my shoulder against the unyielding wood. The only thing likely to give was my shoulder.

I pulled my keys out. This was where I'd come in.

I looked behind me. Did a double take. The figure was now halfway across the lawn. A slash of black silence. For some reason the fact that he didn't move or speak was more alarming than if he'd made some obvious threat that I could respond to.

I turned back to the door. Leaned into the bell.

No response from inside the house.

I glanced over my shoulder.

He was closer still — only three or four yards from me. Even so I couldn't make out his features, nothing but a smudge of darkness where his face should be. But that was the light. The lack of light. But the way he stood there…motionless, staring….

I turned back and pounded the door. "Christ," I muttered. "Open *up!*"

The porch light blazed on above me. The door suddenly swung open and I half-fell into Sam Devlin's arms. For a split second a brawny pair of arms closed around me and my face pressed into a warm hairy chest.

We disengaged hastily. I threw a nervous look behind me. The lawn was an empty stretch of…nothing. I blinked. There was no sign of the man who had followed me.

Nothing. Not a trace.

"What is this, some kind of sleep deprivation experiment?" Devlin inquired in less than patient tones. I straightened my glasses and looked back at him. His hair was a lot more ruffled and the addition of gruesome pillow creases down his face didn't add to his looks.

"Someone was following me."

"From your car?"

"From Berkeley House. I walked over to see it. There was a light in one of the upstairs windows —" I broke off at his expression. "Someone was out there. He was standing there not two minutes ago."

"Are you on some kind of medication?" he asked. "Never mind. Dumb question. Have you maybe skipped your medication?"

I didn't totally blame him. If I didn't know me as well as I knew me, I might wonder about me too. And we hadn't started off on the best footing. All the same, Sam Devlin was getting under my skin like no one I'd ever met. But then I've never been impressed by big macho alpha males.

"You don't believe me? Fine," I said. "Can you just wait here while I bring my bags from the car?"

He groaned and rubbed his eyes. "Make. It. *Fast*."

"Two minutes." I told him. I sprinted to the car, grabbed my laptop and suitcase, and ran back.

Several times I glanced towards the woods and the road, but there was no sign of anyone.

Sam Devlin's long form threw a sinister shadow on the grass as I lugged my bags across the lawn, hiked up the stairs, and squeezed past him. He only stepped aside at the last moment.

"Thanks," I huffed.

"Are you sure you're in the right line of work?" he inquired. "Fear of the dark seems like it might be a handicap in your profession."

"Funny."

"Not really. Are you done for the night?"

"Mission accomplished," I said, heading straight for the main staircase. "Sorry to have disturbed your beauty rest."

Amazingly enough no sarcastic comment followed. I heard him slam the front door and lock it after me. The downstairs lights went off as I reached the upper level.

Keeping in mind that Devlin was in the first room off the left, I staggered down the hallway past the master bedroom and two additional rooms — putting a safe distance between me and Joe Friday.

Finally I opened a door into a room with an empty bed. I guess there was other furniture beneath a sloping roof, but all I cared about was the bed. I dropped my bags, climbed onto the mattress and pulled the quilt over me. Sleep settled over me.

§ § § §

The smell of coffee woke me.

For a few moments I lay there, trying to remember where I was. Not at home. Not at C.K.'s... I waited for the inevitable stab of pain. It would never be C.K.'s again. And then I remembered.

I opened my eyes. The shadow of the wisteria growing outside my window moved against the white ceiling.

I blinked, checked my wristwatch. Nine-thirty. Late for me; I never needed much sleep, and lately my sleep patterns were worse than ever. My nose twitched at the promise of caffeine.

Throwing off the quilt, I padded into the adjoining bath. A quick shower and a shave later, I dug a clean pair of Levis out of my suitcase and pulled on a T-shirt.

The bedroom window looked down on a sparkling pool and a brick courtyard. Flowering vines twisted through the top of a redwood pergola. Tidy green lawn stretched in all directions and vanished into the woods. I could just glimpse the blue of the ocean behind trees. It was a beautiful place. A little isolated, but that untouched quality was all part of the scenic charm. I thought I understood what had inspired the elegant, passionless landscapes of Oliver's early career.

I went downstairs and was making my way across the carpeted hall when Devlin's voice reached me from the kitchen.

"Flakier than pie crust. And a little old for Oliver. Normally he prefers them straight out of the shell."

Silence. He was either talking to himself or he was on the phone.

"Early thirties, at a guess." He added sardonically, "A natural blond. In every sense."

Me. He meant me.

It's not like I hadn't heard all the stupid, close-minded comments before, but my gut tightened anyway. The fact that Devlin thought I might turn tricks for a living sort of appealed to my warped sense of humor, but that he thought I was dumb? I didn't find that so funny.

Maybe the polite thing would have been to pretend I didn't hear him. I guess I'm not that polite.

I strolled right into the kitchen. He stood by the gleaming stainless steel counter, coffee machine bubbling over beside him, and I had the satisfaction of seeing him jump. He recovered instantly, turning away and speaking quietly into the mouthpiece. "I'll give you a call if I hear anything, Thad."

Hanging up, he nodded to me without warmth. "Morning."

"Morning." I nodded at the volcanic spill. "Is it okay if I pour myself a cup of coffee?"

"What's Oliver's is yours. At least for the next ten minutes."

"What happens in ten minutes?"

He handed me a clean mug from the cupboard, his eyes greener than the untidy stretch of woodland behind the house. "Oliver doesn't have a long attention span."

"Can we get this settled here and now," I said, pouring coffee. "I think Oliver's a charming old guy, but I'm here to investigate Berkeley House. Period."

"If you say so."

I gritted my jaw against a lot of stuff that would make future encounters with this asshole awkward, and looked up to meet his gaze. "Look, your uncle invited me to stay for a couple of days, and if there were any strings attached, I'm not aware of them. Since he's not even here, they'd have to be pretty long strings, wouldn't they?"

"Puppet-length."

I took a sip of coffee and nearly choked. "This is *terrible*."

He nodded gloomily. "Yeah."

"It's probably the worst cup of coffee I ever had."

"I know."

I couldn't quite read him. "Do you... prefer it this way?"

He took a mouthful from his own cup and shuddered. "No. It just always turns out like this."

He was permitted to carry a gun but couldn't figure out how to use a coffee machine?

"Would it be okay if I made another pot?"

For a moment I thought he was actually going to smile. "Knock yourself out."

I poured the seething black contents of the current pot down the drain and set about measuring coffee into the machine. Devlin watched me thoughtfully. He wore a black T-shirt and faded Levis that emphasized his narrow hips and long legs. He had a perfect body, no doubt about it. It made an interesting contrast to his homely face.

"Where'd you say you met Oliver?"

"An art exhibit in San Francisco. C.K. Killian introduced us."

"The art dealer?"

I was surprised he knew that. He looked like his idea of art would be calendars with sport cars.

"Yep."

"And what were you doing at an art exhibit?"

I wondered if it were possible for him to ask a question so that it didn't sound like he was interrogating a hostile witness.

"C.K. is – was — is a friend."

He raised those black eyebrows again. "Is he a friend for not?"

"He's a friend," I said shortly. I wasn't about to go into my relationship with C.K. My former relationship.

"And somehow you and Oliver got talking about this book you're writing, and he invited you to scope out Berkeley House?"

"Pretty much. Yes." When I raised my eyes he was watching me narrowly.

Sure, there was a little more to the story — like the fact that I was drunk off my ass and had actually — humiliatingly — cried on Oliver's surprisingly comfortable shoulder about getting dumped by C.K. — but no way was I ever going to share that information with him. Or anyone. I sort of hoped Oliver had forgotten it.

Devlin said reluctantly, "For the record, you were right about seeing someone in the woods last night."

"Are you keeping a record?" I gazed at the coffee machine, willing it to hurry along that precious life-saving elixir.

When he didn't answer, I glanced his way. "So who was roaming in the woods last night besides me?"

"Thaddeus Sterne. Our nearest neighbor — our only neighbor — unless you count your ectoplasmic buddies at Berkeley House."

I ignored that crack. "Thaddeus Sterne? The painter?"

"That's right."

"*Wow.*" I meant it. Thaddeus Sterne was a legend in the art world. Even more of a legend than Oliver de la Motte. Probably because Sterne sightings were rarer than albino whales. He was like the Garbo of the oil paint set. According to C.K., the last time Sterne had made a public appearance was the 1980s.

Then I remembered the stillness, the silence of the man who had followed me through the woods, and some of my pleasure died. Sterne might be a genius, but last night I'd felt threatened.

He said curtly, "Yeah, well, see that you don't disturb him while you're poking around out there. The property lines are clearly marked."

"Correct me if I'm wrong, but he was on your property last night."

"*He* can go where he wants. If you see him, get out of his way." He studied me, his eyes flinty in his blunt-featured face.

I swallowed my irritation — which tasted only slightly better than the bitter coffee had.

"Understood. Anything else I need to know before I head over to Berkeley House?"

Talk about a foolish question. Sam Devlin contemplated me for a long unsmiling moment. "I think we better discuss that, as well," he said. "Are you aware that the property is condemned?"

"The house? Yes."

"Great. Well, if you want to wander around the grounds at your own risk, that's one thing, but it's not safe to go inside the house."

"I already signed a waiver —"

He interrupted, "I don't care what you signed. You saw the place last night. One good push and the building will be in the sea. You don't go inside."

"I've already arranged this with Oliver — the guy who owns the property."

"I don't care what you arranged. You don't put one foot inside that house. Understand?"

What, was the entire *universe* supposed to be his jurisdiction? I stared at him. It was a stare I had perfected through years of dealing with insolent adolescents and asshole adults. He stared right back. I finally managed a terse, "Yeah, I understand."

He nodded curtly. "Good. I've got a call into Oliver, but just so you know, I believe this story of yours about writing a book." He managed to make it sound like he figured I was capable of any lunacy.

"Gee, thanks," I practically stuttered. He was actually going to double-check my story? Who the hell would make up a story like this?

He shrugged. "No offense, but Oliver is a sucker for a pretty face and a sob story."

Unfortunate choice of words under the circumstances.

I smiled. It probably looked more like a baring of teeth, because he blinked. What an arrogant asshole he was. Poor Oliver. I could just imagine the lectures he had to listen to from Mr. Law and Order.

"I'll keep it in mind," I said.

"Do that."

Apparently he also needed to have the last word. I struggled to control myself. I couldn't remember the last time somebody had this kind of effect on me.

"Is there more or am I dismissed?"

To my surprise he gave a twist of a smile. "Not easily," he said.

Chapter Three

"Hey, be careful there!"

I turned away from my survey of Berkeley House's pallid and dissolute face — hollow-eyed windows and gaping broken door mouth. A man in jeans and a plaid shirt hurried across the threadbare lawn towards me

As he reached me, he said earnestly, "You weren't thinking of going inside? It's a death trap."

He was about my age. Attractive. Medium height and comfortably built; hazel eyes, soft brown hair and a carefully groomed beard.

"Hi," I said. I gestured with my camera. "I was just taking a few photos."

He studied me and something changed in his face. In mine too, probably. The old gaydar picking up those high frequency waves. "It's private property, you know." He said it almost apologetically, his smile rueful.

"I know," I said. "I'm staying at Oliver de la Motte's." Remembering Oliver's reputation, I added hastily, "I'm writing a book about haunted houses along the California coast."

"Seriously?" The genuine interest was refreshing after Sam Devlin. He offered a hand. "Mason Corwin. I'm president of the local historical preservation society." His handshake was firm. "So you know the history of the house?"

"Just the bare bones."

"Interesting choice of words. There are plenty of skeletons in the Berkeley House closet."

"I'll bet. David Berkeley was a magician, right?"

"A 20th Century illusionist. By profession and philosophy. He really did subscribe to the notion that the material world was just an illusion."

"Yeah? How does that tie in with his committing suicide?"

Mason smiled wryly. "Beats me. I personally subscribe to the here and now theory."

I smiled back, then glanced at the house, feeling its tug once more.

"Come by the museum," Mason invited. "You can look through our collection. We've got all kinds of photos, newspaper clippings, and memorabilia on Berkeley."

"I'll do that."

He smiled at me again. "How long are you staying for?"

"Just through the weekend."

"Too bad."

"Why?" I caught the meaning of his smile. "*Oh.* Thanks."

His gaze wavered, edged past me. I glanced around. He said, "Old Thad Sterne. He's another reason to be careful around here. He's kind of on the weird side. Take a piece of advice?"

"Sure."

"Ghost hunter or not, don't hang around here after dark. It's not safe."

"Thanks for the warning."

He nodded. Glanced at his watch. "I've got to get back. The museum opens at noon on Fridays." He hesitated. "But I'll be seeing you, right?"

I smiled. "Right."

I waited until Mason vanished into the woods, then I ducked around the back of the house. I could do with less of an audience.

Immediately I saw what Devlin and Mason meant. Originally the mansion must have sat several hundred yards from the cliff, but time and tide had done their work. The back porch stairs were now literally inches from the edge.

One of these days — and not too far in the future — the entire structure was going to tip over the side.

I stared down at the hypnotic green swirl. White foam washed across the bronze rocks below. The wind seemed to sing eerily off the cliff beneath me. That might explain any mysterious noises coming from the house, but I couldn't see anything that would create the mirage of ghostly lights in the upper story windows.

I dipped under the rickety railing, climbed cautiously onto the wraparound porch.

Exposed to the unrelenting elements, the porch was in bad shape, the remaining wooden planks silvery and fragile. I picked my way across, and then pushed open the sagging French doors, which gave with a screech of rusted hinges.

The glass doors opened onto an empty sunny room. Despite the obvious disrepair and smell of damp and mold, the bones of the house — the black wood floor, the arching windows, and graceful architecture — were still beautiful. A giant chandelier, missing crystal teeth and beads, hung from the ceiling, winking and glinting in the light streaming through the windows.

Once this must have been a lovely room in a gracious home. Now...

I stayed quiet, trying to pick up a feel for the house. Listened to the wind moaning down the chimney, keening at the window casements.

The reflection of the water flickered against the bare ceiling and walls.

It was sort of soothing, but I didn't feel soothed. I felt nervous and keyed up. I told myself it was from having to sneak into the house — the mistrustful awareness that Sam Devlin was probably the type to come and check up on me.

Moving to the window, I considered the choppy water, the wind rippling through the grass. Not hard to imagine that unceasing whisper preying on the nerves of a guy who wasn't maybe totally right in the head to start with.

The light was very good in here. I pulled my camera out and took a couple of photos of the cobwebbed chandelier.

I proceeded to the next room, which turned out to be a wide and elegant hallway. Chunks of plaster molding littered the floor. A graceful curving staircase led the second story. I studied it, wondering what kind of shape it was in. It didn't look obviously unsafe, but that didn't mean a lot given the condition of the rest of the structure.

I started cautiously up. Seven careful steps and there was a loud crack. I hesitated. Took another tentative step — my tennis shoe shoved right through a rotten board.

"Damn."

Grabbing the carved railing for balance, I pulled my foot out and started back down. Another snapping sound and the edge of the next step broke off right under the heel of my foot. Only my grip on the rail kept me from pitching forward.

Shit. It really was unsafe, Super Cop hadn't been exaggerating.

I leaned over the railing and looked down at the dusty blackwood floor. An easy drop. I tested the railing, it groaned, but held. I swung a leg over and jumped, landing in a crouch. The crash of my touchdown sounded like I was going to slam through to the cellar, but to my relief the flooring held.

I'd have liked to get some shots of the second story, but it wasn't crucial.

It did make the lights in the upper story windows a little more problematic. I wasn't a particularly big guy and it would have to be someone a lot lighter than me to make it up this staircase. So...natural phenomenon?

Or was there another way upstairs?

Since Berkeley was supposed to have topped himself in his downstairs library, I didn't see why spooklights would be manifesting themselves upstairs, but it's not like the supernatural had to abide by the rules of human logic. Especially since half the humans I knew didn't abide by them.

I spent the next couple of hours wandering through the downstairs rooms, using my flashlight to guide the way through the dark interior, brushing aside cobwebs as long as tattered draperies. I took some pictures and made some general notes.

On the inland side of the house I came to a long room overlooking the woods. Daylight spilled through the cracked windows revealing built-in bookshelves and the cracked and fissured façade of what must have once been an elegant fireplace. Silvery sheets of velvety wallpaper peeled off the scarred walls.

Presumably the library. The room where David Berkeley decided to end it all.

And what a way he'd chosen: using the specially-made guillotine from his stage show. Gruesome but effective.

To me, it felt like an empty room in a dead shell of a house. But then I've never been particularly sensitive — at least, not in the psychic sense. According to C.K I was ridiculously oversensitive in every other way.

On impulse, I sat down in the center of the room, closed my eyes and just…listened.

Wind worked its way through the holes and loose boards: an eerie chorus in a multitude of different tones and pitches.

Was it just the wind?

I closed my eyes, listening…feeling….

"What the fuck are you doing inside here?"

If Sam Devlin wanted to pay me back for catching him off guard that morning, he got his money's worth. It's hard to retain your dignity when you're scraping yourself off the ceiling, but I tried. At least I didn't actually scream — although I'm guessing my shocked expression was just as bad.

Not that he spent time gloating. He leaned in through the open window frame, his face hostile but unsurprised — apparently not much of anything surprised him — and said evenly, "I told you the house was off-limits."

"I told you I've got Oliver's permission."

"I don't give a goddamn. I told you to stay out of the house."

Apparently he read my silence correctly, because he said levelly, "Last warning. Get out before I come in and get you."

I wasn't sure if he would try it or not. If he did decide to throw me out, it wouldn't be much of a contest, he was a lot bigger than me, and I didn't doubt he was a lot tougher. In any case, there was no point continuing now with him draped over the window sill. Talk about blocking reception.

Feeling a little silly to have been caught trying to…well, what had I been trying to do? Commune with the dead? I crossed over to the window and he backed out, looking as grim as though he'd caught me trying to wriggle out of my straight jacket. I started through the open window and his big hand closed on my shoulder dragging me out.

"Come on, pretty boy."

"D'you *mind?*" My shirt — and skin — caught on a nail. "Christ, watch it!"

"All right, all right." He unhooked me. "Hope you've had your tetanus shots."

"Yeah, since you missed your rabies vaccine."

He gave a little snort that might have been a laugh.

I got through the window without any further help. Mouth compressed, Devlin watched me as I checked the tear in my shirt.

"Come on!" he said impatiently after a second or two.

"Go. I don't need a police escort."

"You've got one, anyway."

I raised my head and glared. "What, you're escorting me off the premises?"

He made a sharp gesture with his chin, and turned, obviously expecting me to trail after. So, in answer to my question, yes, I was apparently being escorted from the premises.

Devlin strode off across the patchy lawn and I followed at a normal pace. No way was I trotting after him. I watched him stomping along ahead of me through the shambles of the old sunken garden, his dark head gleaming in the late afternoon sunlight.

I fantasized about picking up a piece of broken statuary and lobbing it at his thick skull. But enough damage had been done to the property without me adding to it.

At the end of the garden he paused, waiting for me.

"I think we'll wait to hear from Oliver before you do anymore exploring," he said when I finally joined him.

"Oh for —! I've only *got* the weekend!"

He shrugged. Clearly not his problem. "I'm sure he'll call this afternoon," he said indifferently.

I shook my head, not trusting myself to speak, and he turned and stalked off again. I guess I should have been grateful he didn't insist that I march in front of him with my hands on the back of my head.

When we reached Oliver's, I went straight upstairs to shower off the cobwebs and filth of Berkeley House.

Devlin called up to me as I was changing into a clean pair of jeans and flannel shirt.

"Hey, professor. Phone call for you. It's Oliver."

I came downstairs and took the phone from him in the hallway. "See," he said laconically. "Told you, he'd call."

"Thanks." I took the phone without meeting his gaze. Waited for him to depart — which after a minute he did.

"Hi, Oliver. It's Rhys. Sorry to bother you."

"Well, my dear. How are you getting along?" I pictured him instantly: tall and elegant with iron-gray hair and amazing green-gold eyes. I figured the connection to the Neanderthal now slamming kitchen cupboard doors had to be by marriage. Probably a forced marriage.

"Well…"

He laughed that plumy laugh. "You mustn't mind Sammy. He has a very suspicious mind. It comes of being a cop. But it's all right. I've vouched for you."

I doubted that meant as much as he imagined it did.

I glanced at the door of the kitchen, through which Prince Charming had vanished. "The thing is, Oliver, he's making it all but impossible for me to step foot inside Berkeley House."

"Mmm. I heard," Oliver said vaguely. "But you can surely work around that, yes? You're a resourceful boy."

I blinked this over. "Uh, yes. I guess."

Oliver sighed. "I was so hoping that you and Sammy would hit it off."

"Hit if off?" I added ungrammatically, "Me and *him?*"

"Yes! Oh, I know how brusque and hard Sammy seems, but he's not like that really. Just a big softie, once you get to know him."

"Sure," I said, not believing it for a moment.

"You'd be lovely together, you know. You're just what he needs. And he's what you need, my dear. Someone you can really count on. Someone steadfast and loyal."

"You make him sound like a St. Bernard." I was joking but I was sort of appalled. Was that why the old reprobate had given me permission to investigate the house? So he could pimp me out to his socially retarded nephew?

"His bark *is* much worse than his bite. I've known Sammy his entire life…" He ran blithely on with a full listing of the Boy Scout virtues, but I'd stopped listening as Sammy appeared in the kitchen doorway.

He gave me a level look. Maybe I'd already used up my one phone call privilege. I said, cutting Oliver off, "Okay, thanks. Did you need to speak to him again?"

"No, no. Just give Sammy my love," Oliver said archly.

I returned something noncommittal and hung up.

"He sounds like he's having a good time," I said into Devlin's formidable silence.

"Oliver knows how to have a good time."

I wondered if he knew Oliver's hopes that we would hit it off. If so, I couldn't blame him for feeling a little hostile. There's nothing like matchmaking relatives. I'd had my own share of that.

"Satisfied that my intentions are honorable?"

His smile was sour. "You've certainly got Oliver convinced."

But obviously not Sam Devlin.

"So is it settled? Can I get back to work?"

"If by that you mean going back into the house, no."

"Christ! What is your problem?"

"Look, it's not safe. You had to have seen that much for yourself today."

I gazed out the window at the failing light. I wasn't looking forward to walking through those woods in the dark.

"I don't get it. I've signed a waiver. I'll be careful. Oliver is okay with it."

He sighed. "Oliver hasn't been inside that place for decades. He has no idea of the shape it's in."

"Fine," I said shortly. "I'll stick to the grounds."

He eyed me skeptically. It began to get under my skin.

"I said I'd stick to the grounds. What do you want?"

"Your word is fine."

He said it mildly, and I ignored the little stab of guilt that went through me. We stood there for another minute and he said slowly, "So, professor. By any chance do you know how to cook?"

Chapter Four

I assumed it was some kind of crack, but as I stared at him I realized he was perfectly serious. Strange but serious.

"That depends. What is there to cook?"

"Follow me."

I followed him through the large and modernized kitchen then downstairs to the basement and a tomb-sized industrial freezer.

"Perfect for storing a body," I murmured.

"Yes. Don't annoy me too much."

I looked at him and he laughed.

"Funny," I said. I stared at the frosty packs of food. "This is all frozen solid. What do you expect me to do with it?"

"I thought we could defrost something in the microwave." He actually looked…conciliatory. Not an expression that fit naturally on his dour face.

"I guess we could. It's not ideal, but yeah, we could defrost something. What did you have in mind?"

He reached right into the ice cavern and pulled out a neatly-wrapped packet in white butcher's paper. "Pork chops?" he said hopefully.

I thought it over. It couldn't hurt to try and make friends with him. Well, *friends* was unlikely. What I pictured was more in the spirit of throwing a bone — or a pork chop — to a big ugly guard dog.

"If I cook, you clean up, right?"

"Deal," he said so quickly I thought it must be some kind of trick.

But apparently he was just desperate for a hot meal. He sat at the kitchen table watching every move I made as though he feared I make take off with his precious pork chops.

I checked out the refrigerator, opened a few cupboards, pretended he wasn't there, but after a few minutes his silence sort of got to me. I leaned against the counter, waiting for the microwave to melt the block of pork chops, "So are you on vacation or something?"

Nothing.

He was an alien life form and I was wasting my time trying to communicate.

The microwave bell rang and I popped open the door.

"Or something." Devlin spoke curtly from behind me. To my surprise, after another long pause he said, "How did you get involved in the ghost hunting racket?"

I searched the spice rack, selected cumin seeds, black peppercorns, coriander and sea salt. "It's more of a hobby than I business," I said. "I mostly teach history."

"How'd you get interested in paranormal studies?"

I realized two things about him: he was a better listener than he appeared to be, and he was not easily sidetracked. I guess that was useful in his line of work.

Combining spices in one of those anchor-sized frying pans, I tried to decide if I was going to be candid or not. On the whole I thought candor with someone like him was a bad idea, so I was startled to hear my voice begin, "My brother was killed…"

I stopped, appalled. Where had that come from?

"Sorry," he said brusquely.

Silence. I pushed the spices around the pan.

"What happened?" Unexpected as it was, Devlin's voice jarred me out of my reflections.

I said, "It was a long time ago. I don't know why I brought it up." And I really didn't know.

He said, "How did it happen?" A cop's curiosity, I guessed.

Easier just to get it over with. I said, "Dylan, my twin —" And was even more startled when I swallowed mid-sentence. I spoke quickly to get past that little stumble. "Was killed when I was eleven. We were riding bikes and a car hit him. It was…fast. One minute he was right there…laughing…and the next minute he was gone."

I stopped the film running in my head. Stopped myself from saying anything else. I had already said too much. I threw Devlin a quick look. Waited for him to say something — bracing for sarcasm or traffic death statistics or, worst of all, sympathy — not that he looked like the sympathetic type. To my relief he didn't say anything. His face was expressionless, his eyes alert and curious.

I stirred the spices and the room grew fragrant with the toasted scents. I said, "It just seemed to me…has always seemed to me…that the line between life and death is so…*fine*…"

"It is fine."

"But it seemed like because it was just a matter of seconds…" I stopped, realizing I was never going to be able to explain it to someone like him. He thought by "fine," I meant fragile — that was natural since he was a cop — and while I agreed that life was fragile, that wasn't what I was talking about. I meant that the dividing line was so flimsy, so insubstantial that it seemed possible — even probable — that you could just reach right across…. If you knew how. If you had the courage.

I flashed him a quick, meaningless smile. "So that's my traumatic childhood. Sorry you asked?"

His brows drew together as I pulled the blender away from the wall, dumped the spices in and turned it on. The whir of the blender made speech impossible, and I was glad of that. I couldn't imagine why the hell I'd told him about Dylan. Low blood sugar, probably.

While the pan grew hotter, I scooped out the blended spices and began to dry rub the meat with them. The smell of the heating pan and the spices, the warmth of the kitchen and the scent of Sam Devlin's aftershave and freshly-laundered flannel shirt had a weird effect on me. I became conscious of my bare fingers deeply massaging the warm raw meat — and that Devlin was watching me with close attention.

I said at random, "So what kind of a cop are you? Oliver never said."

Another tense pause — I wasn't sure why the question should make him tense. He wasn't undercover, right? So what was the big deal?

"I'm a sergeant at the Park police station. Burglary division."

"That must be interesting."

He gave me an ironic look.

I tried anyway. "Do you…like it? Being a cop?"

"Yes." He couldn't have made it any terser. His eyes went back to my meat massage.

I gave up. Nodded at the wine rack on the far side of the room. "You want to open a bottle of wine?" By then I needed a drink.

He rose, opened the wine with quick efficiency, and poured me a glass. Our fingers brushed as I took the glass – and why the hell I would even notice beat me. I took a sip. A very nice pinot noir. I took another sip, set the glass down and placed the chops in the heated pan.

The room began to feel very warm — the effect of wine and the stove.

"What do you want with the chops?" I asked, squatting down to look for a sauce pan.

He cleared his throat. "Whatever you…"

I glanced around. His gaze appeared to be pinned on my ass. He took a gulp of wine and said, "I think there's some canned corn in the cupboard."

"Okay. Toss me a can."

He got up, opened the cupboard, and tossed me the can of corn — across the table. I almost suspected he didn't want to get too close to me. Studying the can of creamed corn — I considered the peculiar likeness of the Jolly Green Giant to present company.

I studied Devlin under my lashes. He was a big man, no question. It was probably handy in his line of work. He looked intimidating, and he had the voice and manner to back it up. I wondered what kind of social life he had, being a cop and looking the way he did. It couldn't be much of one since he was spending his vacation all by himself at his uncle's isolated retreat. Maybe he'd be in a better temper once he was fed and watered. Granted it would take a lot of feeding and watering…

"I could make stuffing," I offered.

His face changed. He looked at me with something close to respect. "Could you?"

I nodded. Maybe when he was in a better mood I could work on him again about Berkeley House. Considering the house's state of disrepair it would be safer to have someone aware of where I was all the time; I didn't want to have to lie and sneak around, but no way was Sam Devlin getting in the way of this book.

Searching the refrigerator I came up with limp celery, a loaf of stale nut bread and half an onion. I set about making stuffing. Sam Devlin watched me all the time, and unwillingly I watched him back, uncomfortably aware of long legs, wide shoulders, powerful arms.

"So why did you become a cop?" I asked into what began to feel like a very long silence.

"I wanted to make a difference," he said sardonically.

I sighed. It really was pointless trying to talk to him, but I like talking to people. Generally the wrong people, according to C.K. "And have you?" I asked.

He was silent. Gee, what a change. I glanced at him and once again he was observing me in that assessing way.

"Maybe."

It took him so long to answer that I'd forgotten I'd even asked a question. I didn't pursue it.

Dinner was ready in just under an hour, and by then I was feeling the effects of two glasses of wine on an empty stomach. When Devlin came over to the stove to inspect the results of my efforts, I felt awareness of him in every pore.

"You really can cook," he said, as though he hadn't believed it until all the evidence was presented.

"My dad's a chef. Or was. He's retired now." I was proud of my impromptu efforts: home-style pork chops and stuffing. It smelled great if I did say so myself.

Devlin made an uninterested noise. "I'm going to build a fire and eat in the study," he said, serving himself out of the pan.

For the life of me I couldn't understand why I felt hurt. He had asked me to cook dinner, not dine with him. And I didn't want to dine with him anyway, right? Because what could be more uncomfortable than trying to choke down food in his silent and disapproving presence. Too much wine, I decided. I was just feeling a little blue, missing C.K.

"Sure," I said. I set my plate on the table and pulled out the chair.

He eyed me for a moment. "It's warmer in the study, but suit yourself." He turned on heel and vanished from the doorway.

I stared after him.

Oh. Okay.

I picked up my plate and trailed down the hall to Oliver's study.

It was easy to picture Oliver in this room – urbane and easy in a silk smoking jacket, pouring cognac from a decanter, and chatting amusingly about art or whatever caught his fancy. If Oliver had ever been a starving hard-scrabble artist, I didn't know about it; this room provided the perfect setting for him. The walls were a deep green, the trim and molding white, the furniture leather and masculine. Paintings covered the walls, mostly oils, but a few watercolors — one or two of them looked like Thaddeus Sterne's work. Not that I was an expert, but you pick up a few things dating an art dealer.

Devlin sat on the floor in front of the fireplace, staring into the flames. His powerful body was relaxed and graceful, one arm resting on an upraised knee, the other leg stretched out before him. In the muted light he looked almost attractive, I thought, and then had to bite back a laugh.

"Something funny?" he asked, catching me by surprise.

"Uh, no." I sat down across from him. Avoiding his eyes, I stared up at the paintings — a small fortune in artwork. I couldn't believe there wasn't a state of the art security system to protect it. Maybe Devlin *was* the state of the art security system.

"He's amazing, isn't he?" I said, meaning Oliver. I thought of his kindness that day at the art gallery, and felt an unexpected lump in my throat. Oliver had most certainly been on the prowl that afternoon, but the minute he'd figured out what was up with me, he'd been absurdly kind.

"Every day in every way," Sam returned. An unemotional tone but I realized that there was a sense of humor in there — a sarcastic sense, which appealed to me, since I was a little on the sarcastic side myself, according to C.K.

I really didn't want to think about C.K. tonight.

We chewed for a while, and he said, "This isn't bad."

"Thanks."

"In fact," he said grudgingly, "it's pretty good."

I nodded, biting back another laugh.

Silence but for the scrape of forks on plates, the crackle of the fireplace and the howl of the wind.

"It doesn't stop, does it?" I said, lifting my head to listen.

"What's that?"

"The wind."

"No. It doesn't stop." His head lifted and there was a gleam in his eyes.

I felt my mouth tugging into a smile. I said, "No, I am not spooked by it. I'm not afraid of the dark, either. Or ghosts."

He actually grinned. He had one hell of smile — when he let himself smile for real instead of that usual sardonic twist.

"Or lions or tigers or bears," I added.

"Oh my," he murmured right on cue.

And we both laughed. For real. A shared moment, and a genuine laugh.

After that it was a little easier — another bottle of wine helped. Sam asked about the other ghost houses I was writing about, and I told him about some of the things that had happened during my research of other houses. He listened politely — unimpressed, I think, but polite — which was an improvement in diplomatic relations.

I was telling him about the elderly owner of a Monterey B&B who had invested quite a bit of money in her resident "ghost," when he startled me by bursting out laughing.

"I'm serious," I said. "She had to be in her seventies and she was climbing along the outside railing of this giant staircase with a long pole and a makeshift rubber foot attached — all covered in phosphorous paint."

"What size foot?"

That struck me as hysterically funny. He watched me, smiling, but his eyes were dark and serious. I eventually got control of myself and said, "I forgot to ask. Anyway, she may have been a fraud, but she made the best oatmeal raisin cookies I ever ate in my life, no lie. The *best*."

His smile widened. He said, "So the fact is, you're actually trying to disprove these ghosts, aren't you?"

That sobered me fast. "Not at all."

"No? Seven haunted houses and every one of them a fake?"

I shook my head. "It's not my fault they're all a bunch of frauds. I'm trying to find proof that these ghosts really exist."

He looked unconvinced, and for some reason it seemed important that he be convinced.

I said, "I want to believe. I really do."

"Then maybe you shouldn't ask too many questions."

I frowned. "That seems like an odd philosophy for a cop."

"You're not a cop. I didn't say it was my philosophy."

Maybe he didn't mean to sound as brusque as he did. Maybe he was just too used to talking to bad guys. I changed the subject. "If you spent summers here as a kid, did you ever go inside Berkeley House?"

"Yeah, and it wasn't safe back then," he said.

"Okay, okay. I get it," I said. "Did you ever see anything…?"

He shook his head like I was confirming his suspicions.

"What's the big secret? Did you see something?"

His mouth did the sardonic thing. "Not really."

"So there *was* something?"

Amused, he said, "How do you work that out?"

"Well, if there was nothing, you'd have said *nothing*, but you said, *not really*, so there is something."

He studied my face for a moment. I'd had a lot to drink, and I wondered if it showed. I wasn't slurring or anything but I felt very…relaxed.

He said slowly, "Yeah, there *is* something…" And he leaned across and kissed me on my open and astonished mouth.

Since Devlin seemed a little on the socially inept side I was taken aback by the skill of that kiss. He didn't look like an expert in seduction, but that mouth — pressing coolly and firmly against mine — had had a lot of practice. I found myself wondering hazily who would have dared kiss him…and what I was doing kissing him when I wasn't sure I even liked him.

"Uh…"

He reached over and carefully removed my glasses. I blinked at him uncertainly. The muted firelight turned him into a fuzzy shadow. I had the impression of gleaming eyes and five o'clock shadow, and then he found my mouth again, parting my lips with gentle insistence. It was the gentleness that undid me.

That, and way too much wine, and not enough sleep, and missing C.K. and…

A lot of excuses for giving into what simply felt…great.

I found myself tipping back, big hands cradling me as I landed on the rug, His kiss deepened, heated. Still gentle, but now exploring…

I lay in his arms responding without hesitation, my hunger surprising even me. I pushed up his T-shirt, ran my hands down his sides. His body was warm and brown and lean; muscles rippled beneath my fingers as he shifted position. It felt good to hold onto someone, to feel bare skin. I wanted more. Needed more. His fingers worked the button of my shirt, his mouth still on mine, his knee insinuating itself between my legs.

He finished unbuttoning my shirt and I half-raised to shrug out of it; he pulled his T-shirt up over his head and tossed it away. His hands went to the button fly of my jeans and I thrust up at him, already so hard the stiff denim was torture. My hands fastened on his belt and I worked it like I had seconds to disarm a bomb — which is what it was starting to feel like. Sweat broke out on my forehead, my breath came fast. I felt wild, out of control with wanting him. Wanting him *now*.

He had me free of the constriction of briefs and jeans, yanking them down where they hung up on my tennis shoes, and I didn't give a damn because by then I had got him free as well, and his dick, hard and thick, was giving the high five to my own.

"Oh, *God*," I groaned.

He didn't say a word, his breath fast and rough and scented not unpleasantly of the spices and wine. Usually I'm a little more vocal, but his silent intensity shut me up.

I bit my lip as we humped and ground against each other, fast and frantic like this had been on our minds from the first meeting — which was crazy. The slide and slap of feverish bodies. It didn't take long at all before I was coming. I yelled and bumped my head into his shoulder, pressing my mouth to the hollow there, somewhere between nipping and nuzzling.

Sam came a couple of heartbeats later in hard economical thrusts, and I felt that blood-hot spill between us.

A shudder rippled through him and then another exquisite little aftershock of pleasure, but he still didn't say anything. Just expelled a long heated sigh against my ear, stirring my hair.

Chapter Five

We lay there a few moments, recovering our breath. Sam's powerful arms felt good about me, comfortable. Right. I like to be held; C.K. hated it, wanted — needed — his space immediately after sex.

And about the last person I wanted to think about right now was C.K.

Not that thinking about Sam Devlin was an improvement because I felt a little stunned at what I'd — we'd — done.

On Oliver's Aubusson carpet no less.

"Wow," I said finally.

He gave a short laugh and let me go. I was sorry about that. Sorry as he lifted off me and moved away. Dazedly, I felt around for my glasses.

"I begin to see the attraction," he said.

"What's that?"

He said clearly and calmly, "Now I understand why Oliver's developed a sudden interest in psychic phenomenon."

It took a moment for the meaning of his words to sink in.

I stared at the dark blur with the even voice. That's what comes of having sex with people who you don't like — and who don't like you. And how stupid was I that I felt like he'd slapped me?

I slipped my glasses on and got up in one quick movement. I thought he tensed — it was hard to tell in the dim light, but maybe he'd had a lot of experience with people wanting to hit him after sex. He stared up at me, apparently waiting for some reaction.

"Yeah, well there's no accounting for taste," I said. "Mine in particular." It wasn't a bad exit line, and I took advantage of it, heading for the door.

He didn't say a word and I left him there in the shadows.

§ § § §

I opened my eyes and groaned.

It was morning. I'd slept through the entire fucking — no pun intended — *night*. Instead of getting my ass over to Berkeley House and doing what I'd come here for, I'd gone upstairs and, feeling stupidly, illogically sorry for myself, given into the urge to lie down for a couple minutes rest. Only my quick nap had turned into the entire night and now it was…I checked my wristwatch…ten o'clock.

I'd lost an entire night. Totally wasted it conked out in Oliver's guest room. The entire night and a good portion of the morning as well.

In a very bad temper I rose, showered and went downstairs. No homely scent of witch's brew coffee this morning, which gave me hope that Prince Charming had taken himself off somewhere — like the cliff behind Berkeley House — but no such luck. There he sat reading the local paper.

He looked up and nodded briefly as I entered the kitchen.

I nodded even more briefly back, felt him watching me as I opened the fridge and scanned the contents. I ignored him.

"I thought you might prefer to make the coffee this morning," he informed me, like this was a concession on his part.

I snorted. "Thanks. I'll just get something in town." I removed a carton of orange juice, poured myself a glass and drank it standing at the sink staring out across the woods at the rooftop of Berkeley House.

He shrugged and went back to his paper. I glanced to see what was so fascinating but the local headlines seemed to consist of a couple of burglaries, the results of the annual garden show, and a successful library fundraiser.

I finished my OJ, rinsed the glass out and left the kitchen.

§ § § §

Ventisca was one of those quaint little seaside villages, though not so quaint that it didn't have a Starbucks, of course, and I headed there post haste to up my caffeine intake to appropriate levels. I ate a pumpkin cream cheese muffin while I got directions to the Historical Society.

I found the Historical Society nestled in between two calculatedly adorable bed and breakfasts. It was the only building on the street that didn't have flower boxes in the windows or a brightly painted entrance. Corwin Mason was unlocking the black front door when I pulled up. I got out of the car, waved, and he waved back, his expression lightening.

"Well, hi there! I was hoping you'd turn up today." He looked relaxed and approachable in a blue striped polo shirt and jeans, and his obvious pleasure was balm to my ego after Sam Devlin.

"If this is a busy time, I can look around on my own."

He chuckled, gesturing me inside. "We're not exactly on the Must See list for most tourists."

I looked around while Mason went about the ritual of opening the museum. There were the usual displays of Indian life and Spanish influence. I skipped over the collection of arrowheads and beads, ignored the sepia photographs of the town's early history, and by-passed the local arts and crafts section. There were a couple of very nice watercolors by local artists — nothing by Oliver or Thaddeus Stern — and a lot of battered antique furniture.

And then I saw the guillotine.

It was roughly twelve feet tall and painted in some kind of shiny black lacquer. Golden sphinxes formed the feet of either side of the two tall guides; tiny jeweled eyes winked at me from the bird-like faces. Egyptian gods and goddesses ambled their way down the sides of the "bed," and the circular collar that held the victim's head in place was covered in crimson velvet. The morning sunshine glinted cheerfully off the sharp angled blade hanging above my head.

"Christ, is that real?" I asked Mason. "Is that the guillotine he used to kill himself?"

He joined me, smiling faintly. "No. This was a second guillotine Berkeley designed to use in his show. See, his assistant's head would fit down here." He leaned across and pressed a small lever. "A dummy head would fall into the basket. The assistant would never be in any actual danger, although it looks pretty realistic from where the audience was sitting."

"It looks pretty realistic from where I'm standing." I added slowly, "It's huge. I don't know why that never occurred to me."

"That's show biz." Mason pointed to the far wall where a large oil portrait hung. "And that's David Berkeley."

I'd seen photographs of this portrait, but the real thing was startlingly vivid. Somber eyes stared out of a long, pale, intense face. Flat black hair and a dapper mustache and beard. The background was green like the sea beneath the cliffs at Berkeley House. I couldn't think how I'd missed it earlier, because once I'd noticed the painting, it was hard to ignore it. I could feel the gaze of those black eyes as though a real person were watching me.

"Creepy," I commented.

Mason laughed. "Yeah. It's painted so that the eyes seemed to follow you wherever you are in the room. I'm used to him now, though."

"Who painted it?"

"No one."

At my glance, he clarified. "No one famous, I mean. It was done by a local artist. Aaron Perry."

"The same Aaron Perry who ran off with Berkeley's fiancé?"

"The same. Very good. You've done your homework. According to the stories, the three of them were inseparable growing up. The girl —"

"Charity Keith," I supplied, and Mason laughed.

"Now you're showing off."

"Yeah. It's an interesting story. Sad. Romantic. Like most ghost stories."

"Pure soap opera, if you ask me. Charity agreed first to marry Berkeley, but then changed her mind and ran off with Perry. Berkeley committed suicide at the peak of his fame and fortune — such as it was. The guy was not exactly Houdini."

He guided me through the rest of the display. There were fragile posters of Berkeley's performances and yellowed newspaper clippings of his modest triumphs. He'd definitely been junior varsity. No appearing before the crowned heads of Europe and his performance at the Pan-American Exposition had been marred by the assassination of President McKinley.

I glanced over the notice of Berkeley's engagement to marry Charity Keith and studied the formal still posed portrait of the happy couple. Apparently not that happy, since Charity had eloped with Berkeley's good friend Aaron Perry.

Even in his engagement portrait Berkeley looked…harrowed. Charity, on the other hand, had that grim expressionless countenance most brides wore back then. Possibly something to do with women not having the right to vote until 1920.

"Are there any photos or pictures of Perry?"

"Not that I know of."

"Too bad." It would have been nice for the book, a picture of the love triangle. I mused, "An elopement must have been socially awkward in a town this size."

Mason laughed briefly. "I bet."

I moved down the row of black and white photographs, pausing at a picture of Berkeley in Paris. I felt a prickle down my spine as I picked out his tall figure standing next to the unsettlingly realistic guillotine. Something about that tall dark figure in top hat and cape caught my attention; seemed somehow familiar.

"This was the guillotine he used to kill himself?"

Mason peered over my shoulder. He smelt appealingly of pipe tobacco and citrus. He was sucking on a lemon drop, and he shifted it with his tongue before saying, "I don't know. There were two of them and they were identical, I guess, until Berkeley doctored one for his own personal use. That one was destroyed after the inquest."

The shudder that rippled down my spine caught me off guard. Mason laughed. "Berkeley's story really got to you, didn't it?"

I laughed, trying to brush my unease off. "Maybe. It's all these gruesome props. Usually I have to use my imagination more. A lot more."

"I can imagine. Have you ever seen a real ghost?"

"Me? No." I glanced over my shoulder, feeling those strange painted eyes again.

"Well, if it's any comfort, it was all about the illusion for Berkeley. He didn't really chop the heads off volunteers."

Mason was teasing, and I forced a smile in response; I had no idea why David Berkeley's story affected me like no other I'd investigated so far. It wasn't a rational response, that was for sure.

He left me to examine the rest of the photos and memorabilia at my leisure, and I spent the morning glancing over the colorful ephemera of placards and postcards, puzzling over birdcages and boxes and other vintage odds and ends. I took photos of the clippings and the portrait of David Berkeley. I had more than enough information on him for the book, but the more I learned about him, the more fascinated I became.

I was the museum's only visitor that morning, and I wondered what Mason did to while away the long hours.

"We get a lot more visitors in the summer," he assured me, when I asked. "Berkeley might never have been a household name, but he's still pretty well known in magic circles." He watched me screw the lens cap on my camera, and asked a little diffidently, "What do you think about lunch?"

"I'm all in favor of it."

I really liked his smile – and the fact that smiling wasn't a struggle for him. "There's a little place down the road that makes terrific meatball sandwiches."

"Sounds good," I said, and was treated to the easy smile again.

I followed Mason to a little Italian restaurant with a great view of the ocean. The tables were covered in red and white checked table cloths and there were candles in Chianti bottles and faded photos of 1960 Rome for ambiance.

Mason ordered the meatball sandwiches and I went for pepperoni and black olive pizza, having no idea when or if I'd have dinner.

"How long are you staying for?" he asked as we sipped beer from chilled mugs.

"Just 'til Sunday night."

"I guess, living in L.A., you don't get up this way a lot?"

I thought of all the plane trips, all the Friday night drives up the coast to see C.K. How come it had never occurred to me that I was the one doing all the driving and flying and jumping through hoops? Never again.

"No," I said.

He nodded, stared at the table top.

Someone had left a newspaper folded on the table next to us, and my wandering gaze lit on the story about the recent rash of burglaries — which reminded me of Sam. Now that I had a little distance from the night before, I could see that a certain amount of cynicism was probably part of the cop job description. And it's not like I was so inexperienced I put undue importance on sex. I was irritated with my earlier reaction to his misanthropic view; what did I care what he thought about me? I put it down to Oliver planting ideas in my head about him.

"What's the crime rate like here?" I asked, to distract myself from the direction my thoughts were going.

"Almost non-existent." Mason followed my gaze to the newspaper headline and shook his head. "Oh, that. That's something new for us. Started a couple of weeks ago with summer houses getting broken into and robbed. Luckily no one's been hurt."

I nodded absently.

We chatted about the usual things. Mason was full of praise for small town living. He had moved to Ventisca from San Jose following the death of his longtime partner three years earlier.

"I'm sorry," I said.

He smiled sadly. "Yeah. People sort of forget that AIDS is still killing us."

I wondered if he had tested positive for the virus or not. I liked him and found him attractive but I wasn't at the point where it mattered to me personally one way or the other. His uncomplicated admiration and openness was refreshing after Sam Devlin. Not to mention C.K.

But I was still unsettled about my stupidity in having sex with a stranger the night before — unprotected sex at that — and it put me on my guard. I returned the conversation to neutral ground. "So what's the local word on the ghost?"

"Ask around and you'll hear plenty of accounts of flickering lights and strange noises. You know: the ghostly slide of a guillotine blade echoing through the woods."

He grinned, and I grinned back, but I remembered the eerie sensation of those silent woods closing in on me.

"Have you ever seen anything?"

He hesitated. "I hate to tell you this, but I'm not a big believer in the supernatural."

"Sure. Which means anything you've seen will be more interesting. Or at least more reliable."

He took a swallow of beer and wiped the foam from his mustache. "I've seen the lights. I go out to Seal Point sometimes with my telescope. The lights are supposed to be Berkeley traveling from room to room searching for his lost bride."

"But she wasn't his bride, right? She ran off before they married, so why would he be looking for her in the house?"

Mason shrugged. "Never thought about it. Maybe ghosts aren't logical. Maybe his ghost forgot what happened. He did chop his head off, after all."

I laughed. "Good point."

I liked the way his eyes crinkled at the corners when he smiled. I said, at random, "Berkeley killed himself eight months after Charity ran off?"

"So the story goes. Yep. That much is documented."

"It seems like a weird way to commit suicide, using the guillotine. You think he'd just throw himself off the cliff or blow his brains out."

"He was a showman up to the end, I guess."

"I guess. So did you ever hear —"

He chuckled. "I know what you're going to ask. Did I ever hear the ghostly scrape of the guillotine ax?"

"Did you?"

His face was rueful. "Nope. I've made a point of never getting that close to the house at night."

"Seriously?" Mason didn't look like the nervous type.

"Seriously," he said, and his eyes were without their habitual twinkle. "And, if you'll take my advice, you'll steer clear of those woods after dark."

Chapter Six

Mason and I talked a little longer, and then I reluctantly declined dessert and coffee and headed back to Oliver's. This time I took the back road, skirting the Oliver's home and parking in the woods not far from the cliffs.

I could smell the sea salt and eucalyptus, and hear the cries of the gulls circling high above the rocks as I unloaded my gear, and lugged it across to Berkeley House. Once I had everything out of the car I lifted it through the broken front windows of the library and began setting up my equipment.

The afternoon was warm and unusually sunny, the wind down to a murmur. I could hear birds singing in the trees. The unease I'd felt the previous day seemed silly now.

I mounted the video cam on its tripod in the corner of Berkeley's library where it wouldn't be easily spotted by anyone peering through the window. Setting the timer, I hurried back to the car.

As I pulled away, I was caught between guilt and triumph. Yes, I'd given Sam Devlin my word not to go back into the house, but I'd been coerced into it, so it didn't count.

Not really.

Besides, Devlin was a jerk.

It took about ten minutes to drive to Oliver's. I parked in the shady front drive, and went inside the house using the key Devlin had given me before I'd left that morning.

There was no sign of him, and that was a relief.

Sitting down at my laptop, I entered my notes from the museum. I worked for about an hour when the sound of splashing filtered through my consciousness. I rose, went to the window and looked down at the brick patio and swimming pool beyond.

Sam was in the pool. I watched him for a while. He swam with a single-minded ferocity. Gleaming brown arms cut glistening arcs in the air, strong legs kicking as he shot through the water. Each time he reached the length of the pool, he did one of those quick underwater summersaults off the wall and started back across the water.

I was struck again by the beauty and power of his body; I didn't want to remember how it had felt to be held by him, how his mouth had tasted on mine, the roughness of his cheek and the softness of his hair. I wanted to forget the night before had ever happened, so it was annoying as hell to find it difficult to tear myself away from the window.

But I did. I went back to work, finished entering my notes and then read them over. I thought Berkeley House was by far the most interesting of my chapters, and I wondered if it would be feasible to use David Berkeley's portrait on the book cover.

"Hey," Sam yelled upstairs some time later. "You want some dinner?"

I opened my mouth to yell my refusal, but my stomach growled, practically loud enough to answer for me. And the answer seemed to be yes.

I closed my laptop and went to the top of the stairs. "Is that your way of asking if I'll cook?"

He stared back, but then his mouth quirked like he just might smile. "It's for your own protection," he said.

"That's what I thought," I said.

His expression altered. "If you want me to cook, I'll cook."

I must have looked unconvinced because he said, "I defrosted a couple of steaks. I can do steak."

I was too hungry to ignore this olive branch — in fact, I was hungry enough to eat an olive branch, so I shrugged ungraciously and joined him downstairs in the kitchen.

"There's beer in the fridge," Sam said, peppering two enormous steaks. "I went to the market earlier."

I opened the refrigerator and saw that he had indeed stocked up. There was plenty of imported beer as well as perishables like milk and bread and lettuce. Apparently he was planning on staying for a good while. It didn't matter to me now; I wouldn't be staying beyond Sunday and I'd already figured out how I'd work around him.

"How was your day?" he asked, his eyes very green in his tanned face.

"Fine."

"How'd the ghost hunting go?"

I stared at him. Was he *making conversation* with me? Why?

"It was okay," I answered warily.

"Learn anything useful at the museum?"

My hand slipped opening a bottle of Beck's and I almost spilled some of the precious elixir. "How'd you know I went to the Historical Society museum?"

He raised thick brows at the suspicion in my voice. "I saw you with Mason Corwin coming out of Mama Louisa's. I put two and two together."

"Oh?"

His mouth twitched a little at my tone. "Is that a touch of paranoia? I was going into the market. I have the produce to prove it."

Well of course he wasn't following me; I hadn't thought he was, but it still gave me a funny feeling, especially since he was being so uncharacteristically cordial.

"Speaking of which, do you want me to make a salad or something?" I offered, mostly to change the subject.

Sam smiled, his expression informing me that he knew exactly what I was doing. "Sure, that'd be great."

It occurred to me that the offer of beer had simply been a ploy to get me to open the fridge and see the vegetables awaiting my expert hand. "Are you sure you're gay?" I inquired. "You seem pretty helpless in the kitchen."

"I'm sure." He gave me an unexpectedly direct look. "My skills lie in another direction."

Anybody else, I would have thought he was flirting. As it was, blood rose in my face remembering exactly how skilled he was — and my own uncharacteristic response.

I busied myself tearing up and washing greens, and Sam took the steaks out to the back patio. Apparently his idea of cooking was BBQ.

I gave myself time, drank some beer, then followed him outside. He was sitting in one of the wooden Adirondack chairs idly swiping at flies with the extra-length spatula while the coals heated. I straddled one of the weathered benches taking a turn at observing him for a change.

"How do you want your steak?" he inquired into the silence.

"Medium — hold the flies."

He turned a gleaming look my way. "Extra protein," he observed.

"Ha."

He resumed gazing at the sun-glittering pool.

I swallowed a mouthful of beer, listened to the sound of the pool filter and the scrape of dead leaves on the bricks. Bees hummed around the bougainvillea winding up the wooden posts of the pergola, brilliant scarlet and yellow flowers.

"So what happened between you and the boyfriend?" Sam asked suddenly.

"Huh?" I stared at him, astonished.

"The art dealer boyfriend," he clarified, as though I had so many I might have lost track.

I continued to stare at him, and his face reddened as though it belatedly occurred to him that maybe this was just slightly intrusive. I figured that Oliver must have filled him in on me — preparatory to handing me over as human sacrifice du jour.

"He didn't do monogamous," I said. "Or long term." I stood up, swung my leg over the bench, aware that he was still watching me with that bright alert gaze. "Are we eating inside or out?"

"What did you want?"

Somehow everything spoken in the last couple of minutes seemed laden with undertones and secret meaning. It took me a second to gather my thoughts. I said, "Outside, I guess. It's nice tonight."

"It is nice," Sam agreed. He rose and applied himself to the grill.

§ § §

The steak at least was perfect.

After his odd question about C.K., Sam seemed to have little to say. We ate mostly in silence, while the little lights strung across the open patio and threaded through the vines blinked into life like fireflies or tiny stars. Pool lights illuminated crystal water. The evening was perfumed with charcoal and chlorine and freshly mown grass.

Every so often I'd glance up from my plate and Sam would be staring at me with a expression I couldn't quite pin down. Each time I'd catch his gaze, he'd look away.

"You want another beer?" He asked on his way into the house.

"No thanks."

We were both sticking to beer — and not too much of it.

"How did your family acquire Berkeley House?" I asked when he returned with his beer. "Berkeley wasn't a relative, was he?"

"No."

"The house was abandoned after Berkeley's death?"

"Near enough. The house went to elderly relatives of Berkeley's back east. They had no interest in moving out west and the house had a bad reputation locally. Finally it was sold off with the surrounding acreage to Cornelius Wagnalls, who built this house. Wagnalls lost everything when the stock market crashed in 1929, and Oliver's grandfather bought the estate in auction."

"And the house was left closed up all that time?"

"Mostly. There are stories about Wagnalls offering the house to his daughter as a wedding present, and her walking inside and walking straight out again." He raised his black eye brows suggestively. "Atmosphere," he said.

"Or thirty years of dust." I smiled absently, reminded suddenly of the previous evening, the way it had felt being together. It was still hard for me to believe that I'd done that. Or that he had.

It seemed risky to even question it. It had been a one off. It had felt good at the time, but now I needed to forget about it. So how the hell come I kept thinking about it?

I said briskly, talking myself away from my wayward thoughts, "Are you ever going to tell me what you saw at Berkeley House way back when?"

Sam tilted his beer bottle up, his eyes studying me wryly over the top.

"Is this going in the book?"

"Not if you don't want it to." That was a rash promise; I wasn't sure if it would go in the book or not, but I wanted to hear what he had to say.

"Okay, well, it's not like I have an actual incident to report. I used to go over to the house. This is about twenty years ago."

How old was he? Late thirties? Early forties? I tried to picture him as a little kid. I kept getting tall, grim-faced with five o'clock shadow.

"What did you see?"

"Nothing."

At my expression he said, "I never *saw* anything, but…it was an…uneasy place. It had a vibe, I'll give you that."

"Did you ever go upstairs?"

"A few times." He shrugged. "By then there wasn't much left to see, but when Oliver was a kid there was still some furniture and bits and pieces of Berkeley's magic apparatus."

"For real?"

"Yeah. No one seriously ever tried to secure the premises, so piece by piece, it all vanished or was destroyed by vandals. Oliver's grandfather donated the best of what was left to the Historical Preservation Society."

"What kind of stuff was there?"

He eyes rested on my face; it was probably my imagination, but for a moment his expression seemed to soften. "Books mostly. A guillotine. A portrait of David Berkeley."

"I saw that guillotine today. Pretty impressive. The portrait too."

He smiled reluctantly. "You love this stuff, don't you? Everything from the magic tricks to the spooky old house."

"Well…it'll make a great chapter for the book and…yeah. I do." I waited for him to say something rude or belittling, but he just grimaced and reached for his beer.

"What was it like upstairs?"

"Like the downstairs."

I opened my mouth to object, and he said patiently, "There was a lot of junk and a lot of cobwebs and dust. A few skeletons of sea gulls that flew in through broken windows and couldn't get out again."

"Did you go through all the rooms?"

"Yes," he said. "I did. And I crawled around in the attic."

Here was a valuable resource if he'd be willing to cooperate.

Correctly reading my expression, he said, "That wasn't the creepy part."

"What was?"

"The cellar."

His eyes flicked to mine and I wasn't sure if he was about to pull my leg or not. "Cold as ice. A cold like nothing I've ever felt. I only ever went down there once. That was enough."

"The cellar? Not the library?"

"The cellar."

"But Berkeley killed himself in the library."

"So the story goes."

I fastened on this. "Is there any reason to think he didn't kill himself there?"

"Not that I know of."

There was nothing about the cellar in any of the stories about Berkeley house, so I couldn't figure why there would be a cold spot in the cellar. Lights in the upper story and an unnatural chill in the cellar: two supernatural manifestations that didn't make any sense.

Whether they made sense or not, I wanted to check the house out, experience its secrets for myself.

Afraid that Sam might read my thoughts — he seemed pretty good at that — I changed the subject again. "How long have you been a cop?"

His face tightened. "Ten years."

Yes, there was something there. Something to do with his job.

"Do you like it?"

"Yeah."

"Are you on vacation now?"

He gave me a long level look, planning, if I read his look correctly, to tell me it was none of my fucking business. But instead, he said neutrally, "I'm on...leave."

"Oh." Medical leave? He looked healthy as a horse. What other kinds of leave were there?

I was still thinking it over as he changed the subject, turning the tables once more.

"Oliver says you teach at UCLA?"

I nodded, reached for my beer.

"You've got a pretty good football team heading into spring practice."

"Twenty returning starters and an experienced core group of players."

"And you teach history?" He really had been listening the night before.

"Mostly. One course on parapsychology."

"How long?"

"Six years."

He nodded thoughtfully.

It was the slightly awkward conversation you make on a first date. I almost asked him how he felt about Oliver trying to set us up, but remembering how quiet and intense he had been when we'd fucked, I held my tongue. It seemed to me that he was not a guy to tease.

I must have been looking at him oddly, though, because he raised his brows. "What?"

I shook my head. "Thanks for dinner. My turn tomorrow night."

"Are you staying for dinner? I figured you'd be taking off early. Beat the traffic."

Meaning he'd *hoped* I would be taking off early? Probably.

"I...was thinking I might stay over Sunday." *I was?*

Sam raised his brows.

"Unless you have a problem with that?"

He shrugged. "It's not a problem for me. You're Oliver's guest."

"Right. Well...good." For some damn reason I couldn't come up with anything else to say. I'd thought — well, I hadn't really thought anything. I'd *hoped* — no. No, I definitely wasn't hoping for anything. In fact, I had no idea what the hell I was thinking or why I had suggested staying another night.

Sam said slowly, "Did you know Berkeley was found just moments after he used the guillotine? The local story is that when they picked up his severed head he opened his eyes and spoke."

I stared at him. I knew it was just a story, but for some reason my face felt stiff as I formed the question, "What did he say?"

"*Dum spiro spero.*"

A chill rippled down my spine. "Which means what?"

"It's Latin."

"For what?" I asked a little impatiently.

Gravely he said, "While I breathe, I hope."

He laughed at my expression, and I was glad it was too dark for him to see that I was red as well.

"Funny," I managed.

He was still laughing.

"So is there actually any story about Berkeley being found after he used the guillotine?"

He sobered. His eyes, black in the uneven light, met mine. After a moment, he said, "No. Of course not."

I realized he was lying.

"You know, there are scientists who believe that when a head is suddenly severed it takes the brain a while to realize what's happened. There are recorded instances of severed heads responding to someone speaking their name or touching their cheek."

He said flatly, "Berkeley was found days later. There's no story about his severed head."

"How do you know when he was found? I've never read anything about it."

"Anecdotal evidence. There are still a few old-timers with stories about Berkeley." He rose and picked up his plate and mine. "Don't let your imagination run away with you, Professor," he threw over his shoulder.

After a moment I stood, gathering the rest of the dishes, following Sam into the house. He had the dishwasher open and was loading it.

"I'll wash up," I told him, and he nodded and left me to it.

It didn't take me long. I finished loading the machine, turned it on and went upstairs to bed.

Setting my wristwatch for eleven thirty I lay down to nap, but it took a long time to relax. I could hear the TV downstairs, little twitches of the house settling down for the night, the wind....

I woke at the creak of floorboards down the hall and the sound of Sam's bedroom door shutting. Raising my head, I checked my wristwatch. Ten-thirty. Early yet. I closed my eyes and drifted back to sleep.

My wristwatch was going off softly next to my ear. I rolled over, peered at the luminous dial in the gloom. Eleven forty-five. Time to get moving.

I sat up, pulled on my jeans and shirt. Found my shoes and socks, holding them in one hand as I eased open the bedroom door. I paused.

Moonlight dappled the floor like silver lily pads on the shiny dark wood.

Not a sound from down the hall.

I tiptoed down the lily pads past Sam's closed door, hesitating at the squeak of a floorboard.

I waited. Behind the door on my right, I could hear Sam snoring, and I bit back a grin.

I continued down the hall, down the stairs and out through the front door, which I locked quietly behind me. I sat down on the porch steps and slipped my tennis shoes on, pulled my sweatshirt over my head.

Rising, I glanced back and the black window of Sam's bedroom.

I hoped to God the neighborhood burglars didn't pick tonight to hit Oliver's.

§ § § §

Berkeley House was, unsurprisingly, quiet as the grave on a crisp and chilly Saturday night.

I crawled in through the library window and hesitated for a moment in the darkness. It was very dark with only my flashlight to guide my way across the uneven floor.

The video camera whirred softly away in the indistinct gloom of the library. I checked the meter. It had only started running two hours ago, so there was still plenty of time and tape.

For laughs, I tried tapping on a few walls. Berkeley was an illusionist. I thought it was likely he might have a hidden room or a secret passageway built into the house. But the place was huge and some of the rooms were no longer even accessible due to broken flooring and tumbled walls. I wondered if it would be possible to lay hands on a set of blueprints for the house. Mason might know.

Remembering Sam's comments about the cellar, I started hunting for the kitchen. There were two doors at the end of the long former dining room. One door turned out to be false, apparently existing only to add symmetry to the room's architecture. The second door led down a short passage to the enormous old kitchen. The flash light picked out where the ovens had stood, the wreck of cupboards, and another door leading into what must have been the pantry.

Staring up, I saw the gallery where the lady of the house would have stood to drop her instructions for the day's menu down to the kitchen staff. Of course there had been no lady of the house in Berkeley's day, so maybe he had stood up there himself.

For some reason the image of that tall, thin figure standing up in the gallery gave me goose bumps. I turned away, making my way to the far end of the kitchen where an empty door frame led out onto a porch.

That couldn't be it.

I started back across the wasteland of dirt and debris.

The flashlight beam picked out another door I had missed when I'd entered the kitchen. It was positioned near the kitchen entrance, set off to the side of the hallway. I studied the peeling surface for a moment and reached for the tarnished knob. It seemed stuck. I tugged harder and the handle came off in my hand.

The door swung gently open.

The dank breath of the cellar gusted out. I could feel clammy stink against my face. A chill wave of sick horror came over me.

Okay. Maybe not.

I shoved the door closed and stood there for a moment panting in the wake of that cold miasma.

What the hell *was* that?

I backed up trying to make sense of it. I'd experienced a few cold spots in my investigations — though nothing that couldn't be explained by underground springs or faulty architecture — and occasionally I'd felt something that prickled the hair on the back of my neck, but this was the first time I'd ever felt anything quite that…extreme.

Mouth dry as sand, heart banging away in my chest in that flight or fight instinct, I began to reason with myself. It was just bad air. Stale air.

It was dust. Mold. Mildew. The damp.

That scene from the movie *The Haunting* flashed into my mind. Gloomy old housekeeper, Mrs. Dudley warning poor doomed Eleanor, *There won't be anyone around if you need help. We couldn't even hear you, in the night. In the dark….*

Right. In the night. In the dark. In the damp.

That seeping damp…pervasive and oppressive…like a gust of swamp gas or the tainted air from a crypt. It brushed against my face like a veil.

Even if there was some kind of presence – no, *not* presence. Presence was the wrong word. Even if there was some kind of supernatural manifestation, that didn't mean there was any danger. Outside of the movies, no one has ever been killed by a ghost.

I was still telling myself this as I stumbled back towards the door opening onto the dining room. I grabbed the handle, relieved when it turned. Why wouldn't it turn? Why was I overreacting over a little bit of moist and mildew?

I made my way through the broken planks and plaster, almost falling over a loose floorboard in my haste.

Christ. I was acting like the very nitwit Sam believed I was.

Blundering back into the hallway, I paused to get my bearings.

Something moved in the surrounding pitch blackness and my heart stopped. I swung my flashlight in the direction of that soft sound. A mouse froze in the glare of my flashlight and then whisked itself away behind a baseboard. I sucked in a sharp breath, told myself to get my shit together.

Okay. There were good reasons not to explore the cellar. It was a foul place, and it wasn't even mentioned in any of the stories about Berkeley House. So no need to prove anything to myself. Logically, there was no reason to go down there.

If I did decide to explore the cellar, it would be better to do that during the day. But actually it would be better to just forget about the cellar because Sam was right. It was dangerous down there. The house really was unsafe. I could break a leg easily. Or my neck.

I reached the library with a feeling of relief.

The relief was short-lived.

As I stood there listening to the breeze through the broken window scuttle leaves or old newspaper around the floor, I got that sensation of being watched.

A feeling of increasing anxiety crept over me. I turned my flashlight into the cobwebbed corners of the room.

Nothing.

I shone it at the black mouth of the doorway.

A prickly shivering darkness seemed to lay in wait beyond the doorway.

Yeah. Right.

Really, what the fuck was my problem?

I resolutely turned from the doorway and scouted out a reasonably clean place of floor space near to the wall. Wrapping myself in my blanket, I sat down with pad and pen.

The spring moon moved slowly across the floor, the shadows lengthened, deepened...

The repetitive rasp of sliding metal, a cold hollow thunk, and the jangling pull of a chain filtered into my dreams.

I started awake.

To a crisp and eerie silence.

I listened tensely.

To nothing.

I rubbed my eyes, checked my watch. Three-thirty. The camera was still running. I took a look at the electromagnetic detector. The needle was trembling, indicating strong erratic fluctuating EMFs.

I watched it in the circle of my flashlight beam. The needle stilled.

I waited for something else to happen.

Nothing did. I jotted down the time and event in my log, then made myself sit down again to wait.

Outside the window I could hear crickets chirping.

Bed sounded better and better. Especially since I couldn't seem to keep my eyes open.

Electromagnetic fields could result from a number of things, but that sound had been so...real. I could still hear the echo of the slow distinct draw of chain, the swift steely bite, and the crunch of blade on...on flesh and bone?

Too much red meat, that's what this was about. A heavy dinner and not enough sleep.

Unfolding painfully, I set my unused pad aside — I wasn't about to write down my dreams — folded up the blanket and crawled out through the window.

I hurried through the shambles of the garden, pausing on the edge to look back at the house. The scent of eucalyptus hung heavy in the night air. I told myself that if I saw lights in the second story windows, I would go back, so it was a relief to see only black and broken panes reflecting the night sky. I started back up the road towards Oliver's house.

It seemed a long way that night — as though the overgrown road were elastic, stretching further and further despite the energetic pace I set.

I began to think about the figure in the road the previous evening.

Except...not a mysterious figure, after all, but rather a famous and well-respected artist. With a penchant for sauntering through the woods at night.

Well, everyone needs a hobby.

But the way Thaddeus Stern had followed me through the woods — that wasn't normal behavior. That was...disquieting. The way he'd stood there watching me, moving closer and closer across the lawn. He'd practically emanated malevolence.

Or had my tiredness and imagination got the better of me?

Given the direction my thoughts were going, I guess it wasn't surprising that when someone stepped out of the bushes right to the side of me, I shot off the ground like I'd had springs installed in my feet.

A blast of fear and adrenaline surged through me, I turned and bolted — slamming right into a thick tree trunk.

Chapter Seven

I was seeing stars.

"Are you all right?" The voice floating above me was soft and alarmed. A black bulk bent over me.

I jackknifed up — and just missed banging heads with the owner of the voice. "I-I think so…" Actually, I felt a little sick in the wake of that rush of fear and adrenaline — not to mention the shock of hitting my head.

I had a blurred impression of massive shoulders and silver fur. It didn't do much to settle my nerves.

Feeling around in the grass, I found my glasses and examined the wire frames doubtfully. The lenses were fine but the frames fit crookedly when I slipped them on. I viewed my companion.

He was big — even bigger than Sam. Tall and broad with a dark hawkish face and long silver hair and beard. Silver eyebrows too.

"Here, let me help you up." Forceful hands fastened on my upper arms and lifted me onto my feet. "I didn't mean to frighten you."

"You didn't." I put a hand to my forehead, brought it away. No blood as far as I could tell. That was good, though I could feel a knot rising beneath my cautious fingers. It pulsed, tender to the touch.

"You're Oliver's little friend." His eyes were very dark, like black holes in his face.

I irritably shook off my fancifulness. An elderly man and the safety of Oliver's house within sprinting distance: there was nothing here I couldn't handle. I bent to brush myself off.

"I don't know if friend is quite the right word," I glanced up. "I don't know if *little* is quite the right word. You make me sound like a pet rabbit."

He chuckled. "Sure you're all right?"

"Mostly. You're Thaddeus Sterne, aren't you?"

"Yes." He did that chuckling thing again.

I said as though we were standing in C.K.'s gallery, "I'm a great admirer of your work."

"Are you?" He sounded amused. "Would you like to come back to my house and see some of it?"

It seemed an odd time for a visit, even if he was one of living legends of the art world. "I should probably be getting back," I said regretfully.

"I think you should come with me," he said gently. "David Berkeley's waiting for you."

"I...what?" I jerked upright, interested at how calm I sounded. Calm and a little faint. Which was pretty much how I felt.

"Look." He pointed down the road. I stared. There in the bend where the trees dipped low and the shadows were deep I could see —

No. I didn't see anything but shadows. And Thaddeus Sterne was almost certainly off his rocker.

But my eyes wouldn't seem to look away, and as I focused I seemed to be able to pick out the tall, faceless figure. A tall man standing silent in the center of the path.

This was what I had seen the night I arrived. Not Thaddeus Sterne at all. The shade of David Berkeley.

Ridiculous. I was just reacting to the suggestion...

"Why would he wait for me?" I asked carefully, unable to tear my gaze away from the umbra in the path.

"I don't know." I could feel Thaddeus's gaze on my profile. "You keep returning to the house. Maybe he thinks you're looking for him."

I was too tired to work this out. And then it occurred to me that I was having a very strange dream. It had to be a dream. I could imagine myself telling Sam about it over dreadful coffee in the morning: *I was standing in the woods talking to Thad Sterne about David Berkeley — and David Berkeley was right there listening to us.*

I said to Thaddeus, "I thought it was you following me the other night."

He said, "You'd better come back with me and let me take a look at that bump on your head."

Yeah, I had to be dreaming. I was tucked up in bed right now. So it was okay to go along with this — it wasn't for real, and I was curious about how it was all going to work itself out.

I nodded, keeping one eye on the dark shadows where I thought I'd seen...Berkeley's specter.

We didn't take the path, though, Thaddeus pushed right through the bushes and I followed him so there was no need to pass that point in the road where Berkeley waited.

"It's not far," he assured me. He moved in long powerful strides once we cleared the shrubbery. I trailed after him.

We walked until we came to a house that looked like an Arts and Crafts masterpiece: a rambling shingle-style in dark wood with a multitude of brightly lit windows. Thaddeus trudged up the interlocking stone front path and pushed open the unlocked front door.

"You're not afraid of burglars?" I asked.

He tittered, holding the door so that I could precede him inside. "No danger of that. What do I have that anyone would want?"

I stared around at an informal wall-to-wall gallery of paintings, a fortune in Thaddeus Sterne art work. It seemed to me pretty obvious what someone might want, but I let it go. There's no point debating with people in your dreams.

Thaddeus led the way to a large room that was also lined with paintings. Obviously the rumors were wrong; he hadn't quit painting. He had just quit exhibiting.

I sank down on the nearest surface: a velvet-covered sofa straight out of a Victorian novel. My head hurt, but mostly I just felt tired and a little woozy. Sterne left me for a few moments and returned with an old-fashioned ice pack. I applied it cautiously to my forehead.

Disappearing again, he reappeared with a decanter. He poured two cognacs, one of which he handed to me. I said apologetically, "I probably shouldn't after a knock on the head."

He shrugged, set the glass on the flimsy table next to the sofa, and then dropped down in a giant brocade chair. He leaned forward, frowning beneath the shaggy silver eyebrows.

"Tell me about Oliver?"

I shifted the ice pack. "Tell you…what?"

"How did he look?"

"Good. Healthy. Happy."

He nodded. Stared at his drink. Had that been the wrong answer?

"Did he say when he was coming home?"

"Not to me." I added uncomfortably, "I think he's in Paris now."

"Yes. He loves Paris." He tossed back the cognac in his glass. "You must have made quite an impression on him."

I said honestly, "I think he felt sorry for me. I'd broken up with my boyfriend and…I wasn't taking it well."

He stared at me.

"He can be very kind," he said at last.

"He was to me."

There was a very strange silence. I realized that more than anything I wanted to lie down on this velveteen couch and go to sleep.

"We grew up together, me and Oliver. We've always been together."

I guess it was all how you defined "together."

I searched around for something to say. He obviously was only interested in one topic. "What was he like back then?"

He said dryly, "Like he is now, only faster on his feet."

"Did you know Sam when he was a boy?" I heard myself ask — proof that I'd been knocked harder on the noggin than I supposed.

Sterne smiled, his face unexpectedly relaxed. "Oh yes. He spent all his summers here when he was growing up. Sammy's a sweetheart."

I made a noncommittal noise. I hadn't seen that side of him yet, but he certainly had the Silver Panther vote.

Sterne chuckled again. I wished he wouldn't. It raised the hairs on the back of my neck. Then he leaned forward and whispered, "You shouldn't go in the house. It isn't safe. Especially for you, I think."

I stiffened. "Why especially for me?"

"Not every door you open is possible to close."

"That's certainly cryptic."

He just eyed me in that calm way.

"Did you ever see…?" I realized it was a foolish question. He had seen whatever I had tonight. The question was what had we seen? How much of it was imagination — or suggestion — and how much of it was bad lighting?

"Sam said he used to play —" I paused, wondering if "play" was the right word to describe anything Sam might have done.

"Boys will be boys," Sterne remarked. He reached for my untouched cognac. "Oliver and I used to prowl through the house when we were lads, too."

"You know the story about Berkeley killing himself in the library?"

"Using the guillotine from his act? Oh yes. The guillotine was long gone by then, of course, but you could still see the bloodstains on the floor."

The ice pack was leaking cold water down the back of my neck. I shuddered, studying Sterne, not sure whether to believe him or not. He smiled maliciously.

"Or maybe we just hoped that's what those stains were." He eyed me speculatively.

I said, "Is there some legend about Berkeley's severed head speaking when he was found?"

He laughed heartily. "Where did you hear that old horror story?"

"So there is such a story?"

"Amor et melle et felle est fecundissmismus."

"Which means what exactly?" Did everyone in this damn place speak Latin?

"Love is rich with both honey and venom."

I stared at him. "That can't be true." Why had Sam lied?

"Of course not." His eyes were puzzled. "It's just a story some fool made up. You know the legend of course? Berkeley killed himself when his childhood sweetheart ran off with his best friend."

"A local painter by the name of Aaron Perry."

"That's right!" He looked pleased. "Have you seen the portrait?"

I nodded.

"It's not bad, is it? Aaron Perry had something. It's a shame none of the rest of his work survived. Berkeley was at the height of his fame when that portrait was painted. Fame being relative. He traveled all over the world: England, Spain, Paris —" his voice was bitter on the word "Paris." "He performed in music halls and carnivals and circuses. Anywhere he could. He didn't come home for years on end, but I suppose he thought the girl would wait forever. She didn't."

The silence was definitely awkward.

"I should probably be getting back," I said.

"Do you know the way?"

"Yes. I think so."

"Take the road. Don't cut through the woods."

I didn't answer that. I wasn't sure that he wasn't deliberately trying to spook me — no pun intended.

Sterne followed me to the front door. "Thank you for visiting," he said politely. "I don't get much company. Everyone thinks I'm crazy." He chuckled and closed the door in my face.

§ § §

"Shit!"

Sunday morning, I studied myself with dismay in the steamy bathroom mirror. A colorful bruise marked my brow bone where the tree branch had whacked me the night before. Now how was I supposed to explain that?

I raked my hair over my forehead. If I didn't mind it in my eyes, it was long enough to cover the special effects. I just had to remember not to move my head around too much. I sighed and reached for my shaving cream brush. Not so pretty a boy this morning.

Lathering my face, I considered last night's adventures. If I didn't have the bruises to prove it, I'd have wondered if I'd dreamed the entire evening. As it was, the events had an Alice in Wonderland quality to them. Or maybe I was thinking of the Jabberwocky. I'd definitely experienced a sinister moment or two in that house. Probably my own overactive imagination, but I couldn't wait to get hold of the video camera and see what might have been captured on tape.

"What the hell happened to you?" Sam asked, looking up out of the paper when I wondered into the kitchen a short time later.

So much for my hair disguising the damage. I walked over to the coffee maker. This morning Sam appeared to be boiling tar in it. Perhaps he planned on working on the roof.

"I — er — went for a walk last night and banged into a tree." I replied, wondering if Thaddeus would confirm my story or whether he'd come up with his own version, which was liable to include details about me climbing out of Berkeley House at three o'clock in the morning.

"A walk in the woods?"

"It's true, believe it or not."

To my alarm he tossed the paper aside and got up, coming over to examine me. I flinched as he raised his hand — and he halted mid-reach. Just for an instant hurt flared in his eyes. "Rhys —"

I had a sudden understanding of how often people reacted to his size and rough-hewn looks, without giving him an opportunity to be anything else. That wasn't my problem, but how could he know that?

"Really, Sam, it's okay," I said awkwardly.

He brushed the hair off my forehead. I went stiffer than a plank of wood, feeling that gentle touch in every cell of my body. I swallowed nervously, my throat making a little squeaky sound.

"That shade of purple just about matches your eyes," he said with wry humor.

I smiled weakly. It felt funny having to look up into his eyes — funnier still was the expression in them. I couldn't make it out but just for a second I thought he was about to...

Actually, I don't know what I thought.

"There's coffee," he said laconically, lowering his hand and moving back to the table.

"Is that what that is?" No wonder he was such a grim guy if he started every morning out with a dose of molten lava.

"I ground the beans myself."

"They have a machine for that, you know."

He grinned a wolfish grin. "I waited for you as long as I could."

Oddly, I remembered Thaddeus saying that Berkeley had assumed his sweetheart would wait forever. Which reminded me.

"I ran into Thaddeus Sterne last night."

His face changed, the friendliness draining out of it. I said defensively, "I wasn't looking for him. Why would I? He stepped out of the trees and startled me. That's how I got this." I pointed at my forehead.

After a moment he relaxed and nodded. I felt a flicker of guilt. And unease. Maybe I should have shut up about Sterne; now it was sure to come up between them as a topic of conversation.

"How was he?" he inquired.

"I think he misses Oliver. A lot."

"Yeah." He sighed. He didn't seem like the type to waste time sighing over what couldn't be changed, but that was the impression I had. Then he jerked his thumb back at the stove. "I fried up some Spam and eggs, if you're hungry."

"No you didn't," I said.

He looked puzzled. "Yeah, I did."

"Spam? Nobody eats Spam."

"I got news for you. Spam is delicious and nutritious."

"I'll give you delicious. No, actually, I can't in good conscience give you either of those."

"Suit yourself," Sam said. "There's probably a stale box of oatmeal somewhere."

I raised the lid on the frying pan and the warm, salty smell of fried eggs and ham hit my salivary glands. I hadn't realized quite how hungry I was.

"Well, I guess I have to eat something," I conceded, reaching for a clean plate.

"You do eat a lot for such a little guy."

"'Little guy?' Excuse me, King Kong, but I'm nearly six feet." His eyes flickered at the King Kong crack, but then he laughed.

"Better keep your strength up then, Cheetah. Especially if you're going to be taking many moonlight strolls." It was suddenly hard to avoid his gaze. "What brought on that sudden desire for fresh air, by the way?"

I could come clean right now. I could tell Sam everything that had happened — or at least everything I had dreamed. But if I told him, I knew without a doubt he'd have my equipment out of Berkeley House and me packed and on my way back to Los Angeles before my Spam and eggs were cold. That's what I told myself, anyway, but what I really shied away from was risking this jokey almost companionable truce between us.

"I wanted to see if I could catch another glimpse of those lights over at Berkeley House."

He was silent. I kept my eyes pinned on my plate while I shoveled in eggs, waiting for him to press it. I tried to decide if lying by omission was as bad as lying straight to his face — and whether I had it in me to lie straight to his face in any case. I wasn't sure I could anymore.

So it was a relief — and a surprise — when he all he said was, "Did you see the lights?"

"No."

He nodded, and then went back to his newspaper.

After my delicious and nutritious breakfast, I went out to the pool to have a heart attack and read over my notes in peace.

Not that Sam was disturbing me, except that somehow his presence was harder and harder to put out of my mind. In fact, I was astonished to realize that I hadn't given C.K. a single thought in almost twenty-four hours.

It was warm and sunny by the pool; summer wasn't far off now, and the events of the night before felt more and more distant and unreal. I turned my laptop on, working while the pool water lapped soothingly against the filter and the sun moved lazily across the bricks.

As I tapped and clicked, I began to wonder about Aaron Perry and Charity Keith. Their story seemed to stop with the event of their running off together; no source ever mentioned them after the elopement. Of course, I had never thought to ask anyone about them before...

I plugged "Charity Keith" into Google, but came up with nothing. "Aaron Perry" brought up musicians, actors and basketball players — none of whom fit the profile. There was quite a bit of information on David Berkeley — a lot it totally inaccurate — and there were several mentions of the runaway lovers, but nothing about what had become of them.

Nothing about the talking head either, for what that was worth. I was pretty sure Sam had brought that up to freak me out, and then for some reason changed his mind and turned it into that silly joke.

Had the eloping couple never returned to their hometown? A little drastic, surely? Or was public opinion so strongly in favor of Berkeley that they had decided they needed a fresh start?

Or had they feared some reprisal from Berkeley?

I thought about this for a moment, eyes narrowed against the sunlight dancing on the water. I wasn't sure why that idea had come to me; perhaps it was the unsettled feeling I had about Berkeley's — alleged — specter. If it *hadn't* been Thaddeus Sterne in the woods that first night...if it really had been the shade of David Berkeley…then there was no denying the sense of threat I'd had.

But maybe the Perrys had returned. Maybe no one mentioned them because David Berkeley was the star of that show, and what interest was there in a couple of ordinary newlyweds settling down to run-of-the-mill domestic bliss?

Why had none of Aaron Perry's other paintings survived if he had continued to live and work in Ventisca?

Maybe they weren't any good? Maybe they had survived but no one recognized them as Perry's since he wasn't a famous artist? Maybe he had stopped painting and got a day job. The absence of other paintings didn't prove the Perrys hadn't returned to Ventisca; it was just interesting, that was all.

I could check out the local graveyard. Maybe check church records?

A shadow fell across the lounge chair. I glanced up.

"Feel like taking a break?" Sam asked.

"What's up?"

He said very casually, "I was thinking of going into town for lunch. Want to come?"

I did — how much startled me — but as I opened my mouth to say yes, I realized I would lose a much-needed opportunity to slip over to Berkeley House and change the video tapes, resetting them for the night. I might not get another chance. Besides, I needed to hear whether the ghostly guillotine sounds had been in my imagination or had actually been recorded.

"I'm not at a place where I can stop," I said reluctantly, nodding to the laptop.

He glanced at his watch and said tentatively, "Well, how about in another hour or so?"

"I — uh — I really need to keep working," I excused. My own disappointment startled me, but I didn't see a way around it. "Rain check?" I said hopefully.

Even as I said it I realized how stupid that was. When would there be time for a rain check? I'd be leaving tomorrow.

"Sure," Sam said indifferently, his face closing up again into its usual hard lines. "See you later."

He went back into the house and I stared unseeing at the computer screen.

The minute I heard his car pull away, I shut down my laptop and ran inside the house.

I pulled on Levis, stepped into tennis shoes, and hot-footed it over to Berkeley House. There was no sign of anyone in the woods — for a change — and my fears of the night before seemed the result of not enough sleep.

Slipping through the broken library window, I quickly changed the tapes, stuck the recorded video in the smaller video cam and started out again.

Leg over the sill, I hesitated.

Why not take a look at the cellar in the daylight?

Last night I had been overtired and, I had to confess, I'd let the atmosphere of the old place get to me. But today the house was just a slightly depressing wreck, and there was no reason not to check out the cellar. In fact, there was every reason to take a look, since it was my job to investigate paranormal occurrences, right?

I ducked back under the sill and made my way down the hall and through the ruined dining room. The chill hit me as I slipped through the dining room side door, but it was cold inside the center of the house, removed from the light and warmth of the day.

Rounding the corner, I stopped, letting my flashlight play over the scratched and battered door to the cellar.

The door was closed again. The knob had been replaced on its spindle. I stared at it for a long time, trying to remember when I'd replaced it.

I reached for the knob and then let my hand drop back to my side.

My skin crawled at the thought of opening the door to that...to that *what?* What was my problem?

I yanked open the door.

Cold. Bitter cold seeping through my clothes, my skin, right to my bones....

I slammed the door shut.

Fuck. I couldn't do it. I couldn't make myself step through that door, let alone go down the steps to the cellar.

And that fact alone seemed to indicate that there was something here, something at least worth mentioning in the book.

I'd never felt anything like it.

Everything else...the shadowy figure in the woods, the lights, the noise of the guillotine, everything else could be put down to fatigue or imagination or suggestion.

But whatever was on the other side of this door....

Suddenly I wanted out of that house about as intensely as I'd ever wanted anything in my life.

As I crossed the hall to the dining room my foot stuck to the floor. I shone my flashlight on the sole of my shoe.

A dime-sized piece of plastic.

Not plastic.

Hard candy.

I could see a candy wrapper blowing inside the house but there was no way a half-sucked lozenge of candy had wafted here on its own. And there was no way David Berkeley's ghost — with or without a head — was eating hard candies.

Someone — a human someone — had been inside the house besides me.

Chapter Eight

Kids, I thought. Not that I had seen any kids around, but candy and trespassing in haunted house seemed to indicate an adolescent hand.

Or perhaps ...Thaddeus? He didn't seem particularly fearful of the house, but he also didn't seem like the candy-popping type. Or maybe he did. How would I know?

There was a reasonable chance I had the answer on the video tape — assuming the candy-sucking intruder had showed up during the hours I'd been recording.

I remembered the floating lights in the attic and the sounds of sliding metal and clanking chains — had someone faked guillotine sounds and a ghostly presence? Why?

The house was already abandoned and no one seemed to show much of an interest in it aside from me — and my interest was temporary. It's not like I planned to move in there. The house itself didn't seem long for this world.

I stick-stuck my way across the floor, the dirt on the wood gradually working the candy loose and off my shoe sole.

Climbing out the library window, I was startled to see that the day had grown overcast, the sun retreating behind heavy cloud cover. A cold salty wind blew off the sea. I crept my way through the overgrown garden and then slipped into the woods, making my way back to Oliver's.

Sam was still not back, but as I glanced at the grandfather clock in the hallway, I saw that it was nearly four-thirty. He might be on his way back now. He'd been gone all afternoon.

I hunted around until I found a television hidden inside a lavish antique armoire. It took a few moments to figure out the inputs, but at last I had the camera hooked up to the TV.

I pressed play and stood back to watch.

Gray snow and the ear-blast of static.

I turned down the sound and tried different channels. No good. I hit fast forward.

The tape was blank.

"Damn."

Camera malfunction? Pilot error? I couldn't make sense of it. I'd used this camera dozens of time without problem.

Could someone have tampered with it? A candy-sucking saboteur? But why wouldn't such a person simply have turned the camera off — or smashed it?

Hearing the sound of a car in the drive, I snapped off the TV. I wiggled the cord free, grabbed the camera and ran for the stairs.

Foot on the bottom step, I heard Sam's key in the front door lock. I froze, spied the hall closet door, and jerked it open, setting the camera inside.

I turned as the door swung open. Sam, was balancing white bags of take out while trying to pull his key from the door.

I felt a weird mix of pleasure and guilt at the sight of him, and although I had been planning to make my escape upstairs with the evidence as quickly as possible, I found myself walking towards him.

"Hi."

"Hi." He smiled a little self-consciously. "How'd the work go?"

"Good."

This was ridiculous. I actually felt...*shy*.

"I thought tonight we'd both get a night off." He held up one of the bags. "You like Chinese?"

"I love Chinese."

He gave another one of those lopsided smiles like he was still practicing getting the expression right.

"Grab some plates and a bottle of wine. We'll eat in the study." He added as an afterthought, "If that's okay with you."

"Yeah, it's okay."

His eyes met mine.

I waited 'til he vanished into the study, then I opened the closet door, grabbed the camera and took the stairs two at a time. I dropped the camera inside the doorway of my room and raced downstairs.

No sign of Sam, but I could smell woodsmoke.

I uncorked a bottle of wine, found glasses, and carried the plates into the study. Sam had dragged a short table over to the fireplace and was setting out little white cartons.

"Cashew chicken, barbecue spare ribs, sesame beef...."

I poured the wine into the glasses and settled on the floor beside him facing the fire.

Something was different. Something had changed. I could feel it, even though I couldn't identify what it was. I knew the change was partly in myself — and I knew the change was partly in Sam. Every time I met his eyes — which was frequently — something in his gaze warmed me, lifted my heart.

Suddenly there was a lot to say, each of us rushing into speech, pausing, smiling, to let the other talk. I let Sam refill my glass a couple of times and I looked forward to the night ahead.

When we finished eating, Sam slipped his arm around my shoulders and I turned my head to find his mouth. I closed my eyes, liking the feel of his mouth on mine, firm and warm, liking his gentleness and liking his assurance. My heart started to pound hard in my chest as his tongue brushed my upper lip.

"I've never known anyone like you," he said against my mouth. It almost sounded like an apology.

I smiled and his tongue slipped into my mouth, a dark and sweet kiss. Our tongues pushed delicately against each other, whorled, withdrew.

I laughed, snatched a quick unsteady breath. It had been a long time since kissing had been a big part of my sexual repertoire. With C.K. time had always been of the essence, both of us busy with our careers and outside demands. I hadn't realized quite how many outside demands C.K. had until one of them insisted he break up with me.

Sam rested his hand on my jaw, turned my face to his and kissed me deeper still, taking my breath away as his tongue touched, tested, tasted. Weren't there something like eight thousand taste buds on an adult tongue? Every one of mine seemed to be experiencing its very first burst of flavor: a smoky blend of alcohol and cashew chicken and something uniquely masculine — uniquely Sam.

The phone rang above our heads.

Sam stiffened. I moaned. He tore his mouth away.

"Who the hell is *that*?" I complained.

He kissed the corner of my mouth, and sat up. "Thad probably. No one else ever calls here."

The phone continued to shrill away. Sam rolled to his feet and picked it up.

I listened to the one-sided conversation. Since that was Sam's part of the conversation, there was basically nothing to hear.

"Yeah…Okay…Sure…No. No problem, Oliver. I'll handle it."

He hung up the phone and studied me ruefully. "Feel like a walk in the woods?"

"Seriously?"

"Oliver says he got a strange phone call from Thaddeus a while ago. He wants me to go over there and check that he's okay."

I sat up. "Okay."

We grabbed jackets from the hall closet and locked the front door behind us.

The moon was lost behind the heavy clouds as we cut through the woods, but our two flashlights provided enough light as we pounded down the dirt path.

"What are you smiling at?" Sam asked during the silence that had fallen between us. If he could tell I was smiling in the dark, he had to be paying pretty close attention.

"I was just thinking I'd put money on you over David Berkeley's ghost any day of the week."

He sounded amused. "I thought you weren't afraid of ghosts?"

"I'm just sayin'." Actually, I was saying too much, but I wasn't used to having to deceive anyone in the course of my work. And I liked less and less having to lie or conceal things from Sam. I tried to think of a way to tell him I'd been sneaking into Berkeley House before Thaddeus brought it up, but I hated the thought of losing this new-found harmony.

And maybe Thaddeus wouldn't say anything. Maybe whatever had us hot-footing it over to his house in the middle of the night would require all his attention. And if he did bring it up, maybe having a third party present would keep Sam from getting too angry, and give me a little time to explain my side of it.

Only one light was on at Thaddeus's house. Remembering the blaze of lamps the night before, it struck me as ominous. Sam banged on the door, but after a pause that seemed long enough to confirm my fears, Thaddeus swung open the door. He was wearing a purple paisley silk dressing gown and his hair looked like he had stuck his finger in a wall socket. He reeked of booze.

"Oliver sent you," he said immediately.

"He's worried," Sam said. "Can we come in?"

Thaddeus's eyes moved from Sam to me. He said, "He's not so worried that he'll come home."

For a minute I thought he was talking about me. He continued to stare at me.

"Can we come in, Thad?" Sam repeated. And after a moment Thaddeus moved aside and led the way into the house.

We trailed him into the room where he'd played host to me the night before. Sam sat down as though it was an ordinary visit, and after a moment, I sat too, choosing a chair off to the side. I was sort of hoping Thad might forget all about me.

We watched as he poured himself another cognac. His hands shook.

"You think that's going to help?" Sam asked.

"It can't hurt," Thaddeus retorted. He poured another glass and handed it to Sam. Looking blearily around, he spotted me. "There you are." He poured a third unsteady glass and I half-rose to take it from him.

Sam savored, swallowed, and said, "What's going on, Thad?"

"I'm old and I'm tired and I'm lonely," Thad said pretty crisply for a guy who'd apparently downed a half bottle of cognac. "I've come to the end of my rope."

Sam didn't have an answer for that, and I recognized it would be best if I kept my mouth shut. I swirled the tulip-shaped glass and then sniffed the volatile aroma.

"I want Oliver to come home," Thaddeus said. "If he loves me, he'll come."

"You know it's got nothing to do with that," Sam said.

Thaddeus turned his dark, bitter gaze my way. "I know what it has to do with. It has to do with using pretty little boys like that one to keep the dark at bay."

I lowered my glass. Granted, I was outside my weight division with those two, but I wasn't a midget, and I was over thirty. I opened my mouth, but caught the warning look Sam shot my way. By now I had an idea of Oliver's track record, so I bit back what was on the tip of my tongue.

"It's still got nothing to do with you," Sam said.

"No?" Thaddeus laughed — nothing like his usual nutty chuckle — and tossed back the rest of his drink.

Sam said quietly, "Thad."

Thad refilled his glass from the decanter at his elbow. "Don't be a boor, Sammy. Allow me my little farewell party." He raised the glass and toasted something out there in the night.

"Oh, that's just great," Sam said disgustedly. "What? You're planning to off yourself because Oliver's a spoiled, overgrown adolescent?"

Thaddeus glared. "This is farewell to *a dream*," he said with great dignity. "I wouldn't give him the satisfaction of killing myself."

"For what it's worth, I don't think Oliver would find your death very satisfying."

"It doesn't matter what he would or wouldn't find," Thad returned. "It's over. I've finally given up. I've been a fool. I see that now. Flesh and blood can't compete with...." Once more he turned that dark hostile gaze my way. "Well, it's finished. Over. Oh, don't worry. I won't do anything drastic. That's why you're here, I suppose. You can call Oliver right back and assure him I'm not going to cut my throat. I'd have to care to cut my throat, and I don't care anymore. I don't feel anything anymore."

And he drained his glass once more.

"Why don't I help you to bed, Thad?" Sam suggested. "You'll see things differently in the morning."

"Oh, go home, Sam," Thad said wearily. "And take *him* with you."

Sam's eyes met mine apologetically. I shrugged. I accepted that Thad's dislike wasn't personal; I just happened to represent everything he blamed for his unhappiness.

We didn't stay much longer. Sam made a couple more attempts to help Thad to bed, but they seemed to piss the old man off more than anything, and in the end even Sam had to concede defeat. Thad seemed to be settling into a boozy doze when Sam nodded silently to me. I rose, setting my empty glass aside.

We let ourselves out, standing for a moment on the porch. The wind had picked up again, rustling the tree leaves around us.

"Will he be all right?"

Sam shrugged. "I guess so. He's not a child. And he's not self-destructive — unless you count wasting your life loving someone like Oliver."

"Oliver must care a little. He called you to come check on Thad."

"Oh, he cares. In his own way." He added quietly, "The best thing for Thad would be if he *could* stop loving Oliver. But how do you break the habit of a lifetime?"

That was a depressing thought. I felt tired and dispirited as we headed back to Oliver's. No wonder Sam was cynical about relationships with a role model like Oliver. And, if I remembered correctly, his parents were divorced as well

"They grew up together?" I asked.

"Oh, yeah. They were boys together, went to art school together, achieved fame and fortune together."

"They were lovers."

"They *are* lovers. That's the weird thing. No one means more to Oliver than Thad."

"I guess I understand Thad's confusion." My own sour memories must have echoed in my voice because Sam glanced my way and then put an arm around my shoulders.

He said, "I don't understand Oliver. I don't understand why being with the person he loves the most isn't enough for him. But it's not. He needs the fame and he needs the adulation — he likes being a celebrity and he likes being a legend in his own lifetime. And if that's all it was, it would be difficult enough for Thaddeus, who doesn't care about any of that."

"But Oliver also likes pretty little boys."

"Yes." He sighed. "Thad isn't in the best of health, although he won't tell Oliver that — won't let me tell Oliver that. So Oliver's going to wait too long, and that will be that."

"And you don't think maybe you should speak up before it's too late?"

I felt him glance at my profile. "No, I don't."

I thought it over, comfortable in the circle of his arm.

"Did you ever hear the story of David Berkeley?" I inquired. "He was a Twentieth Century magician who was so busy building a career based on creating illusions that he fooled himself and lost the woman he loved to another man."

He said wryly, "Okay, okay. I know about Berkeley, and Oliver knows about Berkeley. Oliver knows life is short — that's a big part of Oliver's problem."

"Non-interference. It doesn't seem like a cop attitude."

"I'm not a cop with the people I love." His voice was different, although I couldn't define how. "And if it was me, I'd try to spend every minute with the person I loved, instead of focusing on the pain of losing him one day."

"Is that what it is?"

"I don't know. Partly, I think."

I thought it was funny how easily he spoke of love and caring and commitment. He didn't look like a guy who would waste five minutes on mushy stuff, let alone be able to articulate his feelings. Of course, he didn't look like a world-class kisser, either, but he was that all right. My mouth still tingled pleasantly from our after dinner encounter.

I started to speak but caught sight of Berkeley House through the trees. I stopped stock still. "Look!"

Sam followed the direction I pointed. In the distance we could see hazy lights moving eerily from window to window on the upstairs floor.

He was silent.

"You see that?"

"Yeah." He let go of me, automatically reaching up with his free hand, and I knew he would ordinarily have been wearing a shoulder holster. "I need to check that out."

The last thing I wanted was him investigating the house and finding my equipment. I said, "Unless someone's using a trampoline, I don't understand how that can be of human origin. The staircase has rotted through and the dumb waiters are wrecked."

He snorted. "What, you think that's David Berkeley looking for a lost sock or something?"

"Maybe he's looking for his head."

He glanced at me. "Now that's a gruesome thought, professor."

I shrugged.

"It might be some kind of refracted light. Ships off the ocean?"

I didn't even bother to answer that one.

"Okay, what do you think it is?"

"You can't even *consider* the idea that it might be a paranormal phenomenon?"

He opened his mouth, and then apparently rethought the first words that came to him. "I didn't say that." His spoke painstakingly, and I realized that he was making a conscious attempt not to offend me. "But I need something more than — "

He fell silent as the light vanished. We waited for a few moments but the windows stayed dark.

"The moon reflecting off something maybe," he said doubtfully.

"Whatever it is, it's over for the night." I said. "Let's go back to Oliver's."

He thought it over. "Come on," he said, and to my relief — and pleasure — he put his arm around my shoulders again.

As we continued on I was thinking about my assertion that supernatural forces had to be at work, but what about the lozenge of candy I'd found?

I knew I should tell Sam.

If local kids were fooling around in that house, it had to stop. The place was a death-trap.

But maybe I could wait 'til tomorrow; 'til after whatever was going to happen tonight had developed. We'd have a better chance of weathering Sam's discovery of my deception if things went well tonight. And if I could get my stuff out of the house tomorrow without him finding out, maybe I could find another way to let him know about the house's other trespassers.

"What are you thinking about so seriously?" he asked.

"About the way things work out. I'm glad Oliver invited me to stay."

His hand rested lightly against the small of my back, warm, possessive. "Me too."

When we got back to the house, Sam poured us each a brandy and then called Oliver. It was a brief call, and Sam was unusually curt with his uncle. At least, that's how it seemed to me, listening in.

He said finally, "Maybe you should tell Thad then."

He listened to Oliver, and then said with great finality, "Then I guess it comes down to trust."

Trust. A little frisson of alarm unfurled down my spine, and I was glad I'd kept my mouth shut about sneaking back inside the house. In fact, I was definitely going to get my stuff out of that house without Sam finding out. I could probably pretend to leave tomorrow and then swing back around and park in the woods again.

Sam concluded his call with Oliver. For a moment he gazed down at the phone; his head raised, he met my gaze. "Feel like a moonlight swim?"

"A...swim?"

He smiled — and I found myself smiling too.

§ § § §

We swam naked in the warm buoyant water of the pool behind the house, our voices quiet in the cool empty night air. A tear in the canopy of thick cloud cover revealed the dusting of stars glittering high overhead. Sam had turned on the living room stereo and the music drifted out from the window, a lazy seductive saxophone flirting with a sexy-shy piano.

After a couple of lazy laps, I floated on my back and stared up at the sky. The fleecy black clouds looked low enough to touch. Steam rose from the water. Sam swam up beside me; he moved like an eel in the water, smooth and fast, the water barely rippling around him.

"What time are you leaving tomorrow?"

"I should probably be on the road by lunch time. I have an evening lecture."

He sank down, swimming under me, slick body brushing my own, surfacing so that I was lying across him. His genitals bobbed against my backside; he was half-hard — and now so was I. The languid graze of hands and legs, the bump of bodies, the glide of water on sensitive skin: it was playful and erotic at the some time.

"Do you —?" I wanted to ask if he ever got down to L.A., but he interrupted quietly, "Yeah, I do." And his hands slid under me, turning me without effort so that I was lying on top of him.

He kissed me, his lips cool and tasting of chlorine and Sam. I kissed him back.

His legs wrapped around me, his arms slipped under my own, holding me tight. His mouth fastened on mine again and we slowly submerged, the water closing softly over our heads.

I realized I was out of my depth in more than one way.

Chapter Nine

I breathed out a gentle stream of bubbles through my nose while Sam's breath filled my mouth and lungs. I opened my eyes as we sank past the pool lights, the underwater world washed out aqua and bright as daylight. It was like being in our own sphere, warm as the womb; I let go, let Sam control it, relaxed in his arms as we drifted down. His mouth exhaled softly into mine. Our feet touched against the floor of the pool and he pushed off. We shot back up again in a silver spill of bubbles.

Our heads broke the surface, the night air cold against our wet faces.

It was black as pitch. It took me a moment to realize the house lights were off and the music had stopped.

"Hey," I said to Sam, wiping my face. "That was some kiss. The fuses just blew."

The pool water swelled like ink around us as the wind rose again. Sam's feet and legs brushed mine as we tread water.

"It's an electrical storm," he said, staring up at the clouds.

Sure enough, as we watched, lightning forked against the night. The air around us seemed to crackle with a charge — followed by the boom of thunder.

"Oh hell," Sam said. "Swim, Rhys."

I didn't need to be told twice. We raced for the steps, reaching them as the night flashed white — followed by another ear-splitting crack of thunder.

Sam was up and out, reaching back for me. With one hand he practically lifted me out of the water and onto the cement — and I realized exactly how strong he really was.

"It's close," I gasped, as another flare lit our way acro bricks to the back door of the house.

"Too close," he agreed. He kept a hand fastened on my upper arm, guiding me through the blur of wooden patio furniture and potted plants.

The wet slap of our feet left footprints that vanished on the paving behind us like ghost steps. Sam felt for the door knob and pushed into the kitchen. The curtains billowed in the wind from the open windows, shadowy and indistinct in the darkness.

"Stay there and I'll find candles," he ordered.

I didn't bother to answer, stepping back outside, finding my way to the table where I'd left my glasses. I slipped them on and stood there for a moment beneath the vine-covered pergola watching the lightning flash above the ocean. The air snapped with electricity. The hair on my arms prickled with it.

"Rhys?" Sam called from inside the house.

"Right here," I called back.

Sam appeared in the kitchen doorway holding a thick candle. The flickering shadow cast sinister angles across his face.

I said, "This would seem to limit the evening's entertainment options."

A slow and wicked grin crossed his face. "I wouldn't say that," he said.

§ § § §

"You're beautiful," Sam said huskily. His big warm hand stroked my belly like he'd stroke a cat. It felt extraordinarily nice, and if I'd known how to purr, I would have. Instead I laughed huskily, as my cock filled, twitching like a witching wand.

"So are you."

"You're right. That is funny."

I shook my head, but it was hard to concentrate. I just stirbis hand around me. I dug my heels in the mattress of groaned thrust up a little. Instead his hand slid upwards, He est, scratching my nipples with his thumbnail. I liar."

utiful and funny and smart — and a

My eyes flew to his face. "I'm not lying," I said — and because my conscience was guilty, I sounded abrupt and defensive.

"I'm teasing you," he said. "I know you're not lying. You're trying to be nice. You don't have to bother. This mug of mine is useful in my line of work."

I stared up at his face; there was strength and character in his harsh ugliness. In fact, he no longer seemed ugly. I liked the fact that he didn't look like everybody else. He seemed familiar and increasingly important to me. Too important to lie to.

"Sam," I began hesitantly.

His mouth touched mine, stopping my words as though he knew what I was going to say, as though he didn't want to hear it, as though he didn't want the moment spoiled. And because I didn't want the moment spoiled either — because I *needed* this moment — I let his lips press me into silence, opening to him in another way.

Sam's kisses made me feel like I'd never been properly kissed before, like it was the first time — like the best of all the firsts: the first giddy swoop of alcohol in your bloodstream or the first sweet bite of dark chocolate on your tongue or the first time you saw a shooting star or felt a man's mouth close on your dick.

His hands gathered me close, hard and competent but cherishing too. I could feel every beat of our hearts echoing in my veins and nerves, beat and answering beat. I felt safe and complete in Sam's arms.

His mouth lifted from mine. "What would you like?" His soft words gusted moist and warm against my ear.

I said with simple certainty, "I want to be inside you."

And he nodded, surprising me with an astonishingly sweet smile. "Sure. How?"

We angled around, knees and elbows bumping, but it was relaxed and easy, as though we were already used to each other, comfortable with each other. Sam stretched out before me, long strong and bronzed in the candlelight. Everything in beautiful proportion, the ripple of muscles beneath supple skin, the black dusting of hair over limbs and genitals. His hands and feet were carefully groomed, the nails trimmed and buffed. His hair was neatly cut. He took care of the details, so he did care to some extent about appearances. I felt unexpected tenderness for him, a desire to make up for things.

Bending, I kissed the back of his strong neck, and he shivered.

There was a tube of sunscreen next to the bed, and I squeezed a dollop of creamy white smelling of sea and sand on my fingers, separating the globes of Sam's tight buttocks with one hand and probing that tight little hole with the other.

I pushed one delicate finger in and Sam uttered a long, low groan, his body clenching.

I smiled. "All right?" I leaned forward, pressed a damp kiss between his shoulder blades. The ring of muscle pulled at my finger as I slid in and out.

"Believe it," he grated.

I took my time, although I could tell he didn't really need it, and then I pressed a second finger in, stretching him, seeking that nub of nerves and gland. Sam pushed back at my hand, drawing me in deeper.

"You're so gentle..." He raised his head, smiling. "Knew when I saw those long, sensitive fingers of yours...*fuuuck*..." His back arched as I found his P-spot.

I moved forward, trying to find his mouth at that awkward angle, massaging the spongy bump with careful fingers. My own cock was rock hard, my balls aching. Sam shuddered and moaned as I lowered myself on top of him. I loved the hard heat of his body down the length of mine.

"This feels so good," I said into his muscular shoulder. "I think I've wanted this practically since that first night."

"You're killing me here, professor," Sam muttered. His buttocks humped back against my groin, and I pulled my fingers out, replacing them in that moist heat with my dick. So...*good.* I whimpered as his sphincter muscle contracted around me. Began to push and slide in that hot darkness. I couldn't have stopped to save my life.

Sam let out a deep sound, something between a groan and a growl, and began to rock back hard against me. I thrust back at him, closing my eyes, just concentrating on that welcome velvet grab, trying to push deeper, needing to feel joined, united. Heat on burning heat. His fierce silence in contrast to my own wounded sounds as I pumped into him, reaching further and further for that desperate release —

And finally…after delicious and due diligence…at last…there it was. Rolling up out of the yearning struggle of hungry cock and willing ass, slow sweet climax that pulsed through me, warming me with every heartbeat.

"Sam…Sam…" I couldn't help it. Couldn't help the helpless noises as I began to come, pouring out stupid emotional things while my muscles turned to rubber and my cock spurted sticky relief into the clench of his channel.

I collapsed on top of him, gasping for breath, quivering head to foot. I'm ashamed to admit I didn't even know if he'd come. Although the linens felt soggy enough for several orgasms.

A long, long time later, Sam stirred, tipping me off of him and pulling the covers over us. I wrapped my arms around him, still wanting the closeness, quietly delighted when his arms wrapped around me again, cradling me against his warmth. He kissed my brow bone and my nose, and I smiled, opened sleepy eyes.

Over his shoulder I could see the candle on the bedstand, hissing and guttering hot wax. "Does that candle look funny to you?" I mumbled. "Kind of green and glowing…?"

He half-rolled away, blew the candle out, and pulled me back against his body.

§ § § §

The storm had passed.

I slipped out from under Sam's arm. Slid out of the warm bed, found my glasses, stuck them on my nose. The clock next to Sam read half-past midnight. For a moment I stood there watching Sam sleep in the moonlight, the hard planes of his face relaxed, his hair tumbled, his mouth soft. He was snoring, a tolerable buzz. I found my jeans and tiptoed out of the room while Sam slept deeply on.

Making my way along the hall, I headed downstairs, retrieving my shoes in the hallway.

I was moving fast, refusing to acknowledge any unease. I needed to make this fast, needed to get back in case Sam woke and wondered what happened to me. I didn't know how heavy a sleeper he was and I didn't want to find out the hard way.

So if David Berkeley was lurking in the trees, I didn't see him as I ran through the woods. I came out on the edge of the sunken garden, paused, hands braced on thighs, to catch my breath. The moon, reflected in the black windows of the house, gilded the eucalyptus trees and the broken statues. Cautiously, I made my way down the moss-slick stone stairs, finding a path through the weeds and brambles.

Skulking along the side of the house, sticking to the shadows, I drew near the library window — and froze. Were those voices I heard? I inched closer, trying to see through the shadows and darkness.

I reached the library window and listened.

Silence.

No — there is was. Echoing down the hallway. It sounded like something heavy being dragged along the floor.

Hands on the window ledge, I hesitated. Leaned in.

I heard it again. A voice. Masculine. I couldn't make out the words. I swung myself up, ducking under the shattered window, and the roof crashed down on me....

§ § § §

Cold.

Bitter cold. I shivered — had been shivering if the ache in muscles was anything to go by.

My head ached too, the sick pounding of my temples seeming to rebound through my entire body, pulse hammering, heart thudding too hard. Shell bursts flared behind my eyelids.

What was wrong with me? Was I ill?

I pried my eyes open. Pitch...black...nothing.

Panic washed through me. Was I blind? What had happened to me?

I made an effort to sit up. Sweat broke out on my body, nausea roiled through my belly. I twisted to the side and threw up. I groaned. Threw up again.

When the worst of it seemed over, I scooted back painfully, dropping back shaking onto the cold stone. Why was I lying on the floor? *What* floor?

What...the...fuck...had happened to me?

For a few moments I lay there shuddering, fighting the sickness bubbling in my guts. My head throbbed in time to my heavy heart beat. The cold of the stone floor seeped...

Cold stone?

Where the hell was I?

I forced my lids open again. Passed my hand in front of my eyes. I could just make out a pale glimmer.

It wasn't my vision. At least...it wasn't only my vision. I was somewhere very dark, somewhere with a stone floor...

It didn't make sense. I tried to remember....I recalled swimming with Sam. Warmth washed through my body. I remembered making love to Sam.

That was the last thing I could recollect. It wasn't a bad place for memories to end, but...

I pushed myself up, having to wait on my hands and knees for the next wave of nausea to subside. I dragged myself the rest of the way to my feet, and hands outstretched, tried to get an idea of the size of the room that held me.

Three steps forward and my hands touched wood. Old wood. Rough and splintered. A door.

Dizzily, I closed my eyes and leaned against the wooden surface.

No way.

No. This had to be a nightmare. I was lying next to Sam right now. Dreaming. And hopefully he would wake me up any minute.

I waited in the unstable blackness. My balance was off and I needed the support of the door to stay upright. I needed to lie down again. But not here. I needed out of wherever here was...

Vague flashes of running through the woods, the moonlight gilding the ruined garden, and then...nothing.

My heart accelerated, zero to ninety in nothing flat.

I was in the cellar at Berkeley House.

I knew it as sure as I knew anything...which was maybe debatable considering the dumb ass way I'd managed things so far.

One thing for sure, no ghost knocked me over the head and threw me into the cellar. I told myself this a couple of times in an attempt to distract my awareness of the sickening chill pressing in on me.

Numbly, I moved my hands over the door, trying to find a knob. A handle.

No reason for panic. Even if there was...something...wrong with the house...and there wasn't. Of course there wasn't. Even if there was...it had nothing to do with me. It had nothing to do with my being in the cellar.

I jerked my head around at a whisper of sound behind me.

Was there moment? A breach in the wall of darkness? I turned back to the door, urgently feeling over its surface.

There it was again, the stealthy slide of something metallic. A tinkling like broken glass — links of a chain?

My groping fingers closed on metal. A handle. I twisted it. Tried the other way. The door stayed firmly closed. I yanked hard. The door didn't budge.

Another insinuation of sound. I threw a frantic look over my shoulder and froze.

Movement in this utter darkness?

I turned, planted my back against the wood, facing...the wisp of smoke that seemed to unfurl in the void a few feet from me.

My eyes strained to see.

From overhead came the slow draw of a chain. I looked up, flinched as something glinted overhead.

"This isn't real," I said desperately. "I don't believe in this."

I caught motion out of the corner of my eye, jerked my gaze forward. A filmy, cadaverous mist was gathering a few feet away.

No.

I shook my head to clear it. Mistake. The room slanted sickeningly. I could feel something warm trickling down my face. Blood? Tears? My head swam. I blinked hard.

Above me I heard again the metallic rasp of links through a pulley, but I couldn't look away.

The mist was taking shape before me…a tall figure in old-fashioned garments…shoes with spats…trousers…vest beneath overcoat…a top hat…but all of it indistinct, vaporous, seeming to waver and wane as though moving in a breeze.

The drag of chain was louder, harsher…deafening It was destroying my ears.

The mist seemed to reshape, a familiar face taking form: long, narrow, diaphanous, with hollow burning eyes and a cruel thin mouth.

Overhead the pulley stopped.

"You're not real," I told the baleful haze. "I don't believe in you."

The eyes seemed to find me in the darkness. *It sees me*, I thought bewilderedly. The cruel mouth turned upwards.

I heard the screeching release of chain, felt something heavy hurtle my way. I cried out in shock as something massive and glacial and terrifying slammed into me.

From a distance I heard David Berkeley laughing.

§ § § §

"Thatta boy."

The words trickled through the warm blankness. Someone was stroking my face. My hair. A warm calloused hand smoothing from temple to jaw, a long, slow, comforting sweep over and over.

"That's it. That's better."

Sam.

I unstuck my eyelashes.

An indistinct form leaned over me — and beyond his shoulders, the red ball of the morning sun. I was lying on the ground. I could feel the fragrant tickle of weeds and grass, feel the damp warmth of the earth beneath me. Tears of relief flooded my eyes.

I unglued my lips. "Sam?" I croaked.

"Welcome back," he said. He brushed the back of his knuckles against my cheek, wiping the wet away.

"I can't —" It was an effort to get my lips to form sentences. I felt battered, exhausted. "Are my glasses —?"

"Your glasses are broken. I found them outside the house." He added grimly, "That's how I knew to look for you inside." He repositioned, slipped an arm beneath my shoulders. "You think you can sit up?"

I nodded. Sat up with his help. "Sorry," I said to the blur of his face. "Are you pretty pissed off?"

"Yeah, I am. You want to try standing up?"

I nodded. Rested my head in the warm curve of his neck and shoulder. Closed my eyes.

§ § § §

When I next opened my eyes I was in my bed at Oliver's, and it was late afternoon. I squinted at the clock on the bedside table. Sometime after three? My spare pair of glasses sat next to the clock. I slid them on.

Three-twelve on Monday afternoon.

Shit.

I needed to call the university. I shoved aside the pile of blankets and sat up cautiously. My head ached but nothing like that morning. I reached up, touched a square of gauze and tape. Sam to the rescue, apparently.

I was slowly trying to process everything that had happened since that very long ago night we had spent together, when the open door to the bedroom pushed wide, and Sam, wearing black jeans, black T-shirt and a black expression, looked in.

We gazed at each other for a silent moment. He had the advantage. There's nothing like being knocked over the head and caught out in a lie to take the wind out of your sales — sitting there in nothing but my underwear didn't help, either.

"Hi," I said, subdued.

"Hi. How do you feel?"

"Okay." That was overstating it. I felt like shit.

"Good. Because I want to know what happened. You up to getting dressed and coming downstairs?"

I guess I could understand why he had no wish to sit with a nearly naked me in my bedroom. "Yeah."

"I'll see you downstairs."

"Sam —"

But he was already gone.

I got up slowly, dressed still more slowly, and went downstairs. Sam was in the kitchen, sitting at the table. There was a mug of tea in front of him.

I took a seat at the table, moving with careful deliberation, trying to jar my head as little as possible.

He watched me without particular sympathy. "You want some tea?"

"Please."

"Milk and sugar?"

I nodded and wished I hadn't.

"You've got a mild concussion," he said, observing me. "I had Oliver's doctor take a look at you while you were out."

"Thanks." My spirits sank lower still at his flat tone.

He placed a mug in front of me. I picked it up, hand shaking. I sipped the hot liquid and felt a little better. I wondered if this doctor had left any tablets for my head.

"So fill me in on what happened after you snuck out of the house." He didn't sound angry, exactly, just…empty.

I told him everything I could remember — which wasn't a lot — and I apologized a couple of times for…not listening to him.

"You mean lying?" he asked, the second time I said it.

I cleared my throat. "Yes."

He was silent for a moment. "Have you ever blacked out like that before?"

"I didn't black out. Someone hit me over the head."

"When I pulled you out of that cellar you were...you appeared to be catatonic."

I stared at him.

"Has that ever happened to you before?"

"No." I took another mouthful of tea, concentrated on keeping my hand steady. "I didn't dream it. There's something in the cellar," I said.

His green eyes rested on my face. This was the face that people across the interrogation table from him saw. I'd blown it with him; I knew that. He wasn't somebody to take a light view of being lied to.

"You mean like a ghost?" he asked at last.

"I mean like..." I stopped. "Yes. Like a ghost," I admitted.

He looked sorry for me. "Rhys."

So I told him everything. I told him about seeing the shade of David Berkeley in the woods the night I had arrived, how I thought it had been Thad, but now I knew for sure it hadn't. I told him about hearing the sound of a guillotine when I'd fallen asleep in the library. I reminded him of the horrifying cold emanating from the cellar.

"You said yourself you'd never felt anything like it," I said.

"It's an unpleasant place. That doesn't mean there's a — an *entity* setting up house down there."

"Thad saw David Berkeley too."

"*Thad?* Thad is not what I'd call a reliable witness."

Neither was I apparently. It didn't look like he was going to bother humoring me at this point.

I said, "What happened to my equipment?"

"Loaded in your car."

I nodded, looked down at my mug. My fingernails were torn and bloodied; I must have clawed the door of the cellar trying to get out; I was just as glad I didn't remember that part.

"There's something down there," I said.

He stared at me with those hard green eyes.

"I think David Berkeley is insane — was insane."

"I think he's dead," Sam said with finality.

I said, "If there is such a thing as life beyond the grave —" His wearied expression stopped me. I said, "Is it unreasonable to think that if someone was driven mad in life, their spirit might be...troubled as well?"

"Yeah, it is. Dead is dead. Over. Done with."

I had the sick feeling he wasn't just talking about mortal coil stuff.

I said, still trying although even I wasn't sure why, "There's something in that house. Something that can't rest. Something that won't let David Berkeley rest." I rubbed my head. Speaking of rest, I wanted nothing more than to lie down again.

Distantly I was aware that Sam had risen from his chair. He dropped a hand on my shoulder, squeezing, then letting go. "You should get some sleep," he said. "You've got a long drive tomorrow."

Chapter Ten

I was packing when Mason showed up that evening.

The door bell ring and then Sam bellowed for me from downstairs. When I came down only Mason sat in the front parlor.

"How are you feeling?" he asked, rising as I entered the room. "You look okay." He stepped towards me and then stopped.

"I'm fine. Just a slight headache." I gave him a wan smile.

Had I been interested in Mason? It seemed as vague as everything else that had happened to me since crawling out of Sam's bed Sunday night.

Mason sat back down and so did I.

"The whole town's buzzing with the news you got yourself clobbered by the local burglars."

"I did?"

"Yeah." He looked puzzled. "Didn't you know?"

"I don't remember much about it."

"Apparently the gang was using the house to store the stuff they stole."

I stared at him, dumfounded. "I didn't see any sign of that."

He smiled his nice uncomplicated smile. "They were using a hidden room."

"A hidden room?"

He chuckled at my tone. "'Fraid so. Not so hidden as it turned out. Sam Devlin knew all about it."

"He knew about it?" I didn't seem to be able to do more than echo Mason's words.

"Apparently he spent a lot of time in the house when he was a kid."

I felt irrationally hurt that Sam had not shared this knowledge with me. Had he thought it would tempt me too much to return to the house? Little did he know.

"So they caught the burglars?" I asked.

"No. They recovered some antiques, a couple of stereos and some TVs equipment. They won't catch anyone. I'm sure they wore gloves. Everyone knows that much."

"Yeah," I said slowly. "How would these burglars have known about the hidden room?"

Mason got a funny look on his face. "Now that's an interesting question." He lowered his voice. "It would have to be someone familiar with the house." His eyes shifted to the doorway which led to the room where, from the sound of things, Sam was watching TV — loudly. "Did you know he's on suspension? Something about missing property in a police investigation."

My head was really starting to throb again. I stared at Mason. "You think *Sam* —"

"I just think it's very convenient that he happens to be the guy who discovered the hidden room was full of stolen property right before the sheriffs descended on the place."

I absorbed this slowly, shook my head – unwisely — which made me curt. "That makes no sense at all. He couldn't have been the one who hit me. When I left he was sleeping."

Silently we both absorbed the implications of my certainty on this point.

Mason said, "He wouldn't have been the only person involved, you know."

"He wouldn't have pulled me out of the cellar if —" I stopped because I already knew the answer to that.

Mason said earnestly, "He wouldn't have wanted to kill you. No one would have wanted that."

I nodded. I knew what he was suggesting didn't make any sense — I knew Sam was not part of any local burglary ring — but I was too weary and muddled to reason out how I knew.

Mason rose. "Anyway, glad you're okay. I guess…"

He stopped. I stood up.

"Thanks for coming by," I said. "And thanks for your help…and everything."

"Yeah. You won't be headed this way again?"

"My work here is done." I was trying to put the right note of levity in, but it just sounded dull.

"Sure. Take care," Mason said.

After he left I spent a few moments sitting in the parlor feeling sorry for myself. I listened to the television blasting from the next room.

Finally I rose and followed the sounds to their source.

Sam was sitting in the dark watching some nature program. Snarling tigers and velvet-eyed antelope — the antelope were getting the worst of it, as usual.

"Can I talk to you?" I asked from the doorway.

A noticeable pause, and then he said, "Sure." He pointed the remote control at the TV.

I sat down across from him and said, "I think you should dig up the cellar."

I couldn't read his face in the flickering light of the television set, but he said without inflection, "Is that so?"

"That cold, that…miasma — it's classic outward manifestation of a haunting."

"Look, you weren't hit *that* hard on the head."

"Just listen to me for a moment. A ghost or a spirit is the sentient presence of someone which stays in the material world after the individual dies. Conventional wisdom is that the ghost is the spirit of a murdered person who wants justice."

"Or someone who died violently and is confused about passing over." Sam turned his head my way. "I read plenty of ghost stories when I was a kid. I know the drill."

"I've investigated a lot of so-called haunted houses, but I've never seen or heard anything like Berkeley House. I guess the sounds and lights can be explained by the burglary gang wanting to scare people off — and maybe someone was dressing up like David Berkeley in the woods — but nothing explains that cellar."

"I think a case of concussion explains that cellar."

I was afraid he had a point. "Okay, maybe, but you felt the cold yourself. You said you'd never felt anything like it."

"The house is built on a cliff over the Pacific ocean. Of course it's cold. Of course it's damp."

I said stubbornly, "I can't believe that what I experienced down there was all due to concussion. You said yourself I was in shock when you pulled me out."

He said, "I know you're not the most honest guy in the world. For all I know, you're not the most stable guy, either."

Well, I sort of had that coming. I said, "I'm sorry I lied to you, Sam. I let my enthusiasm for the book get in the way of my judgment."

He was shaking his head, and I knew he wasn't interested in hearing it.

"But don't let your personal feelings for me get in the way of hearing what I'm saying. I've never had anything like that happen, never experienced anything that didn't have a rational explanation."

He moved as though he were going to get up and walk away, but he stayed seated. "Rhys, Jesus. It's a creepy room. All right? I don't think David Berkeley was murdered, and he had plenty of time to figure out what he was doing when he set the guillotine up."

"I think Berkeley is trying to hide or protect something in the cellar."

There was a long moment of silence.

"So what's in the cellar?" Sam asked evenly at last.

"The remains of Charity Keith and Aaron Perry."

"Really." It was not a question. Sam's tone was uninterested.

"I might be wrong —"

"You might."

"But I think the reason no one ever heard of Perry or Keith again, why they never turn up in any of the historical accounts, is that Berkeley killed them. And I think that's why he killed himself eight months after they supposedly ran off. Either he couldn't live with what he'd done or..."

"I'm going to hate myself for asking. Or...?"

"Their spirits were haunting him."

"Okay," he said calmly. "Appreciate the theory. What time did you want to hit the road tomorrow?"

§ § § §

My office phone was ringing Thursday afternoon when I got back from giving a seminar on historical research and interpretation. I shrugged out of my tweed jacket, reaching for phone with my free hand.

"Davies," I said.

"Hello," Sam said. "How are you?"

I sat down hard; I hadn't expected to hear from him again. He sure as hell hadn't indicated he'd be giving me a call when he said his curt goodbye Tuesday morning.

"As good as new," I said. "It's nice to hear from you."

"Yeah. Well. Oliver's on his way home. He liked your idea of digging up the cellar, so he's inviting you back for the weekend."

"Oh." I said. Oliver was inviting me, not Sam; that was clear. And Oliver had initiated the call; it wasn't Sam's choice. My happiness drained away; I was embarrassed to have felt it. Of course it was over. It hadn't even begun, really. We'd fucked a couple of times and it had been nice and that was that. Leave it to me to start building it into something more.

As tactful as ever, Sam questioned, "Is that a yes, no, or whatever?"

"Whatever," I said.

Silence. Nothing new there.

"Is that what you want me to tell Oliver?"

It took a little effort, but I got a grip on myself. "No, of course I want to see whatever there is to see. What time should I be there?"

"They're breaking ground Saturday morning." He added, like he was reading a script, "You're welcome to come up Friday evening."

"Okay. I'll see y — tell Oliver I'll see him Saturday morning."

Silence. "Okay," said Sam.

Another silence. It was torture.

I opened my mouth, but he said, "Drive safe," and hung up.

§ § § §

The sun was shining when I pulled up at Berkeley House on Saturday morning. I could smell the brine and eucalyptus on the breeze. There were a couple of trucks parked in the clearing. Voices and the unmistakable gravelly pound of distant jackhammers echoed from inside the house.

I slammed my car door and started walking, but stopped at the sound of someone calling my name.

Oliver waved to me from the sunken garden. Thaddeus was with him — and the contentment on his face was almost painful to see.

"Hello, dear boy," Oliver greeted, as I came down the mossy steps to meet them. "Have you seen Sam?"

That answered one question; I'd been wondering if Sam would be around for the festivities. I replied, "I just got here."

"He's probably inside overseeing the slaves. You'd better go talk to him. He has some bad news for you."

"In that case I can't wait to see him."

Oliver chuckled, exchanging a knowing glance with Thaddeus, who chuckled right back. I never realized how much alike they sounded.

I hiked up to the house, ignoring the anxiety spiraling through my guts. I wasn't sure if I was more uneasy at the thought of facing Sam or the cellar again, but either way, the best thing was to get it over with.

The boards blocking the front door had been removed and thick brick-colored hoses ran though the doorway and disappeared inside the structure. I stepped over the hoses, following them to the dining room.

It was amazing how the light and noise and bustle diffused the atmosphere. Sam stepped through a side door and spotted me. It seemed to me that he hesitated for an instant. Then he pointed the way I'd come and yelled over the sound of the drills and shattering stone and mortar, "Let's go outside."

I nodded, turned and preceded him back out. The sunlight and fresh air were a relief. I hadn't realized how much I didn't want to go back inside.

And yet…it suddenly dawned on me that I hadn't felt that sick taint flowing from the cellar.

Sam took my upper arm, surprising me, drawing me to a halt. "I wanted to tell you before you found out some other way. Mason Corwin's been arrested for burglary."

"You're kidding me."

He let go of my arm. "No. He turned up on that video tape you recorded Sunday night. Him and another local man."

"Mason knocked me out and threw me in the cellar?"

"Mike Klinger, the other guy, knocked you out. But Mason let Klinger put you in the cellar, which was pretty stupid, since I'd never have started poking around the house if they'd just dumped you in the garden."

I thought this over. I'd wondered what happened to the second video tape. Confiscated as evidence, apparently.

I said, "He must have found out about the hidden room by reading through Berkeley's private papers."

"That's right." His green eyes were approving — and I was sorry to note how much that mattered to me. "He pretty much admitted everything when the sheriffs questioned him. Anyway."

I shrugged. I was sorry about Mason, but… A little maliciously, I said, "He'd suggested that maybe you were involved."

Sam snorted. "Did he?"

"He said you were on suspension because of some missing evidence in a case."

Sam's face hardened. "Small towns. Yeah, that's true. But it's ancient history now. I was cleared and I've been reinstated. I start back at work next Monday."

"Congratulations."

"Yeah." He gave me a funny look from under his heavy brows. Reluctantly, he asked, "Are you…pretty upset about Corwin?"

"Me?"

"Yeah."

"No."

"Because I thought maybe..."

"While I was sleeping with you?" I interrupted, offended.

To my surprise, he grinned. "Not so much sleeping."

"Not so much." I turned my profile to him, stared at the house. The sounds of the drills seemed to have stopped.

He said quietly, "I don't like being lied to. I don't like the idea of being manipulated."

"Manipulated?" My voice rose. His hand closed around my arm again, but the funny thing, I was relieved by that hard grip. Relieved that he seemed to have trouble keeping his hands off me.

"Shhh." He nodded towards the garden where Oliver and Thaddeus seemed to be in deep conversation by an overgrown hedge. "I may look like a dumb ox, but I'm not." He was smiling, but it didn't reach his eyes.

"If you think I was manipulating you, you're dumber than I thought you were," I said.

"That could be," Sam said evenly.

Oliver was laughing. His voice drifted up from the garden. I watched Thaddeus watching Oliver, and even from this distance I could see the hunger and longing on his face. It made me sad.

And I thought I had an inkling where this particular insecurity of Sam's sprang from. He'd had had a lifetime of seeing Oliver operate. And Oliver was quite an operator.

"Is that back on again?" I asked.

"Apparently."

"How long is Oliver home for?" I asked.

"He says for good." Sam watched the two older men. "Apparently Thad scared him this last time. We'll see."

I nodded. I could feel Sam watching me. I said finally, "I'm sorry I lied to you. It didn't seem like a big deal at first, and then when it was, I didn't know how to get out of it. There was no manipulation. I...liked you. A lot. I mean, after I got used to the fact that you can be a real jerk."

He didn't smile as he drew me forward. His mouth brushed mine lightly, and something tight and angry in me relaxed. I kissed him back, and for a moment there was nothing and no one else.

"I realize I'm not exactly your type," he said abruptly. "Guys like me generally don't have a chance with guys like you."

"Is this your unique lead in to asking me out?"

"Yes."

One of the workmen stuck his head through the window. "Hey, you better get in here," he said to Sam. "There's something under this floor all right. It looks like a skeleton. Or maybe two."

Sam's eyes met mine. "Congratulations, professor."

"Kind of gives you a dim view of romance, doesn't it?" I remarked.

He said quite seriously, "I'm willing to take a chance. If you are."

"Okay," I said. "Just this once."

About the Author

Over the past decade, multi-award-winning author JOSH LANYON has written numerous novels, novellas and short stories as well as the definitive M/M writing guide *Man, Oh Man: Writing M/M Fiction for Kinks and Ca$h*. He is the author of the Adrien English mystery novels, including *The Hell You Say*, winner of the 2006 USABookNews awards for GLBT fiction, and co-writer of the Crime and Cocktails series with Laura Baumbach. Josh is a Lambda Literary Award finalist.

You can find Josh on the internet at:
http://www.joshlanyon.com/
http://jgraeme2007.livejournal.com/
http://groups.yahoo.com/group/JoshLanyon

MLR Press Authors

Featuring a roll call of some of the best writers of gay erotica and mysteries today!

Maura Anderson
Victor J. Banis
Jeanne Barrack
Laura Baumbach
Alex Beecroft
Sarah Black
Ally Blue
J.P. Bowie
P.A. Brown
James Buchanan
Jordan Castillo Price
Kirby Crow
Dick D.
Jason Edding
Angela Fiddler
Dakota Flint
Kimberly Gardner
Storm Grant
Amber Green
LB Gregg
Drewey Wayne Gunn

Samantha Kane
Kiernan Kelly
JL Langley
Josh Lanyon
Clare London
William Maltese
Gary Martine
ZA Maxfield
Jet Mykles
L. Picaro
Neil Plakcy
Luisa Prieto
Rick R. Reed
AM Riley
George Seaton
Jardonn Smith
Caro Soles
Richard Stevenson
Claire Thompson
Kit Zheng

Check out titles, both available and forthcoming, at
www.mlrpress.com

Good things come in 3's.
MEXICAN HEAT
LAURA BAUMB
JOSH LANYO
ISBN # 978-1-934531-0
TEQUILA SUNRISE
LAURA BAUMBA
JOSH LANYO
ISBN # 978-1-934531-72-3
SANGRIA WHITE BULL
LAURA BAUMBACH
JOSH LANYON
ISBN # 978-1-934531-73-0
CRIMES & COCKTAILS
MYSTERY SERIES
MLRPress.com
AVAILABLE ON-LINE, AT LOCAL BOOKSTORES & THRU INGRAM